Hea SS
Heart of the home

 W9-CIB-172

$ 27.95

HEART

OF THE

HOME

HEART

OF THE

HOME

Fern Michaels
Brenda Joyce
Bronwyn Williams
Denise Domning

Five Star
Unity, Maine

Five Star Romance.
Published in conjunction with Signet,
a division of Penguin Putnam Inc.

Cover photograph by Tom Knobloch.

July 1998
Standard Print Hardcover Edition.

Five Star Standard Print Romance Series.

The text of this edition is unabridged.

Set in 11 pt. Plantin by Minnie B. Raven.

Printed in the United States on permanent paper.

Library of Congress Cataloging in Publication Data

Heart of the home / Fern Michaels . . . [et al.].
        p.   cm.
    Contents: Meggie's baby / Denise Domning — Sunshine
/ Bronwyn Williams — The awakening / Brenda Joyce —
Hunter's moon / Fern Michaels.
    ISBN 0-7862-1491-0 (HC : alk. paper)
    1. Family — United States — Fiction.   2. Domestic
fiction, American.   I. Michaels, Fern.
PS648.F27H43   1998
813´.54080355—dc21   98-15515

Contents

MEGGIE'S BABY

Denise Domning

Chapter One

A small pipe squealed in ear-shattering announcement, the note so shrill it drove nesting birds from the thatched roofs overhead. The sound stabbed through the heavy crowd that packed Blue Boar Row, as folk moved ever so slowly toward Salisbury's market square. Startled townsmen stopped to look behind them.

"Make way, make way for the world's finest troupe of players, coming to bring you delights untold! 'Tis beneath your fine maypole that our jugglers and jester will play their tricks for you, while our dwarf and our dancer will amaze you. Look upon us as we pass and be entertained!"

This time, when the piper put his mouth to his instrument, it was to release the sweet notes of a familiar lilt. Approval rumbled from the throng. In the next moment, handbells began to ring, the sound reverberating off the dark timber and whitewashed walls of the tall homes at either side of the street. A tambour rolled into a rhythmic beat, the drum's steady thrumming urging the crowd to part. The townsmen did as they were bid, folk at the lane's center moving to its side. That meant anyone unfortunate enough to be at the far edges of the street was shoved back against the shuttered windows of workshops, no matter how big his person or how prominent he'd recently become.

Caught in a relentless tide of bodies, Alexander, master cabinetmaker of Salisbury and new alderman, ducked to avoid rapping his head on the overhanging second story of a cordwainer's house. As he did so, he lost hold of his wife's hand.

He snatched for her elbow, but a crook-backed weaver and his family slipped between them.

"Meggie!" he called. His wife gave no sign she heard him. Either Meg hadn't noticed their parting or she was ignoring him. After their spat this morn, the latter was the more likely of the two.

As the hurt Meg did him once again washed over him, Alex battled frustration. What was wrong with her? She acted as if it would slay her to accompany him to this day's festivities. His jaw tensed. Even if Meg loved him no more, she was still his wife. She owed him her loyalty, especially on this, the most important day of his life.

He watched as Meggie rose to tiptoe to peer toward the lane's end. It made no difference; she was too short to see over the heads of their neighbors. She sidled around a lanky apprentice to get a better view of the coming players and stepped into a brilliant shaft of midmorning sunlight.

Alex caught his breath in appreciation. Reddish streaks took light in the knot of dark brown hair caught at her nape. The tiny golden buttons that decorated her headpiece, a ring of stiffened green fabric perched atop her head, sparked. Caught in the day's sweet breeze, the green silk of her unbelted and sleeveless overgown, set atop a long-sleeved undergown of dark yellow samite, molded itself to the lush curves of her body.

Oh, but Meggie looked as fine as any noblewoman this day. If she ever forgave him for buying her those gowns without asking her opinion, then insisting she wear them, she'd be well pleased. But, until she forgave him . . . Alex pushed past the weaver's threadbare family and once again took control of his wife.

As he fastened his hand on her arm, Meggie looked up at him. Her face was framed by a wisp of silk that passed beneath her chin and covered only her cheeks, leaving her hair bared. This morn's anger yet lingered, or so said the color that touched her pale skin, but her mouth, a perfect pink bow set beneath her tip-tilted nose, was no longer drawn in displeasure. So, too, were her gray-green eyes now wide with interest beneath the gentle sweep of her brows.

"Alex, I cannot see," she complained, her voice barely audible over the noise of the crowd and the approaching musicians.

Since he would have stood upon his head if it served to distract his wife from her earlier and incomprehensible pique, and taking her to the crowd's forefront was by far the easier, Alex smiled. "Then, we will go where you can."

There were times when being tall and strong had their uses. Alex put his shoulder into the back of the man before him and heaved. The man cursed, but gave way, as did the one in front of him and the one beyond him. Alex and Meggie reached the throng's front just as the first of the troupe was passing.

The piper, his small pipe's air-filled bag caught between his elbow and his ribs, strode alongside the drummer, who held his large, circular instrument before him. Both men wore red tunics. Their chausses, the garments that covered their legs from waist to toe, were yellow and their shoes, a dusty green. Tiny bells, sewn to bands that were tied above their elbows and knees, jingled with their every movement. Like many within the crowd, they each wore a ring of spring flowers upon their head.

Behind the musicians came a cart, its two solid wooden wheels squeaking as they turned on dry cobbles. The vehicle was bedecked with garlands of hawthorn branches, heavy with white blooms. Rather than a horse or ox, it was pulled by a pair of men. These two wore motley, one side of their tunics being red, the other yellow, their chausses showing the opposite arrangement of color. Laurel wreaths, streaming with wide strips of colored cloth in all shades of blue and yellow, hung around their necks.

Straddling the vehicle's tongue was a dwarf in a costume that appeared to be naught but brightly colored tatters. In the little man's stubby-fingered hands were two long-handled bells. These he clanged as he threw back his head and howled like a wolf at the hunt.

From farther down the lane, a pleased shout rose in the watching crowd. Alex looked past the cart's end. It was a woman who brought up the troupe's rear, her fair plaits flying as she leapt and capered.

The acrobat wore red gowns that had once cost someone a pretty penny, trimmed as they were in glossy beads. Years of hard usage left them faded, with barren spots in the trim and patches on the elbows and skirt. Their owner had hastened their demise by slitting her skirts from hem to thigh. This not only offered her freedom of movement, it gave those watching a tantalizing glimpse of smooth, white skin above the garters that held her knee-high stockings in place.

As the woman came nearer to where Alex stood, she flipped onto her hands in one swift and sinuous movement, her skirts caught between her legs. Men and women alike gasped as she twisted her body over her head, then lifted herself back onto her feet. She pirouetted and Alex caught sight of her face. Not so many years ago, she'd been a beauty, with fine, even features. Now, haggard lines and sun-dried wrinkles marked her visage, suggesting that hunger and hardship were ofttimes her companions.

Turning a slow and graceful circle, the dancer came to a halt before him. Her gaze caught on the massive golden chain that crossed the breast of his knee-length blue velvet tunic.

She stared at its clasp, a great knob of onyx, her brows lifting in appreciation.

This was all it took to send Alex's spirits soaring into the sinful realm of pride. The corners of his mouth lifted apace. For the hundredth time this day, he reveled in what he'd accomplished.

Who would ever have believed that the runaway son of a louse-ridden serf might one day be named alderman of a city as powerful as Salisbury? Ah, but he'd done better than that. He took his place as one of those who governed the city at the youthful age of a score and twelve, a full decade younger than any of his new peers.

The dancer's gaze darted from his chain to his face. Alex well knew his features lacked the softness that would lend him the title handsome. Despite that, her expression warmed and a new sensuousness filled her movements. Her dance became an offer, saying that for the right price she'd play her acrobat's tricks to tease and please him.

Embarrassed, Alex glanced at Meggie. No matter their present difficulties, he loved his wife. It would hurt and dishonor him if she thought he encouraged a whore.

Meggie hadn't noticed; her attention was yet focused on the back of the players' passing cart. Relieved, Alex gave the whore her answer in the slight, negative shake of his head. His refusal woke no emotion in the faded brown of the woman's eyes. Her attention simply shifted past him, as she sought another man willing to pay for what she offered.

As Alex watched her twirl and leap down the lane, dark thoughts closed in on him the same way his neighbors swarmed into the lane behind the players. Pride died. No matter how great his success in trade or how high he climbed in city government, he was a failure. He was incapable of setting the spark of life into his wife's womb.

The horror of his deficient manhood was so loathsome, Alex scrabbled within himself to find some shield from it. Deeply rooted irritation came to his rescue. Meggie must accept that they would never have a child. Didn't she see that her frantic determination to fill her womb made it impossible for him to lay abed with her? As long as she counted the days, he would never be able to forget that each and every month's passing proved him lacking, over and over again.

He fed his irritation with Meg until he could no longer feel failure's sting. So obsessed was his wife with making children that she scorned what he could give her. This morn, rather than appreciate that she was now one of Salisbury's most prominent wives, she'd tried to refuse to attend this, his first feast with the aldermen. Well, he had had enough of her ingratitude. Not only would his wife sit at his side throughout the meal, she'd do it with a smile upon her face. Alex turned, meaning to once again fasten his hand on Meggie's arm, only to discover that his wife was gone.

Chapter Two

With only her elbows for weapons, Meggie battled those around her in order to retain her place at the forefront of the crowd following the players' cart. Despite the effort this took, her attention never left the vehicle. Or rather, the wee lass perched atop the pile of belongings in the cart's bed.

Never had Meg seen so beautiful a child. No more than two years of age, the girl's wide-set eyes were the same tawny brown as Alex's. Her tiny features were perfectly formed, her lips, cherry red. Fair hair floated in airy wisps around her face. With no hat upon her head and only a sleeveless, unbleached linen shift to cover her body, the girl's round cheeks and chubby arms were already made golden by the sun.

Meggie was so bewitched she'd not have noticed when the players' conveyance entered Salisbury's market square, save that the piper again set his instrument to squealing. It was an attempt to steal both attention and pennies from those already performing in this open area; he succeeded. Rich merchant and ragged, flea-bitten laborer, alike, turned their backs on the town's homegrown and less sophisticated entertainers to watch the troupe's progress around the crowded marketplace.

Past the makeshift ovens, erected by Salisbury's guilds, they went, the wafting air thick with the smell of oxen roasting and baking onions. Canny vendors, their wheelbarrows and hand trucks bedecked with nosegays and colored ribbons, moved aside to let the troupe pass, then hawked sweetened breads and brown ale to the trailing crowd.

The procession halted near to the stocks, at the marketplace's center. The maypole stood there. Tall and slender, the denuded tree trunk was a spire, shooting up into the vaultless blue of the spring sky. Long braids of white hawthorn and early blooming roses swept down from the pole's tip to coil upon the square's well-trodden earthen floor.

Just behind the maypole, the queens of the May held court. Chosen from the fairest of the town's maidens, each lass wore her finest attire and crown of spring blossoms set atop her free-flowing hair. And, behind them stood the great tent under which the aldermen would take their meal.

Meg's whole being tensed in anxiety as she caught sight of the three linen-covered tables beneath that bright canopy. Every one of the aldermen's wives was a mother, some many times over. It was to be expected that, during the course of the meal, each and every one of them would ask her *the question*. Aye, and when she gave her answer, their expressions would fill with pity. Some would offer her cures for her barren womb, as if she'd not already tried every one with no success; others would tell her her empty arms were ordained by God. No matter which bend they took, all of them would shun her for the defective woman she was.

Meg's gaze returned to the child on the cart as the longing for her own babe grew until it was like a living thing within her. It wasn't fair. Even a player, who was lower than a serf in the sight of God, could produce what she could not.

The wee lass was watching Meggie watch her. She wrinkled her nose and smiled, revealing her newborn teeth. Raising a hand, the child pointed to the golden buttons that decorated the useless ring of fabric Alex had accepted from the tailor as "the latest in fashion." "Pretty," she said, her voice unexpectedly husky as if her throat were scratchy with illness.

For the briefest of moments, Meg considered ripping off the headpiece and giving it to the lass as a toy. She might have done it, had she not known how much Alex paid for the silly thing. Meg glanced down at her rich gowns and all of this morn's resentment tumbled in upon her once again.

How could Alex have done this to her? She was no great beauty, who could wear such bright hues. These garments made her feel as if every eye was upon her, not in admiration, but as one might stare at a mule trying to pass itself off as some great lord's warhorse.

"Touch?" the child asked, drawing Meggie's attention back to her.

When the babe raised her arms, inviting this stranger to hold her as she explored the sparkling buttons, Meg could not resist. "You may, indeed," she replied, stepping to the cart's side to lift the child from its bed.

"Avice!" The dancer bounded to Meggie's side and tore the girl from her arms. As Avice molded herself to her dam's boyish form, her mother turned a wary gaze on the wealthy townswoman. In her face lived the certainty that she'd just foiled a kidnapping.

"Nay, you mistake me," Meg hurried to explain. "She but wished to touch my headdress. My pardon for frightening you." When the woman didn't relax, she added, "I can understand your concern. She is a lovely child."

Caution melted beneath a mother's pride. The dancer smiled, revealing she'd once been as beautiful as her daughter. "My thanks, mistress. Aye, my Avice is a pretty one, but she's cheeky, as well. Although I try to teach her better than to beg favors from strangers, she yet trades upon her beauty to get what she wishes, eh, my little sweet?" she teased her daughter. Avice only turned her head into her mother's sweat-streaked neck.

The drummer rounded the cart's corner and set his instrument against the wheel, then glanced between Meggie and the dancer. His plain face twisted in anger. "Unless she's paying you to chat, Hawise, best you take your skinny ass over there." He jerked a thumb toward the folk waiting to see their show. "And do your contortions until Will and Alan are ready to juggle."

When Hawise didn't leap to do as he commanded, his expression darkened in anger. "If you won't bring in coins with your feet, do not complain over how you must spread your legs to feed yourself and your brat." With that, he turned and began digging into the contents of their cart.

Shame burned in Hawise's fair skin, the raw color saying that the title *whore* didn't sit easily upon her shoulders. She bowed her head. "My pardon, mistress, but last month we were robbed and five of our troupe murdered. Dickon says 'twas Avice's crying that drew the thieves, so it is I who must bear the greatest portion of our loss."

Setting her daughter on the ground, Hawise put a hand to the child's back and urged Avice into the cool dimness beneath the cart's bed. "Go, sweetling."

The lass toddled under the vehicle and dropped placidly onto her seat. With tiny fingers, she plucked at the few, brave blades of grass that had managed to sprout through the square's hard earth. Meggie shot Hawise a surprised look. "She'll not wander from there?"

"Nay," the dancer replied as she bent backward until her hands met the ground behind her, "she's a good lass."

Walking over her head, Hawise returned to her feet. The crowd encircling the cart applauded. With a final smile to Meggie, she skipped into a series of flips.

Meg watched her perform, as much awed by Hawise's flexibility as how the thin woman managed to trap her slitted skirts so they slid only a little way down her legs. Still, enough flesh was exposed to win one man's appreciative hoot.

That sent pity for Hawise shooting through her. How horrible it would be to have to lay beneath man after man to earn one's daily bread. Her pity widened to include Avice. It was wrong that a child should have to endure a whore for a mother and a player's life. Avice would never know what it was like to have a home or the comfort of a town's strong walls to keep her safe.

Someone grabbed Meggie's arm. Yet trapped in thoughts of whoring, she gasped in surprise and tore free before she looked up. When she did, she gasped again. It was Alex and he was furious.

Her husband's fine brown eyes were all the darker with his rage, his usually arched brows flattened to straight lines. Deep creases cut into the rugged line of his cheeks and a muscle ticked along his clean-shaven jawline. Beneath a nose that was nigh on knife-edged, his mouth was but a narrow line. He'd pushed his flat brown cap back onto the crown of his head. With its brim off his brow, where it should have been, his thick, sandy brown hair tumbled onto his forehead.

Meg's heart plummeted like a stone in her chest. What a fool she was to let her admiration of another woman's child so bemuse her that she forgot Alex would follow her. He hated it when she looked at children, and reminding him that he'd wed himself a barren wife did her cause no favors.

"Jesu, Meg, how could you do this to me?" Despite his anger, Alex kept his voice to a harsh whisper. "Can't you see she's a whore?"

Relief coursed through Meggie. Alex hadn't witnessed her holding Avice; it was only the conversation with Hawise he'd seen. "She's not a whore by choice," she returned in thoughtless defense of the woman.

Alex's brows shot up as the anger in his eyes melted into horror. Meggie grimaced at what she'd revealed. No honorable

19

tradesman's wife ever spoke to a woman of low morals. Such a thing was terribly improper. Not only had she conversed with Hawise, but they'd spoken of whoring. That was tawdry, indeed.

"Pray tell me you did not discuss her profession with her." His words were a heated breath of outrage.

"Nay, I but overheard another of the players speaking to her," Meg lied, then cringed in shame. How easily falsehoods now slipped from the lips of one who'd once prided herself on her truthful tongue. When had she become so skilled at twisting the truth?

Depression spiraled in on her. It had happened over this last year. The closer Alex came to achieving the wealth and position he'd always desired, the more distant he became. It had been in an effort to protect what remained of her marriage that Meg sought to mask how he hurt her, not only from him and their neighbors, but from herself, as well.

In an effort to placate, Meggie set her hands on the breast of her husband's blue velvet tunic, her fingertips resting against the golden embroidery that trimmed its neckline. She smoothed her hands down the hard planes of his broad chest, neatly tucking the excess into his broad leather belt. The fabric was rich beneath her fingers.

"Peace, Alex," she begged quietly. "I but passed a few words with the woman. No harm has been done you."

Alex was not appeased. His gaze hard, he stepped back until he was beyond her reach. Meggie let her hands drop to her sides, her heart aching.

There had been a time when merely resting her hands upon his chest would have set his heart to pounding. No longer. Where they'd once found great joy in their marriage bed, their lovemaking was now an infrequent and teeth-gritted duty. Now that Alex knew she was incapable of producing the heir

20

he wanted, he no longer desired her. Indeed, it seemed he could not even bear her touch.

"No harm?" her husband hissed at her. "Meggie, all of Salisbury saw you. You must remember you are now an alderman's wife. As such, you are expected to be a model of feminine behavior."

Resentment roared through Meg, strong enough to bury what ached in her. Now that Alex loved her no more, he cared only for how her behavior reflected on his good name. Her eyes narrowed and she fisted her hands on her hips.

"Am I, now?" she retorted, straining to keep her words private between them. "Odd, but I do not recall being asked if I wished to take up such a role, any more than I was asked if I wished to wear garments such as these." She plucked at the fine silk of her overgown.

Alex sucked in air through his clenched teeth. "I'll waste no more of my time arguing about those damned gowns. While I regret that you dislike them, if I say you wear them, you'll do as I bid you."

"Will I?" she snapped back, anger now driving her tongue. "What is it you think I am, some great poppet you can dress as you please, walk where you wish, and command to speak only to those of whom you approve?"

Her husband straightened to his tallest, his eyes afire in an anger that matched hers. "How can you betray me, when you know how hard I've worked to give all this to you?" he demanded.

"*Give* this to me?!" Her shocked cry was followed by rage so deep it hurt. It tore through her like a flood, then poured from her mouth in harsh words. "You spend every moment of your day working, then seek your rest without sharing two words or a touch with me and call this a gift? Well, I do not accept it! I say what you've done, you've done for yourself,

21

without care or concern for me or my feelings. Do not dare pretend it was for my sake!" Her last words shivered in the suddenly quiet air around the cart.

Mortified, Meg glanced around her. Those folk who'd been watching the players were now watching them. The townsmen who knew her and Alex, even in the slightest, were staring at her in shock; those who did not were openly laughing. Meggie looked up at her husband.

Alex stood like a statue before her, his face ashen. In his eyes was a hurt she'd never thought to see in them. Her heart broke. It had been she who'd put the pain there.

"Oh Alex, I am so sorry," she breathed, then pressed her knuckles to her lips.

Her husband said nothing, only stared at her. Horror rocked Meggie. If she had planned to destroy what remained of her marriage, she couldn't have done a better job. Nay, that was not true and it was past time to stop lying to herself. Her childless state had long ago killed her marriage.

A sob caught in her throat. How well she'd blinded herself to the truth. Now that Alex had achieved the material success he craved in life, it wouldn't be long before he replaced her with a woman who could give him sons.

At the thought of life without him, an ache even more terrible than that born of her empty womb woke in Meg. She loved her husband, she didn't want to lose him. A tiny hiccup of scorn shot through her. If that were so, then why had she publicly scolded him like some backward alewife? Mayhap, it would be best for both of them if she freed him from their wedding vows.

Meggie took a step away from him, then stopped, waiting for Alex to stop her. He didn't lift a hand. Tears stung at her eyes. She blinked them away. Why should he stop her when he wanted her no longer?

22

The urge to run as far from this place and what she'd done woke in her. "I think I needs must pray," she whispered, more to excuse herself than in any desire to actually seek spiritual aid. Turning her back on all that was good in her life, Meggie raced blindly for the nearest lane.

Chapter Three

Alex watched the woman he loved leave him, his heart like a stone in his chest. Meggie did not want what he could give her and he had nothing left to offer her. Their marriage was over.

Whirling on his heel, he started toward the canopy that marked the area reserved for the aldermen. Folk shifted to allow him to pass, their gazes fixed on anything but him as they tried to pretend they hadn't seen or heard what they had. Where humiliation and anger should have been his companions on his trek to those tables, there was only sadness. How long would it be before Meggie asked him to release her from their wedding vows, so she might find a man who could fill her aching arms with the child she so desired?

The tables, dressed in fine, bleached linen cloths, were arranged like a square with one side missing. Looping garlands of spring blossoms hung along their edges and wooden trenchers, one per couple, were arranged before each bench. The benches, also meant to be shared by two, sat only along the outside of the tables, leaving the interior free for the servants to come and go with their platters.

Since the time for dining was yet more than an hour distant, only about half of the aldermen and their wives were present. Nursing cups filled with the finest ale Salisbury could offer, these auspicious folk wore clothing of the finest silks, samite, and velvet to reflect their status. Thick gold chains graced the men's tunics, while daintier jewels glinted on the fingers and necks of their wives. Of them all, Thomas Emotteson, a draper by trade, was the finest.

Seated at the center table, the cloth merchant was resplendent in a scarlet velvet tunic topped with a deep green mantle, his cloak an unnecessary affectation on a day as fine as this one. He was a handsome man, nigh on as big as Alex. Beneath his scarlet cap, thick, golden hair fell to his shoulders, framing his well-made features. Just now, the man's blue eyes were alive with snide amusement.

Sharing Thomas's bench was his wife. However fine, Mistress Alice's tawny gowns hung from her thin shoulders. Her hair, revealed beneath her bejeweled headpiece, was grayed well before her time. She sat still and silent, her head meekly bowed.

Master Thomas turned to his wife. "Move aside." It was a harsh command.

Without comment or even raising her head, Mistress Alice slipped from her end of their bench and reseated herself on the next one. The draper eased over to take her place, then raised a hand in invitation to Alex. "Come, sit here beside me, Master Alexander," he called.

Still trapped in his sadness, Alex responded without thought, only realizing his mistake as he settled himself on the bench next to the draper. Of all the aldermen, he cared the least for this one. It was rumored that Master Thomas was a parsimonious cheat, although those he'd supposedly defrauded had little success in proving their charges. Alex suspected the cloth merchant used his power as an alderman to protect himself from censure.

"You look as though you need a drink." Thomas laughed, then signaled the guild member whose honor it was to serve them as butler this day. "Fill his cup and stand ready to keep it filled. He's going to need every drop."

Still grinning broadly, the draper clapped his new peer on

the back as if he and Alex were old comrades, then leaned close. "Troubles at your hearth, are there?" he whispered the impertinent question.

"Not worth speaking of," Alex retorted. If he wasn't willing to discuss his marital problems with his confessor, he was hardly going to spill his troubles to this man.

"That's not the way it looked from here." Thomas smiled, trying for a fatherly expression and failing. "Ah, but you're young; it's the ignorance of youth that's caused you to spoil the vixen. Let me give you a bit of advice. When she raises her voice to you, you must slap her down. If a wife doesn't see her husband's fist from time to time, the devil gets in her. If you allow a woman to forget her position in the world's natural order, there's naught but hell to pay for it, as you've seen well enough this morn."

The thought of beating Meggie made Alex's stomach twist. Words of defense sprang to his lips. "She has just reasons for her complaint."

Only as Alex heard himself speak did the truth of what he said strike him. Where was the difference between himself and Thomas? Aye, mayhap he'd not physically hurt Meggie, but that didn't mean the harm he'd inflicted on her was any less painful. In trying to escape his own failure, he'd demanded his wife accept what he deemed his proper atonement without once asking her if she wanted it, or even if she wished him to atone. How could he have been so arrogant?

Master Thomas raised his hands in mock protest and rocked back on the bench. Contempt gleamed in his blue eyes. "Prickly as a hedgehog, you are. Ah, I have it. She's refusing to do her marital duty, isn't she?"

Alex stiffened at this rude remark. Shifting on the bench to put as much distance between himself and the draper, without moving so far he actually insulted the man, he stared coolly at Master Thomas. "I think that's no matter for your concern." His words were chiseled from ice.

"Mayhap not," the draper returned, his friendly tone belying the vicious shadows that clouded his blue gaze. Alex lifted his chin a notch in new understanding. The merchant was seeking for some weakness in his new peer. "But, in my experience," the man went on, "it's most often bedplay that lies at the root of a man's dissatisfaction in his marriage."

From the players near the maypole, the small pipe bleated out a flourish, the sound so thrilling every eye was drawn in its direction. Alex looked. So did Master Thomas. The piper was heralding the advent of the jugglers.

As the two men began to toss their balls, taking the acrobat's place before the crowd, the dancer moved out into the audience, yet leaping and tumbling. Folk eddied around her, cheering her feats, as she wove her way through the throng toward the aldermen's table. When she was within view of every man beneath that canopy, she once again began her sensual dance, making the same offer Alex had earlier refused.

Master Thomas's face flushed as he studied the thin woman's movements. Realizing his interest, the acrobat moved until she was performing directly before him. At her promise of pleasure, a leer flashed across the merchant's lips. It took but the lift of Master Thomas's chin to transmit his acceptance.

Being judicious in her solicitation, the dancer didn't immediately stop in her performance. She knew well enough that on festival days such as this one a goodly number of the town's poorer lasses were walking the lanes, seeking to earn a few coins by whoring. As the acrobat was not only a stranger to Salisbury, but a player, the lowest of the low, there was the very real possibility of fines and a beating were she to be exposed as their competition.

After a final set of flips, she lowered herself to the ground, her legs opening until she sat with one limb at either side of her. Her exalted audience acknowledged this feat with applause. Barely panting, she rose, bowed, then moved back through the crowd. Alex watched her wend her way toward the marketplace's exit, no doubt in search of a darkened alley where what she and the draper did would be concealed.

Beside Alex, Master Thomas braced his hands upon the table as he lifted himself to his feet. "I'm off to the latrine," he said.

Alex's brows rose, insulted that the man would offer so paltry a shield to his true intent. Not only did the draper flaunt all convention by taking a foreign whore on a festival day, this sort of rutting was a grievous sin for a married man. Mayhap he was wrong, but to Alex's way of thinking those in power owed exemplary behavior to the folk they ruled. However, feeling himself too newly come to his position to openly confront the man, Alex settled for a chiding look.

From her seat at her husband's right, Mistress Alice made the smallest of noises. Her husband's fine features tensed at the sound, then he rapped his knuckles on the tabletop, once and sharply. His wife flinched.

Master Thomas turned a cold gaze on Alex. "Were I you, Master Alexander," he said as he eased around the edge of the bench, "I'd consider the advice I offer you. Believe you me, when a man submits to a woman's rule, he gets no more than what he deserves. In my household, there's no female who raises her voice to me." He shot a final, warning glance at his wife, then strode away from the table.

Alex watched in contempt as the draper crossed the marketplace in the acrobat's wake. There was no doubting the man's unspoken message: he would take a whore, fully aware that Mistress Alice knew what he was doing. To treat his wife with such uncaring and disrespect was beyond Alex's ken.

With that, Meggie's face rose up before his inner eye. Instead of her usual, gentle smile, her features were touched with an aching loneliness. Guilt lodged in his heart. Who was he to judge Thomas, when it was his own uncaring that put the pain in Meggie's eyes? By turning his back to her all these many nights, he'd made it seem as if he no longer desired her. She didn't know, because he had never told her, his reason for doing so was to protect his own beleaguered self-esteem.

Understanding came like a flash and Alex caught his breath, feeling much as St. Paul must have on the road to Damascus. Dear God, but he was a blind fool. If there was pain in Meg's eyes, it meant she yet desired him, not simply in the hopes that his seed might take root in her womb, but because she loved him. It wasn't his confessor to whom he must lay out this matter, but to his wife.

The need to find Meggie brought him leaping to his feet. Alex scanned the square, but there was no sign of her. Impatience nipped at his heart. He would speak to her, he must, this very moment!

"Good morrow, Master Alexander," boomed Master Gareth, the goldsmith, from his stance at the table's far end, his deep voice bigger than he.

Short and stringy, the wealthy smith had red hair that had begun to retreat from his freckled forehead. As the merchant strode over to Alex, his narrow, ruddy face warmed even more with a friendly grin. Catching his new peer by the hand, he pumped with vigor in a grand show of congratulations.

"Well come you to this table. Why do you not come speak with me so I might know you better," he invited, drawing Alex away from where Mistress Alice sat. When they were at the canopy's far end, the goldsmith lowered his powerful voice

29

as he continued. "I saw you conversing with Master Thomas. I think there are matters we needs must discuss."

For a last time, Alex glanced at the place where Meggie had stood, then released his impatience. It was foolish to chase after her when he had no idea where she'd gone. Besides, he needed time to form his explanations. Come nightfall, Meggie would be home; where else had she to go? Aye, and once she was within their walls, she had no choice but to take her place beside him in their curtained bed. She had nowhere else to sleep.

For the first time in months, desire sowed its seeds in Alex's heart. From them grew the need to show his wife how much he yet loved her. He almost smiled. Where better to make his apologies and explanations than in the privacy of their bed?

Content with his plan, he turned his full attention on what Master Gareth was saying. The smith whispered on about his continuing attempts to see Master Thomas dismissed from the council for his unworthy behavior.

In the vain hope she might somehow escape what she'd just done, Meggie let her feet take her where they willed. Down the nearest lane she went, shoving her way through the crowds of folk who yet streamed toward the town's center and the May Day festivities. At last, she burst out onto an open area, only to stop in surprise.

Towering over the few trees that dotted the short plain were the walls of Salisbury's new cathedral. For over two score years, the building of this great church had supported the town's tradesmen. Nay, it had done more than that. The laying of the cathedral's foundation had given birth to Salisbury, its construction becoming the town's lifeblood, making it into the prosperous metropolis it now was.

She stared at the magnificent edifice. Against the bright blue sky and the lacy green of newborn leaves, its stones gleamed a pale gray. Meg let her gaze rise. The church was broader at its base than at its apex. To support the higher portion, ribs of stone rose from thick piers some four or five storys overhead. Like prayers winging their way to heaven, these heavy constructs arched gracefully through empty air to meet the clerestory wall at the tracery on the even higher roof line. The miracle of soaring stone took away her breath, luring Meg into taking a step toward the building. Here, in this holy place, she would find the answer to all that ached in her.

Awe dissolved into reluctance. She didn't belong here; this was the bishop's church. Her own parish was that of St. Thomas's, near Salisbury's center. If she wanted spiritual comfort, it was in that far humbler building that she'd find it.

But when Meg tried to turn away, she couldn't. However reluctant her heart, her feet were determined to see her within this massive building. She stopped before the cathedral's western end and its doorway. Set in a great arch two times as tall as Meg, the thick wooden door was painted bright blue, the color only accentuating the beauty of the wall's proportions.

Flanked by two small square towers with spiring roofs, this west facing wall rose seemingly forever above her. Three huge, arched windows filled with colored glass sat at its center, the middle window taller than the outer two. On this wall, the stonemasons who'd labored on this church had displayed not only their love of God, but their skill as well. Story upon story of pillared arches marched across its width, each arch creating a tiny alcove into which a statue had been placed. It was a full legion of saints and prophets who guarded the door.

A wry grin touched Meg's mouth as she stepped up to the door. It was just as well there were holy sentinels, as someone had left the door ajar. She slipped into the cathedral's cool interior, then paused.

Overhead, the ceiling was a series of great arches held aloft by thick pillars of dark marble. It wasn't dim. Instead, day's bright light shot down in dusty beams through the cathedral's clerestory windows. The sun made the gold decorating the altar's canopy take fire. So, too, did the red, green, and yellow paints decorating the ceiling and walls glow in jeweled tones.

No matter how many times she came here, for festival and holiday, Meggie never ceased to be astounded at what the touch of the sculptor's chisel could do. At every corner, along every line, hard, cold stone had been softened into gentle curves or warm, living images. Decorative vegetation trailed around capitals. Leering, laughing faces stared down at her from overhead, their soundless expressions almost unnerving in the utter stillness of the sanctuary.

She took a step, then froze as a sharp sound rang out from the opposite end of the nave. Only when the echoes died did she realize it was her own footstep she'd heard, the sound sent back to her by a trick of the arched ceiling. With a breath of relief, Meggie started down the main aisle, her intention to visit the lady chapel. After all, who better to spill her troubled heart to than God's own mother, one woman to another?

But when she came to a tiny tomb, a wooden box with a wee man carved upon its face, she halted. This was the Blessed Osmund's tomb. Within that small sarcophagus lay the remains of the see's founding bishop, nephew to the Conqueror. His remains had been moved from his original resting place in the ancient fortress of Old Sarum a mile or so distant from New Salisbury, from whence he'd ruled his see.

A spark of hope came to life in Meg's heart. There were many who claimed cures after praying to the Blessed Osmund. Hope died in the next instant.

"I think you cannot help me," she told the departed bishop. "Unlike the others you have aided, I have no physical ailments, save for my dead womb and a broken marriage because of it.

I think that if the Lord God has not seen fit to grant me a child, so my husband might love me once more, there is naught you can do."

Despite her pessimism, the urge to pray grew. Not one to question her impulses, Meggie gave way and knelt before the box. As did every woman she knew, she carried her beads in her purse, which hung from the embroidered belt knotted around her waist. Opening the pouch, she pulled forth the strand. Cool and smooth, the pretty stones slipped as easily through her fingers as did the litany of her prayers from her lips. Although it took no more than a half hour to finish her prescribed routine, the soothing familiarity of it banished anger and resentment. As the last word left her lips, Meggie lifted her head and stared at the carved man on the tomb.

Panic, sharp and swift, shot through her. Her husband was by himself at town's center! How could she have abandoned him to face such humiliation at the aldermen's table?

Meg drew a quick breath as the magnitude of the wrong she did Alex pierced her. What an idiot she was. In her own selfish resentment and fear, she'd forgotten how important becoming an alderman was to him. From his earliest years, her husband had craved this level of success. Aye, and until last year, when the proof of her barrenness had become obvious, she had supported him in it.

Her panic deepening, she leapt to her feet. Ach, but she'd done worse than abandon him. It was their neighbors who had witnessed their spat. These were the same folk who made Alex their representative. What if, because of her behavior, they now no longer wished to entrust Alex with the responsibility for their neighborhood? Turning, she hurried down the aisle without care or concern for which angels she disturbed. If she was to save her marriage, she must sit beside Alex at that table, no matter what it cost her.

Chapter Four

The passage of another half hour had only made the market-place all the more crowded. Worse, Meggie was entering the square from the cathedral's side, the point farthest from where she needed to be. In the vain hope of speeding her trek, she tried threading her way along the makeshift booths that lined the square's outer edge, where merchants hawked everything from pickled eels to sweetbreads.

Of a sudden, a solid wall of folk rose up before her. Grimacing in frustration, Meg lifted herself onto her toes to peer across the expanse to the maypole and the aldermen's canopy. She sighed in relief. The meal had not yet started. There was yet time for her to make her apologies to Alex.

Her husband stood at the edge of the shaded area conversing with the town's goldsmith. Even from this distance she could see the intensity that was so much a part of Alex's nature radiate from him as he spoke. A frown marked his broad, clear brow. Meg chewed her lip in concern. What if she'd hurt him so deeply he could never forgive her?

The smith leaned near to Alex to make some point. It must have been amusing for her husband threw back his head and laughed. Meg caught her breath in appreciation. Her husband's smile was a thing to be reckoned with, a charming turn of his lips that never ceased to stir her.

Her reaction to him made Meg smile. Although Alex wasn't the most handsome of men, there hadn't been another man for her since her seventh year when their parents arranged the betrothal. Then, he'd been but an apprentice of six and ten, all knobby knees and gangling arms. Ah, but there was nothing gangly about him now.

At a score and twelve, Alex owned a far younger man's physique, something his velvet tunic did nothing to disguise. The rich fabric clung to the broad line of his shoulders and the powerful curves of his upper arms. Even his legs were fine. Exposed beneath his tunic's knee-length hem his calves, clad in brown chausses cross-gartered with blue, were well-formed.

With that, the honest craving for her husband's touch shot through Meg. The memory of every joining that had driven her to the pinnacle of pleasure woke in her, firming her determination to reclaim Alex's heart. If there was a way to rekindle his passion, she'd find it. And, if he refused her?

Meg's eyes narrowed. If Alex thought she would let him discard her, he was sorely mistaken. Their marriage vows had promised forever, not only "until my wife proves herself infertile."

Of a sudden, the folk ahead of her surged back, taking Meggie with them. She stumbled, then yelped as a burly drover trod upon her toes. The big man shifted swiftly to one side, turning as he did to offer her a sheepish grin.

"Pardon, mistress," he said, "but they're pushing from ahead of me." Despite that it was not yet past midday, his words were slurred with drink.

Those he blamed for his false step set to cheering. A viol screeched to life, sawing out a familiar tune. With a collective crow of recognition, the crowd around Meggie began to form a ring. The drover caught her by one hand, his face alive with a broad grin. With a hoot, a ragged beggarman grabbed Meg by the other.

"Nay, release me," she cried to them, trying to break free. "I've no time to dance!"

They paid her no heed, instead dragging her with them

into the circle. The first steps were slow, the ring turning around the violist, who stood at its center. The musician was an old man, his worn tunic decorated by flowers thrust into its many rents. When he grinned, he displayed a mouth as toothless as a babe's. With a stomp and a cry, he quickened his bow's pace across the strings.

With an answering cry, the dancers moved into a skip, those watching yelling their approval at this new pace. Yet again, the violist increased the tempo of the tune. As the dancers' feet flashed to meet his beat, their audience shouted and clapped in encouragement.

It was more than Meg could resist. She snatched up her skirts, her feet flying in time with all the rest, her heart soaring along with the joyous notes. This was May Day's purpose. It was a decadent celebration of the world's rebirth after winter's death, a day for reveling in the simple fact that they'd held body and soul together for yet another year.

The circle had turned no more than a dozen times when chaos awoke in the watching crowd. Men and women cursed as someone shoved through their midst, then Hawise exploded into the ring. A flaming red mark stained her cheek, the color hot enough to suggest it would be a bruise come the morrow. Tears left muddy trails in the dusty coating on her skin. The musician's tune ended on a sour note. Meggie and all her fellows came to a teeth-jarring halt as the acrobat darted across the circle's center.

"Stop that woman!" The man's angry shout rose from the depths of the crowd the acrobat had just departed. "Stop her, I say!"

Hawise tossed a frantic look over her shoulder and tried to plow into the circle's opposite side. Despite the substantial power of her body, Salisbury's folk were now warned against her; they closed ranks. The acrobat rebounded into the empty space at the circle's center, then turned a hasty pirouette seeking another avenue of escape.

"I think not!" the drover shouted, releasing Meggie to leap into the open space. He grabbed Hawise by one arm. Another man, equally as big, jumped forward to take the other. Hawise gave but a tiny shriek of protest, then hung sobbing between them.

Concern for the woman raced through Meg as she glanced at the faces around her. Gone was the previous moment's laughing gaiety, leaving only a sullen distrust for one who was not only an outsider, but a player. The townsfolk were but waiting for a reason to punish Hawise, no matter how minor her misdeed might have been.

"Who is it that raises the hue and cry after this woman," the drover called out, "and for what crime?"

"I do."

It was Thomas Emotteson who pushed his way into the circle. Fed by her earlier conversation with Hawise, Meggie's concern grew. If the alderman had caught her whoring, she was in trouble, indeed.

The draper halted at the center of the ring, his back to the acrobat. His usually fair complexion was dark with rage, his fine tunic smeared and rumpled. A set of bloody scratches tracked down his lean cheek.

At the sight of so feminine a wound, new suspicion took light in Meg's heart. Master Thomas had a poor reputation among Salisbury's housewives, one they did not share with their men. It wasn't for the quality or price of his wares, which were better than most, but because he made untoward advances. She found herself praying he wasn't the man Hawise had chosen to futter.

Thomas aimed a steady, clear gaze at those around him. "I humbly thank you, neighbors. You've done me and Salisbury a great boon by capturing this filthy wench. Look you all upon how she attacked me when I discovered her whoring in yon alley." He turned to make certain all saw the oozing scratches that marred his handsome visage.

"He lies!" Hawise sobbed, now writhing between her captors in desperation. "I was not whoring."

"And I will tell you all that she speaks falsely," the drover shouted, grabbing the acrobat by one plait to hold her still. "I can smell the scent of coupling on her."

"She was whoring?!" another man shouted from the crowd, his voice filled with indignation. "Who does the slut think she is, coming into our town at festival time and taking coins from our own lasses?"

"She must be punished!" Thomas demanded, then fell silent, the corners of his mouth quivering upward into the smallest of smiles.

His hidden grin set new anger to glowing in Meggie. Thomas meant to goad the crowd into attacking Hawise. Aye, and unless someone stepped forward to soothe them, there were folk with ale enough in them to do as he willed.

Meggie waited. No one uttered a word. If Hawise was to be defended, there was only herself to do it.

Fear exploded in her. She dared not speak, not if she wished to keep her marriage. To challenge one of Alex's peers would only treble the injury she'd earlier done him.

"I say we shear her!" A man wearing a long dagger belted over his green tunic staggered into the circle's center. He drew his weapon, brandishing the blade for all to see. "I've a knife sharp enough to cut her locks."

Although his words were so thick with drink it made his ability to do the deed questionable, the crowd howled its agreement, liking this punishment. Hawise shrieked in terror. Grabbing the drover's forearm as a brace, she lifted herself

38

and slammed her foot into the big man's groin. He dropped, gagging, bent over and rolling in pain. The folk around her roared, her attack creating a raging mob out of a cruel but harmless throng.

As Hawise set on her remaining captor, townsmen surged forward. Even as the man released her, no doubt thinking to protect his own shaft from her heel, folk fell on her. This corner of the marketplace thundered with the cry that the whore must be punished.

"Nay!" Meggie screamed as the acrobat dropped beneath their blows. She forgot she must protect Alex's position and drove into the mob. Her dresses tore. An elbow caught her in the head, sending her headdress tumbling.

Blinking away stars, Meg dropped to her knees at Hawise's side, then threw herself on top of the battered woman. A fist caught her mid back. "Nay, stop!" she panted out. "She is punished enough."

With access to their victim blocked, the mob turned, seeking someone else on whom they might vent their blood lust. It was Thomas who pointed the way. "There are the ones who pander her," he shouted. "Look, the players are already running, knowing themselves to be guilty of whoremongering!"

The drover, his pride well and truly bruised, staggered onto his feet as he took the bait. "Do not let them escape, lads. We must show them how we treat their sort in Salisbury!"

Baying like hounds at the hunt, tradesmen and laborers alike turned to race after the fleeing players. As they departed, Meg lifted herself off Hawise to look upon the damage they'd done her. Blood seeped from a gash in the acrobat's head to puddle on the ground beneath her cheek. One arm was no longer straight and true. At least Hawise's dark eyes were open, her gaze pain-filled, but focused. She was a strong woman, indeed.

Meg found hope that she might escape guilt. If there was no worse than a broken bone, Hawise would soon heal. She offered the acrobat a small smile as she lifted the woman's head into her lap to spare her pain.

"Do you remember me from this morn?" she asked quietly.

"Aye, mistress." The acrobat's voice was choked, but her words were clear.

The few folk who had remained behind gathered in a loose ring around Meg. There was the ragged beggarman with whom she'd danced and the musician. At the latter's side stood two scrawny apprentices, neither having seen more than twelve years. From a respectful distance three housewives watched, their gowns neat, their hair covered with clean head scarves.

"Who will aid me in tending her wounds?" Meg boldly asked of them.

The housewives shook their heads, knowing their husbands wouldn't approve. The lads shrugged, knowing nothing of healing, while the beggarman turned and walked away, in the direction the mob had gone. Only the musician came to kneel at Hawise's opposite side.

"Ach, poor thing," the old man said as he set his viol beside him to stroke the acrobat's cheek with a gnarled hand. "You should not have tried to run. They'd have been content if you'd let them take your hair."

Hawise's gaze flickered to him, then back to Meg. Tears pooled in the creases at the corners of her eyes. *"He,"* she coughed out the bitter word, its scornful emphasis leaving no doubt that she meant Thomas the Draper, "wouldn't have let them stop at that."

Her gaze took fire with her need to explain. "Mistress, he refused to pay my price after he lay with me. When I protested, he said he would reveal that I was whoring and see me beaten for it unless I laid with him a second time." What should have been a vehement utterance was nothing but a sigh.

Lifting her uninjured arm, she caught Meggie's hand in her own. "Mistress, I couldn't bear to be used twice," she breathed, her eyes closing. "When he tried to force me, I scratched him and ran."

Meg stiffened as outrage filled her. It was wrong that Master Thomas could abuse Hawise so. It was even worse that the crowd had beaten the woman without ever asking which of their own men had broken with custom to lay with her.

Understanding woke apace with her anger. Here was why the alderman had urged the crowd to violence; Thomas meant to distract the folk, so they would forget to ask after her partner's name. He'd sacrificed Hawise to protect himself.

Guilt followed rage. Why hadn't she stepped forward to speak when she'd had the chance? If so, Hawise might be shorn but yet whole and Thomas exposed.

Hawise freed a sharp cry, her eyes flying open. Her breathing quickened. "Mary save me, it hurts," she moaned, going rigid. This time when she coughed, blood colored her spittle.

The old man looked at Meggie, deep concern staining his watery gaze. "Mistress, I like this naught at all. It speaks of injuries we cannot see."

Meg's guilt burrowed deeper still. "I live but two lanes distant. We'll take her to my house," she told him, ignoring the fact that Alex might object to her taking a whore into their home. To those left around her, she asked, "Who will help to bear her there?"

"Avice!" Hawise cried, panting against what hurt her.

Meggie's heart skipped a beat. In the midst of all this chaos, she had forgotten the child. She raised her head to scan the marketplace for the cart. Now that the square was nigh on empty, she could easily see across its width. The players' ve-

41

hicle lay on its side, ransacked. Only the odd petal and bit of leaf remained of its gay garlands.

There was no sign of the child. Ach, but she dare not tell Hawise this. If the acrobat thought her daughter gone, she might give way to what hurt her and die right there. Meg tried for a soothing smile. "I'll fetch her just as soon as you lie safe before my hearth."

The acrobat coughed again. Her fingers tightened until they were like steel bands around Meg's hand. "Nay, I die. You admired my Avice. Vow to me that you will take her, becoming her mother in my stead," she gasped out.

Meggie stared at Hawise in shock. She wanted a babe, but not at this price. "There is no need for such a vow," she protested, her voice rising as horror ate up every iota of jealousy she'd ever felt for another woman's child. Hawise daren't die. Meg wasn't certain she could bear it if the woman perished, all because she'd held her tongue.

"Vow, I pray you," Hawise pleaded in her breathless voice.

"Swear to her, mistress," the musician urged. "If you refuse, she'll only grow more agitated, when she must be calm."

Meg slumped in reluctant acceptance. "I so vow," she said. The weight of her words hung like a millstone around her neck.

Hawise hadn't heard. Her eyes rolled back into her head. She stiffened, then began to convulse.

With a cry, Meggie again lay atop her, trying to still the racking motions. The old man joined her. After a moment, Hawise abruptly stilled and her breath rattled from her chest. Meggie waited for the next indraw of air, but the moment stretched on without sound. In the next instant, the musician straightened and blessed himself. Still, Meggie willed Hawise to breathe.

"She is gone, mistress," the old man said gently, laying a consoling hand upon her shoulder.

Rearing back in refusal, Meggie stared at Hawise's face. Now that her soul had departed, the woman's features were strangely flattened. Horror grew uncontrollably. She shot a frantic glance at those around her. The apprentices' eyes were wide in their pale faces; the housewives were gray.

Her gaze once more shifted to the cart. Avice was hers, but the child was gone.

What if she couldn't find the lass? What if she did and Alex refused to let a whore's child into their house? Anger rushed back over Meg. She'd be damned to hell for breaking a deathbed oath, that's what.

This was all Thomas the Draper's fault. Hatred for the alderman, not just for what he'd done to Hawise, but to her, and the child, filled her. She shot a blazing glance at the aldermen's table, seeking him. The table was empty. But, of course. The town's elders were bound to follow the mob in the hopes of soothing the situation. Thomas, hypocrite that he was, would be with them.

Rage was a fire in her belly. Meggie leapt to her feet. Her hands curled into fists, ready to give Thomas his due. It took no great amount of deduction to locate where the aldermen had gone. All she need do was follow the distant, echoing cries of "thieves" and "panderers." With a tiny growl, Meg started toward the sounds.

"Mistress," the old man cried after her, "we cannot leave her here. What shall we do with her, now that they've chased off her companions?"

"Send the lads to Saint Nicholas's," Meg threw back over her shoulder. "They should beg the holy brothers to come fetch her, telling the monks that the house of Alexander the Cabinetmaker will bear the fee of her burial."

Meg's rage deepened. It wasn't Alex who would pay, but Thomas the Draper. Of that, she would make certain.

Chapter Five

Frustration and disgust churned in Alex. He crossed his arm tightly over his chest and leaned farther into the scaffolding that lined the walls of this wee church. The merchants of Salisbury were in the process of replacing the wooden chapel of St. Thomas's with a far more permanent structure, Alex contributing along with all the rest of his neighbors. The stones for the new church were being hewn from the same quarry that had supplied the fodder for the cathedral's walls.

Between his height and his stance here at the back of the altar dais, Alex could see the whole of the short nave. Folk were crammed into the small space. Men, who on a normal day would never consider raising their hands against another, were begging for the chance to lay a blow. It was ale that made them shake their fists and howl.

Despite their drunken bluster, not one of them stepped forward to do the damage he threatened, even though those they sought to hurt were within their reach. It wasn't the presence of the town guard, made up from Salisbury's contingent of young men, that stopped them. Rather, it was that every one of the troupe lay prostrate before the altar, their fingers tightly curled around its holy legs — that was, all save for the acrobat; the crowd claimed they'd already given her the beating she deserved.

So long as the players touched that holy piece, those who wished to do them harm would be damned for violating the sanctity of this church, or so Alex's priest was insisting at the top of his lungs. Such a loud and steadfast defense of the troupe only spurred Thomas the Draper to greater volume. Alex's disgust grew. Apparently, the acrobat didn't futter well, for, despite that he'd been the one to use the woman, the cloth merchant was demanding the players be punished for pandering a whore.

As Alex's earlier contempt hardened into something deeper than dislike, the urge to expose Thomas Emotteson became irresistible. Had he owned a shred of proof that the draper had laid with the woman, Alex would have spewed it that moment. His gaze shifted to the rest of his new peers, all of whom were ringed around the altar.

It was their seeming support of Thomas that had driven Alex to the back wall, aye, even into reconsidering his desire to join their ranks. Every one of those men must know what Thomas had done. After all, the acrobat's offer had been flagrant. Still, they stood with him, even the goldsmith, not because they believed the players guilty of any crime, but because Thomas was one of their own.

As new shouts and curses woke at the back of the church, Alex straightened to see what was what. A ragged pathway was opening in the crowd as someone carved himself a passage. Alex's eyes flew wide in shock. It was Meggie who bulled her way through the throng.

Gone was his wife's pretty headpiece. The wisp of silk that had been her chinstrap now hung, a limp and tattered rag, from one side of her head. Knocked from its neat roll, her hair half dangled down her back, the loose deep brown strands curling along her soft jawline. The gowns he'd so wrongly forced upon her were torn and befouled with dirt . . . and blood!

A great smear of it stained her lap. Concern shot through Alex, only to die just as swiftly. Meg wasn't hurt, she was engaged. Never had he seen his wife so angry. Every inch of

45

her was tense, her hands clenched into fists as if she meant to do battle. It wasn't at him that she aimed her ire, although God knew he deserved it for the way he'd treated her. Nay, Meg's blazing gaze was focused on Thomas Emotteson's back.

A touch of righteous satisfaction filled Alex. The certainty that Meg meant to reveal what the aldermen had so ably ignored, Thomas's wrongdoing, grew in him. As his wife stopped before the altar and set her hands on her hips in preparation for loosing the sharp side of her tongue, a smile tugged at Alex's lips. However right Meggie was in attempting the draper's exposure, what she wanted couldn't happen without his aid. And she would have it. Alex started away from the wall, stepping over the prostrate players, to give his wife the support she needed.

Meggie raised her chin to a haughty angle. "Turn and face me, Thomas Emotteson!" she shouted in bold, nay, imperious command.

Thomas whirled, while every man upon the dais, even the sprawled players, looked at her. The draper's golden brows spiked in surprise at being so rudely addressed by a woman. As he recognized the insult she did him and his pride, his blue eyes darkened.

"How dare you shout at me, Mistress Margaret!" It was an arrogant chastisement.

"How dare I?" Meg threw back, her voice steady and strong. It took every ounce of her will to keep herself from flying at him, so deep was her desire to deal him a taste of what Hawise had suffered. "I say how dare you! The acrobat is dead. Since it was you who drove Salisbury folk to beating her, I charge you with her murder!"

Her accusation woke a rolling, almost regretful, sound from the crowd behind her. Death had never been their aim, only the rightful punishment of one who had done wrong.

Master Thomas's pretty face brightened to red. "Slander! Where is Master Alexander?" he bellowed, whirling to scan the aldermen on the altar's dais. "Come you and muzzle your wife," he demanded of Meg's husband.

A flutter of shock tore through Meggie's rage. Mary save her, but what had she done? Publicly humiliated Alex for the third time this day, that's what.

She glanced toward her husband. His head bowed, Alex was stepping off the dais's edge en route to do as Master Thomas commanded. Meggie looked away, knowing the rage she would surely see on his face would destroy her. Instead, she let her gaze dash frantically across the aldermen as she tried to gauge the sort of damage she'd done.

The town's most prominent men all watched her, their eyes narrowed, their expressions harsh in disapproval at such forward and unfeminine behavior. Meg's heart sank. What an idiot she was. She could have taken her tale to Alex, sharing it with him in private. Then, if he deemed her accusation just, he would have confronted Master Thomas as was mete.

Meg closed her eyes in utter defeat. This was the price she paid for losing control of her emotions. This morn she'd argued, both privately and publicly, with her husband. Then, for fear's sake, she hadn't spoken when she should have and Hawise's life had been the forfeit. Now, because she let rage rule her, she spoke when she shouldn't and it would cost her her marriage.

Alex came to a halt beside her. She waited, eyes closed and head bowed, to feel the anger that must surely be gnawing at him. He took her hand, his fingers lacing between hers.

With a start, Meg looked up at him, only to have her breath catch in an astonishment so deep it stole her voice. Alex was watching her, his eyes that warm tawny-gold color she so loved. As the corners of his mouth lifted in a smile, his harsh features softened.

Meggie's worry melted away as she understood. Not only had Alex forgiven her for this morn's hasty, hurting words, but he was pleased that she confronted Thomas the Draper. Her hand still caught in his, Alex turned to face the cloth merchant.

"Master Thomas, I do not choose to silence my wife." His voice echoed in the breathless stillness that filled the church. "I know Margaret to be an honest woman and, judging from the look on her face, I think she has something of value to offer on this issue."

Thomas glared at them both, a mix of triumph and malice glittering in his blue eyes. "Have you so little respect for your fellows, Master Alexander, that you would allow your wife to spew unsubstantiated charges? If so, you'll not long remain a member of this body. Moreover, unless you remove that woman from here this very moment, I will sue you for slander."

"I bow to that possibility," Alex retorted calmly, "but your charges will have to wait until we've heard and judged what she has to say." With that, he turned his gaze on Meg. "Speak as your heart requires," he told her, his voice loud enough so that all heard his command.

However surprised by his unexpected support of behavior unbecoming to an alderman's wife, Meggie was filled with renewed confidence. Turning to face those crammed within the familiar walls, she called out, "Aye, Hawise was a whore, but when has the punishment for whoring been death? Only on this day," she said in answer to her own question, "when Master Thomas urged you into beating her before you thought to ask who it was that lay with her. Well, I am here to name her partner. It was Master Thomas, himself, who used her and so the acrobat confessed to me with her dying breath."

"You lie!" the cloth merchant shouted so swiftly, his words nearly overriding hers. Even at that he wasn't fast enough to stop the uneasy murmur that rolled over the crowd.

"If not you, then who?" someone shouted from the depths of the throng.

Thomas shrugged nonchalantly. "I saw naught of his face for he turned and ran the moment I came upon them."

"With his chausses about his ankles?" his heckler shot back.

"It is not I who lies, but Master Thomas," Meggie called to them, then turned once more to face the draper. "You not only laid with the acrobat, you refused to give her the coins you promised for the service she did you. Instead, you threatened to turn the crowd on her if she didn't submit for a second time. It is because she could not tolerate to be used twice by you for no profit on her part that she now lies cold and still. Once again, I name you murderer, Thomas Emotteson!"

This time, when her charge echoed in the nave, more than a few called out against the wrong the draper had done. Seeing that the tide was turning against the cloth merchant, those aldermen nearest to Master Thomas began to sidle away from him. Thomas did not notice, so deep was his rage at being confronted by one he considered so far beneath him. The cloth merchant's chest puffed out in a pompous display of indignation.

"This is an abomination! I will not listen to a woman spew foul lies about my character."

"Now who commits slander?" Alex returned. His words cut through the crowd's rising complaint. "For myself, I am convinced that you laid with the whore as my wife claims. I saw you leave the table nigh on the acrobat's heels, then follow her out of the square. Nor am I the only witness. The goldsmith saw the same, did you not, Master Gareth?"

Meggie's husband looked toward the goldsmith. The small man glanced uneasily between the draper and his newly come peer, as if weighing which of the two to support. As he made his decision, his narrow face came to life with something akin to approval. Crossing his arms over his scrawny chest, he stepped to the dais's edge.

"Aye, so it is, Master Alexander. I, too, saw him follow the acrobat from the square."

Shock at so unexpected a betrayal drained the color from the draper's cheeks. "You are both mistaken," he cried, his voice breaking on the final syllable. "When I left the table it was but to relieve myself." The rumbling in the chapel lowered into tones of suspicion at this poor choice of words. "My bladder," Master Thomas cried out in amendment, his tone nigh on frantic.

"I doubt that!" A pretty young woman pushed her way from the crowd. Meg recognized her as the miller's new wife. She came to a halt before the altar, her gaze fixed on the cloth merchant, her finger extended in accusation. "You are a man always seeking some new place in which to put your shaft. Twice, have you insulted my ears with lewd offers, daring to do so only when you knew my husband was away."

"He what!" her much older mate shouted, his voice filled with outrage and shock.

Master Thomas turned a sickly shade of green as the miller leapt to his wife's side, his fists clenched. The man looked from his new bride to Master Thomas, as if he wasn't certain who he wished to punish, the man who attempted to trespass or the woman who left him in the dark. "Why did you not tell me?" he finally cried in helpless protest to his wife.

She fell sobbing into his arms. "He is an alderman. I thought he might do you harm if I complained."

The miller glared over her head at his former customer as he led his crying wife back into the crowd. "Damn you, if you ever cross my threshold again, I'll beat you to a bloody pulp."

Now that two of their own had broken the silence over Master Thomas's behavior, women throughout the nave added their voices to the choir; they recognized their opportunity for revenge was at hand.

Their revelations set their menfolk to screaming. Within the moment the church thundered with demand that the draper and his masculine parts be separated in retribution for his insults. Master Thomas shrieked, then dropped to his knees before the priest and his fellow aldermen.

"Aye," he blubbered, "I admit it. I laid with the acrobat, then turned the crowd on her to avoid paying her. If she is dead, then I am surely at fault. Accuse me as you will, but, I pray you, take me into your custody before they have at me!"

At Master Gareth's sign, two of the guardsmen came forward to grab the cloth merchant by the arms. As they hauled Master Thomas to his feet, the draper sagged between them, sobbing in fright. This time, when Master Gareth made a sign, it was to urge his new peer to return to the altar dais.

Alex released Meggie and joined him in facing the angry folk, his hands aloft in a demand for quiet. At last, the shouting in the nave subsided. "Master Thomas has admitted to his crime and is arrested," Alex called out. "Stand aside so the town guard might take him from here."

This only evoked more shouts of protest. Some screamed that there would be no justice for the draper's wrongdoing, that the aldermen always protected their own. Others rejected the arrest, saying the one who had impugned their honor and their wives deserved nothing less than castration.

"Heed me!" Alex bellowed, again lifting his hands. It was a long moment before the crowd acquiesced. "Those of you who know me will attest that I am an honorable man. As you have heard from Master Thomas's own lips, I am newly come to my position, thus I have no great loyalties or ties to this body. I give you my word that Master Thomas will stand trial for his crime.

"Come now," he continued, his tone softening until he cajoled, "it is May Day and we've celebrating to do. The morrow will be here soon enough, bringing with it naught but more of our daily labors. Go, return to your feasting and dancing, content that I will see justice done."

If his words didn't transform Salisbury's folk from mob into the gay crowd of the previous hour, it was reminder enough to lower their shouts to a grumble. Slowly, folk began to turn and file from the church. Alex returned to Meggie's side, settling a bracing arm around her waist. Meg leaned her cheek against the fullness of her husband's shoulder as she watched the nave clear.

Only when the church was empty did the guard step down from the altar dais, their prisoner in their midst. Gone was the cloth merchant's arrogance. Thomas shambled down the aisle, a broken man. It was more than apt vengeance for Hawise.

That thought sent a wave of sadness washing over Meg. Poor Hawise. She was gone, her life and passing having made barely a ripple upon the surface of life. The only one left to mourn her was a missing child. With that, the weight of Avice's life once again came to rest upon Meggie's shoulders. Whether she liked it or not, she had vowed to take the lass. She had to find the child.

Turning in Alex's embrace, Meg stared at the players. The men yet lay prostrate before the altar and there was no sign of the child in their midst. Angry tears filled Meggie's throat at that. Cowards, all! They'd left Avice behind when they came racing here to save their own lives.

"What is it, Meg?" Alex asked, glancing from her to the members of the troupe.

His gentle tone teased her into looking up at her husband. Once again, she was astonished at the change in him. Gone was the distant man who had put his trade ahead of her in his life. This was the man to whom she'd given her heart.

Ah, but even as this change urged her to share her burden with him, Meg hesitated. What if, in confessing that she'd vowed to make a whore's child their own, she sent him back into his previous uncaring? At last, she simply swallowed all explanation over Avice. Besides, there was no point in mentioning the lass, when the child was missing.

Rather than relieve her, this thought only made sadness grow. Meg bowed her head and, in doing so, caught sight for the first time of what had become of her expensive garments. The green overgown's hem was in tatters, a side seam rent all the way to her hip. The body of it was befouled with Hawise's blood. So, too, did dirt and blood stain the slick material of her undergown's sleeves.

As she stared at the blood, the events of the past hour became achingly real. Hawise had died in her arms. Meg's knees weakened. Her stomach knotted as she once again saw Hawise fall beneath the crowd's blows and felt the woman's final convulsions against her own breast.

Meg caught her arms around Alex, burying her head into his chest. Framed in cries of horror, words of every sort crowded into her throat, all of them demanding release. Against their pressure, her mouth opened. What came out was a piteous cry. "Oh, Alex, I've ruined my new gowns."

Threading his fingers into her hair, Alex lifted her face

53

until he could look into her eyes. Concern touched his harsh features as he pulled the remaining pins from her veil and tossed aside the ruined bit of silk. Then, he smiled, his eyes warming to pure gold. "What do gowns matter if we yet have each other?" he asked softly, drawing his fingers down her cheek in a gentle caress.

His touch sent shivers of heat racing through Meggie. When he drew the ball of his thumb across the fullness of her lower lip, she breathed in utter astonishment. Her heart set to tumbling within her chest. Alex's caress said he not only yet loved her, he desired her.

Happiness tangled with the horror of Hawise's death. Meggie's breath caught in a sob. One tear trailed down her cheek. Another followed. As the trickle became a steady stream, she again leaned her head into her husband's chest.

She cried in the joy of finding Alex anew. She cried for Hawise, for herself, and the children she couldn't have. But mostly, she cried for the babe she'd been given and dared not take.

"Come," her husband said as he enfolded her into his strong embrace. "I think we must go home. There are things I need to tell you."

Chapter Six

Alex brought Meggie to a halt before the door to their home. Although his wife yet leaned heavily against him, her sobs had died into quiet hiccups and short gasps. Opening the door, he led her down the two steps into his ground-floor workshop.

As with all the other dwellings on this street, his workroom was recessed a few feet below street level. Thus, when the vertical shutters that ran the length of the narrow front wall were opened, folk passing on the street could easily see him at his work and gauge the quality of his goods. The shutters were closed for the day and so they would stay until the morrow; only the cookshops and alehouses were open on a festival day.

When they were within, he told Meggie, "Once we've found you something fresh to wear, we'll return and enjoy the feast."

Meggie's response was another broken sob. Alex grimaced, dismayed at himself. That had been his pride speaking, making one last and hopeless attempt at congratulating himself for his achievements. He could see that partaking of a festive meal, behaving as if it were naught but a normal day, was not possible for her.

To his surprise, there was only halfhearted disappointment at the thought of dining without Meg at his side. Even his own eagerness to attend the meal was gone. He'd had enough of an introduction to the ways of aldermen for one day. What rose to take its place was the desire to spend the afternoon renewing his relationship with his wife, but that wasn't possible.

But no matter how much he might wish it otherwise, it was his duty to attend the meal. Attend it he would. That was, once he'd freed Meg of her fouled clothing and seen her at her rest within their bed, which stood in the bedchamber two stories overhead.

Alex closed the door behind them. The workshop dropped into a dim quiet, broken only by another of Meggie's gasps. Returning to her side, he again gathered her into his embrace. How sweet it was when she melted against him, wrapping her arm around his waist. He pulled her closer still and her next sharp breath made the curve of her breast move against his chest.

A potent wave of sensation rolled through him, as fresh and new as the first time he'd touched Meg on their wedding night. Desire followed, so strong his knees weakened against it. Alex fought his carnal need. There was barely time enough for speech, lovemaking would have to come later that evening.

He led Meg across the workshop toward the steep steps at the back wall. As workshops went, his was much the same as any other's, what with his workbench sitting at the room's center. It was the saws, planes, hammers, and adzes, all hanging on their pegs on the walls, and the wood stacked beside the stairs that told the world he was a cabinetmaker. That and the wood shavings that usually covered the earthen floor. Just for this day, they were missing, his apprentice having swept before departing to make merry.

Following her up the steps, they entered the house's small hall. Normally, this room, which served them as both living area and kitchen, was the most active in his house. Here, too, silence reigned. Like his apprentice, Meggie's two maids were gone for the day.

Between the servants' absence and the day's warmth, the massive hearth on the far wall was without its usual blaze, leaving the room illuminated only by a hazy shaft of sunlight flowing through the open shutters on the south wall's arched window. It was enough to reveal the hall's every detail and what met Alex's eye pleased him well, indeed.

Because he needed samples of his handiwork, they had more furnishing than most of their neighbors. Placed before the hearth was his chair, its tall, curved back meant to catch and keep the fire's heat within its embrace. The trunk that held their table linens, built while he'd yet been a journeyman in his former master's shop, sat near the window. They stored their dining table's planks and braces behind it.

At the opposite wall, standing beneath the highest steps of the stairway that cut its way upward to the home's third story, was an open-faced cabinet. Painted a bold red, the cabinet's scalloped trim was bright yellow, its shelves filled with those serving pieces that Meg brought with her into their marriage. There were two pewter platters, an array of wooden bowls and, the most precious of all, a saltcellar with a silver knob upon its top.

Beside the cabinet, its outline barely discernible beneath the length of rough hemp nettle canvas, was the cradle he'd wrought early in their marriage. As he looked upon the piece, Alex's disappointment in himself grew. He knew Meg hid the cradle so she need not be reminded of what they didn't have. Despite that, not once had he considered selling the piece. Discarding it seemed an admission of his own failure as a man. Recognizing his callousness only spurred his need to redress the hurt he'd done his wife. Alex hurried her past the cradle and cabinet, then up the stairs to their third-story room.

As large as the hall beneath it, this room had several small windows, their dark wooden frames gleaming against white-washed walls. With the weather so fine, all of their shutters were thrown wide and sunlight shot into the openings to lay tiny squares of golden light upon the wooden flooring. One beam caught on the two distaffs and the basket full of sewing tools that sat next to Meggie's loom.

Across the room stood their curtained bed, the most valuable part of Meg's dowry. Unlike his own handiwork, this piece wasn't elaborate, what with no carving on its four, tall poles, its head and footboard. Still, Alex had never had a desire to replace it. Every time he looked upon its plain red woolen draperies and its thick straw-filled mattress, supported on its network of ropes, he was reminded of how far he'd come from the nest of grass in a mud and manure hovel that was his birthplace.

He and Meg stopped beside their clothing trunk at the bed's foot. Turning her toward him, he reached for her belt, his intention to free her of her befouled gowns before he put her to bed. Instead, he smiled, charmed by her disheveled appearance.

Their walk from church to home had succeeded in completely loosening Meggie's hair. It billowed in a soft, dark cloud around her shoulders. A few, glittering tears yet clung to the thick fringe of her eyelashes. Their sparkle seemed to make her eyes all the greener. Salty tracks now marked her round cheeks. Cupping her face in his hands, he used his thumbs to brush away the trails.

His wife sighed at his touch and leaned her head into one of his palms. Her skin was soft against his calloused palm, her hair like silk where it lay against his fingers. Yet another stab of sensation shot through Alex and desire doubled its strength.

He let his gaze drift to her mouth. The lush curves of her lips were a siren's song he could not resist. Lowering his head, he touched his mouth to hers, forgetting that his intention had been speech, not caresses.

Although Meggie drew a swift, surprised breath at his kiss, her mouth remained passive beneath his. Concern shot through Alex. What if his abuse had destroyed the heat she'd once harbored for him? Ever so slightly, he moved his mouth on hers, until his kiss became a plea that she should prove to him this was not so.

This time Meggie's draw of breath was a sound of pure need, her lips claiming his with the heat of which he knew her capable. Her passion slaughtered Alex's good intentions. What difference did it make if he returned to the feast now or an hour from now?

Matching her desire with his own, he pulled her closer, reveling in how the generous roundness of her breasts flattened against his chest. When Meg rose on the balls of her feet so she might press her hips to his, Alex groaned, more than content to indulge himself in the sensations she awoke in him.

As her husband's kiss deepened, Meggie gloried in this proof of his rekindled desire for her. Happiness and heat made for a heady mixture when he slipped a hand between them to cup the fullness of her breast. His thumb brushed atop its peak and the need to feel his bare skin against hers exploded in her.

With her mouth yet pressed to his, Meggie stroked her hands down the smooth velvet of his tunic until she worked at freeing him of his belt. Alex made a sound low in his throat as he understood her intent. Rather than try to stop her, he combed his fingers into her hair, then loosed her mouth to press his lips to her ear.

Meggie found she couldn't draw a steady breath. His belt, along with the purse and knife attached to it, fell from her fingers. Even as it clattered onto the floor she was reaching to free the loop of fabric from around the jewel that closed the neckline of his tunic.

Alex traced a searing line of kisses down the curve of her neck. Meg's fingers set to trembling so badly she could not manage that simple motion. Then, he nuzzled at the place where her neck met her shoulder, proving that no matter how long it had been, he'd not forgotten how to wake her body. She cried out in pure pleasure and collapsed against him, wanting nothing more than for him to continue what he was doing.

With a laugh, her husband released her, then stepped back to tear off his tunic. Meggie followed his lead, shucking her garments as swiftly as she could. He was bare before she had time to loosen her ribbon garters and remove her shoes.

Meg drew a breath in appreciation, shoes and stockings forgotten as she admired him. Not since the first months of their marriage had they laid together in day's light. Caught in the sun's golden glow, his bared skin gleamed. Oh, but he was wondrous to look upon, all strong arms, brawny chest, lean hips, and long legs.

Alex was watching her, equally entranced, his brown eyes golden in his admiration for her form. "By God, but you are lovely," he breathed as he reached for her.

Meggie allowed him to embrace her, but she set her hands flat against his chest to keep herself a pace back from him. Her gaze flowed downward, until she focused upon his shaft. Even her breath grew heated as she studied the part of him she knew could drive her to ecstasy.

But it was he who needed to rediscover his passion for her, not she who needed to wring joy from him. Her need to assure herself that he would never again forgo coupling spurred Meg into boldness. She let her hands follow her look and curled her fingers around his shaft, touching him in a way she'd never before dared.

Alex froze.

Concerned that she might have either hurt or insulted him, Meg glanced up into his face, only to smile. Aye, she had surprised him, but his gaze was lambent with the sensations she was waking in him. He rested his hands upon her shoulders, freeing all of himself to her touch.

Meg stroked her palm along the length of his shaft. A quiet moan left him. As she continued her caress, his eyes closed and he leaned his forehead against hers. Meg quaked, startled that her nether parts might grow moist and hot because she touched him. Never had it occurred to her that she might find such joy in pleasing him.

Of a sudden, her husband growled and snatched her close. Yelping in surprise, Meggie released him. So swiftly did he lift her into his arms, she gasped.

"What are you doing?"

He made her no reply, only thrust through the bed curtains. Dropping her onto the mattress, he lowered himself atop her.

"Alex," Meggie protested with a laugh. "I yet wear my shoes and stockings."

His mouth took hers. All thought of shoes died. Meg moaned against the heat she'd made in him, then moaned again as her own fire grew to match his. The desire to move tore through her. She shifted beneath him. Mother of God, but his skin felt wondrous against hers; his shaft burned where it touched her thigh.

He wrapped his arms around her, then rolled onto his back, taking her with him as he went. Confused, Meggie tried to slide from atop him. Alex set his hands on her hips, lifting her above him. When Meg knelt astride him, he looked up at her.

"If you can play the game of discovery with me, then I deserve the right to do the same," he breathed, his eyes burning with the need she awakened in him. "Mount me," he pleaded, "and in doing so make me yours, once more."

Shock started through Meggie. Coupling in this way was unnatural. Surely, their priest would never approve. Then again, neither would the father have approved of her wanton caress.

Wanting to please her husband overrode her reluctance. The novelty of lovemaking done in this way sent a shiver up Meg's spine. She forgot sin as she lowered herself onto his shaft, then forgot all else at the sensation of taking him within her.

He released her hips to cup her breasts in his hands. As he teased her with his fingers, the urge to move again filled her. She did not deny herself. Meg rocked atop him, causing an even sharper stab of pleasure within her. Trembling in its wake, she thrust down upon him again, then again. Joy tumbled in upon her, all the stronger for its long absence.

"Alex," she cried out in astonishment.

He pulled her down atop him and caught her mouth with his. His lips slashed across hers as he demanded she not cease her movements. Meg did as he bid. This time, it was she, not Alex, who drove them onward toward the pinnacle of pleasure.

When Alex at last clutched at her hips and arched beneath her to spill his seed, a wave of ecstasy washed over her. The pleasure was so great it was nigh on unbearable. By the time he relaxed beneath her, Meg was panting in a satisfaction so deep that every muscle in her body loosened.

She collapsed atop him, pressing kisses to his mouth, his brow, his cheek, until she caught the lobe of his ear in her lips. Alex shivered, his laugh low and warm. He caught her close and eased to the side so they might face each other.

Yet trapped in the sensations he'd made in her, Meg watched him in smiling silence. The afterglow of joy left his eyes the color of amber, but as it ebbed, his gaze darkened with something that might have been embarrassment.

Worry quirked to life in Meg. What if she'd been too bold? "What troubles you, Alex?" she whispered.

"Say that you love me," he begged softly.

Relief washed through her and she traced the outline of his lips with a fingertip, following her caress with a brief touch of her mouth to his. "I love you. I always have and I always will."

Although his expression eased at her words, he didn't return her smile as he threaded his fingers into her hair. "Aye, so you do. Now that I am blind no longer, I can see that." It was sorrow, not embarrassment, that tainted his words. "Ach, Meg, but I am amazed that you can love me still after I have been a horse's ass."

"Alex," she protested, as if there was no reason to call himself such, when, of course, there was.

He pressed his forefinger against her lips. "Nay, love, hear me out. Meg, somehow, I came to believe your love for me destroyed because I could make no babe in you. I sought to once more win your affection by making you an alderman's wife, complete with fine gowns to wear."

"It was for me." Meggie sighed as she understood. Awe filled her at how he'd tried to show her his love, only to be followed by disappointment in herself. If Alex blamed himself for her barrenness, then every tear she'd shed over her fruitless womb must have deeply hurt him. Why hadn't she seen his distance had been born out of pain?

"Oh, Alex, it is I who have been blind," she cried softly, "yet you love me still."

"Of course I do," he retorted, as if startled that she would doubt his heart. "Did I not vow to honor and love you forever? This I shall always do, despite the fact that I cannot give you the one thing your heart most desires."

The need to reassure him was strong. "Alex, you mustn't blame yourself for my barrenness. How can it be your fault, when I can feel your seed entering me? Nay, I fear it is I who cannot provide your seed a place fertile enough in which to take root."

He offered her a lopsided smile. "You are kind to say so, but both your sisters have goodly broods. Since yours is not a family given to barrenness, I suspect it is I who am incapable."

Amusement shot through Meg at his proclamation. She eased closer until she pressed every inch of herself against him. Raising herself on an elbow, she whispered into the cup of his ear, "Incapable? How can you name yourself so, when there is no pleasure like that I find in your arms."

Alex laughed and pulled her close. "Ah, how I love you," he told her. "Tell me you will love me forever, even if we never bring forth children."

This made a different sort of concern shoot through Meg, for they did have a child now. The need to tell Alex about Avice died nigh on as swiftly as it was born. She dared not confess her vow to him, at least not just this moment, in case doing so destroyed what was so newly repaired. It was far more important to reclaim Alex's love than to speak of a child who may not be found.

With that, Meg turned her back on the hope of ever having a child of their own. "I will love you always, Alex, whether I am barren or not," she vowed to him, then smiled. "We shall simply have to find other ways to fill our days."

Of a sudden, the image of just how they might occupy their empty hours awoke. As desire was reborn in her, Meggie slid her hands down her husband's chest. Her palms tingled with the feel of him. Passion grew, fed by the discovery that there were two ways in which to couple.

And if there were two, was it possible there were three? In her innermost reaches, the embers of the fire she knew for him flamed. As its heat roared through her, she tried to lower her fingers below his waist. Alex caught her hands.

"Aye, but not this day," he told her, his voice deep and husky, "as I have a feast to attend."

Meg waited for him to rise. Instead, his thumbs moved against her palms, the sensation thrilling. After a moment, she raised a scornful brow. Were Alex truly intent on stopping her, he should have leapt from the mattress and been hard at dressing.

It was another moment before she comprehended the message behind his words. Her lips lifted. Alex did not wish to return to the square; he wanted to remain here with her. To allow himself to stay, she needed to seduce him beyond his control. She met his challenge, already assured of victory.

"Must you go?" she asked, moving her hips against his. Her taunt woke life in his shaft. "You will be an alderman for at least a year. There will be other meals," she breathed into his ear, then used the tip of her tongue to trace its whorl.

"Wanton!" Alex chided, but the huskiness of his complaint belied it.

She again sucked at his earlobe. He groaned and tore away to roll atop her. "Who cares for feasts or aldermen?" he growled, then set to kissing his wife in earnest.

Once more dressed in her green and yellow gowns, Meggie stood in the cathedral's aisle. For the life of her, she couldn't understand how she'd come to be there. Last she remembered it had been late evening. The maids had laid out their pallets, while she and Alex had pulled their bed curtains closed to wait until the snores of their servants had filled the bedchamber. Then, they'd tried once more to outpleasure each other.

Trapped in confusion, Meg started down the aisle. It was neither light nor dark, giving her no hint as to the time of day. She stopped at the cathedral's most auspicious tomb, that of William, Earl of Salisbury, bastard uncle to England's present king.

"Daughter of Eve, you are the most perverse of women," a man chided her. His voice, filled with compassionate irritation, rang in the high-flung vaults of the cathedral's ceiling.

Startled, Meggie whirled on the speaker. He was a man of middling height, his nose big, his hair pale beneath an oddly formed hat. Although the style of his clothing was strange to her, the manner of his address told her he must be a churchman. The jewels on his fingers and oddly formed cap suggested he was a man of some rank.

"I beg your pardon," she said, her words more a reflexive reaction to the potential of his power than in any thought that she'd done him some wrong.

"And, so you should," he agreed, his dark eyes filled with a kind amusement. "You came asking for favors, then will not lift a finger to achieve what you so desire."

Meg stared at him in blank astonishment. He raised a brow at her lack of understanding. "Did you not ask me to give you a child? What you want can still be yours. Rise, Margaret, and tell Alexander of Avice."

Awe and terror tangled in Meggie. This was the Blessed Osmund, taking her to task for not honoring the vow she'd made Hawise. With a horrified scream, she turned to escape certain damnation; instead, darkness closed around her. Made frantic by fear, Meg fought to free herself from the cloying shadows.

"Meg!" Alex cried, his voice filled with concern as he dragged her into his embrace. "Love, you are dreaming."

As his voice penetrated her terror, Meggie calmed. She leaned her head against his shoulder, her heart yet hammering in her chest. It was a long moment before her vision cleared and the homely outline of her bed appeared out of the night. She stared at the grayed form of the bed poles in relief. Then, through a tiny crack in the bed curtains, the first hint of dawn appeared as a pink glow that pierced the dark in the bed's interior.

"What was it that so frightened you?" her husband asked with a yawn. He stroked his hand down her back in an effort to soothe.

The thought of ever again having to experience a ghostly chiding destroyed all Meggie's reluctance to speak to him of Hawise. "Alex, I forgot to tell you something," she whispered.

Chapter Seven

Alex listened as words tumbled from his wife's lips. She spilled the whole of the tale, starting with how she'd admired the acrobat's child, then prayed at the blessed bishop's tomb after their spat. When she related Hawise's dying demand that Meg vow to take Avice, admiration woke in him. The acrobat must have truly loved her child if her final moments had been consumed in the effort to secure a life for her child, rather than in concern for her own immortal soul.

As Meggie finished with Bishop Osmund's visitation to her dreams, her lips set to trembling and tears filled her eyes. "I am so sorry, Alex, but when I vowed to her that we would take her child, I truly did not believe she would die."

"So, the babe is to be ours," he murmured.

Alex leaned back against the bed's head, yet musing over the fantastic tale. As he did, an odd sense of rightness flowed over him. Now, why hadn't he ever considered adopting an orphan? If they were truly incapable of making a child between them, this was the obvious solution. Meg cared for nothing save that she had a babe in her arms and all that mattered to him was that she had her heart's desire. In making Hawise's child their own, the thorn would be pulled from this infected wound of theirs, allowing the injury to heal while peace and contentment were restored to their house.

"Alex, you should know that although I vowed we would take the child," Meggie was saying, enough sorrow in her voice to tease Alex into attending her as she rambled on, "Hawise never heard me. I think I would not dishonor my vow if we but made Avice part of our household. You are an alderman now. As such, I know you cannot take a whore's child as your own daughter."

Alex's eyes flew wide in shock as he came upright on the mattress, deeply stung by her words. "Meg, what reason have I given you to think me so shallow or so cruel?" he cried, more than a trace of harshness in his voice.

Startled confusion dashed through his wife's pretty eyes. "I meant no insult, I only thought, well, that there may be those who will recognize Avice as Hawise's daughter. Surely, the other aldermen will disapprove of you making the spawn of a player and a whore like unto our own."

"May the devil take them for uncharitable fools if they do," he retorted stoutly. Meggie but stared at him. "I am surprised at you, my love. How is Avice so very different in origin from I, who came from a situation nigh on as low as hers? Nay, if we find this child, we will make her ours, scorning anyone who speaks against us for doing so."

With that, he threw open the bed curtains and rose, taking his everyday wear from the clothes pole on the wall behind their bed. When he glanced at his wife, he found Meg yet sitting in the tangle of bedclothes. She watched him, her eyes yet wide in disbelief. He raised his brows. "Come, wife, there's a lass out there who waits on us to find her."

His words broke the spell. With a squeal, Meggie threw herself out of the bed and caught him in a tight embrace. "How I love you!" she cried between kisses as she showered her heart's affection on his face.

Alex caught her by the arms and set her a step back from him. Oh, but there was joy to be had in making Meggie happy. "And I you. But I think we best be swiftly at this. The trail only grows colder by the moment."

Meggie took his warning to heart, thrusting away from him

to tear her everyday gowns from the pole. Yanking the pale blue undergown on over her head, she didn't bother to tug it into place before she followed it with the sleeveless brown overgown she always wore atop it. "Hie, Alex," she shouted from within the body of her garments, "faster! We must find our daughter!"

"Nay, we don't have the brat, nor do I care what becomes of her, as long as it's not us who're burdened with her. That wee bitch has been naught but trouble from the day of her conception." The drummer's hard voice grew steadily louder as he spoke. His hateful words echoed upward out of the copse, until they slipped through branches not yet fully cloaked in summer's raiment and into a sky of glassy blue.

She and Alex had spent the whole morning searching, questioning nearly every soul in Salisbury, but they were still no closer to finding Avice than when they'd arisen. As each hour ended with her arms yet empty, desperation had set its talons into Meg. It was in a final attempt to find the child she now wanted with all her heart that she'd urged Alex to locate the troupe. No matter that she'd seen for herself that the child wasn't in their midst yesterafternoon, the certainty that the players had found Avice would not die.

No doubt thinking only to set her mind at ease, Alex had agreed. Finding the troupe had been far easier than expected. The players had escaped Salisbury's city walls, taking refuge in a copse of trees but a furlong off the road and only a half mile from the city's gates.

"Unfairly said, Dickon," the dwarf called out, his voice surprisingly manlike. He sat in the cart's bed; what with most of their belongings stolen during the attack, he was nigh on the only thing in it. "Avice was no more trouble than any other child would be," he went on, his words sharp-edged in chastisement. "You only complain because Hawise refused to become your woman after Roger's death. It's her rejection, not our losses, that turned you against her."

The drummer whirled on his heel to face the small man. "I've had enough of your blame, Ned," he hissed. "It was that brat's bawling that brought the thieves down upon us and killed Roger in the first place. I was in the right to demand Hawise take responsibility for a greater share of our losses."

"Right or wrong, you knew Hawise had but one means by which to restore that loss, Dickon." This was the piper. He sat on a fallen log before the ashy remains of their campfire, his gaze aimed at his clasped hands, which hung between his spread knees. Grief etched deep lines into the musician's thin face. "Now, because you made her whore, we've not only lost all we owned, but Hawise, herself, may God have mercy on her soul. All else we can replace, Dickon, but not her."

This sad proclamation won a choked sound from the drummer. His glaring gaze darted across the faces of the few who remained in the troupe, then he turned on his heel and stormed off into the trees. "I am going to piss," he shouted over his shoulder. "Best you all be ready to travel by the time I'm returned."

"Aye," the dwarf threw after him, "dragging an empty and useless cart along with us. You'd best consider selling it to feed us, else I'll be finding myself a new troupe!"

The piper ignored their bickering to turn his mournful gaze on Alex. "Master, last I saw, the babe was seated beneath yon cart in your town's square, just where Hawise left her. Avice did not wander. If she is gone, it is because someone took her." His lips quivered downward, the hollows beneath his eyes seeming to grow darker still. "Would that I had more to offer you. My heart breaks at the thought of that lass being used by one with evil in his heart. She was such a cheery babe."

"What's to be done with Hawise's remains?" the dwarf asked. "It feels wrong to leave her behind as if she were but a bit of offal. Not that there's even a ha'penny we can offer on her soul's behalf." This last was a scornful aside.

"She's with the holy brothers at St. Nicholas's," Alex told him. "We'll stop there on our return to Salisbury, making an offering to see she's cared for."

With that, he opened his purse and brought forth two silver pennies. These he offered to the piper. "Yours is a talented troupe. Yesterday's chaos gave me no chance to reward your skills. I do so now, wishing you well in your endeavors."

The piper solemnly accepted both compliment and payment. "My thanks, master. I, too, bid you good fortune in your quest. Your kindness and concern does much to recommend you to me on Avice's behalf."

"I give you my word that we'll keep searching until we find her."

With a final nod, Alex came to join Meggie at the copse's edge. Aching beyond tears or words, she could only gaze up at her husband. His harsh features softened in recognition of her pain. Laying an arm across her shoulders, he led her from the copse. As they left the shelter of the trees, the wind buffeted them, warm but fierce. Meg's skirts were forced against her legs, the air tearing at the plain head scarf covering her plaited hair.

As if it rode on the wind, depression drove deep into her. Why, oh why, hadn't she trusted in Alex from the first? If she'd told him about Avice yesterday, the babe might now be cradled, safe and warm, in her home.

"Take heart, Meg. We'll find her yet," Alex told her as they made their way across the grassy field, aiming for the wider dirt trail that was the road to Salisbury.

Rather than comfort her, his words played havoc with the

jumble of emotions within her. Fear, hurt, and anger poured from her heart, then tumbled from her lips in a river of words. "Have faith?! What of that blessed bishop who so wants us to find her? I say the least he could do is offer some clue as to her whereabouts. Ach, but is this not the way of churchmen? They are ever so swift to tell folk what to do, while never giving a word of guidance on how such tasks are to be accomplished."

"Do you mean that?" Alex said quietly, a touch of concern tinging his voice.

Meg caught back her emotions, grateful that only he and the birds had overheard her tirade. Blasphemy such as this could make naught but trouble for her, or Alex. "Nay," she sniffed. "But it felt good to say it."

Alex laughed. "You cannot know how startled I am to discover my sweet Meggie can be so outspoken. What is it that has finally loosened your tongue?"

Meg caught her breath as she glanced up at him. There was nothing in Alex's face to indicate that he disliked her boldness. "I was never so angry as yesterday. If it displeases you, I shall endeavor to take greater care with my speech."

"You need not do so on my account," he replied.

Love for him once more flowed over her. Meggie freed herself from his arm, then caught his hand, twining her fingers between his. Hand in hand, they proceeded on their walk in a comfortable silence.

There was no mistaking St. Nicholas's Hospital. The verge at either side of its gateway was lined with beggars, all of them assiduous in plying their trade. As Meggie and Alex drew near, every one of them thrust out their hands.

One of the more hapless among them broke from their ranks to hobble after them. The man's right arm was withered, his left foot turned inward so far he shuffled, rather than stepped. Toothless and ancient, his face was so wrinkled his eyes nigh on disappeared into folds of skin. He lacked chausses or footwear and, beneath the tatters of his robe, he was gaunt to the point of starvation.

"Master and mistress," he cried, "you seem kind folk. Take you pity upon me! I am too old to fight the others for the crusts the monks throw in our direction."

Alex drew her closer to him, meaning to hurry past, but Meggie held back, her hand dropping to her own purse at her belt. "Might I?" she asked of her husband.

"What is this, trying to ease your guilt at chiding a saintly churchman?" Alex teased, then shrugged. "You know your household accounts better than I. Do as you see fit."

The moment Meg's purse opened, the crowd converged on her. Their clamor was deafening as each one tried to outplead his neighbor. Swiftly pressing a penny into the old man's grimy palm, she began to back away, already shaking her head in refusal to the others, when a child's husky wail pierced the din.

Meg's heart lurched. Avice's voice was also husky. She whirled to scan the throng. Lifted high over a beggar's head, no doubt so as to make sure the townswoman saw, was a babe. The child flailed and kicked at being so rudely held.

Hope splintered yet again. This couldn't be Avice. Where Hawise's daughter was fair haired, this babe's tangled locks were nigh on as dark as Meggie's own. The child's skin, at least what Meg could see of it beneath the oversized and ragged tunic that covered the babe, was a leathery brown, as if burned to it by the sun. Suppurating sores oozed on the wee one's filthy face.

Noting her interest, the beggar who held the babe fought his way to the forefront of the crowd. "Mistress, I beg you, a pence for my daughter's sake," he pleaded.

Meg stared. It was the same man who held her hand in yesterday's dance, then had turned away after Hawise fell. It seemed he did not recognize her without her finery, for he continued with his piteous plea.

"See how she ails, mistress. I need salves for her sores and food to warm her belly."

With that, he thrust the child out before him, shuddering and gasping for breath against her tearful protest. The lass raised tiny fists and scrubbed at her eyes. When her hands came away, one of the sores was naught but a smear.

Meg's heart took flight. The sores were but painted! Now that she looked closer, she saw that the brown color of the child's hair was unnatural, the darkened skin splotchy and uneven. Both were either dyed or painted. But there was no way to disguise the perfection of feature that Meggie remembered from yesterday. Nor, the color of the babe's eyes. It was here that Meg found her proof. Hawise's daughter had eyes the same tawny brown as Alex's.

"Avice!" Meg shouted, wrenching the child from the beggar's grasp. Even as the man grabbed for her, she was barreling her way through the beggars to the safety of Alex's arms.

Epilogue

"Is that my brother?"

Lying upon the freshly made bed, Meg turned from considering the beauty of her sleeping son, only hours old, to look toward the door. In the opening next to Alex stood the daughter she'd made her own. There was no need for a penetrating gaze to find Avice's beauty; it glowed for all to see. Despite that her origin was common knowledge, three tradesmen had already approached them, suggesting betrothal.

"Indeed, it is," she said to her lass, then patted the mattress in invitation. "Why not come you and look for yourself?"

Avice raced to the bed's side, then stopped, making no effort to clamber up onto the tall mattress by herself. Instead, she turned to her adopted father, who had followed her more slowly across the room. "Help me, Papa," she commanded, her five-year-old voice piercing.

Amusement and astonishment warmed Meg's heart as Alex did as Avice bid. Even after three years, the depth of his affection for Hawise's child could still startle her. Where Meg loved Avice, as any mother might love her child, Alex adored her. It was she, never Alex, who disciplined the cheeky girl; her husband could not bear to make their daughter cry.

When Avice was content with her seat on the mattress, she peered down at the swaddled infant sleeping in the crook of Meggie's arm. Her brows dropped in disgust. "His nose is flat."

"What a thing to say about a lad who looks so much like his mother," Alex chided in laughing protest as he seated himself beside her on the bed.

"He does not resemble me," Meg cried. "It's you he favors, save for his dark thatch."

"Poor lad." Alex shook his head as if disappointed. Gone were the deep furrows of worry that had marked his face during the long hours of her labor. It was joy he hid behind his facade of dismay.

"I think his coming set more gray in your hair, my love," she teased him, knowing it was not her delivery that whitened his hair, but three years of laboring as hard for Salisbury as he did in his shop that put the streaks at his temples.

"Two days trapped in helplessness will do that to a man," he replied. Reaching out, Alex caught her free hand and raised it to his lips, then pressed a kiss on her fingers. "A daughter and a son, two children. That is enough. We need have no more."

Avice leaned forward to peer more closely into her brother's face. "I like him," she pronounced after a long moment, then fell back onto the mattress so she lay beside her mother.

Meggie turned her head to kiss her daughter's forehead. The lass wriggled in pleasure at the caress. Avice tasted like wood shavings and dirt, typical for a lass who rarely left her cabinetmaker father's side.

"Your mama is very tired just now, my sweet," Alex warned her. "Why do you not come and sit with me?"

The lass wrestled herself around, then crawled across the bed to find her place in her father's lap. When she was settled, she peered over his arm to again consider her sibling. "Will he be able to play with me tomorrow?"

"Nay, you must give him time to grow," Alex told her, gently tugging on one golden plait.

Their daughter frowned in thought as she pondered this. After a moment, she leaned back in her papa's arms, her frown deepening into one of true worry. "Will you love him more than me?" It was a tiny question.

Meg almost laughed aloud. Where Avice might be willing to share her mama, she'd let no one trespass with her papa.

"I will love him because he is our lad," Alex told her, "just as I love you because you are our lass."

"But, he didn't come like I did. My coming was special and not like any other child's," Avice said. In her voice lived the absolute confidence that she was and would always be superior to her new sibling. This was the aftereffect of Alex so often telling and so deeply embellishing the tale of her arrival into their family.

"After my first mother died, you lost me. You and Mama had to search all the world for me. It was the Beggar King and his band who took me and held me captive. When Mama flew into their midst to rescue me they took her captive, as well." Avice leaned back against her father's chest, her dark eyes, so like her adopted father's, glowing in excitement. "Tell me again, Papa. Tell me how you slew ten of them to save Mama and me."

SUNSHINE

Bronwyn Williams

Chapter One

If there was one thing Mary Rose McGuire possessed — and at the moment, she possessed very little — it was a talent for landing on her feet. Sitting on a mossy creek bank in eastern Tennessee one late March afternoon, she reminded herself of that fortunate fact as she dangled her bare feet in the icy water, soothing blisters, allowing some of the ache and trail dust to be washed away.

Her stomach growled. It had been growling at her for the last five days. The next time she had to run for her life, she thought with a whimsical amusement that was hard to come by under the circumstances, she would make sure it was in midsummer, when wild berries were ripe for the taking.

Reluctantly, she reached behind her and collected her sack and her boots. She'd been walking for four days now. Or was it five? Ever since old Sam Guthrie had come to tell her that Uncle Hiram had been killed by a pack of vigilantes over near Catons Grove and that they were headed her way at a hard gallop, looking for hidden loot.

Sakes alive, as if she knew anything about any loot. She didn't even know what loot looked like, although it didn't surprise her that her uncle did. Had. He was gone now. Her last living relative. The miserable old sod.

Rosie's parents and younger brother had died of the diphtheria. The only survivor, she'd been shipped off to live with a great-uncle she'd never even heard of. Grief-stricken and still in shock, she'd soon found herself stranded hundreds of miles away from all that was dear and familiar, living in a two-room hovel in Dead Mule Valley, Tennessee, with an old man who hadn't wanted her any more than she'd wanted him.

But they'd been stuck with each other. And Rosie, determined to hang on to the only kin she had left, had set out to make herself indispensable to the dour old man who spent half his time drunk on popskull whiskey and the other half away on unspecified business. From the day her world had fallen apart when she was eleven years old, to the day she'd walked out of the valley with only the clothes on her back and a few small treasures from the past, she had done her best to raise herself as a lady, the way her mother would have wanted her to do.

It hadn't been easy. Over the years, her memories of the big white house overlooking the Tennessee River, and the beautiful woman who had been her mother, had grown dim. Still, she'd done her best, working with the few resources she had. For all the good it had done her.

Somewhere in the distance, a hound began to bay, the sound echoing out across the valley. Rosie thought, as she stood on one foot and shoved the other one into a boot that was several sizes too large, the soles crudely restitched with coarse twine, that it was about the lonesomest sound she'd ever heard. Looking back the way she'd come, she thought about her uncle and old Miz Guthrie and Eckerd, who'd been her friend. Likely, she'd never see them again.

And then she thought about the last meal she'd had. It had been five days ago — rabbit stewed with wild onions. Just thinking about it made her want to cry. All she'd had to eat since then were a few shriveled turnips she'd found in an abandoned root cave.

Gathering up her hair, she twisted it into a knot on top of her head, anchored it with her uncle's old straw hat and started up the ridge, eager to get as far away from Dead Mule

Valley as she could before nightfall. She was aiming to go all the way to North Carolina because, while she wasn't entirely sure, she didn't think anyone would follow her into the next state.

She'd been traveling for perhaps an hour when she paused and sniffed the air. Was that smoke?

It was smoke! And where there was smoke there was fire — and where there was fire, there might be food. . . .

Stumbling over twisted roots, ducking low branches, Rosie McGuire set off at a run toward the tantalizing smell of wood smoke, her mouth watering in anticipation. A mile or so farther on, she spied a pair of horses and a mule in a rough pasture halfway down the far side of the ridge. Slithering down laurel slicks, over rockfalls, she caught a glimpse of a cabin.

Moments later she spied the graves. Two of them, one with a few sprigs of grass beginning to sprout, the other obviously fresh. "Oh, my mercy," she whispered, trying to think proper sorrowful thoughts. Instead, all she could think of was huge platters, sagging baskets and big bowls of funeral foods brought by caring neighbors. Chickens, hams, cakes, and sweet, sugary pies . . .

Davin Banister was closer to tears than he'd been since the day eight years ago when he'd parlayed a royal flush into a boatload of East Lake whiskey and then watched the boat sink slowly to the bottom of the Currituck Sound after a dozen or so pious souls had attacked it with pitchforks and axes.

The baby continued to cry. It had been crying ever since he'd set foot inside the cabin early that morning. He'd heard the pitiful wails all the way out to what passed for a road. "Hush, now — God help us both, boy, crying don't make it better."

Davin would have cried, too, if he thought it would help,

but nothing could help now. Paul was dead. He'd known that when he'd first set out over a month ago. What he hadn't expected was to find Paul's woman dying of cholera.

The baby, too, would probably be dead by morning of the same scourge that had swept the entire valley, according to the blacksmith who'd given him directions to Paul's cabin. "If I was you, son," the wiry old man had warned, "I'd light outta here and not look back."

But Davin had had no choice. He'd had to go on. He had promised his father to find Paul's widow and child and bring them back to Seven Oaks. It was the first request his father had made of him in twelve years — the first time they'd even spoken since the old man had turned him out, a half-grown boy, with only a horse and the clothes on his back.

"Hush now, baby," he murmured, jiggling the miserable waif in his arms. "There's no more beans left in the pot, and I don't reckon you've got teeth enough to tackle raw onions."

He paced and jiggled, wondering what to do next. Stay on and bury the boy beside his parents, or ride out of here and pray he wasn't carrying the sickness with him. He was still pondering his course when he heard a noise.

Thunder? Someone knocking? Placing a hand gently over the baby's mouth, he whispered, "Shh — stow it, son." And then he felt something warm and wet suckling on his finger. He started to swear even as he strode to the door and flung it open.

Rosie hefted the chunk of firewood, fixing to bang on the door again, when it suddenly opened. She stared up at the tall man with the bloodshot gray eyes and a dark layer of stubble covering half his face. Her mouth fell open as she remembered the handsome prince in a book she'd once cherished.

Only this prince's hair was black, not yellow, and he wasn't wearing fancy bloomers over long blue stockings. And he didn't look any too happy to see her, either.

Thrusting a noisy, smelly, soggy bundle at her, he snarled, "Do something, dammit! He's been like this all day!"

Too stunned to protest, Rosie clutched the squirming bundle to her breast. A pair of small wet fists waved frantically. Two tiny feet were kicking her in the belly. "A baby?"

It was certainly no glass slipper. She stared down at the wet, red face. Its eyes were tightly shut, its mouth wide open. Its belly was stiff as a board and it was screaming at the top of its lungs. "Mister, I don't know ary a thing about babies."

"You're a girl, aren't you?" The man peered up at her face under the wide-brimmed straw hat. "A boy? A woman? Hell, I don't care if you're old Scratch himself, do something for that poor mite and I'll pay you whatever you want."

"Food?"

"You want food?" Taking her arm, the man practically dragged her inside the stuffy little cabin. "Fix what ails him and you'll have my undying gratitude and all the food you can lay hands on." Davin didn't bother to tell her that that would be damned little. They could settle the score later. Once the poor miserable babe had given up the ghost, he thought, and winced at an unexpected shaft of pain.

It had never occurred to him when his father had first summoned him and sent him off on this wild-goose chase that the boy was his own flesh and blood — that he would feel such a powerful connection.

By this time Rosie was pretty sure what ailed the small bundle. It was wet. It stunk to high heaven, and even as she patted its tiny backside, it released copious quantities of gas.

"Where's its mama?"

The man in the black frock coat, buckskin britches, and the tall black boots nodded silently toward the two graves visible through the open door. "Both his folks are dead. He's my nephew."

"That's awful," she whispered. "What about milk?"

"What about it?"

"Don't you have a goat or a cow?"

"Hell, so far as I know, there's not even a chicken."

"Well, what are you feeding it?"

"It's a him, and I fed him beans, mashed up with a fork and watered down some. He liked 'em once he got used to the taste."

Which gave Rosie a pretty good notion of what ailed the baby. She might not know much about babies, but she did know what beans did to a body, and when that body was as small as this one was . . .

They were still standing in the open doorway. Now that the sun had sunk behind the mountain, the air had a bite to it. The man took her by the shoulder and she allowed herself to be led inside. She wasn't stupid enough not to recognize the dangers, but right now, he needed her even more than she needed him, which gave her an edge. Besides, he had food and she'd likely die if she didn't get something to eat soon.

He lit a lamp. She looked around, still holding the grizzling baby, who was gnawing on her shoulder and farting in her hand. The place showed signs of having been cared for once, but not lately. A chair, a bentwood rocker, reminded her of one her mother used to have, and she could feel her nose starting to get red, the way it always did just before she set in to cry.

There was a row of pretty teacups hanging from nails on one log wall, and a china vase of dead wildflowers. The bed was stripped, the ticking stained. There was no sign of a crib or a cradle. Dust lay thick on the floor, trails clearly visible where someone had walked through it.

She sank down onto the rocker and set it into motion. "I reckon the first thing to do is find something to eat," she said, thinking more of her own belly than the baby's.

"There's not much here. I don't know if they ate up all their supplies and then got sick, or what. I found some honeycomb, a few onions, and some withered mushrooms. There was a pot of beans on the range, no more than a cupful. I've been feeding the boy those, doling them out to make them last until I can get him somewhere, or he . . ."

Rosie knew what he was going to say. She didn't want to hear it. Decent folks didn't sit around waiting for a baby to die. "He don't seem real puny. Kicks like a mule."

"He's hungry. Gnaws on anything he can cram into his mouth."

"Did you give him honey?"

"Not yet. He just finished up the beans. I thought I'd save the honey for tomorrow."

Rosie got up then. It was all she could do to drag herself across the small room to the cupboard, but the thought of honeycomb was a powerful incentive.

She could feel his eyes on her back as she rummaged through the clutter on the shelves. Three plates, a cup holding seven spoons — real silver, she noted with some surprise. An old newspaper and a basket holding three dried peppers, a few small onions, and a dozen or so puckery, blackened mushrooms, too old to identify.

"Who are you?" he asked quietly. His voice was deep, dark, and slow. Different from the handful of folks back in Dead Mule Valley. She tried to remember the way her father had spoken, but as usual, the memory slipped away before she could latch onto it.

One thing she did know. It wasn't real smart to talk to strangers. The fewer who knew her whereabouts, the safer she would be. "Well, lookee here," she exclaimed, reaching for the jar that was half filled with comb, oozing precious, golden honey. Sourwood, from the color. Her favorite kind.

Grabbing one of the spoons, she scooped out a dripping chunk of honeycomb and crammed it into her mouth, then she dipped the tip of the spoon in again and offered it to the baby.

"He likes it," she cried, delighted. Small feet and fists pumped furiously as the infant demanded more in the only way he knew how. Rosie gave him as much as she dared, feeding herself in between. "There, dumplin', let's clean you up a speck before we set to whompin' up supper," she murmured.

"Whomp away. I'll go bring in the horses."

She glanced around in time to see the man disappearing out the door and thought, my, he was a sight to behold, even if he wasn't a real prince. If he'd been a real prince, he'd not have looked twice at a freckle-faced redhead wearing second-hand overalls, much less have invited her in to take supper with him. All the same, she surely did admire the set of his features and the way he was put together.

The baby wanted more honey, and so did she, but first she had to do something about the stench. "You're not all that homely when you stop crying, dumplin', even if you do smell worse'n buzzard bait. I bet your mama set some kind of store by you, didn't she?"

She sorrowed up a bit, thinking of the two fresh graves outside, but then she set to peeling off layers of wet clothing. Wet and worse! He didn't much like being washed, but she did it anyway, and then dressed him in a tiny gown she found in a basket beside the bed, marveling at the ruffles and fine stitching.

She wondered about the gray-eyed man, and about the two

people buried out beside the pasture. She'd passed a few farms on her way east, but hadn't seen a barn outside of this place.

Of course, a few trappers lived out away like this, too, but this didn't look like any trapper's cabin she'd ever seen. Besides, this time of year a trapper would've had his pelts pegged to a wall to finish curing. She hadn't seen any sign of pelts, or traps, either.

Of course, the man might've been in the same business as her uncle. Uncle Hiram hadn't run a still himself, but he hadn't exactly been a stranger to the trade.

With the baby sucking on a rag soaked in honey water, Rosie did the best she could to make herself more presentable. She didn't hesitate to borrow soap, a comb, and a small mirror, but couldn't bring herself to borrow anything else. From years of sharing a tiny, two-room shack with a mean-spirited old rascal, she had developed a powerful sense of privacy.

At least her face was clean now, even if her clothes weren't. She'd long since outgrown the dresses she'd worn as a child, and as her uncle had never seen fit to replace them, she was used to wearing a pair of his old overalls and whatever she could piece together from printed feed sacks. Her hair she simply coiled into a rope, tied in a knot, and jammed her hat back on to hold it.

Then, while the baby continued to suck on his honey rag, she set to making supper from onions, mushrooms, peppers, and honey, and did some more thinking about the man.

She wished she'd thought to ask his name, but then he might've asked hers. The fewer who knew her name, the fewer could point out her direction once she'd gone. And she had to leave as soon as she'd filled her belly — and maybe her pockets, if there was anything left over. She was bone weary, and so lonesome she could howl, but she hadn't come far enough yet to feel safe.

"I'm a-gonna miss you, little dumplin'," she whispered. He was sort of pretty when he wasn't crying, with eyes the color of wild chicory and a nose no bigger than a chigger bite. She thought about the doll she'd once had, that had been lost somewhere between Chattanooga and Dead Mule Valley. She'd cried a whole passel of tears over that doll. "You're a real live doll baby, aren't you, sugar pie?"

Rosie thought about lingering for a while, wondering if she dared take the risk. Even if they were following her, they'd hardly be looking for a man, a woman, and a baby.

She decided to study on the matter while she got on with supper. After building up the fire in the range, she poured a gourdful of water into a pot and set it to boil. The baby had fallen asleep and dropped his honey rag. Impulsively, she leaned over and kissed him. He was so small, so miserable. What was going to happen to him?

Sighing, she plopped his soiled napkins into a pail of cold water to soak. Poking at the shriveled mushrooms, she crumbled one in her fingers, sniffed it, then tossed the whole lot into the fire. They might be fine as George's shine, but she hadn't lived all these years by taking foolish chances.

She ended up boiling the onions and dried peppers together and adding a dollop of honey for seasoning since she couldn't find any salt. It was the best she could do, she told the man when he came back inside. "Take it or leave it."

He took one taste and decided to leave it. Rosie's feelings weren't hurt. Her uncle had been a persnickety man, too, when he'd been home. She was so hungry, even after eating her fill of honey, that she ate until she couldn't hold another bite. If her belly knotted up on her in the night, at least it wouldn't be from starvation.

Chapter Two

Several times in the night Rosie woke to hear the baby scream-ing with pain, his little body red and stiff as a board.

"God in heaven, can't you do something?" the man pleaded.

"He needs his mama."

"Then *mama* him!"

In desperation, she scooped the poor mite off the bed, her own tears mingling with his, and walked the floor until even-tually he stopped sobbing and fell into a fitful sleep. Again and again she woke to the pitiful wails. She did the best she could with warm water and honey-soaked rags. After the first few times, she was too tired to walk the floor without stum-bling, so instead she rocked. By trial and error she discovered that he liked it when she laid him across her lap facedown and thumped her feet on the floor. The small jolt seemed to bring him relief. After passing quantities of gas, he usually fell asleep, and Rosie would put him down again, crawl back un-der her table, and roll herself in the quilt.

The last time she was roused from a deep, troubled sleep, gray light was seeping in through the window. She lay still a moment, trying to collect herself. The baby was crying again. The man was pacing the floor with him. In the early-morning light she watched as his big booted feet passed back and forth, so close she could have reached out and touched him if she'd wanted to.

Sleeping under the table had been her choice. Neither of them had been eager to sleep in a bed where a woman had died only hours before. But he told her that when he'd first stepped into the cabin, the baby had been lying there wet and crying beside his mama. He'd said it couldn't do him any harm to sleep there one more night. Possibly his last night on earth. He didn't say that last part, but it had been there in his voice, in the sorrowful way he'd looked down at the poor, miserable little waif.

Rosie thought it was the saddest thing she had ever heard. She did know, because they had talked some in the hours before she'd taken one of the two quilts and crawled under the table, that the man — she'd taken to calling him Blackie in her mind — had been living away from home for years when his father had sent for him and told him that Paul, his younger brother, had died, leaving a widow and child somewhere west of Asheville, he didn't know where.

So Blackie had set out to track them down and fetch them home, only it had taken him longer than he'd expected because they'd kept moving on. He told her he'd arrived barely in time to promise the woman he'd look after her baby. She'd rolled back her eyes then and breathed her last, and he'd buried her beside her husband.

Rosie had cried when he'd told her that. His face had closed up tight. He'd told her the last thing he needed was another young'un bawling her eyes out, and she'd told him it didn't mean a thing, she cried easy. "But you don't need to worry, I'm not fixing to stay." Truth was, she hadn't made up her mind yet.

He had muttered something wicked under his breath, but with the baby crying again, she hadn't quite caught the words, only the wickedness. Cussing didn't bother her. Uncle Hiram could cuss a boar hog right up a tree. She could do a right smart job of it herself, come to that.

The feet paused beside her head. "So you finally decided to wake up."

That startled her, because she hadn't moved a muscle. She knew hunters who could sense when an animal was sleeping or awake — that is, they could when they weren't full of pop-skull whiskey. But Blackie wasn't a hunter. She could tell that right off. It had been more years than she could count since she'd been to a city, but she still remembered how city men looked, smelled, and talked.

She thought she might've talked that way herself a long time ago, but Uncle Hiram had made fun of her, so she'd tried to talk more like the folks in Dead Mule Valley. Now it came natural.

"Want me to take him?" she asked.

"He's wet."

"Want me to show you how to change his drawers? I already figured it out."

"I know how to change his drawers," he said, sounding offended, "but you might as well make yourself useful while I go see to the horses."

Having used the few clean napkins she could find, Rosie didn't hesitate to rip a bedsheet into squares. They didn't belong to her, but she'd worry about that later if she had to.

Nothing belonged to her except for her papa's gold ring and a jarful of buttons her mother had given her to play with when she was a little girl. Jet ones, glass ones, and gold ones that had long since turned green. She'd had some money, but it was long gone.

With a sigh, she crawled out from under the table, rubbed her eyes, and reached for the leaky baby. The man stared at her as if he'd never seen her before, and then she remembered her hair. It was hanging down her back, and it was red. *Real* red. And long. If anybody came around asking questions, he might mention that long red hair, and then they'd know for certain sure they were on the right track.

She should've passed right on by when she'd seen the cabin, but she'd been so hungry. And lonesome. Mostly she was used to being lonesome — folks in Dead Mule Valley weren't real sociable. But she didn't much like going hungry, and she hadn't dared slow up long enough to catch and cook something on account of they might've caught up with her.

If Uncle Hiram hadn't taken all her sang money she could've bought one of those horses out in the pasture. She'd worked hard for that money. She'd been getting sang — ginsing, that was — for years, earning ten cents a pound for green, eighteen cents a pound for dry. In half a day she could fill a tow sack. Eckerd Guthrie had told her once that she was the best sang-getter in the whole valley.

She missed the valley even though it had never felt like home. She'd sort of hoped it would, but it never had. It was better here, even with the two fresh graves out in the pasture. Mostly, she guessed, it was the baby. And the man. She'd almost forgot how it felt to talk back and forth, all nice and friendly. Not that Blackie was friendly, but at least he wasn't outright *un*friendly. And when the baby gazed up at her like a solemn, blue-eyed owl, her heart melted right down to the nub, even when he stank worse than a polecat.

He needed her. No one had ever needed her before.

It was while Blackie was bringing the horses down closer to the house that Rosie made up her mind that if he was fixing to ride out, then she was riding out with him. For the baby's sake. Because he needed her. "You do need me, don't you, pun'kin?"

Her mind made up, she set to heating water, peeled another dripping napkin off the squirming infant, and sluiced him off again. He still didn't smell too sweet, but then, neither did she.

Blackie, now — he smelled like horsemint and lemongrass.

It amazed her, it surely did, that a man could look so pretty and smell so good and still be a man. A woman could learn a lot from a man like that. About how to dress and how to talk. Things that had never seemed important before.

The baby's gown was wet. She looked around for a fresh one without finding it, then rummaged through Blackie's saddlebags. She found a shirt, clean, dry, and neatly folded. Without thinking, she lifted it to her face and breathed in the scent. Half-forgotten memories of starched pinafores and ruffled lawn petticoats flickered in her mind like heat lightning, and she felt herself start to pucker up all over again. "Lord-a-mercy, I'm worse than you are, sweetnin'," she said, laughing, and lifting the baby, she swaddled his small, wigglesome body in Blackie's clean white shirt.

"There," she murmured. "That feels better, don't it?" At least he wasn't crying the way he had cried during the night. Mostly he just whimpered, like he was tired, or coming down with something. "Don't you go and get sick on me, sugar pie. We'll find you some milk if I have to hogtie a' old mountain lion. You'd like that, wouldn't you? Yessirree, lion milk would set you on your feet again in no time."

Rosie was pretty sure he was too young to walk, but it never hurt to give a body something to live up to. She wished she knew more about babies. She could scarcely remember her younger brother, and the youngest child in Dead Mule was Eckert Guthrie. He was sixteen and a half, two years younger than she was.

Holding the baby on one hip, she spooned a bit of honeycomb into a small square of linen and knotted the corner. "Here you go, sugar, you suck on this till Uncle Blackie finds you something better." Dragging the rocker over to the open door, she rocked and sang snatches of half-remembered lullabies while the baby sucked greedily on the knotted linen. After a while he dropped his sugar-tit and commenced to rooting around the bib of her overalls. "Lordy, honey, you need a mama real bad, don't you?"

Davin led the two horses and the mule back down to the house. He'd searched for a wagon of some sort, knowing Paul would've had something to drive.

He'd found it. A smart-looking gig, not at all suited to the terrain, but then his brother had never been overly practical. The buggy was smashed to flinders, tipped halfway down a ravine.

He'd visited the graves, wondering if he should have done more than carve their names into wooden crosses. Although given the circumstances, there wasn't a lot more he could do. He lowered his head, but no words came to him. "Well . . . I guess this is it, then, brother. I'm sorry as I can be things turned out this way. Your wife must've been a pretty woman. I hope you're together now."

What did a man say in a case like this? Dav couldn't remember the last time he'd tried to pray. If God even recognized his voice, He'd be laughing His head off. "So long, fellow. You, too, ma'am. I'm sorry I couldn't have got to know you, but I promise to take real good care of that boy of yours. So far, he's not showing any sign of sickness. You put in a good word for him where it'll do the most good, and I'll do my part."

He was surprised the little fellow had lasted out the night, but he had. So now, Dav told himself, all he had to do was devise some way of carrying him that would leave one hand free for the horse. A sling, maybe.

For all he knew, he was carrying the sickness himself. He had handled the woman's body, after all, wrapping her in a quilt to bury her. He wasn't sure how such things spread, but

96

when one person came down with it, more than likely the entire community would soon be struck down.

He was sorry about the girl, though. He should have turned her away at the door, but then, if the sickness was traveling through the mountains, she'd have come across it sooner or later anyway.

Maybe he could give her some money — he'd need the spare horse to trade for transportation, and the mule to pull it, otherwise he'd offer her something to ride. Not that he owed her anything. Hell — a ragged, runaway kid, he'd be lucky if she didn't steal both horses and anything else not nailed down.

Davin's plan was to head for the nearest community, hire himself a woman, explain the circumstances, and let her decide whether or not to take the risk. With a little luck and someone to look after the baby, they just might make it all the way home. He wasn't worried about carrying the sickness to his father. If either he or the boy was sickening, they'd likely be dead long before they ever reached Currituck County.

He had already written his father a letter to be mailed as soon as he reached a town with a post office, explaining what had happened. Not that the old man deserved such consideration, but he'd done it anyway, for Paul's sake.

God, it didn't seem real. He hadn't seen his younger brother in years, but it was hard to believe he was gone.

Rosie, who possessed a great deal of common sense and an even greater instinct for survival, knew the moment Blackie walked through the door that he'd made up his mind about something. "You're fixing to light out, aren't you?" There was a patch of wetness on his shoulder where one of the horses had nuzzled him, and his eyes had a raw look, as if he was hurting, but he was still about the finest-looking man she'd ever seen. Even scowling he made her feel safe. Or if not exactly safe, at least a whole lot safer than she'd felt since she'd left home on the run, one jump away from the men who had killed her uncle.

Squaring her shoulders, she put on her best smile. "We're all ready to ride. I've washed out the baby's napkins and tore up all the sheets to make more. I'll jest have to wrench 'em out in creeks along the way."

"I'll give you half the money I have on me. It should get you wherever you're going."

"Why would I need money? You're not fixing to leave me behind, are you?"

"Not here. I mean to burn the cabin in case there's still sickness lingering here, but the baby and I are headed east."

"I'm headed east, too."

"We're going all the way to Currituck County." His voice had gentled some. Rosie took heart.

"I've been meaning to ride over and see the Currituck Mountains."

He rolled his eyes. "It's on the water. The nearest mountain's two hundred miles away. Besides, you don't even know me. A girl can't just go riding off with a stranger. It — well, it's not safe."

"It's safer than staying here."

Davin thought she meant the sickness, and he couldn't deny it. "You can take the money and go to the nearest town — you can ride along with us that far, and I'll see you settled before we move on." God knows where, or how, he thought, wondering why he was bothering to explain. He didn't owe her anything. She'd looked after the baby last night, and he'd fed her. They were square.

But she stood there looking at him, Paul's baby straddling one hip, and he found himself seeing her — really seeing her

— for the first time. Not that she was anything special. Red hair. Freckles. Eyes that were either light brown or muddy green, he hadn't gotten close enough to tell which.

Didn't intend to, either. She was just a kid, a ragged, runaway kid. He had troubles enough without adding hers to the list.

Reaching into his coat pocket, he drew out several bills, counted them, and laid seven of them on the table. "This should get you to the next town and see you through until you find work."

She didn't move. "Are you fixing to tote the baby all the way to this Currituck place?"

"I plan to hire a nanny in the next town and trade in the mare for some kind of transportation." He'd had the gelding, Rackum, for years. He wasn't about to give away the best horse he'd ever owned, and he'd need the mule to pull the wagon.

She had a way of squaring her shoulders that he might have found amusing under other circumstances. "I'll be your nanny." He started to argue, but she didn't give him an opening. "Better the devil you know than the one you don't. I remember that from somewhere. What's your name? I reckon if we're gonna be riding out together I'll need to know how to call you."

Hands on his hips, he slowly shook his head. "You're a stubborn thing, you know that? How the devil did I get stuck with two young'uns, as if one weren't enough?"

"I'm full grown. I'm eighteen and a half years old. I'm no trouble, I don't eat much, and I never complain. I'm a hard worker, I'm real good with babies —" At least, she would learn to be. "And if you don't take me with you, I'll probably starve or get shot by vigilantes or be eaten by a mountain lion."

There. A little guilt never hurt anybody, she thought smugly. Let him try to cast me off now.

She knew from the way he shook his head that she'd won. Before he could think of another argument she shoved the baby into his hands, grabbed her sack, and darted back inside the cabin. "Forgot something," she yelled.

"Dammit, girl, come back here! I'm getting ready to fire the place!" he called after her.

Rosie was back before he could come fetch her. "I'm ready," she said, reaching for the baby. The cup and saucer might not make it, even though she'd wrapped them in paper before packing them in her sack, but the teaspoons would. A child needed something that had belonged to his parents. She had her mama's buttons and her papa's ring. Now little Paulie would have something of his own to touch and think back on when he was big enough to understand about family.

Blackie spilled coal oil around the cabin and set it ablaze. "It's a real nice cabin," she said wistfully, watching from the hill a few minutes later as it began to burn. "Maybe somebody could've used it."

"Better this way. The sickness," was all he said, and she wondered if he was thinking the same thing she was. The couple buried out in the pasture. She hugged the baby closer, liking the warm softness of his small body. "I know how you feel, sugar pie," she murmured. "My folks are gone, too. Uncle Hiram wasn't much, but he was all I had left." They were now traveling single file on the narrow trail, the man riding the big gelding, leading both the mule and the mare. Rosie was mounted on the mule. With both arms free, she was holding onto the baby, but now and again she looked back over her shoulder, half expecting to see a passel of wild mountain men riding her down.

"It's Banister." Blackie's voice startled her. Neither of them had spoken in a while. "You asked my name a while back. It's Banister. What's yours?"

"Charmaine Duvallier," she said without a second thought. She'd read it in a book one time and thought it sounded grand. Besides, if she was going to have to make a fresh start, she might as well start with a new name.

She thought she heard Mr. Banister snort, but she couldn't be sure because a flock of crows had cut loose, arguing among themselves, and the creek they were following was kicking up a real ruckus. The air was as clear as white corn liquor, and twice as sweet. For no real reason, she felt like singing. So she did.

"Hesh lidd-ul bay-be, don't you cry, Mama's gonna feed you bye and bye . . ."

The baby stared up at her as if he'd never heard anything like it, and Rosie wondered if his mama had ever sung to him. She traced one of his colorless eyebrows with a finger. He sneezed, and she laughed and hugged him to her.

He *liked* her.

So she began to sing even louder, her voice ricocheting out across the valley, mingling with the crow-calls.

Riding up ahead, Davin winced. "God have mercy, what am I going to do with two of them?"

Chapter Three

Davin Banister had long been considered the black sheep of his family. His mother had died soon after the birth of Paul, his younger brother. Davin could remember the leaf-brown color of her hair, but not her face, nor even the sound of her voice. His father, a successful cotton grower and a staunch member of the Methodist church, might have smiled at one time in his life. If so, Davin had not been privileged to see it.

For as long as he could remember he'd looked after his younger brother, teaching him to ride, to shoot, to swim. Protecting him from their father's notion of discipline, which was a caning for the least offense. It was Davin who'd taken the blame when Paul had allowed a shaggy Banker stallion to cover a neighbor's prize Arabian mare. Three days without food, a broken finger, and bruises that had still been visible three weeks later.

When Paul had followed a trapline into the swamp, replacing every trapped mink with a dead rat, it had been Davin who'd been blamed. The mink had been found in the Banister's corncrib, and Paul, the old man said, wasn't strong enough to spring all those traps alone. So Davin had been hauled outside by the scruff of his neck and caned until he couldn't stand up, while Paul watched through the window and cried.

Davin knew he wasn't helping the boy by allowing him to escape responsibility for his misdeeds. At fourteen, he'd lectured him about respecting the property of others, about admitting his sins, and taking his punishment, and for a little while it had done some good. Paul had confessed to setting fire to old lady Meechum's outhouse while she was in it. Marshall Banister had sternly reprimanded him, but hadn't caned him.

He had confessed to stealing the preacher's sermon just before the service and leaving the poor man to sweat and stammer before his congregation, and to ringing the church bell an hour early one Sunday morning. Half the folks in the neighborhood had scrambled out of bed, convinced they'd overslept. His allowance had been cut.

But two years later, when word got out that a boy from the next county had been found dead of a self-inflicted gunshot, with a note in his pocket that said, "I owe Banister $750," Paul was nowhere to be found. Davin, knowing his brother's habits too well, had found him in a neighbor's duck blind out on the sound. He'd been trying to gather enough courage to drown himself.

Because Paul had been truly devastated, Dav had once more taken the blame. And Marshall Banister had once more accepted his eldest son's guilt without question. But this time, instead of caning him, he had cast him out with only his horse and the clothes on his back. One rotten apple in a barrel, he'd claimed, was one too many. Davin had been a bad influence on his younger brother long enough.

At just over sixteen, big for his age, Davin had thought cockily that he knew all there was to know about life. Not until he faced the world alone, scared enough to beg, but far too proud, did he realize just how unready he was. For the next few years, an embittered and grossly ignorant Davin had done his best to live down to his father's low expectations. At twenty-one he'd been well on the way to becoming a drunkard and a gambler when something had happened that had turned his life around. He'd become instead a successful business-man, more or less by accident.

It had started the night he'd won half interest in a freight boat plying the inland waterways between Delaware and South Carolina. As he'd always liked messing around in boats, the project had caught his fancy. Several years later he'd been in the process of buying his third schooner and an old warehouse on the Elizabeth City waterfront when his father's agent had tracked him down and told him that his father had received word that Paul was dead of blood poisoning. The old man was ill and wanted to see his eldest son one last time before he died.

Davin had come within an ace of refusing, but somewhat to his surprise, he'd discovered that it wasn't in him to deny anyone a deathbed request. Not even the father who had dis-owned him.

A few days later, seeing the sickly old man he remembered as being bigger than an oak and twice as hard, he'd found himself wondering if his father had ever hugged him. If so, he couldn't remember it. Couldn't remember his mother hav-ing hugged him, either, but then, he'd been so young when she'd died . . .

So he'd agreed to go after Paul's widow and son and bring them to Seven Oaks, where they belonged. He'd thought to himself, once I belonged here, too, but he hadn't said it aloud. He didn't belong anywhere in particular now. It was a com-fortable way to live. No expectations — no disappointments.

Which made it all the more curious that he found himself here in the middle of the Appalachian Mountains some five hundred miles from home, with an ailing, squalling infant and a dirty, stubborn girl who lied about her name, her age, and God knows what else.

He glared at her, and then his gaze softened. Well . . .

104

maybe not about her age. As a shaft of sunlight slanted down through the tall balsam firs, splintering on her fiery red hair, he thought, she's a woman, not a child.

Rosie looked around her with growing interest as they rode into the sparsely settled community. It was nothing at all like Chattanooga. But then, her memories of Chattanooga were sparse and spotty, at best. She remembered the funeral — sort of. She remembered being told that a man from the bank now owned her house, and that she was going on a long journey, but the woman who'd told her had a great big mole beside her nose, and she'd stared at that so hard she hadn't heard much of anything else.

She did remember riding for days on end with a big family in a crowded carriage — they talked a lot about Christian duty, and she'd formed the impression they were talking about her, but she'd been too timid to ask. She remembered being handed over to a circuit-riding preacher for the last leg of her journey. The poor man had ridden into Dead Mule Valley looking scared enough to wet his britches. He'd barely taken time to discover the whereabouts of one Hiram McGuire before dumping her and her bundle out beside a tumbledown shanty and rattling off down the road in his buckboard.

Now she didn't know quite what to expect, but she was ready for it. If Blackie Banister thought he was going to abandon her here and go on without her, he was flat out wrong. She'd come this far without getting murdered by vigilantes — she had herself a man and a baby and the whole state of North Carolina spread out before her. The way she saw it, from here on out, it was downhill all the way.

Squaring her shoulders, she started humming. And then she started singing. She'd learned a long time ago that if she tried real hard to be happy, pretty soon any fearful miseries she felt would go away. "Hesh, lidd-ul bay-bee, don't you cry," she howled, jiggling the small body that lay sleeping trustfully in her arms.

"Miss — Duvallier!"

"Maa-ma's gonna feed you, bye and —"

"Charmaine!"

Startled, she looked around to see Blackie Banister glaring at her. "Did you say something?"

He looked tired. They had slept out last night, and once the sun had gone down, she'd been shivering fit to crack a jawbone. She'd taken one quilt and bedded down under a balsam branch with the baby — Blackie had taken the other one and gone off to himself. About the time the night was darkest, just before day broke, the cold had come creeping up from the ground, and Blackie had crawled under her shelter and covered her and the baby with his quilt. She'd puckered right up, but she hadn't said a word. What could a body say in the face of such downright kindness?

Next time she woke up it had been light. Blackie had been huddled up against an old stump, trying to stay warm in only the clothes he was wearing, and she'd lit into cussing to keep from crying again. "Dadburn if you're not crazy as a one-eared bat! Either that or you're coming down feverish."

Naturally, she couldn't leave him there. After carefully tucking the sleeping baby in the quilts, she'd crawled out from under the sweeping branch and placed her hand on his brow. His skin was as cool as a creekbed rock, but for all she knew, he could be burning up inside. He'd slapped his hand over hers and held it against his face, and for the longest time they'd glared at each other. She'd thought then that she might be the one coming down with a fever. Neither one of them had said anything beyond the purely necessary as they'd broken camp and prepared to ride out again.

Long before they'd stopped to rest the horses, her bottom had been worn plumb down to the bone. Riding, she was learning, was near about as wearisome as walking.

He pulled up beside her on that great ugly gelding of his, and she smiled just as if she weren't aching, nodded at the babe in her arms, and whispered, "He's sleeping like a baby."

"He *is* a baby. If I remember correctly from my last trip through here, there's a livery stable of sorts, and a general store. I'm going to leave you at the store while I go see if I can find some kind of a vehicle. This is too hard on the baby."

On the baby! What about her? Still, he hadn't said a word about leaving her behind. Hiding her relief, she said airily, "Long as you're fixing to get us a wagon, I'd like a Cabriolet." She thought her father had one once, but she wasn't sure.

"You wouldn't know a Cabriolet from a cabbage head," he jeered, but he was smiling, so she smiled, too. "While I'm doing that, I want you to buy provisions enough to get us through the next few days. Get whatever the baby needs. I'll pay the tab when I come to collect you."

Davin left both his passengers at the general store, wondering if he shouldn't have simply taken the baby, given the little heathen some money, and left her to make her own way.

But she was entertaining. And she was also useful. Besides, there was something about her that didn't quite add up, and he'd always been a sucker for a good mystery.

At the livery yard, he spelled out his needs, offering Paul's showy little mare in exchange for something solid that could carry in reasonable comfort a man, a woman, and a child.

The sharp-eyed liveryman said he'd ask around and see what was available, and when Dav inquired about the possibility of renting a tub and a few cans of hot water, he was directed to the saloon.

Some two hours later, thoroughly disgruntled, Davin drove

the mule and an ancient farm wagon back to where he'd dropped off his passengers. They were waiting for him. The girl, still in her dirt and overalls, stood beside a stack of provisions. The baby, wrapped in something that looked like a horse blanket.

And the cow.

She was grinning, her eyes bright as wet agates. "Lookee here what I found!"

"What the devil do you think you're going to do with that animal?"

Her grin faltered, which made him almost regret barking at her, but dammit, he'd just been gulled out of two good horses for a piece of junk. "I'm aimin' to feed your baby, that's what I'm aiming to do," she said, daring him to argue.

Which he did, even knowing he'd lost. "I'm not hauling any damned cow down the mountains. Do you know how fast a cow walks?"

"Not very, I reckon, but the storekeeper says a baby can't eat sausage and beans and pickled eggs and cheese without it gets stuck in his craw. She says if I polish his bottom with lard and feed him milk and boiled cornmeal, he'll likely stop crying so much."

"Oh, she did, did she? Tell me, did this storekeeper of yours drop any more pearls of wisdom?"

"I reckon that's about all. I told her his name was Paul, account of that's the name carved into that grave marker. Paul and Mollie. But since he's a boy, I thought it'd be better to call him Paul."

Davin shook his head slowly. Either the girl was simple, or she was about as clever a piece as he'd ever come across — and he'd met a few opportunists in his day. He couldn't make up his mind what she was all about. He did know from riding behind her when he'd taken the baby for a spell to rest

108

her arms, that she wasn't built to wear trousers. He'd stared at that heart-shaped behind of hers swaying and bobbing up and down on the mule's back until he'd found himself thinking things no decent man would think. No sane man, certainly.

Disgruntled, he climbed down from the wagon and loaded the provisions. The storekeeper came out and hugged Charmaine, who hugged her back and promised to stop by and see her if she ever came this way again.

Davin swore, tied the cow behind the wagon, and swore some more as they set out. Charmaine smiled that sunny smile of hers and turned and waved the storekeeper out of sight.

"She's a real nice lady, Blackie. I wish we could've set an' visited with her some, but I reckon we'd better get on down the mountain 'fore it gets too dark to see. Her name's Daisy — the cow, not the storekeeper. But I'm a-gonna call her Cecille. I almost had me a teacher named that once, but she fell in the river and drownded."

Sure she did. Davin wondered if this maddening creature would recognize the truth if her life depended on it. At least riding beside her, he didn't have to look at her backside. He did have to smell her, though, and he wondered why he hadn't thought to offer her a bath, too. But then, the saloon didn't cater to women.

"You smell," she said.

"*I* smell! The *hell* I do!"

She turned to him and sniffed. And then she sniffed the baby, who was sleeping peacefully for once, full of milky gruel. "Yep. You smell. My daddy used to smell like that. Sort of sharp and sweet at the same time."

Bay rum. It had cost him a dime extra, but he'd needed something to lift his spirits. Not for a single minute did he believe her old man had ever smelled of anything except possibly pig manure and moonshine whiskey, but he didn't argue.

He'd argued with the livery attendant over the cart and lost. He'd argued with the girl over the cow and lost.

Losing arguments wasn't something he enjoyed. The sooner he got shed of this business, the better. About a week and a half — maybe two. A man alone on horseback might make forty miles a day. The way he figured it, they might reach Seven Oaks late next week, as long as the road held up. As long as it didn't rain. As long as none of them sickened and died along the way.

"That damned cow of yours is slowing us down," he grumbled.

"Paulie needs milk."

He didn't have an answer to that. She had won. They both knew it, but Davin didn't have to like it.

And he didn't have to like her. Which made it all the more baffling that as they rattled along hour after hour on roads that were bumpy, dusty, and badly rutted, they found themselves talking about things neither one of them had ever discussed with another living soul. He told her all about his early dreams of sailing around the world, seeing foreign ports, sending ships of his own to China and the South Seas.

She told him her dream of having a home and a family again. You'd have thought from the way she talked she was fully expecting a fairy-tale prince to swoop down and carry her off to his castle.

Whenever the baby grew fretful, she sang to him. Her voice was truly awful. Davin winced, but he didn't comment. Little Paul seemed to like listening to her. Or maybe he was just stunned to hear such caterwauling emerging from such a sweetly shaped mouth.

She shut her eyes, and when he asked if she was sleepy she told him she was trying to picture her old house so that she could describe it to him. "Right where the stairs turn we

110

had us a little round window with colored glass in it."

A stained-glass window. Oh, yeah. No moonshiner's shanty should be without one.

"We had us a piano, too, and I was fixin' to learn how to play, but the piano teacher fell in the river and drownded and then Papa got real sick with the diphtheria, and then everybody else did too, exceptin' me, and the preacher said it was because God had set me aside to do something, only he never said what it was. Maybe it was jest to do for Uncle Hiram. He was such a mean old coot, nobody else'd come near him."

She sighed and took off her hat. Her hair was like living flames as it tumbled down her back. He wondered if it would burn his fingers if he were to touch it. "You're going to freckle," he growled, uncomfortable with his thoughts.

"You reckon so?"

He nodded and tried to redirect his thoughts. She was already covered with the things. He wondered how far down her neck they went. All the way to her breasts? Lower still? Surprisingly enough, they did little to mar her features. Her nose was sunburned, but small and nicely shaped. She had nice cheekbones, a delicate chin, and a pair of large, intelligent eyes set in a dense thicket of pale lashes. As for her mouth . . .

"My mama used to read books in French," she confided, and Davin tore his eyes away from her mouth and frowned at the road ahead. "She used to read out loud to me. I couldn't understand the words, but it sounded real pretty, sort of like music."

He glanced at her, ready to make some mocking remark, but she looked so wistful that instead, he reached out and squeezed her hand. But then the trail angled sharply downhill. The mule jogged along with the flow of gravity. Cecille dug in her hooves and bawled a protest, and Davin gripped the

111

reins with both hands and started swearing.

After a few minutes she said, "My papa was double-jointed, did I ever tell you that?" She smiled tentatively, testing his temper.

"No, you didn't."

"Well, he was. It embarrassed Mama, but sometimes for a special treat, he let me see him bend the wrong way. He had eyes the same color as mine, did I tell you that?"

"No, you didn't. Whoa there, you bone-headed old bastard!" Dammit, she didn't have to sound so dejected. What the devil did *she* have to be dejected about? At least she was no longer reduced to eating beeswax. She had a job as a nanny. If things worked out, the old man might even keep her on for a while.

If anyone should be feeling dejected, Davin told himself, it should be him. He'd had to sell both horses. Hadn't wanted to, but once the old pirate at the livery had learned that he was traveling with a woman and a baby, it had been a seller's market.

"Next shady clearing we come to, I need to change Paulie's napkin and boil up a batch of gruel. He's done et all I made up."

"Dunnette. Is that French?" The taunt was deliberate.

"No, it's not. Alley a dee-able. Now, that's real French."

Davin nearly swallowed the stub of his cigar. Could she by any chance mean *allez a diable?* Go to the devil? He'd never claimed to be much of a hand with languages, but with an office on the waterfront, he picked up a few choice phrases.

"Did your mama teach you that?"

"Uh-uh. John James taught me that. He was our butler. He used to work for a Frenchman down in New Orleans before he came north to Chattanooga."

112

"Your, uh . . . butler. I see. Was all your staff French?"

"My staff?"

"Maids. Cook. The people who took care of you."

"Oh, no. Mostly, I was took care of by the Irish."

And that, Rosie told herself, was true enough. Uncle Hiram, her grandfather's brothers, once bragged that his own father had brought the recipe for his whiskey all the way from Dublin, and Uncle Hiram had given her a roof over her head for nearly eight years. That qualified as caretaking, didn't it?

They turned off the rough trail into a rocky clearing beside a rushing stream. Davin jumped down, secured the mule, and lifted his arms to take the baby. Before he could lay him on his blanket and turn back to help his other passenger, she leapt down as nimbly as a mountain goat.

"Whooee, my daree-ear is sore as a b'iled possum!"

Her *derriere?*

Davin stifled a burst of laughter. The little minx was entertaining, he'd hand her that. Couldn't believe a word she said, of course. All the same, she made the time pass more quickly.

He mused on the odd inconsistencies he was beginning to discover in her words — not only the words themselves, but what they implied. How would a girl — no, he no longer thought of her as a girl — how would a woman who'd been raised the way she obviously had even know about such things as butlers and maids and French novels?

Chapter Four

The next day they rode silently for several hours. Davin had a lot on his mind. The baby was fretful, demanding all Charmaine's attention. Yet she was patient, he'd hand her that. Never a word of complaint. He pulled in beside a stream near midday, unhitched the mule and rubbed him down, and then watched her set about the task of milking, mixing up gruel, and spooning it into the baby's mouth, a messy job, at best. While she changed napkins, rinsed out soiled ones, and spread them over the wagon bed to dry, Davin found himself watching her. For a scruffy little barbarian, she was surprisingly graceful. And he had to admit, she was good with the boy.

Which was the only reason he'd allowed her to tag along, he reminded himself. When it came to women, his taste ran to something a little more civilized.

He'd built a small fire to heat the water for the gruel. Now he scooped up a basin of water and set it over the coals, figuring he might as well rid himself of his itchy stubble. When he turned around again, Charmaine had removed her boots, rolled up her trousers, and stepped down into the icy stream.

"Lady, you're plumb crazy," he called out.

She shot him a sunny smile, then, standing calf-deep in the middle of the creek, she closed her eyes and lifted her face to the sun.

Davin stared at her bare limbs, which were pale and remarkably shapely. He lifted his gaze to her face and was immediately struck by her look of . . . what? Pain? Pleasure? A mixture of both?

Of all things, he found himself remembering the last time he'd made love to a woman. "Come on out, Charmaine, it's too cold."

"It's tolerable once you get used to it."

It wasn't tolerable, it was damned cold. When he'd washed his hands after unhitching the mule, his arms had ached all the way up to his shoulder. He continued to watch as she bent over and splashed water on her face, reluctantly admiring the graceful arc of her back, the vulnerable nape where her hair fell away on either side. Swearing under his breath, he said impatiently, "Here, this water's warm." Gesturing to the basin perched on three rocks over the fire, he told her he had changed his mind about shaving. "You might as well use the water," he grumbled.

Another day's itching wouldn't kill him.

With the wild, tantalizing grace that continued to surprise him, she scrambled up out of the stream, an eager smile lighting her face. "Can I borrow your soap, too? Are you certain sure you can spare it?"

"I'm certain sure," he said dryly. "I have to ride upwind of you, remember?" Which wasn't a particular tactful thing to say, but he said it all the same. His tone sounded almost defensive.

Taking the basin and soap, she disappeared behind a thicket. Once she was out of sight Davin did something he'd been wanting to do ever since they'd left the cabin. Something of which he was not particularly proud.

He snooped. For no reason save the curiosity that had been growing ever since he'd first laid eyes on her, he opened the small cloth sack she'd been carrying when she'd first turned up at the cabin — the sack that had been somewhat larger and lumpier when they'd left.

The first thing he found was a jar full of . . . *buttons?* He

115

glanced at it, shook his head and set it aside, along with something small and hard that was knotted in a handkerchief. A pretty pebble, he figured.

And then he found the spoons. The same spoons, unless he was mistaken, that he'd last seen in Paul's cabin. Come to think of it, she'd been using one of those same spoons to poke food into the boy's mouth half a dozen times a day, only he hadn't thought anything of it.

Dav swore. He'd been doing a whole lot of that lately. Why in hell hadn't she spoken up if she'd wanted the damned spoons? He'd have given them to her gladly, not that they were his to give.

Jesus. Disappointment cut through him like a knife. He didn't recognize the cup and saucer wrapped in old yellowed newspapers, but he was pretty sure they, too, had belonged to Paul's widow.

"Ah, hell, Charmaine."

He didn't want her to be a thief. Sure, she was dirt poor. Being poor was no crime. God alone knew what she'd come from — it couldn't have been much. She had tagged along with him only because she obviously had nowhere better to go — either that or she was running away from something. But a thief . . .

Ah, hell.

He was still trying to make up his mind what to say to her when he noticed her shoes. They were wide, far too big for her small feet. He picked one up and the sole flapped loose where the crude stitching had come undone. Nailheads poked through the inside. She'd tried to pad them with rags.

Davin had been broke a time or two in his life, but he'd never been reduced to wearing boots made by a blind, one-armed cobbler using a flat iron for a last.

He was still holding a shoe when she came back again.

116

Intending to tackle her about the spoons, he heard himself saying, "Who the hell makes your shoes?" Which was a stupid question, only when it came right down to it, he couldn't bring himself to ask about the things she had stolen.

Her mouth opened and closed like a beached fish. She stared first at him, then at her naked feet, and then at the boot he held. "My shoes? I'm not certain sure. Why? Does it matter?"

"What the devil are you doing wearing these things?"

At first she looked puzzled, then pride took over. "The onliest reason I'm wearing those boots is because I've got the smallest feet in Dead— in the place where I come from, and when Eckerd Guthrie outgrew them, his ma gave them to me, so there!"

"So there," he repeated softly, stripped of his anger before he was ready. She was a sight to behold, hands on her hips, wet-agate eyes glistening in beds of pale copper lashes. He thought about confronting her with the stolen spoons, but then he thought, what the hell? They wouldn't do poor Mollie any good where she was.

"Put on your shoes. There's a settlement over the next ridge if I remember correctly. If we don't waste any more time, we might make it before dark."

It was late in the afternoon when they reached the settlement. Davin studied the huddle of houses, wondering if there was a boardinghouse among them.

As it turned out, there wasn't, but he managed to bargain with a farmer for hay and oats and a place in his barn to sleep, and with the gentleman's wife for supper, a bath, and a change of clothes for Charmaine. He told them she was his sister — that her house had burned and he was taking her and the baby to their father, which made him almost as big a liar as she was.

Expediency, he told himself as he forked clean straw into an empty stall and covered it with one of the quilts, could make a man do peculiar things. He'd lied, paid through the nose for a rag hardly better than a dust cloth, paid even more for a night in a drafty barn and two meals, all in advance. "You and the baby can sleep in here. I'll take the loft," he said, and found himself wondering if she'd be warm enough. If he shared the stall with her, they'd all three sleep warmer, but he didn't suggest it.

The next morning she was wearing her new finery. The dress, several sizes too large, was a faded red calico. You'd have thought it was China silk from the look of pride on her face. The slat bonnet he'd paid two dollars more for would shade her face, and while it owed nothing at all to fashion, it was a damned sight better than that ragged old straw hat she'd been wearing.

Davin was touched by her look of shining pride. It made him wish he could have given her something a bit better. The farm woman's feet had been even bigger than his own, else he would have talked her out of a pair of shoes.

Meanwhile, Rosie was doing some trading of her own. Back in the kitchen after watching the woman hand-feed a motherless calf, she brought out her jar of buttons and dumped them out onto the table. "My baby's a orphan, too. I feed him cornmeal mush and milk from a spoon, but sometimes he wants to suck on something real bad. If I had me one of them bottles, I could make pretend he was a-nursing, jest like that calf. Now, I got me these buttons that come all the way from Chattanooga, maybe even Paris."

Some twenty minutes later, both women were beaming when, after a few messy attempts, Paulie remembered how to suckle. Rosie thought about the woman named Mollie, who'd had him for such a brief time. It was then that she made up her mind to find out all about her so that she could tell little Paul when he was old enough to understand.

If she was still around.

Blackie was eager to get on the road, so she didn't dare linger over the best breakfast she'd had in more years than she could remember. Quickly, she gobbled down a stack of pancakes, three fat sausages, and a mess of scrambled eggs, and when she couldn't find room for a third biscuit, she waited until no one was watching and shoved it into her pocket.

Blackie, when he'd come in from hitching up the wagon, hadn't said a word about how pretty she looked in her new finery, but she didn't take it to heart. Men were naturally grouchy creatures. It was against their principles to be happy.

The farmer, though — he gave her a good looking over when he followed them outside. "That there frock never looked half as good on my Marthie. Obliged if ye wouldn't tell her I said it, though."

Rosie beamed. Blackie harrumphed. He didn't speak a word until they were well down the road and she took out the nursing bottle.

"Where the hell did that thing come from?"

"The bottle? I traded Miz Marthie six jet buttons for it. She said she could use a bucket and a glove for the calf until she could send off for a new one."

Buttons. It was the opening Davin had been waiting for to bring up the theft of those seven silver teaspoons. Instead, he heard himself saying, "I suppose now you'll be wanting me to stop every half hour and milk that damned cow."

"Name me one time when you milked Cecille." The truth was, the old thing was nearly dry. It took all Rosie's skill, which wasn't that great, to get her to let down even a few drops.

"Is it my fault she won't let me near her?"

119

"I 'speck it is. You frown at her. Cecille's real sensitive."

"Sensitive my — !"

"Shhh, the baby's nearly 'bout dozed off."

They headed on down the mountain, with Davin scowling and Rosie humming and occasionally bursting into song. She had cut holes in the brim of her old straw and fitted it on the mule, who didn't seem to have a name, but who could now boast a custom-made hat trimmed with a bouquet of wilted dogwood blossoms.

Just after noon they passed through another small community. There were several fresh graves visible from the road. "Cholera," Davin said grimly.

It was the first time in more than an hour he'd volunteered so much as a word. Rosie sighed with relief. She didn't much care what they talked about, as long as they talked. Uncle Hiram had been a stingy man with words, their handful of neighbors no better.

"That's real sad. It was the diphtheria that took off my family. Did I tell you that? Not Uncle Hiram, though. He got shot. Or maybe hanged, I don't know for certain sure."

The look he gave her said that either he didn't believe her or didn't know what to make of what she'd said.

She couldn't much blame him. Uncle Hiram wasn't a relative a body could be proud of, but at least she was far enough away from Dead Mule Valley now that she didn't have to worry so much about being chased down by vigilantes, herself.

After a while, he asked if she was still feeling all right, and she nodded. "Fine as George's shine."

"Dare I ask what George's shine consists of?"

"I couldn't rightly say what it consists of, 'sides cornmeal and sugar, but he gets near 'bout twenty dollars a gallon. That's real good money."

Dav nearly strangled. When he'd cleared his breathing passages again, he thought it best to change the subject. In his particular social set, whiskey making wasn't the done thing. The whiskey itself was greatly in demand, but the making of it was generally left to others.

"Paul still feeling all right?"

"Fightin' fit."

They rode on in silence for another mile or so. Then, he said, "I'm not sure, but I think we might have missed getting infected."

Rosie knew right off what he was talking about. "You're still thinking Paul's ma died of the cholera, aren't you?"

"Well, hell . . . what else? I doubt if she died of childbirth, not after that long."

"It was likely toadstools."

"I beg your pardon?"

"I said she likely died of eating them toadstools."

"You mean the mushrooms?"

"Kissin' kin. I can't say for certain sure, but they didn't look right to me. A body can't be too careful c'lecting mushrooms. From the look of her things, she was a city-bred woman. She might not've knowed better."

Davin thought about it for a while and decided it didn't really matter what had killed her. The woman was gone. And Paul was gone, too, and Dav was still wondering just how much of what he'd learned about his younger brother to tell their father.

He had tracked Paul from Winston-Salem, where he'd married and promptly run through his bride's money, to Raleigh. In Raleigh he'd gone into business with a partner, cleaned out the till after some six months and high-tailed it to Asheville, where he'd soon gambled away everything he owned. From there he'd fled westward with his wife and newborn baby, one step ahead of his creditors. Somewhere along the way he'd injured his leg. It had gotten infected, and afraid to seek out a doctor, he had died of blood poisoning.

His wife had managed to get word to Marshall Banister, who had sent for Dav to find his daughter-in-law and grandson and bring them back to Seven Oaks.

God, what a sorry tale.

Almost as if she knew what he was thinking, the woman beside him reached over and patted him on the thigh. He was astonished. There was nothing at all sexual in the gesture. It was meant to be comforting, and against all reason, he found himself being comforted.

Then the baby started to whimper, and she rocked him in her arms and sang him a doleful song about bare trees and blackbirds. Dav winced, but he didn't try to shut her up. Actually, he was coming to enjoy her caterwauling. Or if not enjoy, at least tolerate. He had to admit that thief or not, she had her good points. No matter how much sleep she lost, how many napkins she had to wash out in icy streams — how long it took her to squeeze a cup of milk from that contrary old cow, with the baby howling fit to raise Jerusalem — she never complained. He knew damned well she grew tired. He could see her shoulders slump, but she soldiered on.

Shaking his head in reluctant admiration, Dav thought, given sufficient time and motivation, a man might even be able to civilize her.

Chapter Five

Rosie's memories of Chattanooga, embellished over years of a hand-to-mouth existence in Dead Mule Valley, vanished in the blink of an eye the moment she caught sight of Asheville. In the golden glow of a setting sun it was purely magical, all the fine houses, the fancy wrought-iron fences, the elaborate cupolas and lightning rods with their big glass balls. There were gardens and flowering trees, and gentlemen in suits and dapper hats riding fine horses, driving snappy little runabouts or strolling with beautiful ladies in lace-trimmed silk gowns, enormous hats, and pointy-toed shoes.

"Oh, lookee there, Blackie! That lady's got a turkey buzzard on top of her hat!"

"Blackie?" Her companion sent her a quizzical look.

Rosie was practically bouncing up and down on the hard plank seat as she gazed at all the sights of the city. Catching her excitement, little Paul began to bounce and chortle and wave his tiny fists.

"Settle down, you two, before you fall off the wagon. I'll bespeak us a pair of rooms in the boardinghouse I stayed in last time I was through here. It'll be more than a pleasure, I can tell you, to spend a night without rocks under my backside, or straw tickling my neck and a damned rooster crowing me awake before daylight."

Rosie settled down, but she didn't stop looking. Oh, my, no. There was too much to take in. She had so much to learn now that she was all grown up. Of all the lovely ladies in their pretty gowns, not a one of them was wearing faded calico. A young girl skipped past rolling a hoop, wearing a white dress that came down just below her knees. She wore white stockings and high button shoes, and a wide pink sash around her waist.

Rosie thought, once upon a time I had a pretty white dress . . .

In her heart, or wherever such memories were stored, she heard the echo of her mother's voice. *One of these days, cherié, you will put up your hair and let down your skirts, and every gentleman from Chateauroux to Chattanooga will come to pay you court.* She'd called it Shattanooga. She'd always said it that way, and Papa had always teased her about it.

Rosie had long since put up her hair all by herself. She would have chopped it off except that Papa had always said long hair was a woman's crowning glory. But before she could let down her hems, she had outgrown all her pretty dresses and pinafores. Uncle Hiram had bought her a pair of Eckerd Guthrie's outgrown overalls, fussing because he'd had to pay fifty cents for them. She'd been wearing hand-me-downs ever since. Eckerd's and Uncle Hiram's.

Now she sighed and gawked, and gawked some more. By the time Blackie pulled up in front of the boardinghouse, she was exhausted by her own excitement. The cow needed milking, the baby needed feeding and changing, and she was acutely conscious of the stares of all the well-dressed people milling around the front room of Mrs. Smith's Fine Boarding & Dining Establishment.

"My niece," Blackie muttered to the man behind the desk. "And nephew. Brother's child." He looked embarrassed, which embarrassed her in turn. She hugged Paulie close, and he rewarded her by spitting sour milk down her back.

"You and me had better be on our best behavior, little

dumplin'," she whispered. "Else we'll be sleeping in the barn again tonight."

A snippity maid led the way upstairs. Blackie followed with his saddlebags, into which he'd crammed the baby's things and Rosie's bundle. She hoped he didn't break the dishes. She had wrapped them in newspaper and been real careful, but men didn't set much store by lady things.

On the landing halfway up the stairs, she glanced up, almost expecting to see a stained-glass window, but the neat pattern of tan stripes and medallions on the maroon wallpaper was broken only by a framed lithograph of dead rabbits, a gun, and some onions.

The prune-faced maid opened a door and said with a sniff and a jerk of her head, "Her and the baby can stay in here. Bed's been aired. Coal in the grate. Extra blankets is ten cents apiece."

And then, while Rosie lingered in the doorway, her weary arms sagging under the weight of the squirming infant, the woman led Blackie to the far end of the hall. "I put you in here, sir. It'll be nice and quiet. The bathroom's right across the hall, and we have a furnace in the basement, so you can have all the hot water you want. Most of the rooms is empty."

Davin had soaked in the big claw-footed tub for nearly half an hour, enjoying a cigar and a glass of surprisingly decent Bordeaux, before it occurred to him that as a gentleman, he probably should have offered Charmaine the first bath.

Only then he'd have had to look after the baby and maybe even milk the cow, and God knows, she was better at both those chores that he was. That was the reason he'd brought her along, wasn't it? And he had to admit she'd done a good job. She was a cheerful little thing, too. Nothing fazed her, not even the baby spitting up all over her shoulder or leaking on her lap, both of which events occurred on a more or less regular schedule.

Still, he should've offered her the first bath. The trouble was, he'd been a loner for too long. He wasn't used to thinking about anyone except himself. In his younger days he'd shared everything with his brother, putting Paul's interests ahead of his own, and look how tragically *that* had turned out.

Face it, Banister, you're a heartless, self-centered bastard.

Propping a pair of hairy, muscular legs on the rim of the tub, he considered ways of making amends. First of all he'd arrange for someone else to do the milking tonight. Next he'd make sure the little heathen had time to eat her fill of supper, if he had to pay a maid to take care of Paul. The way her eyes had lit up when she'd seen the plain fare the farmer's wife had prepared, you'd think she hadn't had a square meal in the last ten years.

He reminded himself that it might be a good idea before they left town tomorrow to ask directions to the nearest ladies' emporium. He could well afford to buy her a decent pair of shoes. He'd seen the way people stared at her when they'd first walked into the lobby. She'd stared right back, her eyes big as saucers, not a bit self-conscious in her faded calico dress and her clumsy, worn-out boots.

He didn't want anyone thinking he couldn't afford to dress his own niece. Or sister — or whatever he'd thought to call her this time. So maybe he'd buy her a new dress, too. One that wasn't faded, outdated, and five sizes too big. And some underpinnings. For all he knew, she didn't wear a stitch underneath. If she did, it was probably made of feed sacks, like that godawful shirt with the faded lettering across the back.

Sliding lower in the tub, Dav admired his own long, narrow feet. Banister men ran to long bones, broad shoulders, and narrow hands and feet. While the water cooled, he relaxed in sheer hedonistic appreciation of hot water and scented soap, a decent wine, and a fine cigar. Another week and he'd be home, his obligation to the old man at an end. It was about time he got back to his own interests.

"Lordie, you look dapper as a riverboat gambler," Charmaine declared later when he rapped on her door after dressing in freshly polished boots, a freshly laundered shirt, and freshly brushed coat a short while later. He'd told the maid to take the lot and do the best she could for him.

"And just how many riverboat gamblers have you known, Miss Duvallier?"

"None, I reckon, it's jest something my pa used to say. Are they gettin' ready to feed us now? Do I have time to milk Cecille first? Paulie's gettin' hungry. He sounds right fretty."

Davin felt another chunk of the dam he'd built around his heart crumble away. God knows why, but the little witch was beginning to get under his guard. An unkempt thieving liar she might be, but she did have her good qualities. Besides which, he would never forget seeing her silhouetted against the flap of canvas he'd hung over the wagon bed as a makeshift tent a few nights ago. He'd been greasing a wagon wheel on one side of the wagon, the campfire on the other. Behind the flimsy wall she had first washed the baby and tucked him in, then peeled down her overalls and shirt to bathe in what was left of the warm water.

And he'd watched. Like the low scoundrel he was, he'd watched as she lifted first one arm and then the other, her small breasts clearly silhouetted against the flickering firelight. If she'd been wearing a single stitch of underwear, it wasn't evident. He'd had to tramp in circles around the camp for damn near an hour, going over shipping manifests in his head, before he could tame his raging libido.

When she'd poked her head out from under the wagon

and asked what he was looking for out there, he'd told her he was guarding the camp. Making sure there were no predatory animals in the vicinity. Knowing damned well there was at least one. Himself.

He hadn't been able to sleep. After wrestling with the mule all day along roads more suited to a mountain goat, he should have passed out the minute his head hit the ground, only he hadn't been able to get his mind off the vision of a small, decidedly female figure silhouetted against a fragile canvas barrier.

It was not only embarrassing, it was downright worrisome. He liked women as much as the next man, but he liked them beautiful, willing, and experienced.

Not to mention clean and well dressed.

At least she was clean, now. By the time they left tomorrow she'd be well dressed. He told himself he was doing it for the sake of his pride — no other reason. What possible other reason could there be?

One stern look was enough to end any curiosity when Davin escorted his two charges into Delphine's Ladies' Wear the next morning. If the woman who introduced herself as Delphine suspected him of having plucked the pair of them off the orphan train, she had better sense than to mention it.

The first thing they tried on was shoes. He bought her a pair of sturdy lace-up boots, and because he saw her gazing at them longingly, he told Delphine to include a pair of low-cut opera pumps with tiny spool heels. "You'll probably break your neck trying to walk in the things," he whispered. She was so overcome with excitement he was afraid she was going to burst into tears. "Here, give me the baby while you look at the dresses. She'll need something sensible for traveling," he instructed the proprietress.

Charmaine nodded eagerly. "With lots of lace and one of

those poochy little things that pokes out the back of the skirt."

Dav wondered why he hadn't simply asked her size and ordered a pair of shoes and a couple of outfits delivered to the boardinghouse.

"You mean a dress improver," he heard the older woman say as they disappeared into a fitting room. "Of course, they're not really in style any longer. The new fashions are —"

The door closed behind them and Davin crossed his legs and prepared himself for a lengthy wait. He wasn't particularly embarrassed, having visited such establishments more than a few times with various women. He'd always prided himself on being a generous lover.

But this was different, he reminded himself sternly. Entirely different.

Time passed. Muffled voices emerged from the fitting room, and from time to time the voluptuous Miss Delphine darted out, grabbed another armload of fripperies, and dashed back in again, sometimes offering him a wink and a smile in passing, sometimes only the lift of a penciled eyebrow.

Paulie grew fretful. To entertain him, Dav dangled his pocket watch by the chain, but the baby seemed more interested in sampling his silk cravat. By the time the fitting room door opened again and the two women emerged, his necktie was in ruins, his patience in little better condition.

He stood, gently disengaging his tie from gums and tiny fists. "All done? Come along then, we've wasted too much time as it is."

And then he took a good long look and swallowed hard.

She was dressed in a navy skirt that made her waist look no bigger than his wrist and emphasized the swell of her hips. With it she wore a shirtwaist the color of strawberry ice cream. No lace, but a ruffle around the stand-up collar. With her flaming red hair, the color should have looked awful, but somehow, it didn't.

"Aren't I beautiful?" she asked shyly. And dear God, she was. Davin could only stare. She lifted her skirts and stuck out one small foot in a foolish, high-heeled pump. "Lookee here, aren't these the prettiest things ever you saw?"

Delphine, holding a green dress and several layers of frothy white garments over her arm, looked pleased as punch. The baby burbled gleefully and spit up down the front of Dav's coat.

"I bought me two petticoats and a nightshift and some drawers with little ruffles on the —"

"Charmaine!"

"Well, I jest wanted you to know I mean to pay you back for everything."

"That won't be necessary," he said grimly, mopping off his coat with a handkerchief that was already soggy and sour.

"Has he been troublesome?" She held out her arms and Paulie lunged toward her. "Come here, sweetpea, look at Mama's pretty new frock."

"Charmaine!"

"Madam! Your blouse!"

Davin quickly paid the tab and got her out of there before anything more disastrous could occur. They'd already lost half a day's travel. At this rate it would be Christmas before they ever got home.

"I'm sorry. I didn't mean to disrespect Paulie's mama," she said once he'd settled them into the wagon. "It jest slipped out."

She sounded so chagrined he didn't have the heart to correct her. And what the devil — if she wanted to pretend for a little while the baby was hers, where was the harm?

"It wasn't that, it was your new clothes. We — uh, that

is, Miss Delphine and I didn't want to see all your new finery ruined before you'd even had chance to break it in."

Tears spilled over her thick coppery lashes. "That's jest about the sweetest thing ever I heard."

Dav rolled his eyes. Still holding the baby, he untied the reins and climbed up beside her. "Look, I'm going to drive you back to the boardinghouse and then see if I can't find us something more comfortable to travel in than a farm wagon. We've lost so much time, we might as well stay over another day." She was too busy flicking her skirt to admire her petticoat ruffle to argue, so he went ahead and shot his wad. "And forget trying to pay me back, Charmaine. You don't owe me anything. Consider it part of your salary."

Up came her head. With a regal air that should have been comical but somehow wasn't, she informed him that McGuires didn't cotton to being beholden.

Paul took the opportunity of his distraction to lunge at a passing dog. Dav hung on to him, just barely, then handed him over to Charmaine, wet chin, wet bottom, and all. "Beholden?" he repeated once they'd wheeled out into the main thoroughfare. "And just what the devil is a McGuire?"

Chapter Six

Charmaine, it seemed, was a McGuire. Not only was she not a Duvallier, she wasn't even a Charmaine. She was a Mary Rose.

"Why the devil did you lie to me about your name?" Davin demanded the next morning, even though he'd suspected all along she'd made it up.

"I didn't want to leave no trail."

He was flummoxed. For one long moment he simply stared at her. Which wasn't all that difficult, as she was looking rather spectacular. In a wholesome, bright-eyed sort of way. She'd spent so much time bathing — three baths in less than twenty-four hours, to his count — that he'd been late getting shaved, which meant they'd been late getting off.

Which meant he was already in a foul mood, without this.

"This trail thing — you want to explain that for me?"

He watched as she played with Paulie's feet. He had long feet, long toes. When one of them went into his toothless mouth, she sighed and said, "Uncle Hiram was a McGuire, too," as if that explained everything.

By the time she'd finished telling him about her uncle Hiram and his various enterprises, most of which Dav gathered were on the shady side of the law, and how he'd met his infamous end, he could only stare at her, slack-jawed.

"You lived in that place — that —"

"Dead Mule Valley," she supplied.

"— for eight years, *by yourself?*"

"Well, Uncle Hiram came home from time to time. He

132

didn't much cotton to having me there, though, so mostly, I tried not to talk."

She tried not to talk. For eight years! "So what did you do?"

She shrugged. "Miz Guthrie showed me how to make soap and wash and cook and such. Eckerd showed me how to set a rabbit gum and how to find bee hollers. Old Crackcorn showed me how to tickle trout, and when he took a bear he always give — gave me a mess o' bear meat. I got on jest fine. I think Uncle Hiram was right glad of me a time or two. Leastwise he ate my cookin'."

"Jesus." Davin closed his eyes in reverent amazement.

"I sewed some. I was a real good sang-getter, too, 'bout the best getter in the whole valley, Miz Guthrie said. Eckert took mine along with his when he went across the ridge to the buyer, and I give him a penny ever' time out of my savin's."

"Your savings."

"I was savin' up to go back to Chattanooga, only I reckon Uncle Hiram borrowed from my savin's jar. It weren't — wasn't there when I looked." Lately, Dav had noticed that she'd been working on both her grammar and her diction.

Taking a deep breath, he waited for the picture to clarify. "Then it was true? All that business about your folks, and living in Chattanooga? And the stained-glass window above the stairs?"

"It was jest a little one. I used to think it was big as Lookout Mountain, but now I'm all grown up, I know better. It was real pretty, though. Mama used to let me stand there and get colors all over my dress."

He thought about an innocent child with a family, a nice home — probably even a nanny — playing with shards of colored light. He thought about that same child being wrenched from her small, safe world and being sent to live with a surly old hermit in the back of beyond, where she'd had to *try not to talk*.

It damn near broke his heart.

So he told her about his father's home — about the place they were headed, vowing silently to force his father to let her stay. The old man owed him something after all this.

"The place I'm taking you — I think you'll like it, Char — Mary Rose. It's got stained glass, but it's beside the front door, not on a stair landing. There's a pretty garden — at least there used to be — and lots of big trees . . ."

"Paulie can have a swing. I had me a swing when I was little. Papa used to swing Mama there, too, when I was supposed to be taking my nap."

A happy family. Well, he couldn't promise her that. The old man had always been cantankerous. Now that he was ailing, he'd be worse than ever, but at least he wouldn't cane her. Dav would break his cane over his head if he ever lifted it against her.

"It's called Seven Oaks," he told her. "Our farm. They're water oaks, not turkey oaks, so the leaves turn yellow instead of red along about Thanksgiving. My brother and I, we used to rake 'em up into piles and then land belly-floppers right on top of the heap."

"I don't think our house had a name." She scrunched up her eyes — in the green dress, they were more green than hazel, he'd noticed. "Or maybe it was called two oaks, some pines, and a sycamore. Those are the only trees I can remember besides Mama's rosebushes."

He nodded gravely, trying not to smile. Not for the world would he embarrass her by laughing at her earnest confidences. So far, he was more inclined to cry than to laugh.

She kept reaching up to adjust her hat. Delphine had called

it a skimmer. He'd gone back early that morning before they'd left town to buy it on account of he couldn't see her wearing her old slat bonnet with her new finery.

"Have I told you how nice you look this morning?" Before the words were out, he realized what a whopping understatement that was. She looked like a cross between a big-eyed kid on Christmas morning and the angel on top of the tree.

An angel who wanted to be called Rosie. A redheaded angel with freckles, a sunny smile, and the gracious manners of a muleskinner.

Although that was rapidly changing. He'd seen how she watched other women wherever they went. Already she'd learned to cross her ankles when she sat instead of turning her toes in or spreading her knees and flopping her feet over onto the sides. He suspected that had been her way of taking the pressure off those damned nailheads poking up through her shoes.

"I think he likes it," she said, and Dav nodded. Indeed he did. A little too much. "That there basket bed you made for him."

"Oh. Paulie, you mean. Yeah, he looks pretty happy to lie there and watch the treetops go past."

She grinned, and he grinned back at her. *Slow down, Banister. This one's off limits. Way off limits!*

They stopped at an inn and he sold the cow and bought a picnic dinner, and then had to deal with Rosie's tears over the cow.

"We can find milk most anywhere now that we're back in civilization," he reasoned. "They even sell it in stores these days. Trust me, Paulie won't go hungry."

"Cecille'll think we didn't like her."

"Cows don't think, honey. They kick and litter the roads and break wind, and they come in handy now and again when

135

you need milk and there's no store around, but mostly they're a bloody nuisance. We'd have been halfway to Raleigh by now if it hadn't been for having to drag that old animal along behind us, and having to stop at every crossroad to milk her."

"It weren't — wasn't that often. You didn't even let me say good-bye," Rosie wailed tearfully. She'd told him right from the first she was an easy cryer. Since then she'd more than proved it.

"Come on now, honey, dry up. I sold her to a nice family with a whole quiverful of young'uns. Their cow died, and they were in desperate need of a replacement. She'll be happy there."

"You're certain sure?"

Her eyes would be the death of him yet, Dav told himself. Big, earnest — too damned beautiful, even drowning in tears. He took her hand, feeling the strength, the delicacy of her bones, the leathery calluses in her palms. "I'm certain sure," he promised her.

Okay, so they'd had only two kids, but they'd agreed to buy the old bag of bones for a third of what he'd paid for her. He figured it was the best deal he was likely to get.

They picnicked on the banks of the Broad River. Rosie held Paulie on her lap and fed him from the nursing bottle with milk Dav had purchased at the inn. Leaning against a tree, he watched lazily, admiring the picture they made, contrasting it with the first time he'd ever seen them together. A skinny, frightened kid in dirty overalls and a stinking, squalling baby.

Could that have been only a week ago? It seemed like months. Years. But then, they'd been together, the three of them, constantly since then. That added up to a whole lot of together.

She brought up the baby's wind and then laughed and hugged him, and Dav tried to remember the last time he had been hugged, other than in a sexual context. Had his father ever hugged him? He couldn't remember a single time. His mother might've, but he'd been too young to recall if she had or not.

Not that it mattered.

The baby, now lying on his belly across her lap, let out another satisfying belch, and she looked up, beaming as if it were the most outstanding accomplishment of the century. "I was scared he weren't going to take to store-bought milk, but he likes it jest fine. Just, that is. Davin —" He'd told her his name — after her confession, he'd felt obliged to — and now she called him that instead of Blackie. "Davin, will you tell me all about Mollie and Big Paul so I can write it down for him? A boy ought to know his own folks, and it's awful easy to let things slip away."

He didn't want to talk about it. Luckily, he had a good excuse. "I never knew my sister-in-law. I'm not sure if my father ever met her, but he's the one to tell you whatever you want to know."

"You could tell me about your brother. I could start with that and write it all out, and then write what's happened since I come along so when Paulie's grown up and living in all those oaks, he'll know who fetched him there, and then your pa can tell him his side of the story, and about his mama."

So in Wilkesboro he bought her a pencil and tablet. And a slew of baby napkins, because her hands were red and rough from washing constantly in cold streams. He checked them into the town's finest inn, glad he'd disposed of that damned cow and traded the mule and wagon for a pair and a nice little buggy. At least he didn't feel like he ought to sneak in through the back door.

"Yessir, Mr. Banister, sir, I've put you in our best room, and Miss — Mrs. —"

"My ward, Miss McGuire, and my nephew," Dav filled in smoothly. He was getting used to it after a week on the road, but it was becoming more and more awkward to explain the presence of an attractive young woman traveling with a baby and a man not her husband.

"Your ward. I see, sir. And will you and your ward be wanting adjoining rooms?"

Dav felt the muscles at the back of his neck tighten as he took in the oily gleam in the young clerk's eyes. "Actually, I'd appreciate being far enough away so that if the boy cries in the night, my sleep won't be disturbed."

There, he thought with grim satisfaction. That should cold-cock any notions in your nasty little mind, you damned grub-worm. For good measure, he said, "There's a pail of dirty napkins out in the buggy. Send someone out to collect it, will you? Tell your laundress there's a tip in it for her if she can have them done up by nine tomorrow morning."

They met in the lobby for dinner. Dav had sent a maid to sit with the boy. Rosie, wearing her opera pumps, skirt, and shirtwaist, negotiated the stairs cautiously. She'd done something with her hair. He'd sent a maid out to buy her some hairpins after he'd noticed her attempts to emulate the new hairstyles. This time she'd got it about half right. The effect was glorious.

"I'm going to pay you back for everything," she promised again as they sat down to eat. "I still have —"

"Stop it, Rosie." He didn't want to be reminded that she still had a bundle of stolen silverware. "We'll settle everything when we get to Seven Oaks."

"I just didn't want you worrying I was costing you too

138

much. I know you spent a passel on these clothes, and —"

"I told you to forget it!"

"And I told you us McGuires don't take to bein' beholden."

He sighed. "You're not beholden, Rosie. I could hardly have brought the baby this far without you, now could I? He trusts you."

"Babies trusts ever'body."

"He didn't trust me. You heard how he screamed whenever I tried to do anything with him that first day or so."

"You fed him beans."

"He was starving."

"Yes, well — you like to busted his precious little gut," she informed him. Then, for no reason except that they'd weathered the worst and were on the homeward stretch, they both started laughing.

"Lawsy," Rosie gasped when she could speak again. "That's about the best tickled I've been in a coon's age!"

Dav wiped his eyes and nodded. He'd never done much laughing, at least not since he'd been on his own. It certainly felt good. He wondered if he should plan on spending a day or so in his old home, just long enough to see Rosie and the baby settled in. If the old man would even allow it. He might not, now that he had what he wanted.

Better not. Better to let her go. He'd miss the laughter, though, and the feeling of sharing something good. It'd been a long time since he'd shared anything that mattered.

Rosie missed sleeping in the same bed with little Paulie. After sleeping on a thin pallet in a drafty lean-to for years, she liked the friendly feel of a warm soft body beside her.

But the hotel people had rolled in a baby bed, and it seemed a shame not to let him sleep in it as long as Davin

139

was paying extra for the use of it.

She flopped over onto her back and then had to tug her twisted nightgown out from under her body. It took some getting used to — wearing so many clothes. For almost as long as she could recall — at least since her bosoms had swelled up and she'd commenced her womanly flow — she'd worn overalls and homemade shirts, and in the wintertime she'd worn a pair of Uncle Hiram's old longhandles underneath. She'd slept in those, or in a feed sack with armholes cut out.

She wiggled her toes against the silky, sweet-smelling sheets, wondering if she was dreaming it all, and would soon wake up back in her own familiar corner.

Sometime later, eyes staring up into the darkness, Rosie listened for whatever had roused her from a disturbing dream.

Not the baby. Baby noises didn't leave her all sweaty with the blood racing through her like a spring-thawed creek.

"Oh — oh — oh, oh, *oohhh!*"

Lord ha' mercy, it was right next door!

On and on it went, breathless little yelps and a whole long string of whimpers and oh-ohs. Some poor woman was being beaten to death, right in the room next door!

Rosie sat up, wondering if it was already too late. She'd give anything for her uncle's hog rifle, but all she had was a chair and a chamber pot. She'd have to get real close to use either of those. Slipping out of bed, she crept across the room and pressed her ear against the wall.

Silence. Maybe the poor thing was already dead.

But no — she was fighting back! Rosie distinctly heard the sound of a man's groan. And then he commenced to yelp like a coon dog hot on the trail.

"Serves you right, you sorry skunk," she muttered. "I hope

140

she ties a knot in your tail and hangs you up for buzzard bait!" Pausing only long enough to determine that Paulie was sleeping soundly, she slipped out into the hall and ran silently to Davin's door. Not even bothering to knock, she darted inside and felt her way to his bed.

"Davin," she whispered. "Wake up right now!"

"Whaaa . . ."

"There's a killing goin' on! You've got to do something real quick, before it's too late!"

Dav sat up and rubbed his eyes. He'd been dreaming about Annie, his last mistress. Before he realized that the warm, sweet-smelling female tugging on his arm was Rosie, not Annie, he had her under him and was burying his face in the warm curve of her neck while he tugged her nightgown up around her waist.

She kept trying to say something, so he kissed her. There were only two ways to silence a woman like Annie, and at the moment he was fresh out of jewelry.

The scent of heated woman rose up around him, driving him almost over the edge. He found her breasts — had they always been this small? This firm? Funny — he didn't remember them that way.

She kept right on talking — trying to talk — so he was forced to keep right on trying to silence her. And God, it was sweet. He couldn't remember a time lately when he'd wanted her the way he did now, almost as if he'd never had a woman before.

She jerked her head away, causing his mouth to trail across to her ear, so he nibbled on that. "Davin, wake up!"

"Shhh, spread your legs for me, darling, I need you again. Ah, no, not like that — !" Her thighs clamped tightly on his roving hand. She kept going on and on about . . .

"A *killing?*"

"I keep trying to tell you, he's whomping her something fierce right in the room next to mine! I heard it plain as day. She was a-yelling and he was a-groaning, and I could hear the bed slamming up against the wall like he was pounding her something awful. You've got to *do* something!"

Reluctantly, Dav sat up and rubbed the back of his neck. He blinked at the figure in his bed, her nightgown twisted up around her neck. No way in hell could he have stopped himself from looking. Her breasts, small and high — her narrow waist — the womanly flare of her hips, her full thighs and . . .

Even in the near darkness he could see the color of her hair. It was red . . . everywhere. He swore softly and abruptly jerked the covers up to her chin. "Jesus," he whispered, partly from guilt, partly from frustration. "I'm sorry as I can be, Rosie. I didn't know — that is, I didn't realize —"

"You c'n wrassle some other time, but right now you got to stop him from killing her!"

"Honey, go back to bed. It's all right. He's not hurting her."

It was the wrong thing to say. She sat up and grabbed him by the shoulders, twisting him around to face her.

He didn't want to face her, not tonight, not tomorrow — not a hundred years from now. God, this was Rosie, and he'd almost —

"Damn your sorry hide, there's a woman bein' mommicked to death right down the hall, and if you don't do something —"

"What the hell do you want me to do?"

"I don't know — tell him to stop! Borrow a gun and shoot him! Jest don't let him hurt her. I don't hold with hurting folks."

Gently, Davin clasped her shoulders and eased her away from him. He was still hard as a rock. Embarrassment didn't change that, unfortunately. "Listen, Rosie, nobody's hurting anybody. Five'll get you ten they're only making love. Do you understand? Hasn't anyone ever told you the facts of life?"

In the thin gray moonlight, he could see her eyes. Not the color, but the wide, disbelieving stare. Didn't she know *anything?*

But then, who would have told her? This Eckerd fellow she talked about so much? Her mother? That damned no-good uncle of hers?

He sighed, raked a hand through his hair, and wondered exactly when his life had gone off the rails. He'd been well on his way to establishing himself in the shipping world — in a modest way, at least. He'd taken a few weeks off to do a favor for his father, which made him feel good about himself, because he didn't owe the old bastard the time of day.

And now, here he was, through no fault of his own, getting ready to explain the facts of life to a woman who was beginning to affect him in a way no woman ever had before.

"All right, Rosie, we may as well start at the beginning. Now, when a mare comes in season . . ."

Chapter Seven

He might have known it wouldn't be that simple. Where Rosie McGuire was concerned, nothing was ever simple. Davin didn't know which he would less rather do — knock on a stranger's door and inquire if the man was murdering his wife or making love to her, or try to explain the facts of life to a full-grown woman. A woman who was beginning to appeal to him far too much.

"Go back to your room," he said gruffly. "I'll meet you there as soon as I get dressed."

"She could be dead by then."

"I'm not going anywhere in my damned drawers!"

Lord, where had that haughty look come from? You'd have thought she was to the manor born.

Which, he thought ruefully, she might well be. "Rosie, trust me," he said gently. "If the woman dies, it'll be only temporary, and no — don't even ask me to explain that. I'll tell you all you need to know once I get some clothes on."

Some armor on, he might well have said. Ten minutes later when he rapped softly on her door, she was ready for him. Wearing her feed-sack shirt over the imported lawn nightgown Delphine had cleverly added to the pile, she sat cross-legged on the bed, just as if she hadn't come within a hair of being seduced.

"Is that the way a man and a woman kiss when they make love? Like you did with me?"

"Sort of — yeah, I guess it is, but Rosie, you have to understand. I was asleep. I, um — didn't know what I was doing. If I frightened you —"

"You didn't. I thought it was real interesting. Now . . . you were telling me about this mare of yours. You mean folks do it jest like horses and dogs do it?"

"Stop saying jest, Rosie! The word is *just!*" Which was an indication of just how close to the edge he was.

She nodded solemnly. "I know I embarrass you. I'm trying to remember how to talk right, but I haven't heard a whole lot of talkin' since I left Chattanooga. Mostly je— just Eckerd Guthrie. Him and me used to —"

"He and I."

Her jaw — small and delicately formed — dropped like a shot. "I didn't know you knew Eckerd."

Dav hung on to his reason by a thread. "I never had the pleasure. What I meant was, the proper way to say it is he and I, not him and me. Unless —" She stared at him, waiting to soak up whatever pearl of wisdom he might impart. "Forget it. The proper way to say it is that he and I did . . . well, whatever it was you did together." And he was beginning to wonder about *that,* too.

"Most ever'thing, I reckon. We used to pretend like he was my baby brother when we were little, on account of I had me one once and still missed him something awful. There wasn't no other children in Dead Mule Valley, jest Eckerd and me."

He let it pass. Rome wasn't built in a day. Turning away, his gaze encountered the crib, and he reached down and pulled the covers up over his sleeping nephew, his hand lingering briefly on the tiny upturned rump. What the devil am I doing here? he wondered. Panic threatened to set in, but then he thought about the sleeping infant and the woman waiting on the bed — waiting to learn the facts of life. Waiting for him to tell her about making love, God help him. They're

145

mine, he marveled. They're both completely helpless, completely dependent on me.

The thought was both scary and gratifying. He couldn't recall the last time anyone had depended on him for anything. Once, a long time ago, he'd had a brother, too. He hadn't been aware of it at the time, but he'd loved him. Not his father — at least, he didn't think he'd ever loved him, but then, love wasn't something you thought about, it was either there or it wasn't.

With Paul, it had been there. Paul used to come running to him, begging him to rake his chestnuts out of the fire. And Dav would always do it, and feel ten feet tall for his troubles. If he'd stayed around longer, he might've taught him a few of life's basic lessons — things about sowing and reaping. Responsibility. Never drinking and gambling at the same time.

But then, he'd been only sixteen when he'd been sent away. It had taken him years to learn those lessons himself. Paul never had.

Rosie sat silently, her knees drawn up under her on the bed. Waiting. Finally she said, "You reckon they made a baby in there?"

"Do I reckon *who* made a *what?*"

She nodded toward the west wall. "A baby. The way they were rarin' and snortin', I bet they made a whole litter. Eckerd's ol' hound, she got hung up one time and Eckerd had to throw a bucket of —"

"Rosie," he warned.

"Well, anyhow, 'fore we knew she'd even caught, out popped a passel of the runtiest, ugliest pups ever I did see. Their eyes were all scrunched up, and they were all wet, and —"

Dav held up both hands in a gesture of surrender. "Just hold it right there. I want you to promise me something, Rosie.

146

Starting now, I want you to forget you ever lived in a place like Dead Mule Valley, and that you ever knew any of the people who lived there. I want you to try hard to remember how it felt to live in a house with a stained-glass window over the stair landing, and what it sounded like when your mama read to you in French."

She nodded, and he went on. In for a penny, in for a pound. "And then I want you to think about all the people we saw in the dining room tonight and try to remember what I said about table manners." Someone was going to have to tame the little heathen. It looked like he'd been elected.

"I remember. You said, don't reach across the table, don't talk with your mouth full, don't pull the bones out of your chicken with your fingers, even if you can't get the meat off any other way, and don't set there with your elbows on the table."

Had he truly said all that at dinner tonight? Hell, he broke every one of those rules on a regular basis.

At least she didn't pick her teeth at the table. His father did. It occurred to him that her breeding might be better than his, not that his was anything to brag about. His father had been a farmer before he fell ill. He still owned several hundred prime corn and cotton acres, all of it leased out now, but a farmer was a farmer. His grandfather had owned and operated three windmills in Currituck County. His mother's people were merchants from Elizabeth City. Not a one of them, to his knowledge, spoke French.

"We're leaving early in the morning, Rosie," he said, his voice more gentle than it had been. "I want you to go back to sleep now, and if you hear any more noises, ignore them. Nobody's getting hurt."

"I will. But Davin, you never did tell me about making love. I 'spect it's different when folks do it, isn't it?"

147

"Yes, honey, it is. If they care for each other it can be a beautiful thing." How the devil would he know? He hadn't even known the last names of some of the women he'd bedded. "One of these days you'll understand."

"Will you show me?"

He got out of there before he could disgrace himself. Leaning against the door of his own bedroom, he told himself it was the altitude. He wasn't used to it. Once he got back down to sea level, he'd come to his senses and all these crazy urges he'd been having lately would disappear.

Rosie McGuire. Charmaine Duvallier, for God's sake! A hayseed from the backwoods who bathed in a creek and ate with her fingers. A woman who butchered the king's English, who could swear like a longshoreman. . . .

A woman with eyes that could melt a glacier. A woman who took a smelly, leaky, noisy baby to her heart, putting his needs well ahead of her own.

Yes, and a woman who had not only stolen the silver, but had lied to him consistently. Who knew more about making moonshine whiskey than any law-abiding person should know, and if President Cleveland were to ask her himself, would guilelessly describe the entire process.

But bootlegger or not, she had the sunniest smile and the warmest heart of any woman he'd ever known. And God help him, he was dangerously close to falling under her spell.

Forty miles a day, he vowed. Maybe even fifty. The roads were pretty good heading east as far as Raleigh. He'd be too busy driving to talk, and too tired once they stopped for the night to get into too much trouble.

Not that getting into trouble didn't appeal, but because it appealed far too much. The minute they reached Seven Oaks, he'd drop her and the boy off with the old man and get the devil out of there. He'd been in the process of adding a

148

Chesapeake bugeye to his inland waterway fleet, and buying the warehouse next to Globe Fish Market. Once he'd immersed himself in business again, he'd soon forget all about the redheaded witch who had managed to turn his life upside down for a little while.

The farther east they traveled, the flatter the land became. Rosie marveled at the endless fields that seemed to stretch on forever. She knew better than to ask questions, though, because for the past few days Davin had been too busy driving to talk. The road was congested, with buggies and buckboards, dog carts and runabouts, and men on horseback dodging in and around the wheeled traffic. She was constantly twisting around to see the sights until Davin had to remind her she was supposed to be taking care of a baby.

"As if I ever could forget that." She kissed the fuzzy, sweet-smelling head, bare now in deference to the milder weather.

"We'll be there before dark."

They were waiting for a ferry across what he called The Narrows, in a town he told her was Elizabeth City. "Right over there," he said, pointing to a new brick building on the waterfront, "is where I'm thinking about buying a warehouse and setting up an office once I've delivered you and Paulie to my father."

"Oh." Like a piece of unordered freight. She held the baby close as they drove aboard the ferry for the short trip across the river. Not until they reached the other side could she bring herself to ask, "Do you visit your papa very often?" *Will I ever see you again?*

"No, not often." *Not ever.*

"If I had a papa, I'd visit him a whole lot. Family's important."

He nodded, his eyes focused on the narrow, boggy road ahead.

"Did I tell you I wrote a story for little Paulie, all about how you came and found him, and asked me to help take care of him, and I did. I told him about those seven oaks and how you and his papa used to bellywhomp on the leaves. I made up about his mama, about how beautiful she was, and how everybody loved her, and how much she loved everybody back, but him most of all. I reckon it won't make no difference by the time he's big enough to read it, and it might make him feel better some. A boy needs to know about his folks. He needs to know he was thought right much of, once upon a time."

Davin was quiet for a long time, and then he said, "It's getting chilly. Why don't you reach in the back and get out that shawl?"

He'd bought her the shawl in one of the towns they'd passed through. She couldn't remember the name of the town, but she remembered how his hands had lingered when he'd placed the shawl around her shoulders, and how he'd looked into her eyes for the longest time, as if he wanted to say something.

But he'd only asked if she was hungry, and she was, but she'd said she wasn't, because she could tell he was wanting to move on.

What she wanted was becoming more and more clear in her mind. She wanted things to go on the way they had for the past two weeks. She wanted Davin and she wanted little Paulie, and she wanted them to be a family. She wanted Davin to teach her how to make love, and to care about her so that it would be beautiful. She wanted to make some babies with him. They both liked babies.

But she didn't say that. With so many people to watch along the journey, and so much time to think about what she saw, she understood some of what it meant to be a woman, at least on the outside. What she still couldn't figure out was what to do about all these new feelings inside her.

They rode on in silence, and after a while they turned in between two long rows of pecan trees. There was a big white house at the end of the drive path, and Rosie counted seven oaks in the yard. "Well," she said, forcing a smile, "I reckon we're home."

Davin's palms were sweating. He'd been tense when he'd come home two months ago for the first time in twelve years. This time, however, there was an added element. Rosie. If the old man mistreated her by so much as a harsh look, he'd get her out of there so fast . . .

And do what with her? he asked himself.

Marry her?

Suppressing an oath that was more than half prayer, he swung down from the buggy and held up his arms for the baby. And then old Crank was there to take the horses, saying, "My, my Mistuh Davin, if you ain't a sight for sore eyes."

"Glory, it's big as a castle," Rosie whispered, gazing warily up at the square, hip-roofed house he had taken for granted all his life, porticoes, pillars, and all.

Glory? Her vocabulary was improving beyond all recognition. He almost wished she'd cut loose with a few choice mule-skinner phrases, just for old times' sake. "It's only a house," he told her.

"What if your papa doesn't like me?"

Dav led her up the broad front steps. She was carrying the baby, holding him in front of her as if for protection, and suddenly, he didn't want to be here. Didn't want the journey to have ended.

"Rosie, my father's been ill. He might sound cross, but he doesn't mean anything by it, it's just his way." *If he shouts at her or whacks his cane on the floor, I'll strangle him.*

"Will you stay for a little while, or do you have to leave?"

He'd planned to pay his respects and then leave. The house might be big as a castle, but it wasn't big enough for two strong-willed, hardheaded men, both with too much pride to back down.

He opened the door without answering. He'd find the old man, deliver the goods, speak his piece and then . . . well, then we'd see, he thought. He might stay a day or two, just to make sure they were going to settle in all right.

The initial interview was every bit as bad as he'd expected. Marshall Banister might be old and ailing, but he was still a force to be reckoned with. "How do I know you didn't bring me one of your fancy pieces and try to pass her off as Paul's widow?"

"I wrote you what happened. Paul's wife died. I buried her. This is their son." So far, the old man hadn't even bothered to give more than a cursory glance to the baby. Rosie stood by the door, looking ready to bolt. Dav couldn't much blame her. They'd had to go all the way up to the old man's bedroom. It was hot and stuffy and needed a good cleaning.

"So you say. Come over here where I can see you, gal!"

"Stay where you are until he asks you politely, Rosie."

"Ha! This is my house. Anybody stays under my roof dances to my tune. That goes for you, too, boy."

Davin could feel the pulse beating at the side of his neck. He clenched and unclenched his fists. Once he was sure he could control his voice, he said calmly, "Take Paulie downstairs, Rosie. Find someone to show you where the kitchen is. You'll both want something to eat. I'll be down in a couple of minutes."

"Goddammit, boy, you don't give orders in this house!"

"You're getting red in the face, Marshall. If I were you, I'd try to hold it down."

"That's my damn grandbaby you're talking about, no matter if it's Paul's or one of your own whelps! Hand him over to the housekeeper, then go or stay, suit yourself. The boy stays, though." With a look of sheer malice, he started to chuckle, and then he commenced to cough.

Rosie, holding on to Paulie, backed through the door, her face flushed with anger. "Hateful old buzzard," she muttered. She was halfway down the stairs when Davin caught up with her.

"I'm sorrier than I can say, Rosie. He's never been easy, but — I guess it's the sickness. Whatever ails him, I've never seen him quite this bad."

"I understand."

"Do you?"

"I lived with Uncle Hiram."

Paulie was beginning to fuss. It had been hours since he'd eaten, and he was wet, soaked clean through. Davin said, "I'll see if Arvilla's still in the kitchen. She'll feed you and find someone to show you where to go. So far, the only familiar face I've seen around here is old Crank. I guess the others have all either died of old age or got tired of taking the old man's guff."

Chapter Eight

Davin left her at Seven Oaks. He'd had no choice. He'd gone back to visit the old man in his room after seeing to Rosie and the boy, and things had gone from bad to worse. His letter had never arrived, so he'd had to go over the whole story again. About finding Paul's grave, finding his widow on her deathbed, and the baby on the verge of starvation.

He'd explained about Rosie, glossing over the rougher places, saying only that the uncle she'd been living with had died and she'd needed a job. "Paulie loves her," he'd told the old man. "We figure he's about five or six months old now — no way of knowing for sure. But she's been with him day and night ever since she — ever since I hired her. You might want to keep her on for a few days."

He knew better than to tell the old man outright what to do. He'd do the opposite just to be contrary. But he'd keep her on, Dav was sure of it. Certain sure, as Rosie would say. The servants were all new, a lazy lot, at that. He doubted any of them would want to take on any additional duties.

She'd be all right, he told himself more than once on the ride back to Elizabeth City. She had more backbone than any woman he'd ever known. She'd be more than a match for the old man. She wanted a family? She could have his, with his blessing.

A voice inside him, a voice Dav had deliberately ignored since the first time it had whispered in his ear, said, yes, and she could have you along with them if you weren't such a bloody coward.

was all fired up. "You been a-cussing and a-beating on the floor with that stick ever since I got here. You been yelling your head off and throwin' things — don't think I didn't hear about it. They talk about you downstairs something awful, and I don't blame 'em one bit. You're a hateful old man, and you'll likely choke on your own bile."

She took time out for a breath, and Marshall Banister, his eyes bulging, his face red as raw beef, told her to get out, only he added some words to make sure she understood he meant it.

"I'm going, all right, but first I've got something to say, and you're either going to have to hear me out or get up out of that bed and make me hesh."

She waited. He didn't even let out a squawk. She nodded and set in to say her piece. "You're not near as sick as you let on. That old woman down in the kitchen says you eat like a plow horse and drink whiskey and smoke stinking old cigars. She says you'll likely set the house on fire one of these days, but you don't have to worry about Paulie. I told Melly the first whiff of smoke she smells, to take the baby and go find Davin."

"Ha! I'll tell you where she'll find him, he'll be lying abed in that room he rented across the river with some floozy he picked up in a gaming house. Boy hasn't changed a damned bit. Always was a no-good, gambling, whoring —"

"He is not! He's a better son than you deserve, you measely old rumpskullion! And let me tell you something else, if I ever hear of you mistreating that baby, I'll come back and peel your speckled hide right off your bones and nail it to the barn!" The old man was sputtering so hard she hadn't even heard the door open behind her. "What's more, your housekeeper's a-robbing you blind and your house is dirty and too big for one mean old man when there's orphans out there

157

wearing rags and stealing food from root caves to keep from starving, and besides that, that nasty temper of yours is going to gnaw holes right through your gullet!"

She planted her hands on her hips and glared at the withered, red-faced old man in the enormous canopied bed. "There. I guess that's about all I had to say. You don't owe me no wages on account of Davin bought me some clothes and shoes, and he's fed me real good. I offered him some buttons and my papa's gold ring, but he wouldn't take it, so I reckon we're even."

She waited, quivering in her boots. If only he knew. It was flat out going to break her heart to leave that baby, but Paulie wasn't hers. She had no claim on him. If she stayed, she'd like as not say things she shouldn't and get in trouble and the old man might take it out on Paulie. Uncle Hiram had been like that. He'd go off and get drunk and come home feeling mean and ornery and then he'd take out after her with his bullwhip. Luckily, she could outrun, outclimb, and outlast anything on two legs and some on four. Once he passed out, she'd go back home and by the next day when his head got unswole, he'd likely have forgotten all about it.

Behind her, someone began to applaud softly. She swung around, her heart in her throat. The old man began to cackle. Down the hall, Paulie tuned up for his midnight bottle.

"Measely rumpskullion?" Davin repeated softly.

"Where in tarnation did you come from! Don't you know no better than to sneak up and scare the daylights out of a body?"

"Did I scare you, Rosie? I thought you might be needing me about now."

"Why would I need you?"

He was standing too close. Which was peculiar considering they'd been close as two peas in a pod for the past two weeks.

158

She'd been right in the bed with him that night in the board-inghouse when he'd kissed her and touched her all over.

But this was different, the way he was looking at her, like he knew something she didn't. "Are you feeling all right?" she asked warily. She backed up a step, and he followed her.

And then the old man snorted and said, "Bless me if this ain't better than a cockfight. Go at him, woman! Take him down a peg or two. Always was a damned sight too big for his britches."

Rosie thought he looked just fine in his britches. She started to say so, but then Davin said to his father, "You're a fine one to talk, you stiff-necked old bastard."

"Hesh," Rosie said.

"Hesh?" both men repeated.

"He's your papa, even if he is a worthless, mean-minded old coot. It's all right for me to call him on it, 'cause I'm no kin, but you're obliged to respect him whether he deserves it or not."

"Listen to what she says, boy. She'll set you straight."

"Oh, pipe down, you old troublemaker," Davin growled. Taking her by the arm, he shoved her outside into the hall, leaned against the door, and before Rosie could regain her balance he was hugging her and kissing her until she couldn't remember where she was, much less where she'd been fixing to go.

"Where's your room?" he growled. "We've got a few mat-ters to sort out."

Cheeks blazing, she licked her lips, patted her hair, and stuffed her shirtwaist into her skirt. She couldn't think how on earth it had come out. "I'm sorry for what you heard. I reckon I should've showed the ol' bastid more respect, even if I'm not his kin, seein's how I'm still under his roof."

Dav chuckled. "You handled him just right. He'd have

159

walked all over you if you'd given him half a chance. Pity I didn't learn that sooner."

"I 'speck he's lonesomer than he lets on. Lonesomeness can make a body downright contrary."

"Lonesomeness can do that, all right," Davin said softly. He backed her into the room that had been his as a boy. It was little changed since he'd last seen it more than a dozen years ago. "As it happens, I know a sure cure for lonesomeness."

"You reckon it'll work on your father? He's in a bad way."

"I doubt if it works with old men, but I'd be interested to find out if it works with prodigal sons."

"Is that the one in the Bible that run off from home, and they killed a batch of cows for him?"

"That was one of them. I'm another."

"Are you fixing to stay? Because I'm leaving, but I'd feel easier in my heart if I knew you were going to be here to watch over Paulie."

"I'll watch over him."

"And your papa? He's not real mean inside, it's mostly on the outside. It might even wear off some after a while."

Davin hadn't come racing back to talk about his father, or Paulie either. He'd ridden the poor gelding damn near into the ground because he'd had a crazy hunch she might run away. He led her across to the bed, and she went with him willingly. "You weren't actually going to leave before morning, were you?"

She nodded solemnly, and he said, "Rosie, that's crazy. You're five hundred miles away from your valley now. It's dark as pitch outside. Where would you sleep? How would you travel? I'm afraid you wouldn't get very far on a jar of buttons."

Rosie couldn't meet his eyes. The truth was, she'd had some notion of finding her way back to Elizabeth City, where

160

he'd said he was buying a building. If she could find work there, she might even get to see him. And Paulie, too. But mostly Davin.

"If I stay here," he asked, "would you stay with me?"

"To look after Paulie?"

"To look after me. Paulie'll grow up and leave one of these days. He won't always need you. But Rosie . . . I will. I need you the way a man needs a woman, the way I've never needed another living soul. You're my sunshine, my —" With a deep groan, he reached for her, and while Rosie was still trying to remember how it had been with her father and mother — the way they had laughed together and hugged and kissed, and how her father had fed her mother bites of Rosie's last birthday cake, he kissed her again, and now that she knew how to do it, it was even more wonderful than the last time. "Oh, my glory," she panted when she could finally speak again.

"This time, open your mouth and kiss me back," he growled, barely lifting his lips.

"Are we going to make love now?"

Instead of answering, he started to laugh, and right while he was laughing he kissed her again, kissed her the way a man kisses the woman he loves.

And then neither of them was laughing.

A long time later, he got around to answering her question. "Yes, sunshine, we're going to make love."

"Can we make it right now?"

"We can make it just as soon as I can possibly make the arrangements . . . maybe sooner."

"Will I like it? Will it be beautiful, like you said?"

Davin closed his eyes, leaning his forehead against hers. "Unbelievably beautiful, my love."

And as it happened, it was even more beautiful than that. . . .

Epilogue

The spacious bedroom was too crowded. Davin had insisted on calling in a specialist from Norfolk. Marshall had insisted on calling in a midwife from Moyock. Melly the maid refused to be pried away from Rosie's bedside, and Davin himself alternately paced the floor and fell on his knees beside the bed, clinging to Rosie's hand.

"It's taking too long," he anguished. "Dr. Felder, it's taking too long! Something's wrong, isn't it?"

The midwife looked at the physician, who looked right back at her. Husbands, the look said. They ought to be banished by law at times like this.

Rosie prided herself that she was handling things rather well, considering it hurt like the very devil. Lucky she was tough as rawhide. She'd already picked out a string of names and painted the nursery. She'd wanted blue for a boy. Davin had wanted pink for a girl. They'd settled on yellow.

"Sunshine, you're going to be all right," he assured her earnestly.

Rosie wasn't the one who needed reassuring. Davin, her strong, capable prince of a husband, had fallen apart at the first hard pain. "I know I am, it's you I'm . . . ah, devil take it!" She shut her eyes tightly and bit her lip. "Oh — possum cods! Hellacious damnation!"

Davin glared at the doctor. "Do something! She can't take much more of this!"

"Shh, hesh now, sugar, it won't be much longer," Rosie said, panting for breath. "I've run flat out of cusswords."

162

When the pain took over her whole body, she cussed. Otherwise, she did her best to comfort those around her. "Where's Papa and Paulie?"

"Fishing. Pa took him down to Bullyard Creek."

"You don't reckon they — Oh! Ow! Merciful chicken sh— shoes!"

"Move aside, boy. Miss Romie, you'd better get ready to take him — her —"

Rosie screamed. Davin quietly fainted. From downstairs, Paulie yelled, "Mama, Mama, come look at the turtle Grandpa and me caught! Grandpa says I can keep him, so can I please?"

It was left to Melly the maid to beam down at little Charmaine Elizabeth Louise Banister. "Welcome, honey. You ain't much to look at yet, but you done got yo'self a real fine fam'ly. Yessirree bob, you done landed yo'self in high cotton. Reckon Melly better get you cleaned up some 'fore your daddy wakes up and starts carryin' on again."

Charmaine Elizabeth Louise Banister stared solemnly at the homely face above her. Finally! She was here where she was supposed to be, safe and secure. First she needed a nap. After that, she would look around and see what life was all about.

THE AWAKENING

Brenda Joyce

Chapter One

"Stop her!" he shouted. "Stop her! She's killed him!" He looked up, aghast.

Meg didn't pause. The grog shop was dark, crowded, and noisy even though it was well before noon. No one heard Timothy. The body separated them. She whirled, tripping over one burly thigh, pushing past a group of men swigging Irish whiskey and arguing amiably about a horse race that was centuries old. Her heart thundered in her ears. Her mind was frozen with one thought.

Oh, God, he was dead. She had killed O'Leery!

"Stop her!" Timothy shrieked.

Meg ran as heads began to turn and whip her way. Eyes caught hers, surprised — accusing.

"Stop Meg O'Neil! She's killed Robin!" Timothy screamed.

Panting, a cramp piercing her side, Meg shoved through shoulders and hips that suddenly seemed to bar her way and fled out of an open doorway into the bright morning sunlight, Timothy's cries behind her. Other voices had joined the younger man's. Meg leapt off of the grog shop's porch. She did not have to look back to know she was being followed. The tattered shawl she was wearing slipped, sharp stones and pebbles hurt her feet where her shoes had worn paper-thin, but she did not notice. Red hair unbound and flying behind her, she ran from Fort Hill and the men who would catch her in order to kill her.

The sidewalks were congested with crowds of shabbily dressed, unemployed Irish, busy shipwrights, coopers, cordsmen, and sailors, their paths broken by merchants, brokers, and other dark-suited gentlemen hurrying about their business affairs. The street was clogged with horse-drawn drays, lorries, and carts. Even though Meg was a few blocks away from the wharves, beyond the jumbled skyline of tenement buildings, offices, and warehouses, she could see the smokestacks of steamers and ferries and the high, towering masts of a clipper with her sails unfurled. Meg stumbled along the dirt street, pushing past some young men carrying bales of cotton on their shoulders. She thought she heard Timothy shouting behind her.

God, she hadn't meant to kill him! Or had she?

Rushing harder, she mistakenly collided into the back of a man in a top hat. He turned and, espying her, stiffened. "I beg your pardon," he said with no small amount of condescension.

Meg knew she looked a fright. Worse, she knew why he was appalled. "I'm sorry, sir," she said, her brogue as thick as the day she had arrived on Maverick Island six months ago.

He recoiled.

"There she is!" a husky male voice shouted. "Nab her, boys!"

Meg whirled, saw a group of men that included Timothy bounding off of the sidewalk. Her heart sank like a stone. Her terror was overwhelming.

Timothy caught her gaze. "Bitch!" he shouted, shaking a fist at her.

She turned, darting across the street. In her panic, she hadn't even looked to see if there was a clear path through the two-way traffic. Too late, she saw the fine carriage pulled by a racy black Thoroughbred bearing down upon her. In that moment, Meg knew she was going to die.

She had come this far, all the way to America, to be run

over by some gentleman in his high-class rig, to be buried in some anonymous grave that would not even bear a headstone.

But instead of freezing in her tracks, she dug in as hard as she could, somehow using muscles starved from lack of nourishment and weak from fatigue. Her thighs and calves stretched, burning. Her hips felt as if they would snap. Her lungs were about to burst.

The driver, a tall, broad-shouldered man, stood, sawing on the reins. Meg saw his face. Darkly tanned and high cheek-boned, it was set with determination. He shouted not at her, but at his horse.

The beautiful animal halted, rearing in its traces. Meg did not stop running. Tripping, she made it to the opposite side-walk.

"God's blood!" he shouted after her. "Watch where you are going before you get yourself killed!"

Meg almost burst into tears. She turned the corner, fleeing down a narrow alleyway lined with wooden flats, the kind of neighborhood where she had lived since her arrival in Boston. She had been looking for a job for six achingly long months, so she knew almost every inch of the city, including this neighborhood, so close to her own. She raced past clusters of men drinking beer and whiskey outside of grog shops, women and children sitting on their stoops. A vendor was trying to sell fresh eggs, but no one had the money to buy. Behind his back, two small boys in torn breeches dipped into one of his buckets, making off with a handful of the eggs.

Ahead of her the thoroughfare changed. Rows of warehouses and office buildings fronted India Wharf. The harbor stretched out, lined with every kind of imaginable steamer, ferry, fishing vessel, passenger and cargo ship.

Meg could hardly breathe. She had to pause, gasping for air, her knees beginning to give out on her. She looked back over her shoulder, but did not see either Timothy or his friends. *Oh, God. Was O'Leery really dead? But hadn't she sworn to kill him?*

Another cramp pierced through her. Meg clutched her stomach, bending over, still gasping for air. She needed a place to hide. She started across the street, trying to run but staggering now. She desperately needed to rest.

She dodged an omnibus, then a coach filled with gentlemen, and two more gentlemen on horseback coming from the opposite direction. She felt as if she would never make it to a safe haven. Finally an elegant, open carriage containing a single occupant — a lady who appeared to Meg to be royalty in her silks and cashmere, her jewels and veiled hat — swerved by her. Meg ignored the driver, who shouted an insult at her. Across the street was a huge brownstone building five stories high. The masts from the clipper she had remarked before loomed over the building from behind. Meg barely saw the name engraved atop the two front doors on the second-story pediment: ZACHARY HOLLANDER SHIPPING, WORLDWIDE. The office building adjoined a far larger, lower warehouse where tremendous activity was going on inside as men shifted merchandise. Next to it was a huge loading area filled with hundreds of boxes, barrels, and crates. Meg hurried behind the stacked crates, each one as tall as she, and sank to the ground in a small heap. Her thundering heart did not subside.

She covered her eyes with her hands, which were sorely in need of a good washing. "Oh, Mama," she said, not even realizing she spoke aloud, "I'm so sorry. God forgive me!" But she refused to cry. Not because she was proud, her pride had died when her mother, brother, and sisters had died in County Clare, but because she did not think she could ever stop if she did cry. She rubbed her abdomen. The cramp was gone, thank God.

Meg sat there for a long time.

Eventually she began to listen to the dock workers singing and conversing. Some of the conversation was crude and rough, making her blush. But most of it referred to the clipper ship. The men were placing wagers.

"If he says she can do it, then *Cyclone* can," one man stated loudly in a brogue as thick as Meg's own. "He says she's the best ship he's ever built, and no one builds 'em as fine and fast as Zach Hollander."

"*Flying Cloud* has the record. Eighty-nine days to San Francisco. She'll be hard to beat," someone rejoined.

"I'll lay down a week's wage on the *Cyclone*," the first worker said with a laugh. "You don't know Hollander. He don't know the meaning of failure, my friend."

Their voices faded. Meg was finally relaxed now, her body so tired she wondered if she would ever be able to move. So there was a race. And that man had a job, a man who was as Irish as she, one secure enough for him to wager an entire week's salary on the race's outcome. How she wished she were in a similar position. But no one wanted to hire an Irishwoman, not for respectable work, that was.

Meg thought about O'Leery. She'd finally gone to him. And he'd gotten her the promised job, oh yes he had. Tears filled her eyes. Not because she'd been reduced to sewing piece after piece of linen in a small, airless room fourteen hours a day for less than a dollar. How she hated him. God forgive her, because she could not really be sorry that he was dead.

Meg's stomach rumbled loudly. She was starving, a condition she faced each and every day, often all day. When had she last eaten? Yesterday morning she had stolen a small loaf of bread. She had been reduced to thievery, dear God. And worse, she regretted that more than she did O'Leery's death.

171

Meg tried not to think about the farm. Those days felt like a different lifetime, one belonging to a stranger. But when she was a little girl, before the landlord had evicted them — before her father had lost everything and had taken up drink, finally losing his life in a drunken brawl — she had worn clean gingham dresses every day while doing her chores, had eaten hearty dinners, and slept in flannel nightclothes scented with the lavender bathwater her mother had so loved. And on Sundays there had been muslin dresses trimmed with lace, patent shoes, ribbons in her hair, and a feast fit for any king.

Her stomach hurt her now so Meg forced herself to her feet. Looking up at the blazing sun, Meg judged it to be about high noon. She had been hiding for at least an hour, if not more. Surely by now the coast was clear. She would have to leave the wharves, leave this side of town, forever. Because they all knew her, and now they would be looking for her. O'Leery's death would not be taken lightly.

Meg peeked past the corner of the stacked crates. The street was busier than before with vehicles, pedestrians, and laborers. Meg wondered where she would find her next meal. Begging was out of the question.

She saw no sign of Timothy and his friends. And there was so much traffic now, surely she was safe. She adjusted her shawl over her shoulders, retying the ends. She tried to rebraid her hair, but it was so tangled from the horrible morning, that she gave it up. Instead, she forced it into a single knot, one that would not last long without the pins she could not afford. Meg stepped out onto the street.

Some dock workers were just rounding the corner and they gaped at her. Meg knew that a woman like herself, one pretty and young, even if she was thoroughly disheveled, was not a usual sight in this area. She ducked her head and hurried past the office building.

Two gentlemen were speaking in front of the brownstone, standing on the front steps. Meg was hurrying by when she stiffened at the sound of a very distinct low voice. She stumbled and glanced up. God! It was the man who had almost run her over with his fancy carriage and Thoroughbred horse.

He was shaking the hands of an average enough gentleman in a top hat and whiskers. He had shed his dark brown jacket, stood only in his lawn shirtsleeves and waistcoat. He was tall, well over six feet, and broad-shouldered. His trousers were immaculately cut, and could not hide the fact that his legs were long, hard, and strong. Meg's strides faltered.

He had seen her. His eyes, which were amber, widened as he recognized her.

She was mesmerized. He had one of the strongest faces Meg had ever seen. It was the face of a man who had power and honor. Meg knew it without having to know him.

She jerked her gaze away, suddenly frightened, trembling, although she did not know why. She clutched her shawl more tightly, intending to flee, yet strongly reluctant to do so. She forced herself to continue on her way.

"Madam, stop," he called.

Meg glanced backward in disbelief and saw him striding toward her. Panic rose. She knew how much these Brahmins hated her and her kind. She could not take too much more today, not when O'Leery was dead, killed at her own hands. She could imagine the talking to this stranger would give her for interfering with his driving. Perhaps she had even injured his fine horse. He would verbally abuse her, if not physically.

Meg's strides increased.

"Madam." It was a command. He caught her from behind, seizing her elbow, falling into step with her. Meg looked up at him and saw O'Leery's rough, red face instead. Her heart froze over. She tried to pull free, but was so weak he did not seem to notice. "Please," she whispered.

"Did I hurt you? Good God, are you all right? I could have killed you!" he said, his golden gaze piercing.

Meg began to breathe. She could not believe that he was inquiring about her welfare. Was it a trick? Or had she finally been reduced to insanity? "I beg your pardon?"

He stared, studying her face. "You do not appear well. I am very sorry for almost running you over. How can I make amends?" he asked. He spoke in a direct commanding fashion, as if he were in a rush and had little time to spare.

Meg swallowed. He wanted to make amends, when she had carelessly run in front of his carriage. Did she dare ask for a meal? Apparently she had some pride left, because she could not do it. "I am fine," she managed. He continued to stare, but so did she. She realized that he was an incredibly attractive man. Not that he was handsome in any common sense of the word. But his features were arresting. And he made her feel remarkably small and petite at five foot six inches, a tall woman in her own right.

He released her and reached into the breast pocket of his waistcoat. It was dark maroon; the finest wool Meg had ever seen up close. Suddenly he had silver in his hand. "Take this. It is the least I can do to assuage my conscience."

Meg blinked. But the coins he held did not go away. He was offering her, she thought, twenty silver dollars, more money than she had earned in the entire month she had sewn pieces in the factory. "No thank you," she somehow said.

His eyes widened in surprise.

"Hollander," a jovial male voice called.

The dark-haired man with the amber eyes did not look away from Meg.

"I've got hundreds of dollars riding on *Cyclone*, my friend." The younger gentleman sat in a carriage that he drove himself.

He tipped his low-brimmed felt hat. "Tell me I am not wrong."

"If Mckay is not unseated, then it is not through lack of effort on my behalf," the amber-eyed man said easily. But even in casual repartee, he spoke with an intensity a child could not miss, a conviction and strength that was not just a matter of words, but came from the man's character. Meg stared at his perfect profile.

"*Cyclone* will win?"

"I believe so," Hollander said.

The gentleman grinned and waved and drove on.

The man called Hollander turned his gaze slowly back to Meg. Meg realized she had been staring. Rudely, perhaps.

"Here," he said, pressing the coins into her hand.

"No." Meg did not take them, shaking her head, backing away. She had to leave, not just India Street, but this man. She did not know why, only felt it with all of her heart, her soul. Yet she could not seem to get her feet to move and obey her mind.

He stared after her.

Meg finally turned. This time she waited for a path to clear between the oncoming horses and vehicles. Out in the harbor, a boat's horn sounded. More faintly, she could hear the bells of the Mill Street trolley, just to the south. Above her head, gulls wheeled and cried. She felt his eyes upon her back.

She was shaken.

Meg gripped her shawl and crossed the street. She wanted to look back one last time at the strange man, knowing she would never see him again and oddly sad about it. But she did not have the courage.

Someone shouted, "It's her! There she is! Get her!"

Meg froze, but only for an instant. She was more than halfway across the wide commercial street, and she saw one

175

of Timothy's friends on the corner of the opposite sidewalk. And then she saw Timothy, racing at her from the adjacent block.

Meg cried out, whirling, running not back to the office building and warehouse, but toward Fort Hill. But she had no energy left to spend, and she stumbled. An instant later she felt a hand seize a hank of her hair. Meg cried out as she was brutally dragged up short.

Her buttocks slammed into a hard male body. A thick forearm pinned her from beneath her breasts. A hot voice said something lewd and crude and cruel in her ear. And then Timothy was there, in front of her, his hand raised to strike her down. Caught in his friend's iron grip, Meg could not escape the blow, or even duck.

Timothy's fist nearly smashed her face, when he was grabbed from behind. Meg cried out as Hollander picked him up as easily as if he were a rag doll. He threw him down onto the street, heedless of the traffic swerving around them. Eyes wide, Meg watched Hollander coming toward her, his face filled with controlled fury. For one heartbeat, Meg thought he might even attack her.

But his target was not Meg, it was the man who still held her in a ruthless grip. Hollander seized the man's arm and Meg suddenly found herself free. She scooted aside as Hollander slammed his fist into the man's face, breaking his nose, blood spurting wildly, even onto Hollander's own hand and starched cuff. He struck again. A left-handed blow to the man's abdomen that doubled him over and sent him reeling into the dust.

Meg watched in growing disbelief, her fear abating somewhat, then saw Timothy on his feet, approaching, a knife in hand. "Mr. Hollander!" she screamed. "Behind you!"

But her words were not even out before Hollander turned,

176

smiling grimly. Timothy lunged, knife outstetched. Hollander stepped aside, and in one lightning motion his leg came up, his arm came down. As he kicked the knife out of Timothy's hand, he struck Timothy's shoulder in a chopping blow. Before Timothy hit the earth, Hollander caught him and flipped him over onto his back, where he landed hard like a sackful of bricks on the ground.

Hollander straightened. Both Timothy and his friend lay unmoving. Slowly, he looked up.

Meg was as motionless as her assailants. Her gaze locked with Hollander's. His eyes were hard, harder than she had ever seen a man's eyes before. Hard and blazing and something more — something indefinable.

"Are you all right?" he asked, for the second time that day.

Meg meant to say yes. Instead, no words came out. She took a step backward, absurdly enough, ready to weep. And then another step, and another one.

"You are in trouble," he said flatly, watching her.

"Yes," Meg said. And she turned and fled.

Chapter Two

Her hair was neatly braided. It had not been an easy task. And she had washed her face and hands, using water from a private well. That had been even more difficult, for she had felt exactly like the trespasser that she was, expecting to be noticed at any moment by a servant in the kitchens of the fine brick home whose property she was on.

It was now midafternoon and she stood on a quiet residential street not far from the Commons. Her determination was ebbing as it always did by this time of day. Meg blamed it on hunger, but suspected it had more to do with the obvious hopelessness of the situation. She had already knocked on a dozen doors since she had run away from the wharves — from him.

Meg glanced at the crumbled piece of newspaper in her bare hand. It was yesterday's news — obviously she could not get a free copy of today's *Chronicle*. Dozens of families were advertising for domestic help — for maids, nannies, and governesses. But the last line of every ad was the same: *No Irish Need Apply*.

Meg blinked back hot tears, folding the worn, torn page and slipping it into her bodice. This home, No. 15 Chestnut, had not advertised. But maybe they would need a maid or a nanny anyway, and maybe her heritage would not matter. Meg doubted it.

A wrought-iron fence separated the three-story brick house from the elm-shaded street. The gate was open. Meg walked through, trying not to trudge like an old hag. She knew she had reached the limits of her endurance and wondered how long she could go on.

And what if Timothy and his friends found her?

O'Leery owned the grog shop at the foot of Fort Hill. Or, he *had* owned the grog shop until this morning. He'd owned it and a half dozen more scattered around the wharves, all catering to Meg's countrymen and women. He'd owned a few brothels, too, and a textile mill just north of town. His home, unlike those of his people, was far removed from the wharves. In fact, it was a stone mansion not far from where Meg now applied for a job.

Timothy O'Leery was his son. Timothy was going to kill her and he could afford to hire all the thugs in the world to do the job. That man, Hollander, had saved her this time, but next time he would not be around. Meg had thought about it. She needed employment desperately for obvious reasons. And what better place to hide than in someone's posh Beacon Hill home?

The problem was, she had been trying to gain such employment ever since arriving in Boston. These snooty blue-bloods were every bit as bad as the English, and in some cases worse. The Bostonians felt that the Irish were an invasion; they despised an impoverished people who were only looking for honest work and wages and freedom.

Meg sighed and knocked on the door. It was cracked open by a manservant impeccably clad in dark trousers, a tailcoat, and a white shirtwaist. His gray brows arched.

"I beg your pardon," Meg said softly, her pulse racing. "I was hoping the lady of the house might be at home."

The servant did not even deign to reply. He pushed the door closed in her face.

But Meg was a seasoned veteran of these wars, and she was desperate, and before he could accomplish his goal she had shoved her thin body between the door and the jamb. "I beg your pardon!" she exclaimed, her temper briefly slipping. "I asked for the missus of the house!"

"And what would your kind be wanting with her?" the manservant asked disdainfully.

"I am looking for employment," Meg said quickly. "I had a little brother and two little sisters and —"

"We do not hire Irish," he said. And this time he forced the door on Meg, who had no choice but to withdraw or be crushed, as his strength was far superior to hers.

She turned blindly away, so exhausted that she sank down on the front steps of the house, craddling her face in her hands. She was beaten, beaten down into the ground. Finally, she had lost all of her hope.

She cried softly.

When she finally looked up she realized that the sun was beginning to set. She was on elevated ground, facing north. Across the many steeply pitched roofs of the neighborhood, the numerous church spires and the flatter four- and five-story brownstone buildings on the wharves, lay Boston Harbor, which wrapped almost entirely around the city. Vessels were moored to their docks, while a steamer chugged down the Charles River, toward the Canal Bridge. Meg thought about all that had transpired that day. Her gaze drifted to the east, toward the India Wharf. Of course, she was too far away to make out either the tall office building of Zachary Hollander Shipping, Worldwide, or the even taller, naked masts of the clipper ship berthed on the wharf just behind it.

What was she going to do? She was not going to find respectable employment, not in Boston. She wasn't ready to give up — she had given up. And she had just killed a powerful man. Even if Timothy O'Leary and his friends didn't catch her themselves, the authorities would. Boston was no longer a place she dared remain.

But where could she go, and how? New York City seemed obvious. But would Timothy be able to find her there? And how would she get there when she did not have a single penny to her name? Was New York City even far enough away?

Meg shoved herself to her feet and started walking, not caring which direction she went in. The sun was lower now, burning orange behind her as it sank over the Charles River and Beacon Hill. Meg wiped her eyes with her fingertips. She desperately needed food. Too late, she regretted not taking the twenty silver dollars. It would have fed her for a month and seen her all the way to New York. How stupid she had been. Pride was for the fortunate, not for her.

Meg avoided the Commons at this time of night. But now she kept recalling how he had pressed the money into her hand, and how strong and warm his palm had been. Her heart had leapt right into her throat when he had done that. "To ease my conscience," he'd said. He was not, she decided fiercely, like the others. Another man would have cursed her clumsiness — or would have run her down without a second thought.

Suddenly Meg paused. Recalling hiding behind the stacked crates, recalling the conversation of the dock workers. One of them had bet a week's salary on a ship. And hadn't that younger, bewhiskered man said that he had hundreds of dollars riding on her, too? What was the name of that ship? *Cyclone*. Yes, that was it. Meg began trembling. There was a race. A race to San Francisco.

She hugged herself, absolutely energized now. It would be dangerous for her to go back to the wharves near Fort Hill. But she could no longer remain in Boston. Meg wasn't sure when *Cyclone* was leaving but what did it matter? She would stow away. And until the ship left port, it would be the perfect place to hide. Timothy would never think of looking for her there.

The home he had built for his bride was not on Beacon Hill, where most men of his wealth, power, and social standing would have chosen to reside, but on Charles Street, overlooking the river. Zachary Hollander could not imagine waking up each morning, or going to bed each evening, without being able to gaze out over a body of water.

He drove his carriage down the street, the fine black gelding in the traces pulling at the bit, eager to reach the stables. Zach had had a usual day, one filled with the details of the cargoes he was shipping and receiving, with deals begun and concluded for future voyages, and negotiations over current merchandise with numerous brokers. But his mind was no longer on the tea one of his ships was bearing out of Canton, bound for Liverpool, or the passenger ship that was halfway across the Atlantic, or even *Cyclone*, which would depart for California tomorrow on the earliest outgoing tide. He was wondering why she had run away from him, and why those thugs had been chasing her.

Not that it was his affair. Unfortunately, he had to keep reminding himself of that every so often. Why was she haunting him? He had always had a soft spot for those who were weak and unfortunate, for those who were helpless and under attack. Zach could not stand to see any creature in fear or pain. And that included a thin, young woman with huge gray eyes and a face that was, in spite of her generally untidy appearance, beautiful enough to launch a hundred ships and fill the dreams of a thousand lonely mariners.

He sighed. Hoping she would find a sanctuary, and with it the peace she so clearly needed. But it was for the best that she had run away. What could he have done for her other than to offer her more money? She was not some stray cat, to be adopted into his home. Rebecca would have an apoplexy.

His house was ahead. It was three stories high, a square, whitewashed structure with wide columns supporting the veranda, brick chimneys jutting from the steeply pitched rooftop. Green lawns surrounded the house and stable. Oaks shaded the circular white drive. Zach had built it ten years ago, with great joy and even greater pride, but now he approached with a numb feeling, a complete indifference, an absolute detachment. The only reason he had not sold it was because Rebecca had insisted he keep it, because, he knew, of all the expense he had incurred in building it. And he had shipped out for two years shortly upon its completion. When he had returned from his voyages, he'd discovered that she had redecorated every inch of the interior. How well she knew him. It had eased the pain. When he passed through the front door, then and now, it no longer seemed like the same home. Old hopes and dreams no longer rose their heads to mock and torment him.

Grooms ran out of the stables to greet him, their boots crunching on the white shells of the drive. Zach leapt down from the carriage, handing the reins to one of the servants. "He's had a trying day," he told the head groom, still thinking of the woman he had almost run over, dear God. Her eyes, wide and frightened, so terribly vulnerable, kept reappearing in his mind. "Rub him down well and feed him hot bran tonight," Zach said.

"Aye, Captain, sir," the groom said smartly.

Zach turned away, his own low boots crunching on the drive. He had but entered the spacious, parquet-floored foyer when Rebecca came flying out of the salon, smiling widely. "Zach," she cried, embracing him. She took one look at him and her expression changed. "Something is wrong. What is it?"

183

"Just a difficult day," he lied.

She studied him, then turned and walked back into the salon. Zach followed her into an elegantly appointed room, in the center of which was a dark salmon-colored marble fireplace and a crystal chandelier almost directly above a wide grand piano. She handed him a cognac. "What has happened?" she asked quietly.

He looked at his younger sister, the only family he had left. When their father had died, many years ago, he had sworn to look after her, and he had been doing just that ever since. But she was twenty-four now. And she knew him too well, almost the way a wife should, not a sister. Zach had promised himself last year that he was going to find a good husband for her by the following summer. Well, summer was just around the corner and he had not devoted much effort to the task. He hadn't had the time.

But Rebecca deserved a home of her own, a husband, and children. She did not deserve to grow old doting on him, running his empty, sterile household. The problem was, he knew her as well as she knew him. He knew that she wished to do just that — take care of him until he grew old and died, because she still felt sorry for him.

Zach had never regretted anything more — other than the fire itself — than breaking down in front of her on a subsequent night. If only he had been more manly. If only she hadn't witnessed the extent of his grief.

"What is wrong?" Rebecca asked, guiding him to a damask chair. She did not resemble him. Her hair was honey-colored, her features delicate, as their mother's had been. Only her eyes were the same, that odd golden amber that had been passed down through many Hollander generations. "Is it *Cyclone*? Has something happened to Jackson?"

Zach sighed, stretching out his trousered legs. Jackson

would be *Cyclone*'s captain as she tried to set a new record to the Gold Coast. "No. She will depart tomorrow, as planned, and Jackson is the best captain I know."

"After you," Rebecca amended with a soft, proud smile.

Zach did smile, then. "After myself," he admitted with no vanity.

"You should go," she suddenly said, sitting down across from him in a plush chair, one wide enough to accommodate the pink skirts that belled about her. Pearls dangled from her ears and glistened against the skin of her throat. "It's not too late to change your mind."

How he wanted to go. "I cannot. I have too many obligations here." Not the least of which was seeing that his sister was engaged — and happily so — by the summer's end. And that was but four months away. "I almost ran over a young woman today."

Rebecca gasped. "I do not believe it!"

"She was distraught." Zach met his sister's concerned gaze. "She rushed in front of my carriage without looking either right or left. Fortunately, I halted King and she was not hurt."

"Well, that is good news."

Zach stared down into the golden liquid in his snifter. "She was running away from some rough thugs. She was in trouble."

Rebecca stared.

Zach looked up, met her eyes, and shrugged.

"Then she was not a lady," Rebecca said. "If thugs were chasing after her."

Zach lowered his gaze. "She was Irish, and if I do not miss my guess, not long in this country." Her voice had been soft and musical, enchanting.

Rebecca stood. "Well, I am sorry she was being chased, sorry that you almost hurt her, but forget about it now. It is over with, no harm done. Shall we eat? It is half past seven. I know Cook. He is undoubtedly pacing the kitchens in a frenzy, worrying about his soups gone cold and his salads wilted."

Zach stood, staring at his sister, whom he loved more than anyone, more than anything. "It may be over for myself, Rebecca, but it is not over for her. I am here, preparing to dine, while she is out there somewhere, being sought by dangerous men. I think they would have killed her."

Rebecca whirled, eyes wide. "She is not one of us, Zach. It is not our affair."

Zach did not answer. But it was several moments before he followed her into the dining room.

"Where are you going?" Rebecca asked.

He had thought her abed and asleep by now. Zach paused in the foyer, clad in breeches, high riding boots, and a worn jacket he had carelessly tossed on. He had a revolver tucked into the waistband of his pants, a knife in his left boot. Rebecca stood on the stairs in her nightclothes. "I cannot sleep," he said. "I am going for a ride."

Her expression told him she was thinking about the first weeks after the fire, before he had shipped out to make the first of many fortunes, when he had spent each and every night in the saddle, riding like the wind, as if he could outrace the present, forgetting the past, denying the future. "It is nothing. I want to think. About *Cyclone*," he elaborated.

She finally nodded. "Be careful," she said, turning.

He did not watch her go upstairs. He hurried outside and to the stables, quickly taking a big, rangy white roan out of a box stall. He spoke quietly to the stallion as he tacked him, then led him outside. He mounted under the quiet regard of a perfect half-moon, and gave Saint his heels. The Thorough-

186

bred pranced down the drive and through the front gates, snorting eagerly, ears up. Finally Zach let him run.

Zach cantered the huge horse south down Charles all the way to the Commons. He did not skirt the park, but galloped through it, almost one being with his horse. There was only one thing he wished to do more on this particular moonlit night — stand at the helm of the greatest ship he had ever built, and race *Cyclone* through the Atlantic seas on her way toward Tierra del Fuego.

Saint ran. Zach bent over his neck, aware of each and every reason why he was not captaining *Cyclone* on such an important mission. Hollander Shipping had become a huge entity in the past five years, ever since it had become one of the few American companies monopolizing the tea trade from China to England. His clippers, being the fastest, brought in the freshest teas, and commanded the highest rates. And now the San Francisco run was proving as lucrative. If *Cyclone* set a new record for the San Francisco run, his rates would go even higher, both for the tea trade and for the frenzied passengers seeking gold in California.

No one else could be at the company's helm, while he did have a handful of great captains to whom he could entrust his ships. Like Jackson. And then there was Rebecca, and the promise he had made himself.

Zach slowed the white roan as they left the Commons. Mill Street was quiet now, all the shops closed, locked up, shades drawn, the trolleys parked for the night. Saint's shod hooves clicked loudly on the cobblestones. Laughter and drunken conversation could be heard in the distance, from the grog shops and saloons on the side streets nearer Fort Hill. Zach couldn't help hoping that the Irishwoman with the big gray eyes and wild red hair was unhurt and sleeping peacefully somewhere.

187

Ahead lay India Street, his offices, his warehouse, his wharf . . . and *Cyclone*, a ship he loved almost as much as he loved anything in the world.

Behind the deserted warehouse, Zach dismounted. He tied the roan to one of the pilings on the wharf, patting his dampened neck. For one long moment, Zach just stared at the ship he had designed, personally overseeing every single inch of her construction. She was long and lean, her masts 130 feet high. She was 229 feet eight inches long to be exact, and just 40 feet wide in the hull, while her official tonnage was registered at 1,778 pounds. She had been built for swiftness and speed. She had been built to race the wind, and the worse the weather, the more violent the storm, the faster she would run.

Zach stepped across the dock and walked up the ramp onto *Cyclone*'s immaculate decks. He was smiling now as he lifted his face to the blinking stars and the wet, salty air. The moon seemed to be smiling back at him.

Cyclone rocked a bit at her moorings, wood creaking against ropes, one of the most lulling, serene sounds Zach had ever known. He crossed the decks to stand at the bow, staring across the harbor, past Maverick Island, imagining the cheering crowds that would gather tomorrow. Men, women, and children would line the harbor as *Cyclone* finally got underway. There would be whistles and cheers, more wagers, picnics, balloons, and even fireworks. Then the Irish girl's image crowded into his mind again, and he frowned.

Perhaps he should have questioned those two thugs when they had regained consciousness. Instead, he'd had the police cart them off to jail. Maybe he would pay them a visit tomorrow and ask a few pertinent questions. He shook his thoughts free of her with difficulty.

Zach retraced his steps, but instead of leaving the ship he went below to the captain's cabin in search of a brandy. He could make his way around *Cyclone* blindfolded, and it was not until he entered the cabin that he reached for and lit a lantern. The desk Jackson would use for the eighty-odd days it would take him to complete his voyage — if he broke *Flying Cloud*'s record — was opposite the bunk, beneath a porthole. Zach found a bottle of brandy and a glass, and poured himself a libation. He turned to leave, about to snuff out the wick of the lantern.

He froze. Surely his eyes were deluding him.

Zach set the glass down, held the lantern higher. A person was sleeping on the bunk bed.

His jaw flexed, he withdrew his gun. He set the lantern down and soundlessly approached. And then he saw a long, thick red braid. His heart skipped wildly as he realized it was a woman — a woman with fiery red hair.

In disbelief, he leaned over her as she slept. He had only to glimpse her turned-away profile to realize who it was. But for some odd reason, he had known it the moment he had seen her braid, even though there must be hundreds of women with the same color hair in Boston.

What in God's name was she doing there? And was it a coincidence? His pulse pounding now, Zach stared at the woman who slept in the bunk in a state of complete exhaustion — as if she were dead.

Chapter Three

Zach hesitated. His gaze moved to what he could see of her chest. It was rising and falling slightly but rhythmically — she was hardly dead. Relief filled him.

But then he noticed the skin exposed where her shawl had slipped. Her dress was badly ripped on one shoulder so that almost the entire strap of her chemise was visible. He went rigid. He did not have to think very long to know that one of those thugs had laid his hands on her in a very ungentlemanly manner.

Zach shoved his gun into the waistband of his pants and touched her shoulder. She did not stir.

Aware that his heart was still racing unnecessarily, he shook her again. There was no response. He felt pity rising inside of him. She was truly exhausted.

"Madam?" he said, shaking her again. "Madam, please, wake up." Her lashes fluttered. They were a dark auburn, far darker than her bright red hair. Grimacing, he slid his arms beneath her, calling for her to awaken again. And as he helped her to sit up, he felt the moment when she responded to him.

Her entire body stiffened. Eyes wide, her startled gaze met his.

Before he could speak he realized that it was not surprise he saw in her eyes, but abject terror. She cried out, shoving both fists hard against his chest, small blows, but blows nonetheless.

"It is only I, Zachary Hollander," he said, releasing her and standing above the bunk.

She had already scooted backward, pressing her spine into the wall of the cabin, her bosom heaving, her face starkly white. Then she recognized him and said, "Oh!"

Suddenly color flooded her cheeks. She pulled her shawl over her shoulders, her bosom, her body. She did not move. She reminded Zach of a doe, stunned at discovery and caught in his gun sights.

He managed a smile. "This is my ship. What are you doing here?" He wanted to kick himself for being so callous. She was frightened, with good cause. It was fairly obvious what she was doing there on his ship. Beyond getting a good, safe night's rest, she was hiding.

She stared, not replying.

But he could see that she was trying to come up with a suitable response. "Perhaps introductions are in order?" he said.

She finally nodded. "Meg O'Neil."

"I see. And I am Zachary Hollander, as I have said." He began to feel uncomfortable in the confines of the cabin. As directness was a part of his nature, he knew no other way to proceed. "What did those men want? Why were they chasing you? And why did you choose my ship to hide on?"

Her mouth opened, closed. She breathed again. Her body remained tight with tension. "I don't know what they wanted," she whispered, and Zach knew it was a lie. When tears filled her eyes, he also knew that they were not theatrics. "I am so tired. I . . . . thought I could sleep here," she said.

"And you chose my ship — of all the hundreds in the harbor?"

She nodded. Her stomach growled quite loudly and she blushed.

"When did you last eat?" he asked, recalling how thin her shoulders were, poking out of her torn dress.

Her chin lifted. He saw the lie forming there on her tongue, in her eyes. He saw it there with the pride. Zach held out his hand. "Come. I will take you home. But on the way, we will have some supper. You see," he said, also lying, "I have missed supper myself."

She looked confused. "Why? Why are you doing this?"

He smiled reassuringly and his hand remained extended.

She shifted, leaning forward, and took it. How easily her small palm slid into his. It was rough with calluses. Zach pulled her forward and she slid to her feet.

They went topside and crossed *Cyclone*'s shining, moonlit decks in silence. A buoy in the harbor was ringing; a foghorn sounded. Water lapped the ship's sides.

The roan snorted as they approached. "Can you ride?" Zach asked, certain her answer would be negative.

"Of course," she said, as if any other reply were impossible. She smiled at his surprise.

It was the first time that he had seen her smile and he actually stumbled as she moved to the roan's side. He kept staring, aware of how his heart was lurching. He finally recognized the depth of his attraction to this unthinkable girl. Was he mad? Or had it merely been too long since he had been in the presence of a pretty woman?

She turned slightly. "But I can walk. I don't mind."

"I have the American House in mind. It is too far for either one of us to walk — especially you."

"It's not that far. Just over on Hanover Street," she replied.

He wasn't used to being contradicted. As he took up Saint's reins he asked, "How long have you been in the city?"

She hesitated. "Six months."

"You know the city well." He closed his hands on her waist, felt her stiffen in surprise. He swung her up and into Saint's saddle before she could protest.

192

He swung up behind her, trying not to think about his thighs wrapping around hers. Saint moved forward eagerly. "And where are you employed?"

She hesitated, then spoke in a hushed voice. "I am not."

He heard her dejection and his tone softened. "I am sure you will soon find a place," he said.

She did not reply.

Saint had moved past Zach's closed offices before Meg spoke again. "I am Irish," she said flatly.

He felt it then, all of her hurt, her bewilderment, her misery. It was not his affair but he was angry. He did not agree with most of his townsmen. Editorials ran daily and weekly, protesting the invasion of the Irish, accusing them of being lewd and crude, unwholesome and wretched, a detriment to the city as well as a cause of rising crime. Zach could not approve of the ghetto neighborhoods which had arisen to accommodate them, nor could he condone any excessive immoral behavior, but was fully aware of why an entire population had fled their native land — they were a starving people. And he had faith in the common man — in all men, of all creeds and colors — he always had. He was a loud advocate of hiring those Irish who met employment standards.

"It is a difficult situation," he said slowly, choosing his words with care. "I am appalled by the prejudice of many Bostonians, but you should know that those who speak the loudest often do so because their views are not as commonly held as they wish to make them seem."

She shifted in the saddle. "You are wrong again," she said, causing him to jerk, amazed. Her angry gaze held his as she regarded him over her shoulder. Her alabaster cheeks were flushed. "I have knocked on hundreds of doors and the response is always the same. I am Irish, and unfit for the homes of your kind." She faced forward.

He winced. "I am sorry," he said, meaning it.

She tensed, shot him a disbelieving glance, then quickly turned back. They rode down Hanover Street in silence now. Saint's hooves clopped loudly on the pavement.

"Where do you live?" he asked.

When she spoke, he knew she was lying again. "I have lost my room."

Had she lost her room — or was she afraid to go back to it? "You must have family here, or friends, where I can take you after our meal?"

She wiggled, trying to increase the distance between them. Her ploy failed, his hard thighs continued to mold her softer ones. "My family is dead. They died . . ." Her voice caught. She did not continue.

"I am sorry," he said.

She gripped the pommel of the saddle.

"And friends?" he prodded.

She remained mute.

He leaned forward and looked over her shoulder at her thin, set face. How long had it been since a woman had stirred up so many emotions inside of him? He reminded himself that he was attracted to her only because he had not been interested in any woman for so very long, but he was a humanitarian, and that was legitimate. He suddenly wheeled Saint abruptly around, in the opposite direction.

"Where are we going?" she cried in alarm.

"Hollander House."

"Hollander House?" Gripping the pommel tightly now, she shifted to stare wide-eyed at him. "Not . . . your home?"

"My home."

She panted. "No. Halt this horse. I want to get down." A sob worked its way into her tone.

He pulled Saint up. "Madam, what ails you? I am offer-

194

ing you the finest hospitality."

"I know what you are offering me," she shouted, throwing one of her legs over the pommel and sliding abruptly to the ground. She landed in a heap and immediately crouched there on all fours.

He understood and turned red.

She remained crouched, like a sprinter he had once seen at the starting line of a country fair race. She was going to sprint away from him.

He sat his stallion like a statue. "Miss O'Neil. I am an honorable man. I am offering you a meal and a bed. I am not offering you *my* bed."

She stared.

He stared back.

Slowly she rose to her feet. "Oh, God," she whispered. "You have rescued me and I am accusing you of being like them. Oh, God." Tears slipped from her eyes. She hugged herself. "Please. I beg your forgiveness. I don't know what came over me." She was shaking.

"I think you are overwrought and it is more than understandable." Zach extended his hand, his gaze on her face. Pity and sympathy blended inside of him.

She looked directly into his eyes. And then she put her palm in his and Zach swung her into the saddle, this time riding behind him.

He left her in the dining room, telling her he had servants to rouse.

Meg was in shock. She blinked many times, but the huge room with the pastel yellow ceiling, the blue and gold rug, the gleaming oak table that could seat twenty, and the massive crystal chandelier, did not go away. Was she supposed to sit down in one of those fancy, brocade-covered chairs?

195

She looked at the silver candlestick on the table. It was almost half the size of her body. She glanced at the dark ebony side table, which was twice as tall as she and about as long. She stared at the royal blue velvet draperies, open in spite of the night. Gold cords tied them back. And through the windows she could see a skyful of stars and the darker, shimmering water of the Charles River. Was she dreaming? Or had she died, killed by Timothy and his friends, and gone to heaven?

Her savior returned. "Please, sit down. James is bringing our meal," he said.

Meg stared at him, knowing he probably thought she had lost her mind. She wet her lips and finally spoke in a husky tone. "Is there a place where I could wash my face and hands?"

Crinkles appeared around his golden eyes. "Yes, there is. Let me show you to the powder room." A small smile had formed on his face.

Meg looked at him and had the sensation of falling. But to where? And why? It left a hollow feeling inside of her. That, and a feeling of real fear.

"What is going on in here?" demanded a woman from behind.

Meg turned to see a stunning woman in pale blue satin nightclothes standing on the threshold of the room. Her heart sank instantly. The woman had to be his wife, of course he had a wife, and why should she care? Why did she feel so completely crushed? So terribly dismayed?

"Rebecca," he said, moving to her. He gripped the woman's arm. The woman was staring at Meg now with absolute shock.

Meg cringed inwardly. She knew what was coming.

"This is the young lady I told you about," Zach Hollander

196

said quietly. "The young lady I almost ran over this morning."

"Young lady?" Rebecca repeated, aghast.

"Rebecca," Zach Hollander said, his tone like the lash of a whip. "I have invited Miss O'Neil in for a late supper. Perhaps you wish to go back to bed?"

Rebecca turned her wide golden gaze from Meg to Zach. "Are you mad?" she said.

Zach's jaw flexed.

Rebecca gave Meg one last horrified look, then whirled, practically running from the dining room. Her slippered footsteps sounded loud and swift on the stairs as she raced up them.

"I apologize for my sister's behavior," he said.

Meg could not believe her ears. "Your sister?"

"I am sure she will apologize to you in the morning."

Meg could not find air. "That isn't necessary." As if that woman would apologize to her! What kind of man was Zachary Hollander?

Her thoughts were interrupted as two servants entered the room, carrying covered silver platters. Meg froze, forgetting to breathe. The platters were set down and uncovered. She saw a haunch of venison, a side of pork, fillets of cod, an entire salmon. Saliva wet her dry mouth and her stomach growled loudly.

"Why don't you sit down?" Zach said, an amused light in his eyes.

Meg kept her chin high, refusing to look at the food now, afraid of not being able to stop staring. She could feel her cheeks burning. "The powder room?"

"Ah, yes," he said.

Meg followed him back into the spacious foyer and then down one hall lined with several magnificent paintings. She let herself into the small washroom he indicated. The vanity

197

was marble, dear God, the mirror rimmed in gold. Meg flinched when she faced her reflection.

Was this what he saw when he looked at her? A gaunt face with spots of dirt and huge circles beneath her eyes, snarled hair, a torn and shabby dress, an even shabbier shawl? She inhaled, fighting for self-control. She would eat in his elegant dining room, but then she would leave. She did not belong here.

Meg reached for a faucet and was confronted for the first time in her life with running water. How wonderful it was. She began removing every speck of dirt from her face and hands, then proceeded to spot-wash her clothes. As she did so, visions of venison and salmon danced in her head, along with visions of her host. It was very hard to have the discipline to spend fifteen minutes grooming herself when she desperately wanted to attack all of that glorious food.

He was waiting for her in the hall when she stepped out, and she noticed his guarded surprise at what she hoped was her improved appearance. Meg murmured her thanks and kept her eyes down as she followed him back to the dining room. More platters had been added to the table — roasted potatoes, buttered bread, sugared yams, and marinated beets. And half a luscious cherry pie.

Meg suddenly realized that he was holding a chair out for her while she was mesmerized by the feast laid out for them. She jerked, more shocked now than she had thus far been. He was not just treating her like a human being, he was treating her as if she were a fine Brahmin lady.

"Please," he said.

Meg sat. He sat at the table's head, adjacent her. Meg reached for her napkin, hoping he would not notice her shaking hands. The fabric was very fine, the embroidery exquisite. She itched to reach for the food, but she didn't move.

A servant came forward and offered to serve her. Meg hesitated, looked up, met his gaze, which was frankly assessing. "Yes, James, you may serve Miss O'Neil."

Meg watched discreetly as her plate was heaped with a little bit of everything that was on the table.

"It is Miss O'Neil?" he asked.

She clenched her fork. Meeting his mildly penetrating gaze and thinking about O'Leery. "Yes," she whispered, praying she would not blush now.

"After you," he said.

Meg realized that both of their plates were full and she should begin first. She took a bite of the venison. It was so good she was afraid she would burst into tears. She took another bite, trying to keep a grip on her control and her dignity. She took another bite and another and another — until she realized he wasn't eating a thing — he was watching her.

"It's all right," he said, unsmiling. "And do not tell me you last ate this afternoon. You are famished." His gaze moved to her shoulders. And briefly began a descent — which he abruptly ended by looking at his own plate.

She set her fork down. Somehow knowing the time for lies must end. "It has been very difficult for me, being here with no work, no family," she said. "I cannot thank you enough for tonight. And for this afternoon."

"I understand." He fidgeted with his dinnerware. "Miss O'Neil." His gaze was piercing. "There is an obvious solution to your dilemma," he said.

Meg thought her heart had stopped. Would he offer her free passage to San Francisco? But she had not told him of her plan to stow away. Suddenly San Francisco seemed so very far away. "There is?" she asked cautiously.

"Yes. I wish to employ you here at Hollander House."

★ ★ ★ ★ ★

Rebecca was up, waiting for him in the hallway outside of his suite of rooms. Her arms were folded tightly against herself. Zach sighed.

"Where is she?" Rebecca asked tersely.

"James has shown her to her room, and you owe her an apology."

Rebecca's eyes widened. "What!"

He did not bother to repeat himself.

"Zach, I am in shock. I do not know what you are thinking of. To bring that Irishwoman here. Are . . . if you wish to dally with her . . ." Rebecca could not continue. Her eyes had become moist.

He stiffened. "Is that what you are thinking?" He fought to mitigate his tone, which was razor sharp. "I am not dallying with anyone — and if I were, it is none of your concern."

She cringed.

But he was not going to apologize, not after the living hell his personal life had become. "I know you have been inclined to share the sensibilities of some of our more outspoken citizens, but I expect charity from you, Rebecca, when those less fortunate than ourselves are reduced to poverty and helplessness. I have offered Miss O'Neil employment in our home. I expect you to treat her as kindly as you do the rest of the staff. And this is not a negotiation." He was struggling with his temper again. He rarely lost his temper with Rebecca.

She was ashen. "You have employed her *here?* An Irishwoman? What will the neighbors say? What will my friends think?"

"Perhaps they will reassess their prejudices and follow our example." He reached for the door to his bedroom. "Good night, Rebecca."

She stared after him. She continued to stare when the door

closed solidly behind him. She was trembling. How could Zach speak to her in such a manner? More tears, real tears, filled her eyes.

She had only his best interests at heart. She had sacrificed her own happiness in order to take care of him. And didn't he care that their neighbors would be offended by an Irishwoman working in their midst? Didn't he care that *she* was offended?

Rebecca was neither a fool nor blind. That O'Neil woman, while wretched in some ways, had a lovely face. Far too lovely, Rebecca thought, far too uncommon. All men, including her brother, would notice her.

Rebecca hurried down the hall and downstairs. James was putting out the lights in the foyer when she arrived there. "Where is she? The new maid?"

"She is in the servants' wing, Miss Hollander. I have put her in Annie's old room."

Rebecca nodded, fighting tears, hurrying through the house. She had not entered the servants' wing since she had fired Annie for stealing silverware some months ago. It was dark and quiet, as most of the staff had been asleep for some time now — as well they should be. It was almost midnight.

But at the end of the corridor light was coming out from beneath one closed door. Rebecca did not falter. She intended to set this O'Neil girl straight on the rules of decorum in this house — and that included staying away from her brother. She swung the door open. Knocking did not occur to her.

The girl was in the midst of undressing. She was clad in nothing but her drawers. She whirled with a gasp as Rebecca entered the room, then tried to cover herself — to cover the small but protruding mound of her abdomen.

Rebecca could not believe her eyes. For one long moment, she could not speak. And then she cried out, "You are with child!" It was an accusation.

Chapter Four

"You were already asleep. I didn't want to wake you. She is pregnant, Zach," Rebecca said with censure.

He had just come downstairs for breakfast, a meal he took at seven-thirty while looking over his daily agenda. Rebecca did not take her breakfast with him — she dined several hours later at a more fashionable hour. But this morning she was up and dressed and waiting for him in the small breakfast room that looked out on blooming gardens. Her hands were on her hips.

Zach stared at her, about to take his seat. "What?" Had he misheard?

"She is with child," Rebecca said hotly. "I went to speak with her last night. I saw her condition myself."

Something twisted inside of him. It was far more than pity, far more than concern. He suddenly lost his appetite.

"We must dismiss her," Rebecca said firmly.

"Send her to me in the library," Zach said, striding grimly out of the breakfast room. Mild, early-morning sunlight was streaming through the French doors he passed as he made his way down the oak-floored corridor. Robins, blue jays, and sparrows were in a mad contest of song in the oaks outside of the house. Beyond the back lawns, a tugboat was visible on the river, sending a cloud of dark smoke into the otherwise unblemished blue sky.

She was pregnant. And he had guessed her to be fifteen, which perhaps she was. And she was so thin, too thin for a woman with child. He entered the library, a wood-paneled, book-lined room that was exclusively his domain. He did not realize that he was pacing, raking a hand through his thick, dark hair, until Rebecca appeared on the threshold, with Meg in tow.

Zach paused. Meg had been staring at him; she quickly studied the floor. But her hands, he saw, were clenching the folds of her dark skirt. He took a good look at her midsection. Her tummy was slightly swollen, he supposed, for such a thin girl. But had Rebecca not brought it to his attention, he would have never noticed. "Please come in and sit down, Miss O'Neil," he said. He gestured to one of the large upholstered armchairs in front of his oversized mahogany desk.

She darted a glance at him, but immediately looked away. It was obvious that she was terrified of what he was going to say and do.

"Rebecca, I wish a private word with Miss O'Neil," Zach said.

Rebecca started. But before she could formulate a protest, Zach gave her a severe look. She nodded, clearly displeased, and left the room. "Please close the door," Zach called after her. Rebecca obeyed.

Zach moved in front of his desk, not behind it. He leaned his hip against it. "Is it Miss O'Neil or Mrs. O'Neil?"

She finally glanced up, wetting her lips. Speech failed her.

He forced his tone down, softening it. "Is my sister right? Are you with child?"

She nodded. She was gripping the padded arms of the chair. "Yes."

"I see." A knife seemed to twist inside of him again.

"My husband is dead," she said abruptly.

He met her gaze; she looked away. He stiffened. She was lying. He knew a poor liar when he saw one. But he also sensed a ring of truth in her words, and he could not make sense of that. He shoved his hands into the pockets of his trousers. "When is the child due?"

"Four months," she said, low. "I . . . I never meant to deceive you, sir."

"Of course you did not," Zach said. And then he fell silent. He could not help wondering if one of those thugs had been her husband. And if that was the case, then he was not sorry he had taken her into his home. "How old are you?" he finally asked.

She continued to regard her lap. The tips of her auburn lashes seemed spiky and wet. "Twenty."

He was surprised.

She glanced up, meeting his gaze boldly for the first time. "I will leave now, sir. But thank you for the fine meal and the fine bed." Her tone was choked.

"Wait," he called, straightening as she stood. "Where do you think you are going?"

She was frozen. "I . . . don't know . . . sir."

"Do you not have a day's work to perform?"

She blinked. "Oh. Yes. Of course. Payment for my supper, for the bed. I'll be gone then by evening." She quickly turned away.

He thought he'd seen tears in her eyes. He reached out impulsively, his hand closing on her wrist. "Meg. I mean, Mrs. O'Neil. I am not dismissing you."

She slowly faced him. Eyes wide, and shimmering eerily silver in the early light. "You're not?"

"I am a man of honor," he reminded her. "I have offered you employment. You have accepted. Your condition should not interfere with your work for several more months. And clearly you need this job. Unless," he smiled slightly, "you have received a better offer since last night?"

She stared up at him. "I have not," she whispered.

He realized he still held her arm and he released it. It crossed his mind to tell Cook to fatten her up immediately.

"Thank you, sir," she said, curtsying. "Thank you." She turned, almost tripping in her haste.

"One more thing," he said, amused.

She paused uncertainly.

"Today my ship sets sail. The tide will be high at one-eighteen this afternoon. It is a tradition in this household to behold the departure of a maiden voyage. The entire staff has been included in that tradition since my father built his first ship in 1816. In fact, you have probably heard them discussing *Cyclone*'s departure this morning." He was smiling, filled with excitement at the prospect of *Cyclone* setting sail for her very first voyage.

She was not smiling, though. "Yes. There were some wagers. I . . . cannot go."

His smile faded. "Those two men are in the jailhouse," he said.

She was stunned. "They're in jail? You had them arrested?"

"They were breaking the law," he said flatly.

"I still mustn't go," she said in a rush. "But thank you for your generosity."

He stared. He could not understand her, could not understand why she refused to witness the launching of his extraordinary ship. "What did they want with you? Why are you still afraid?"

She backed up, her shoulders pressing against the door. Her smile, the first of that day, was forced. "I don't know what they wanted. I never saw them before. But . . . I just can't go."

She was lying again. Zach nodded curtly, and she escaped the room.

The kitchen was in chaos because the entire staff was preparing to witness *Cyclone*'s departure. Knives were flying, pans clattering, fires going, as the evening supper was prepared well in advance. Meg had been given the task of peeling potatoes. She hardly saw the spud in her hand as her knife flew over the skin. She remained in utter disbelief. He hadn't dismissed her.

He was the kindest man she had ever met in her entire life. Kind and honorable, she thought, something warm rushing over her, through her. His darkly handsome face filled her mind.

"Luv, I know the perfect spot to watch *Cyclone* leave the harbor."

Meg jerked. A young man stood at her elbow, two pails of water in his hands. He was grinning at her.

They had met earlier. She could not recall his name, but she knew he was one of the houseboys, given numerous odd tasks to do. Blond and blue-eyed, as thin as a rail, he was about her own age.

"So what do you say? Walk with me? I'll even buy you a candy apple," he said, smiling.

Meg stiffened. "I'm not going, er . . ." She trailed off.

"Peter," he said, his expression quizzical. "How come? Everyone's going. Captain's orders, so to speak."

"I'm not going," she repeated firmly. But she imagined Hollander standing there on the wharf beside his magnificent clipper ship. Her heart was suddenly tight. "I am very tired," she said, and it was only half a lie.

Peter regarded her with disappointment. "Well, if you change your mind," he said, and shrugged and walked away.

Several hours later, Meg found herself sitting alone at the rectangular wooden table in the kitchen where the staff ate.

The house was deserted and silent. It felt eerie, and Meg felt achingly alone.

She laid her head on her arms. It was noon. In another hour *Cyclone* would set sail. It was hard to believe that she might have been on that ship and bound for California, even harder to believe that she was now employed at Hollander House, with her employer fully aware of her pregnant condition.

Meg wished that she could go. Even though she was tired, it wasn't the bone-weary, absolute exhaustion of yesterday and the days before that. She'd slept like a log last night, had eaten a breakfast big enough to feed four men that morning. She couldn't remember when she'd felt so full, had slept so well, had been so safe.

Hollander House was the perfect place to hide.

But why couldn't she go? Zachary Hollander had had Timothy and his friend arrested. Meg shuddered at the thought of how furious Timothy must be. Of course, there were other O'Leery cohorts about, and she would be recognized the moment one of them spotted her — recognized and chased. But there would be hundreds of citizens gathered at the wharf today. What if she bound her hair back very tightly, and wore a covering on her head? What if she wore her uniform, the simple black dress and white apron she'd been given that morning? What if she borrowed the housekeeper's reading spectacles?

Meg sat up. She was trembling. There were so few pleasures in her life, and the departure of *Cyclone* was going to be as festive as a County Clare summer fair. And hadn't he said she could — should — go?

And he would be there.

Meg was surrounded by a throng of strangers. She was

207

in disguise. Class lines seemed to have been blurred for the event; a cluster of finely dressed ladies and gentlemen stood on Meg's left, arguing amiably about *Cyclone*'s chances of breaking *Flying Cloud*'s record, while a farmer in dungarees and his buxom wife, clad in a pink gingham dress, stood on her right, a small lunch basket in the woman's hand. In front of Meg an Irish boy in pants four inches too short for his legs held a straw to his mouth and blew tiny pebbles at the passing throng, competing with a boy somberly dressed in a black, wool Sunday suit, also using a straw. A group of burly stevedores were already soused, and a reverend was trying to get through the crowd to bless the ship. Someone had set off fireworks from the roof of one of the buildings on India Street, and they whistled, whirred, and exploded overhead.

Meg smiled as the two boys took perfect shots at an unsuspecting matron in a fancy, pinstriped walking suit. She cried out, clapping her hand to her cheek. The boys giggled and escaped into the crowd.

Meg sobered. How long would it take for the two boys to grow up and realize that they should despise each other? The thought was depressing; she refused to entertain it.

Meg had managed to push her way through the festive crowd to the very edge of Bowe's Wharf, which was just across the wharf from *Cyclone*. Sailors were scrambling all over *Cyclone*, untying lines and hoisting massive, pristine white sails. Meg searched the wharf beside the ship. Her heart screeched to a stop.

He was so *impressive*. Zach Hollander stood on the dock an armspan from his ship, chatting with a group of elegant ladies and finely dressed gentlemen. Although he wore the same trousers, white shirt, and dark jacket as everyone else, he stood out, and not because he was so tall or so powerfully built. His presence, Meg decided, commanded instant attention.

Her pulse was pounding now. She covered her heart with her hand. The realization struck her full force. She was hopelessly in love with him.

Meg could not move, could not breathe.

Hollander laughed at something one of the women said. She had never seen him laugh before and Meg came out of her shock. He was striking, devastating, mesmerizing. He was an extraordinary man. Her gaze shifted. The woman was platinum blond, her figure lush, fabulously dressed in yellow-sprigged lawn, her veiled hat matching the gown. She had placed one gloved hand on Zach's arm and had yet to remove it. He did not seem to object.

It was hopeless. How had this happened? He had rescued her, saved her life, but he was stations above her. He might be kind, but what he felt for her was pity, nothing more. The woman he would one day love and marry would be someone like that blonde. A Boston blueblood, Brahmin-born, Brahmin-bred. Meg knew that she must not have these feelings. She must strike them from her heart.

Besides, she was pregnant with another man's child.

Meg swallowed painfully. But she could not tear her gaze away from him.

Hollander was speaking now with another man, and Meg heard excited whispers around her. "That's him, Jackson, the man Hollander handpicked to captain *Cyclone!*" someone said. Meg saw nothing unusual about the man, who was short and burly, his face covered with whiskers. But Hollander was speaking very seriously now, undoubtedly giving him last-minute instructions. And then he clapped him hard on the back.

They shook hands, and Jackson went aboard.

The crowd began cheering. Someone whistled. Another

round of fireworks whistled high up in the air. Popping, exploding. Drums rolled.

Hollander stared at his ship, his hands in his pockets now. As the last lines were being untied, a huge "Hurrah" went up from the crowd. *Cyclone* was moving, her sails filling out, and a band of wind instruments began to play.

And what a sight she was. So long and lean, her sharp, jutting prow slicing through the bay, her huge white sails completely full now as she began to pick up speed.

Meg hugged her arms to her chest. She hadn't realized it, but she had pushed herself even farther forward, and now stood trembling at the very edge of the wharf, with no one in front of her, just the dark blue lapping waters of the bay.

Hollander shifted and glanced around as *Cyclone* began streaking through the harbor. People were jumping up and down now, shouting and screaming, and someone was making a frantic last-minute wager. Another explosion filled the brilliant April sky and the band played on.

Suddenly Hollander turned, away from his ship, staring toward Bowe's Wharf.

And across the distance of water separating them, perhaps a hundred feet, no more, Meg met his eyes. Her heart went wild.

He did not move.

Meg pushed the spectacles she had borrowed higher up on her nose, turned, and disappeared into the crowd.

The jail was at the foot of Cambridge.

Zach strode swiftly across the street, having left his carriage in front of the Court House in the only available space he'd found. He remained exhilarated, an image of *Cyclone* flying out of the harbor engraved upon his mind. Yet another image was also there in his memory, competing for his attention.

Meg O'Neil, in uniform, wearing a pair of spectacles. So she had come to witness *Cyclone*'s launching after all.

Why did she remain so frightened? And was one of the imprisoned men the father of her child? The more he thought about it, the more likely it seemed to be. Yet he could not imagine her in the arms of either of those men. The very idea was impossible.

Town was still abuzz, even the city center. Zach stepped onto the sidewalk and entered the stone building that was the jail. Inside it was cool, the air circulating from one large overhead ceiling fan. Only one police officer seemed to be in attendance, and he immediately set aside his lunch and sat up straighter upon seeing Zach.

"Good afternoon," Zach said.

The police officer, a middle-aged man with an iron-gray handlebar mustache, was on his feet. "Mr. Hollander, sir. Congratulations."

Zach did not know the officer, but was not surprised that the officer knew him. He and his company frequently made the news, and in the last year, he'd made numerous headlines when he'd begun to build *Cyclone*. "Thank you, Inspector. Yesterday two unidentified thugs were arrested at India Wharf. I wish to speak with them."

The officer blinked. "Jail's empty, sir."

Zach stiffened. "How is that possible? I was there myself when several officers carted them off. They were still unconscious."

The officer seemed to pale. "They were released on bail this morning just after I came in. O'Leery and Dugan."

Zach stared. He recalled Meg's fear and her abject refusal to come to the wharf. Now he was beginning to understand. The men who were after her had been released, and were, perhaps even now, searching for her on the streets.

"How much was the bail?" he asked.

"One thousand dollars."

Christ. Zach stared, not seeing the officer. Those two were not common thugs — and Meg was clearly in trouble.

"Sir?" the deputy inspector said. "O'Leery's pressed charges himself."

Zach started. "Against myself? I was defending the woman."

"No, sir. Not against you. Against the woman."

He was in disbelief. "And just what charges have been pressed?"

"She's been charged with assault — and attempted murder."

"That's insane," Zach snapped. "She was fleeing those two brutes. If anyone was attempting murder, it was this O'Leery character and his friend Dugan."

"No, sir. The attempted murder charges pertain to O'Leery's father. Apparently she tried to kill the elder O'Leery yesterday morning in a grog shop on Fort Hill. And there's a warrant out for her arrest, sir."

Zachary did not move.

"You wouldn't know where she is, would you?"

Zach's gaze did not waver. "No," he said.

Chapter Five

The last-minute preparations for the evening meal were underway. Meg had been charged with setting the dining-room table along with Betsy, another housemaid her own age or thereabouts. Apparently the Hollanders were having guests, for the housekeeper had specified that a dozen places be set, and they were using, according to Betsy, the best silver and crystal the master and his sister owned.

"You should have come," Betsy said, continuing the non-stop chatter she had been subjecting Meg to ever since they had begun their task. " 'Twas a grand sight, let me tell you! I never seen such a ship afore." She laughed as she smoothed down an exquisite lace place mat. "We didn't have any place for ships like that back home."

Meg paid little attention. She'd been beset with nerves all afternoon — witnessing the *Cyclone*'s launching had been a terrible idea. For she'd somehow come by incredible feelings for the man who had been so kind to her. The man who was now her employer. His image remained seared upon her mind. But love, she'd thought, was supposed to be a wonderful experience. Holding hands underneath a rainbow, that sort of thing. Instead, Meg felt like throwing up.

She did not want to continue working at Hollander House, but she had no choice. And if she left, she knew she would never see him again.

"That's not the way you do it," Betsy said, interrupting Meg's thoughts. "Them big spoons are for soup and they go up top, like so."

Meg nodded, rearranging the silverware. "How long have you worked here?" she asked cautiously, in a whisper. She wasn't sure if Rebecca Hollander had returned to the house.

"Four years now," Betsy said happily. "An' I hope to work here my whole life, even after Ivan and I marry. They're good people, Meg. I truly like 'em. An' I have friends, you know, across the street and over on Beacon Hill. We get paid better than them, and we get our vacations, too, plus ever' single Sabbath. An' I never went to bed even once hurtin' from workin' too hard or hungry from eatin' too little." Betsy nodded vigorously.

"Yes, I can see that they are good people," Meg agreed, and it was partly true. Betsy would probably not be so lavish in her praise if she were Irish. Meg was the only Irish servant on the staff, and the few times she'd encountered Rebecca, the woman had made it clear that Meg was no better than the dirt under her feet. "But neither he nor she is married," Meg said, a leading question.

"He won't ever marry." Betsy rushed around the table to Meg's side, speaking in an excited whisper. "It's so sad, though — she won't marry because she thinks she has to take care of him."

Meg gripped the back of one of the chairs — exactly like the one she had sat in as she dined at the table the night before. "I don't understand."

Betsy was eager to share what she knew. "Ten years ago he married this woman, this terribly beautiful, sweet woman — a woman he truly loved and adored. And she had his child, a little girl, exactly as sweet and beautiful as she was. But there was an accident. They were living in his father's house just a short ways from here. His father died a few years earlier, you know. It was a Sunday. The staff was off. He was off, too, on a voyage to Canton. That's China, you know. He

214

trades in tea. And there was a fire. To this day, no one knows how it started, but they say it started in the baby's room. Maybe a candle had been left on, and it tipped over. Half of the house burned down, Meg. And they found her — Angeline — with the baby — so she'd gone to rescue her poor child. But they were nothing but blackened bones."

Meg stared, more nauseous than before. "Oh, dear, dear God," was all she could say.

Tears had filled Betsy's eyes. She nodded. "He came home maybe one week afterward — and that's what he found. Half of a home — and two small graves."

Meg stared. Horrified. She knew the anguish of losing those you loved. How well she knew. And she felt for him now with every fiber of her being. In that moment, all she wanted to do was to go to him and hold him and tell him she understood, and that, while the pain would never go away, one day it would diminish, becoming almost bearable. She would stroke his brow. She could almost feel his skin under her hand. She felt that she could heal him with her love.

An absolutely absurd thought.

"May I ask what the two of you are doing, gossiping in whispers in the dining room?" Rebecca Hollander asked. "Our guests are due in less than an hour."

Meg stiffened. Betsy turned red. Both women curtsied, murmuring downcast apologies. But it was Meg who received the cool warning look from Rebecca before she turned and walked away.

Betsy faced Meg, wide-eyed. "Gawd! She hates you, she does!"

Meg tried to smile, and failed. "I'm Irish, and to her, that means I'm scum," she said.

Zach paced his library, no longer thinking about the launch

215

of his magnificent clipper ship. Some of the shock he'd felt at the jail had dimmed, but not all of it. He had only just returned home, because he'd stopped at the offices of the lawyer who had freed O'Leery and Dugan on the thousand-dollar bond. And he had learned that Robin O'Leery was a powerful man among the Irish living in Boston. He owned and operated a dozen grog shops, a textile mill, a boardinghouse-cum-whorehouse as well as a few other questionable enterprises. He had accumulated far more than money, he'd accumulated authority and power. The Irish considered him something akin to a king.

And she had hit him over the head with a full bottle of Irish whiskey. She hadn't even come close to killing him, but he'd been knocked unconscious, and had thirty-three stitches from brow bone to jaw.

O'Leery was not going to drop the charges, the lawyer said.

And that made Zach an accomplice to her crime. But he wasn't particularly worried about that.

Zach strode to the closed door of his library. The time had come for a confrontation and the truth. His expression implacable, he started down the hall. He encountered Rebecca in a magnificent apricot taffeta evening dress as she was entering the formal salon.

She paused. "Zachary! Our guests shall be here at seven and you have not changed your clothes."

"Do not concern yourself — I will be ready by seven. Where is Meg O'Neil?"

Rebecca became motionless. "I last saw her setting the dining-room table. She is very busy, Zach. All of the servants are."

Zach ignored the innuendo in her words, as well as the questioning light in her eyes. In the dining room he paused, watching Meg place crystal glasses at each place setting. He knew the exact instant that she became aware of his presence.

216

While she did not cease what she was doing, her movements slowed. Her cheeks became flushed. She finally looked slowly toward the threshold where he stood.

And while she was just a too-thin housemaid, his heart lurched. He was insanely affected by her and there was no possible way of denying it. "I would like a word with you," he said quietly.

She froze. She had seemed somewhat pale, but now she turned ghostly white. He saw fear in her eyes. But he was relentless. He gestured for her to precede him.

She left the table, moving through the doorway, her skirts brushing his trousered legs as she passed by him. Zach felt himself stiffen. "To the library, please," he said.

Her shoulders squared, she moved down the corridor. When they passed the two open doors of the formal salon in single file, Rebecca stared at them. Zach ignored her. He closed the heavy library door behind him. "You may sit down," he said.

She faced him. "I will stand," she returned.

He knew she was afraid, could guess why, and had to admire her spunk. He also thought her face had taken on an oddly green cast. "As you wish." He hesitated. "You came to the wharves today." That was not what he had intended to say.

Her eyes widened. A terrible silence separated them. He was standing at least a dozen feet from her, but he could feel tension knifing between them. "Yes," she finally replied. And then, slightly, she smiled. "It was spectacular."

He smiled, unable not to. "She is the finest ship I have ever built."

"A beauty," she said. Then, "Will you do it?" Pink colored her cheeks, as if she was surprised by her boldness in asking such a question.

"Yes." There was no indecision in his tone. "*Cyclone* will

make San Francisco in less than eighty-nine days."

"Then I am happy for you," she said, her voice strangely soft. She glanced away, her fingers creasing her ebony skirts.

How had the room become so warm and airless? Abruptly he walked past her to push a window open as wide as it would go. Outside, he noticed a freight train on the Canal Bridge crossing over the Charles.

He turned. "Is Robin O'Leery the father of your child?" he asked.

She cried out, paling, reaching for a chair. Zach rushed to her side and gripped her arm, holding her upright. Her knees had buckled. "I see that you have managed to answer the question," he said grimly, feeling ill.

She shook her head, tears filling her eyes, and pulled her arm free. She sank down into an armchair. "It's not what you think."

Her tone was so low, so choked with tears, that he could hardly understand her. "Is he also your husband?"

Meg looked up, openmouthed. She did not speak.

Exercising a patience he did not feel, could not feel, as well as an iron control that was ingrained in his character, Zach repeated the question.

"No." Meg covered her face with her hands.

An urge to commit violence surged through him. But he merely walked back to the window, staring at the river as it ebbed into the ocean, imagining in its stead two passionately entwined lovers. "So you have had a change of heart. You must have loved him once." Perhaps she still did. She had tried to kill him. A crime of passion, no doubt. And why was he so distressed?

Meg looked up. "I don't understand."

"He was your lover. You loved him once. Or will you deny that?"

218

She stared at him, unmoving, and then she was on her feet. "You are mad!" she cried. And she turned, rushing across the room.

Zach caught her from behind. Her shoulder felt bony beneath his hand. He did not release her. "Tell me the truth!" His voice was harsh now. "You carry his child, and you tried to kill him. Do you still love him?"

Her eyes were wide, confused, and once again, that pale, odd silver hue. "I never loved him. Never! I never, ever," she halted, panting, "asked for his attentions! All I did was to beg for a respectable job!"

Zach stared, searching her face. And suddenly he understood. "He forced his attentions on you," he said, aghast.

But if she heard him, she did not respond, for suddenly she was gripping his arm with surprising strength. "You said I *tried* to kill him!" She was shouting, nearly hysterical. "Oh, God . . . you do not mean . . ." She stopped, incapable of completing her sentence.

"Yes. He is still alive."

Meg cried out in dismay.

"Meg!" He reached for her again but she evaded him with lightning speed. "He will not hurt you again," Zach said.

"No!" She seized the handle of the door, pulling on it wildly. And when it swung open, she ran out — and he let her go.

For he came face to face with Rebecca.

Chapter Six

Meg watched the guests arriving through a window, using the draperies to make sure that she could not be seen. The parlor was far smaller than the grand salon, far more intimate, perhaps used only by the family and it had been left dark and unlit. Guilt tugged at Meg. She had things to do in the kitchen, and she did not mean to be a lackadaisical employee, but she was compelled.

A couple alighted from a large carriage. The gentleman wore evening clothes, including a cloak, top hat, and white gloves, and he carried a silver-knobbed cane. The lady wore a fabulous green gown beneath her cashmere mantle, and white gloves reached her elbows. Meg saw jewels sparkling around her throat and at her ears.

More carriages pulled up in front of the house, each beautifully polished, appointed in brass and velvet, and accompanied by a pair of footmen. Several more couples entered the front door, each dazzling, and finally a trio arrived. Meg tensed as she realized that the third person in the party was a pretty dark-haired woman no older than she herself. Clearly the brunette, resplendent in a rose-colored dress, was the elderly couple's daughter. Meg's pulse was pounding.

She had counted ten guests so she turned away from the window, for one moment standing alone in the dark. She was jealous. It was absurd. But that brunette had everything Meg did not, including elegance and respectability, and Meg imagined that Zach would not be immune to her good looks and social standing. After all, he was a single man.

Meg paused at the door, cracking it open, glancing to her left, toward the front foyer where the guests had arrived. Directly opposite was the salon where even now the guests were gathered — Meg could hear high-spirited laughter and conversation.

She did not see a soul, so Meg decided that it was safe to return to the kitchen. She knew that Rebecca would be furious if she ever found out that Meg had dared to watch her guests arriving. Meg slipped out of the parlor, careful not to make a sound. At that exact same moment, Zach came down the stairs and into the foyer, devastatingly handsome in his black tails.

Meg was so surprised she faltered, instead of making a dash toward the kitchens. At least twenty-five feet separated them, and he was not looking at her, but approaching the salon. She could have made it to safety undetected.

But he paused and turned. Meg still had her hand on the brass knob of the parlor door. Their eyes met. His went wide. Meg felt a guilty flush covering her cheeks. She did not move.

His gaze went to the darkened room she had just left, and then back to her face. Meg knew he understood exactly what she had been about. To her shock, he smiled at her. And then, adjusting his lace cuffs, he strode into the salon.

Meg was left alone in the hall. She began to breathe again, her hand on her racing heart. He hadn't reprimanded her, or worse, called Rebecca out to do so. And what had that odd smile meant?

As Meg returned to the kitchens, she had the strangest notion that he might even like her.

"You are clearing tonight, Meg."

Meg was horrified. "Mrs. Green," she began, a throaty protest.

The buxom housekeeper shook her head. "I know. You have no experience. I am in complete agreement. But it is not my idea. Miss Hollander has specifically ordered you to clear."

Meg hardly heard as the housekeeper explained to her what she must do. Clear the table? After every course? What if she spilled a plateful of leftover food on one of the guests? Yet hadn't she cleared her own kitchen table hundreds of times, back at the farm in County Clare? Of course that was different. Then it had been her mama, her brother, and her sisters. Everyone had helped. It had been a warm, loving time. It had been far from an elegant, formal dinner.

Meg was told to change her apron. She ordered her hands to stop shaking, but they would not obey. She knew why Rebecca had demanded that she clear the table. She wanted Meg to make a mistake, one big enough for her to be dismissed. She wanted to humiliate her in front of Zach.

"First course is done," James announced cheerfully. He was one of the servers.

Meg prayed she would not disgrace herself, but she was feeling nauseous. She had yet to vomit since becoming pregnant, but she'd been fighting attacks of nausea for weeks now.

Meg followed Betsy into the hall with great trepidation. Betsy squeezed her hand reassuringly as they crossed the threshold of the dining room.

The first thing Meg saw was Zach. He was seated at the table's head, directly facing her. At the foot was Rebecca, her back to the door and the two housemaids.

Meg's heart lurched. He had seen her, and although his posture was relaxed as he listened to the chatter of the matron on his right, Meg noticed him stiffen ever so slightly. And his eyes were upon her, not the auburn-haired lady he was listening to.

Meg hadn't realized that she'd halted in her tracks. And

222

Betsy was already clearing plates. Rebecca turned and shot Meg a glance.

Meg recovered, moving forward, then nearly tripped. The woman sitting next to Zach, on his left, was the young brunette and even one quick glance told Meg that she had vastly underrated the other woman. She was more than lovely; she was one of the most enchanting women Meg had ever seen with her dark sultry eyes and rosy, pouting lips.

Meg reached for the empty plate of a gentleman.

"Miss O'Neil," Rebecca said coolly. "We remove the ladies' plates first."

Meg's cheeks burned. She returned the plate to where it had been placed, staring at her toes. "I am sorry," she breathed. She went to the lady adjacent the gentleman, taking that place instead. The utensils on the beautiful, gold-rimmed china clattered noisily. Meg took another two plates and hurried from the room — aware of Rebecca watching her with a catlike satisfaction.

And Zach had been watching her, too.

"It's always the ladies first," Betsy hissed in the hall as they headed for the kitchens, their hands full. "And don't forget to replace the silver if it's left on the plate!"

Meg nodded, feeling close to tears. Rebecca was succeeding beyond her wildest expectations — because Meg could not stand to see Zach beside that perfect brunette.

On their way back to the dining room, their feet flying across the parquet floors, Meg whispered, "Who is she? That girl seated beside Mr. Hollander?"

"Her name is Annette Eaton. She has been to the house before," Betsy whispered back.

"Is he her beau?" Meg asked, certain that the answer would be yes.

"Not yet, but he will be — if Miss Hollander has anything

to say about it." Betsy smiled as they rounded a corner. "She has been pushing women on him for as long as I can remember."

Meg faltered. "She wants him to marry?"

"Of course she does. It ain't natural, him being alone all these years."

Meg followed Betsy back into the dining room, not having time to absorb Betsy's words, and saw the brunette leaning close to Zach, conversing with him, a beautiful smile on her face — which made her even lovelier. And Zach was listening intently to her every word.

Meg felt sick, far sicker than before. As she picked up a gentleman's plate, she watched them from the corner of her eye. Annette had her gloved hand on Zach's arm. The white lambskin stood out starkly against the black wool of his coat. Meg realized she was not being careful; a wedge of lemon was sliding off of the plate. She righted it before it could fall into the gentleman's lap. As she gathered up two more plates, she ventured another quick glance, wondering if she was going to make it through the evening, beset as she was with nerves, her nausea having never been worse.

Zach was staring at her.

There was something in his eyes that Meg could not comprehend. Was it quiet encouragement? Meg decided her imagination was running wild; she turned and fled.

In the kitchens she thought she would throw up the dinner she had eaten earlier. She panted over one of the sinks.

"What is wrong?" Mrs. Green asked sharply. "There will soon be another course to clear."

"I am ill," Meg said, her hand on her stomach. "I think I might retch."

Mrs. Green's expression softened. "Dear girl. Very well. I

understand. It can't be easy, without your man at your side. Sit down until the sickness passes. It *will* pass." She smiled and turned. "Lucy, you clear with Betsy — change that apron first."

Meg could not believe the housekeeper's kindness. She sat down in relief at the large rectangular kitchen table. The nausea did not subside. Meg wondered if the entire staff knew that she was with child. Mrs. Green was clearly in no doubt of the fact.

Betsy and Lucy left to do the next round of clearing and Meg thought about Annette Eaton and her employer. Surely Zach would fall for her if he hadn't already. Meg covered her face with her hands, feeling tired and sad, her sickness not even beginning to subside. Suddenly the kitchen fell absolutely silent.

Until that instant, twenty servants had been scurrying about, pots banging, knives chopping, plates clattering, kettles boiling, the chef yelling near-hysterical directives.

Meg looked up and saw Rebecca.

Hands on her apricot satin-draped hips, pearls stark white against her flushed neck, she stared furiously at Meg.

In astonishment, Meg rose to her feet.

"What is this?" Rebecca cried. "Did I not specifically state that you are to clear tonight? Is this how you intend to comport yourself while employed in my house? Do you wish, perhaps, to be waited on yourself?"

Mrs. Green sailed forward, ashen but determined. "Miss Hollander, I beg your pardon, the poor girl is not well. I thought —".

"I do not care what you thought," Rebecca interrupted coldly. "Until now, you have done a very good job for me, Mrs. Green. *Until now.*" Her eyes flashed. "I expect her to finish what she has begun. And I do not ever want to have

to set foot in the kitchen again when I have guests present."
Rebecca whirled, her huge skirts belling about her so widely
that they brushed the bricks of the huge hearth. As she swept
away, Meg saw a dark stain upon them.

Her knees were so weak that they knocked together. She
glanced slowly at the housekeeper. "I am so sorry," she managed.

Mrs. Green faced Meg, her color returning. "In the ten
years I have worked here, I have never seen her in such a
state — and I have also never seen her enter the kitchens in
the middle of an evening. I'm sorry, Meg, but you must go
back out and attend the guests."

Meg nodded, incapable of speech. Betsy joined her and
they started down the hall. Meg ignored the other maid, who
cast anxious glances at her. Finally Betsy said, "You're so
green. Are you sure you can do this?"

"What choice do I have?" Meg asked.

They fell silent as they entered the foyer. Laughter came
from the dining room. Meg refused to allow herself to be sick.
As she passed Rebecca's chair, she could feel her triumphant
satisfaction. Meg picked up Annette Eaton's plate. Her gloved
hand lay on the table, close to Zach's arm. She must not care,
she told herself. She must only focus on the task at hand. But
she thought she saw him watching her with concern from the
corner of his eye.

Meg felt it then, her stomach turning over.

Zach rose abruptly to his feet.

Plates in hand, Meg ran from the room. She had barely
crossed the threshold and turned the corner when she began
to retch, somehow holding onto the plates.

When the illness passed, Meg became aware of Betsy staring at her in horror. Worse, there was not a single sound
coming from the dining room, and the silence was glaring.

226

Shaking and weak, Meg looked at the mess, then at Betsy. And she heard Rebecca exclaiming from the dining room, "Zachary!" very sharply.

Betsy yelped.

Meg jerked as Zach took her arm from behind. Turning, she met his gaze and wanted to die.

"Miss O'Neil, you are not well," he said without censure.

Meg blinked. She saw no anger in his eyes, only compassion and concern. But that was impossible.

He continued to hold her arm — actually supporting her with his strength. "Give me those," Zach said, indicating her plates.

Meg was now more than horrified.

With his free hand he took the plates from Meg, piling them up in Betsy's arms. "Miss, go get Mrs. Green and a mop and a pail of soap and water."

Betsy turned and fled with her arms full.

Suddenly Rebecca appeared. She took one look at the floor and flushed. "Zachary, we have guests. You must come back to the table — as if anyone can continue to eat now." She glared at Meg. "This situation is intolerable."

"Little in life is intolerable, and certainly not a small, innocent accident. Please return to the table, Rebecca," Zach said calmly — but it was a command. Before Rebecca's widening eyes, he slid his arm around Meg. Meg truly did not mean to, but she was so exhausted now that she leaned against him, relishing his strength. "Come," Zach said, and he began walking with her, leaving his sister aghast.

Meg realized that he was taking her to the library. She did not think he intended to dismiss her, yet she could not fathom his purpose. The walk down the corridor seemed endless. Meg had to glance up at him. His expression, seen in profile, was implacable — impossible to read. But she would never forget the light she had so recently witnessed in his golden eyes. "I'm sorry. I am so sorry. I . . ."

"You are not to blame. Sickness in your condition is more usual than not. Mrs. Green should have known better than to ask you to work when you were clearly green around the gills." His jaw was firm as he glanced down at her.

Meg held her tongue, not about to tell him who had wished this disaster upon her.

He pushed open the door to the library. His arm around her waist, he guided her to the emerald green damask sofa in the dark. Meg found herself lying there on her back. He lit one of the lamps on his desk. She watched him, unmoving and wide-eyed.

He returned to her side, a pitcher of water in hand, which he set down. He removed her soiled apron and set it aside. Then he produced a handkerchief, dipped it in the water, and handed it to her. Trying not to give in to tears, Meg accepted it and began to clean her face. Now she completely understood why she had fallen so hopelessly in love with him.

"Are you feeling any better?" he asked, holding a glass of water out to her.

Meg sat up just enough to accept it. "Actually, yes." She sipped the water, watching him move to the liquor cabinet. He poured himself a cognac and returned to her side. He sat down on the sofa by her feet.

"I am fine," Meg lied, trembling now. It was not her place to tell him to return to the dinner party, but she recalled Rebecca's wrath, and knew it would be triplefold by now. He did not appear to be in any rush to leave. He was regarding her with his piercing amber eyes as he sipped the cognac.

"You are still pale," he said.

"I am so ashamed," she blurted.

"There is nothing to be ashamed of. You are with child,

228

and not by choice. You have deported yourself admirably. Few women would have your courage and pride given the circumstances of your life."

Meg stared at him. His gaze locked with hers. She finally said, "There is nothing admirable about being with child and unwed, poor and hungry, and desperately afraid of the future."

He sat up straighter. Meg wished she hadn't spoken so impulsively — so honestly. "You are safe here in my home," he said flatly.

Meg looked at her hand clutching the water glass. "Thank you," she said softly. She peeked at him. "Perhaps you wish to return to your guests? I am much better now." It was true. Her stomach felt fine. But not her heart, oh no. It would never be the same after this evening. And even her body felt odd, her pulse racing, her limbs trembling. Her slippered feet were nestled against his thighs. The couch was not long enough for the two of them.

He smiled slightly. "I prefer being here with you."

Meg almost gaped.

He sighed. "I abhor these dinners my sister is so fond of. The conversation is vapid."

Meg felt hope leaping in her breast. "But — surely not all of the conversation is dull?" Annette's lovely image filled her mind.

He glanced at her, the corners of his eyes crinkling — as if he knew her thoughts. "It is *all* dull," he said firmly. Suddenly his smile faded. "You are neither dull nor vapid, Miss O'Neil."

Meg finally slipped her legs over the side of the sofa and to the floor. "That is a very special compliment."

He stood. "I only say what I mean." His gaze was direct, and bolder than she had ever seen it before.

Meg did not know what to say, or do, or think.

Once again, he rescued her. "I will return to my sister's guests, or she will have my head upon one of her silver serving platters." His eyes twinkled then. He sobered. "I shall tell Mrs. Green you have retired for the night. Rest here, if you wish." His gaze transformed, becoming unreadable.

Meg nodded, her heart racing, her limbs weak, watching him set the unfinished cognac down on the side table. He crossed the room with his characteristically long strides. Everything he did, everything he said, made her aware of his strength, his integrity, his power. Meg knew she stared and was helpless to look away. He did not look back as he closed the door carefully behind him.

Chapter Seven

Supper was finally concluded. Zach stood with Rebecca in the foyer saying good-bye to the last of their guests, the Eatons. They had lingered well over a half hour longer than anyone else. Zach had eventually stopped listening to a conversation that ran the gamut from the expected hot summer weather to a poor performance recently remarked at the Opera House. And he was tired of smiling politely at Annette.

Indeed, his thoughts kept returning to Meg O'Neil. How tenderly he felt toward her. He had already informed Mrs. Green that the Irishwoman was to rest whenever she felt ill. But he was just beginning to realize that he was growing very uncomfortable with her in his employ. And his discomfort only had a little to do with her pregnant condition.

"Zachary, thank you for a wonderful evening," Annette said, smiling, her dark gaze seeking his. When he met her eyes her smile increased, just before her thick lashes lowered. Annette was one of the most beautiful unmarried women in town — and she knew it. She had undoubtedly perfected the art of flirting many years ago. Zach was unimpressed.

Still he bent gallantly over her hand, thanking her for coming to supper and ushering her and her parents to the door and finally through it. The first order of business on the morrow, he decided, should be getting Meg to a physician.

He closed and bolted the front door, only to face Rebecca. "Zachary," she said, smiling. Her use of his full name signaled her displeasure. "I wish a word with you."

"If you think to set me down as if I were a child, think otherwise," he said calmly.

Her eyes widened. "Have I ever set you down?"

"Only recently," he said, shoving his hands into the pockets of his black trousers. Satin piping trimmed the length down the sides of each leg.

"Zach." She smiled again. "Having a housemaid who is expecting a child is intol— incorrect. You saw what happened! Not only is she incompetent, she ruined the entire evening."

"She did? I didn't notice our guests rushing to leave." He refused to entertain his temper, for this was his sister, whom he loved. "I am disappointed in you, Rebecca," he said, and meant it.

"You are disappointed in me?" He saw her surprise, followed by her confusion, and then her hurt. She touched his arm. "Zach, what have I done? What have I done other than to run your house in the best manner I know how — and to stand by you so that you do not have to live alone with painful memories?"

"I am glad we are on this subject," he said. "You know I appreciate all that you have done for me, but it is time you ceased this self-sacrifice. I do not mind living alone." Meg's sultry, fiery-haired image came instantly to mind. "I am compiling a list of suitable prospects for you, Rebecca. It is time that you wed."

She did not gasp, gape, or widen her eyes. But she colored ever so gently. "Of course it is time that I wed — I am already twenty-four. In a few more years, no one will have me." Her color increased. "But, Zach, I cannot marry, not unless you do so as well."

"No." His reply was automatic, firm. And for the first time in days, Angeline's image came to his mind but her perfect features were faded now. He instantly became still. Why could he not recall the exact angle of her nose, the exact shape of her eyes? Just a few days ago, he had dreamed of her and seen her, as always, with utter clarity. And all he could see of his daughter was big blue eyes and a headful of platinum curls. He was disbelieving.

"Zach? Are you ill? You have turned white!" Rebecca exclaimed.

Zach realized that his surprise overshadowed his grief. He focused his attention on Rebecca. "I intend to find you a husband, a man whom you respect, admire, and might come to love. A man who will feel the same way about you."

Tears filled Rebecca's amber eyes. "Oh, Zach, I do yearn to be a wife, a mother. But how can I leave you here, alone?"

"You can, and you shall. I am not marrying, Rebecca, it is the furthest thing from my mind." He smiled at her, kissed her cheek. "Goodnight." And as he started down the hall, toward the library, he paused. "And Rebecca. Please. Cease bringing young ladies like Annette Eaton around. I am not interested in her or anyone else, not in the least."

Zach stood in the foyer as Rebecca whispered good night, her eyes suspiciously soft and dreamy, walking upstairs, one hand trailing on the smooth, teakwood banister. Zach was disinclined to sleep. He was overstimulated by the entire day — first *Cyclone*'s magnificent departure, Meg's appearance on the wharves, her illness, and now the fact that, no matter how he tried, Angeline's image was eluding him. But surely it would return to him tomorrow or the next day.

He slipped into the library, which was utterly dark. He moved to his desk to turn one gaslight on. He had had several glasses of fine French wine that night, but was in the mood for a sip or two of cognac — he was as sober as when he had woken up that morning. In any case, he did not think he could sleep just yet.

On his way to the liquor cabinet Zach froze. Meg lay sleeping on the sofa.

After his initial surprise, something inside him softened. He did not move, capable now only of staring. Then he realized he was smiling.

He feasted his eyes upon her face. Her skin was alabaster, her lashes long and thick and auburn-colored. Her brows were strong, slashing high at the corners, but he liked them — they suited her courageous nature. Her nose was straight and small, classic, not perky, and dusted with a few pale freckles. Her cheekbones were high, her jaw a bit wide, but again, its strength suited her. Her mouth was exceedingly full. A honey-colored mole tipped one corner. Zach's gaze lingered there.

He had not meant to follow his thoughts with actions, but he was suddenly tasting her lips beneath his own. He was not a shallow man. Unlike many men his own age, of his own acquaintance, he did not keep a mistress, nor did he frequent Boston's brothels. In fact, he had lived much of the past decade in celibacy, focusing all of his energy upon Hollander Shipping. But he was certain that Meg was a woman of deep passion.

He could suddenly envision her in his bed.

His thoughts agitated him to no end. But Zach only tore his gaze from her mouth in order to allow it to travel down her slim body. Her belly hardly protruded, but now he noticed how full her breasts were, especially for a woman so thin. One of her hands dangled over the edge of the sofa, limp in sleep. And then he remarked the empty snifter on the floor just below her fingertips. Zach smiled.

He had left behind half a glass, perhaps, of cognac. He could not blame her for taking the remaining sips.

He walked around the sofa, drawn as he had never been drawn to a woman before, or at least not since his wife. He wanted to touch her, just a caress across her pulled back hair, but he refrained. Should he wake her? So she could go to her own bed? Rebecca would not be charitable about Meg spending the night on the sofa in his library. Zach reached down and touched her shoulder. But she did not stir.

"Meg," he said softly. "Miss O'Neil." She remained motionless, except for her breathing, which was deep and even. His eyes wandered over her exquisite face again. His body had long since had a definite reaction to her. He had lost Angeline a long time ago, but he was still entirely a man.

He found himself sitting by her hip, his knee pressing against her side. He shook her gently again. "Meg. Can you wake up?"

Her lashes fluttered and she sighed.

He stared at her parted lips. The urge to kiss her while she slept was overwhelming. Had he gone insane? He wanted to taste her, just once.

Before Zach could think about it, before he dared, he bent lower and feathered his mouth over hers. Guilt warred with desire. His actions were entirely dishonorable, and out of character. But it had been years, ten years, in fact, since he had been this attracted by a woman.

Her mouth was soft and yielding beneath his. Zach lifted his head, suddenly out of breath, trembling hard, and fully aware of it. Her lashes fluttered, drifting open. She stared sleepily up at him.

"I am sorry," he said low, itching to close his hands upon her shoulders. "I . . . do not know what overcame me." No words could suffice.

Some of the haze left her eyes. She smiled softly at him. "Zach. Am I dreaming? Did you kiss me?"

"You are not dreaming," he said, aware of his knee pressed against her hip, aware of the soft, gentle rise and fall of her bosom. He would not respond to her second question. "Come. It is time to go to your own bed."

She continued to smile up at him.

"Come," he said, slipping his arm beneath her to help her to her feet.

She sat up but did not stand, and suddenly their faces were but inches apart, her eyes on his. Inwardly, Zach was frozen, suddenly knowing what was about to come the way one knew that the sun must rise every day, and then set. Yet a part of him refused to believe it.

She smiled again. And her hand cupped his cheek. "I know this is a dream. But it is the most wonderful dream I have ever had," she whispered. "Will you kiss me again?" she murmured.

Zach could not move. Her simple caress, even simpler request, had inflamed him. He could not even breathe.

The invitation was shining in her eyes. Zach thought that he moved first. He wasn't sure. He leaned toward her as she leaned toward him and suddenly their lips were brushing, soft and sweet.

And Zach heard his sharp intake of breath. His hands closed on her shoulders and his mouth firmed on hers. Suddenly he could not get enough of her taste. Meg moved closer, clinging to his broad back as Zach kissed her openmouthed, insistent, hot, almost greedy, and she fell back onto the sofa. Zach came on top of her. Kissing her now as if there were no past, and no tomorrow.

"I love you," she said when he began kissing the soft column of her throat. And she moaned in undisguised pleasure.

He could not think. Not when his lips were brushing the cotton covering her erect nipples, not when she moved restlessly beneath him, not when she whimpered in pleasure again and again. Yet he knew he must stop — for what he was

236

doing was wrong. But why was it wrong? She was beautiful and brave, smart and strong, everything a woman should be. His hands smoothed over her breasts, down her waist, over the small, hard mound of her belly and beneath her behind. Zach buried his face against her bosom, panting, trying to regain his sanity and his usual iron control. Fighting desperately to do so.

An animal side of his nature that he had never recognized before wanted her so much. An image of his making love to her upstairs in the master bed invaded his mind, refusing to retreat. But he was not a beast, he was a thinking man. He finally reminded himself that he was her employer, for heaven's sake. Zach shoved himself to his feet.

Some of the urgency lessened, some of the desire became controllable. He came around the sofa to look at her; she lay with her eyes closed, smiling slightly, once again soundly asleep.

Zach stared down at her for God only knew how long, the brief, passionate interlude and its ramifications playing over and over in his mind — and then he strode decisively out of the room.

Meg awoke to streaming sunlight and gentle birdsong. At first she thought she was in her narrow bed in her tiny bedroom. But a moment later she realized where she was — on the emerald green sofa in the library. She sat up, crying out, fully awake now — and she remembered all of last night.

She did not move. Horrified and humiliated, she recalled becoming ill outside of the dining room — and being rescued once again by her employer. Dear God. She recalled his amazing concern and compassion, his stunning kindness. How could she have slept the entire night there on his sofa? Meg also remembered Rebecca's anger. If Rebecca found her now,

Meg would be fired on the spot. She sat up, eager to leave the room.

And then she recalled the dream.

Meg slid her legs over the couch, her feet to the floor. She sat very still. Recalling a hot, hungry kiss, firm, strong hands, oh God. It had been a dream — hadn't it?

But she could taste his mouth — he had tasted like wine and cigar — and she could smell his scent — leathery, spicy, musky — and most of all, she could recall his mouth wreaking havoc on her senses, inflaming her body as never before. The memory alone was enough to make Meg's temperature instantly rise.

It hadn't been a dream.

It was too real, and she was almost certain of it.

Meg stood up, breathing hard — as if she had just run a distance. But Zach Hollander was an honorable man. He was not the kind of man to pursue one of his housemaids. So perhaps it had been a dream after all. She prayed that was the case.

But Meg did not think so.

She closed her eyes in despair, recalling every single kiss, from the nibbling at her throat to the pressure of his lips on her breasts. There was just no explanation for his behavior — or for hers. There was no explanation — and no excuse. Her horror — and misery — increased. Dear God, now he had more than enough cause to dismiss her. Surely he would. If Rebecca didn't do it first.

Meg hugged herself, walking over to the window to gaze out upon the quietly moving, azure waters of the Charles. She was still flushed and breathing far too rapidly. She could not shake Zach's kiss from her mind. How had her life become such a mess? she wondered. So complicated and confused?

She thought about Robin O'Leery, the fat bastard. Zach's

238

kiss had been nothing like Robin O'Leery's slobbering, which she had, of course, fought to ward off. But he had struck her hard across the face when she had opposed him, then he'd caught her chin in his hand, forcing his mouth hard and hurtfully on her. And then he had raped her. Meg had screamed, oh, she had screamed, but no one had dared barge into the backroom behind the grog shop to intervene.

Meg shuddered. That had been five and a half months ago and the memory still made her violently ill. She had not thought she would ever want a man to touch or kiss her again. She had thought her body would remain dead forever. But last night, Zach had awakened her the way she had never dreamed possible, even before O'Leery's rape. Last night, she had discovered a different side of love — she had discovered true passion.

But what should she do now?

She loved him far more than before. It seemed that her love, along with her desire, was growing in leaps and bounds. But she was a mere housemaid. She could not allow him to use her, she must not, for it was wrong and she would be hurt, yet she wanted him so badly — but not just physically. Meg did not know what to do. And how could she face him again? Perhaps he would blame her for the kiss. Yet Meg knew him somewhat by now, and she did not think so.

With great trepidation, Meg left the library. As she traveled down the hall she feared that she would encounter Rebecca, but it was far too early for her to be up and about. Judging by the angle of the sun outside Meg thought that it was not much past seven. She had almost made it to the foyer undetected. She began to breathe more easily. It was only a short distance to the kitchens now.

But just ahead, on the other side of the foyer, Meg saw James hurrying toward the dining room, holding a tray containing a teapot. She halted in her tracks, but he hadn't seen her. Then she heard James inquiring from within the dining room, "More tea, sir?" Which could only mean one thing.

Meg froze. She was not ready to face Zach just yet. In fact, he was the very last person she wished to see.

As she debated what she should do, she heard Zach decline another cup of tea, his chair scraping back. Her heart sank even further. She was going to be caught. She felt like a criminal. She backed up, against the wall.

But it was James who appeared on the threshold, and this time he saw her and his eyes went wide beneath his bushy white eyebrows. "Meg? What are you doing?"

Meg did not reply. Because Zach had come to stand just behind the servant. Her heart lurched.

And so many images and sensations tumbled through her mind. So many emotions and feelings whirled about in her heart. Meg swallowed, staring at him, not knowing what to do, what to say.

But he did not even pause as he walked past James. In fact, he did not look at her, not even once.

Meg was halfway into a curtsy when she realized that he was striding through the foyer, and reaching for the door. He swung it open. "I will be back this afternoon," he said to James. And without a single backward glance, he left the house.

It was worse than anything Meg could have imagined. He had treated her as if she did not even exist.

Chapter Eight

Rebecca ignored Meg as she entered the dining room to remove her mistress's breakfast plates. She appeared to be immersed in a newspaper. Meg hardly cared — she was numb.

Two full hours had passed since Zach had left, treating her as if she meant no more to him than a fly upon the wall. Meg was crushed.

She gathered up two plates, a huge lump wedged in her chest. But she was not going to cry. She had cried when her mother had died, and then when, within days, her baby brother Roddy had followed suit. By the time her two sisters had been buried, Meg was stoic. Sometimes anguish was too deep for tears.

As Meg straightened, about to turn to leave the dining room, Rebecca snapped the *Courier* shut and leveled her golden haze upon her. It was assessing but cool.

Meg met the other woman's eyes, then quickly looked away. She was afraid that her emotional distress would be too obvious.

"Is something wrong, Miss O'Neil?" Rebecca asked. Her tone was clipped and not sympathetic.

"No," Meg lied.

"If you are going to have another accident, I suggest you exit this room." Rebecca stood abruptly. "Somehow you have bewitched my brother, but you have not bewitched me."

Meg's mouth dropped open.

"And if you think even for a moment that you could be anything more than a passing amusement — and I do mean *amusement* — to him, then you are not half as bright as you appear." Rebecca was pale, her fists clenched. "There is little in this house that I am not aware of." She was trembling.

Meg could have mumbled a reply, but she just stood there, her hands full of plates, for the first time realizing that Rebecca felt threatened by Meg. Yet she found no room for sympathy within herself for the other woman. Meg could not accept her condescension, which was based on close-minded prejudice. Besides, the woman wanted to do battle.

"I know where you spent the night, Miss O'Neil," Rebecca said. "And I can guess why."

Meg's pulse was pounding now. "I . . . was ill. I fell asleep."

Rebecca made a sound very much like a snort. "I will not have you drag my brother's good name through the mud of this town."

"That is not my intention."

"No? Then what is your intention? To warm his bed out of sheer generosity? Or sheer carnality?"

Meg inhaled. She could not reply. She was not about to tell Rebecca that she had fallen miserably, hopelessly in love with Zach.

"I know the kind of woman you are," Rebecca said. She shot a disparaging glance at Meg's midsection, making her meaning clear. "I am prepared to offer you a thousand dollars — if you vacate these premises and Boston."

Meg almost dropped the plates.

Tears filled Rebecca's eyes. "It is not enough? Five thousand, then. Why, that would take you all the way back to Ireland and keep you there forever if that is where you wish to go."

Meg fought for air. Her own gaze was blurred. "Miss Hollander, you have no idea how much I could use the money you are offering. Not for myself, but for my child — for his or her welfare and security. But my answer is *no*." Meg did not wait for Rebecca to reply or to dismiss her. She walked past her, head high. But inwardly she was quaking.

Rebecca followed her to the door. Meg knew that she stared after her as she left the room.

Zach had returned to Hollander House in order to finish some paperwork. Concentration eluded him, as it had all day. He remained preoccupied, his thoughts on Meg and his behavior last night. He was still shocked by what had happened, and for the very first time in his life, he was confused and at a loss. He had feelings for Meg O'Neil, which he should not have, but what was he to do?

And did she return his feelings?

Years ago he had loved and lost, and he had assumed he would never love another woman again the way he loved Angeline. Yet without his even knowing it, another woman had entered his life and somehow managed to get a grip on his emotions, a toehold on his heart. He did not want it to go any further, he did not. But . . . he was tired of being alone. Meg had made him realize that he was tired of being lonely. And he was quite certain that if he allowed it, Meg could take over his heart the way Angeline once had.

Zach was afraid.

And what if she did take over his heart? There would be so many problems, due to their different backgrounds and stations in life. But Zach could handle his sister and really did not care what his neighbors thought. No, there was another very real haunting fear consuming him now.

He sighed and tried to force her out of his thoughts, no easy task. But the pages on the desk in front of him kept blurring as he tried to read. He was almost ready to give up.

Rebecca knocked and entered the library. Zach was glad

for the interruption — until he realized that her eyes were glittering and that her face was flushed. "What is it?" he asked, beginning to rise out of his chair.

"The police. Deputy Inspector Rutherford is here, Zach, and he wishes to speak with you!"

Zach faltered, then sat back down, quickly controlling his expression. "Send him in," he said.

Rebecca turned and left.

Zach knew there could be only one reason why the police had come to speak to him.

The inspector entered, an iron-haired man in a dark suit. He nodded to Zach, who rose and shook hands with him. Rebecca hovered in the hallway as the inspector took a chair in front of Zach's desk.

"I am sorry to interrupt you, sir," Rutherford began, "but this will only take a minute. We are pursuing a female fugitive from the law and it has come to our attention that she might be employed in your household. Do you have a housemaid named Meg O'Neil employed on your staff, sir?" Rutherford asked.

Zach's pulse was racing, but he was very calm, the way he would be if a huge northeaster had appeared on the horizon while he was at the helm of one of his ships. He smiled at the policeman. "Actually, Miss O'Neil *was* in my employ, but last night she was dismissed for incompetence," he said smoothly.

"I see. So she's gone?"

"She had no belongings but the clothes on her back. Yes, she left last night, around nine or ten, I believe." Behind Rutherford, Zach saw that Rebecca had turned starkly white, her eyes wide with disbelief.

"Well, if you happen to hear of her whereabouts, please let us know."

"I shall. Does this mean that the charges brought by O'Leery still stand?"

"Indeed, they do," the inspector said. "Again, I am so sorry to have intruded upon you. Oh, and by the way, I have heard the good news, that *Cyclone* set a new record to New York."

"Yes, she has, thank you," Zach said.

Zach stood and the inspector assured Zach that he could see himself out. Rutherford nodded to Rebecca and left the library.

A silence grew taut. Rebecca faced Zach, her eyes flashing, tight-lipped. She did not say a word until the inspector's retreating footsteps could no longer be heard echoing in the corridor outside. When she spoke, it was in a hushed, accusing whisper. "You lied!"

"Indeed," Zach said easily, but he was angry. "And may I ask just how the police came to know that Meg was employed by us?"

Rebecca turned even paler than before.

Meg hid in her room.

The entire staff was buzzing with speculation about why a police officer would come to speak with Zach. No one seemed to have a clue, except, of course, for Meg. She knew.

O'Leery had died. She was now a murderess. There was no other explanation.

Meg's imagination was running wild. She could see herself in handcuffs and drab gray. Worse, she imagined giving birth to her child while locked up in prison.

She stiffened when there was a knock upon her door. Terror immoblized her. But would the police even bother to knock?

Meg's room was windowless. Otherwise, she would have climbed through the window a long time ago. As it was, she had trapped herself. Meg did not know what to do. But now, surely, her employer would not rescue her a final time.

"Meg?" Mrs. Green's voice sounded on the other side of the door. "Are you there?"

Relief almost swamped Meg. She stood up. "Come in," she said weakly.

The door opened. Mrs. Green smiled at her. "Mr. Hollander wishes to speak with you in the library, Meg."

Meg stared. "Are the police still here?"

Mrs. Green had been about to leave, now she started. "No, the inspector is gone. Why do you ask?"

Meg blinked back hot tears. She shook her head, unable to answer, and followed the housekeeper out of the servants' wing, then continued on alone through the kitchens and into the foyer. Outside, the crushed shell drive was vacant. Meg relaxed just slightly. The police were gone, but what did her employer intend to do?

Meg halted on the threshold. Zach was seated behind his heavy rosewood desk. Meg stared, reluctant to come any closer. His rejection of her that morning made the situation even more difficult. And for a heartbeat, he continued to read the papers on his desk. Meg swallowed. His rejection felt far worse than the possibility of being arrested by the police.

Zach looked up. For the first time since the night before, their gazes locked. Meg almost lost her balance. She had expected to see indifference in his eyes, or hostility or accusation, but instead, she saw grave concern. Zach stood up. "Please come in."

Meg hesitated, then did as he asked. He walked around her to shut the door. Meg realized that she was hugging herself, but she could not stop. She faced him, not sitting down.

He shoved his hands in the pockets of his riding breeches.

"I hope you are feeling better than last evening."

Meg started. "Yes."

Incredibly, he seemed flustered. There was a pink spot high up on each of his cheekbones. "The police were here."

Meg did not breathe. Her anxiety made it impossible to do so.

"O'Leery has pressed charges against you and a warrant is outstanding for your arrest."

Meg's gaze remained upon his face. "Timothy?"

"No, Robin."

"He is still alive?" she cried, inordinately relieved. As much as she hated him and hoped he would go to hell, she did not want to be the one to send him there by her very own hand.

"Yes." Zach studied her. "You thought that he died?"

Meg nodded, and then her fear tripled. "Oh, God. He will not rest until he gets even with me. He is far worse than his son."

"I will take care of him," Zach said.

Meg jerked, astonished.

"I will seek him out immediately and convince him to drop the charges and let bygones be bygones," Zach said flatly.

Meg looked at him in utter disbelief — yet she saw his resolve, felt his absolute integrity, and knew he meant every word that he spoke. "Why?" she heard herself ask.

His gaze was riveted upon hers. "After last night," he finally said, "how can you even ask?"

Meg covered her racing heart with her hand. "I am not sure I understand."

"No?" His smile was fleeting, sardonic. "Do you think I am in the habit of making love to the housemaids in my employ?"

Meg slowly shook her head.

"You are a very brave woman, Meg. A very strong, brave, beautiful woman," he said.

247

His words, sheer praise, heartfelt, went right to Meg's head — and on to her heart. Something joyous bubbled up inside of her breast. Yet this could not be happening. "I'm Irish," she whispered. "My father was a farmer. And . . . I carry another man's child."

"And my grandfather was a fisherman," Zach said. Suddenly one of his palms cupped her cheek. "Do you think I care about such things?"

She had never been more moved, more overwhelmed. "No. I should have known. You are a man of honor," she said.

"Yes," he returned evenly, dropping his palm.

So many questions — so many dreams — were competing for attention in Meg's mind. Did he love her? Was it possible? Was there another option — given his integrity? And if so, where did that leave them?

"What should I do?" she heard herself say.

He smiled at her, a smile that came from his eyes. "I told the police that you are no longer in my employ. A small lie, actually, being as I think that now it is a good time to terminate your employment."

Meg made a sound. "I need this job — desperately."

"Didn't you hear a word that I said?" he asked. "Meg, for the next few hours, stay out of sight. I shall inform Mrs. Green that you are no longer staff, and I am going to deal with O'Leery. And then we shall have a more frank discussion."

"A more frank discussion," Meg echoed, praying for a future that seemed impossible — one filled with the love of this extraordinary man.

He smiled again. "Out of sight," he reminded her, and then he took her chin in his hand and kissed her fully on the mouth. And a moment later he was gone.

Meg sank down in one of the armchairs, shaking. Her life had been so bleak, so utterly without hope. And suddenly all was reversed. Suddenly the world was nothing but sunshine, birdsong, rainbows. Eternal rainbows.

Meg smiled.

But her thoughts were interrupted by the squeak of a door — or a window. A draft of cool air came from behind her. Meg turned.

And saw Timothy entering through the window, an ugly grin on his face.

Chapter Nine

Meg cried out as Timothy shoved her forward, into the small, dark room. And then she saw Robin.

He sat behind a small, rickety table, his hands clasped in front of him. He made an incongruous figure in the dark, airless backroom, filled with casks of ale, for he was clad in a suit, his hat and gloves resting on the tabletop, his cane against his chair. He was a burly, middle-aged man. His hair was silver, balding, and he had heavy muttonchops. A jagged pink scar ran from his right temple to his right jaw. Meg had just missed his eye. She was sorry she hadn't blinded him.

"Hello, Meg," Robin O'Leery said.

Meg could hardly breathe, and she was so frightened that her heart was trying to jump erratically out of her chest. Timothy shoved her forward again with the flat of his hand in the middle of her back. Meg stumbled. "What are you going to do?" she asked.

He rose. "I haven't decided. But you will be punished." Then his eyes changed. "You tried to kill me."

Meg knew she should deny it. Say it had been an accident. But he had put his hands on her again, perhaps intending to rape her again, and she had meant to defend herself even if it did mean killing him. "And if you touch me, I'll do it again," she said hoarsely.

He nearly lunged over the table but caught himself and stepped around it. He caressed her cheek. "You mean, like this?" His gaze held hers.

Meg did not move. Her words had been bold and meaningless, because there was nothing she could do to defend herself. She stared back at him.

"Or like this?" he asked, and then he struck her hard across the face, sending her flying to the floor.

Meg did not make a sound, but the effort cost her dearly, for she bit her lip and tasted blood. She was not going to give him any satisfaction, no matter what he did. She knew he would eventually kill her. But now, now she had something to live for. She had her child — she had Zach.

Meg closed her eyes, her face pressed to the floor, fighting her pride. She was hauled upright from behind by Timothy. She faced Robin. "Let me live. I'll do whatever you want."

"You'll do whatever I want whether I let you live or not," he returned.

She hesitated. "No. I'll do anything you want. . . ."

"You overrate yourself. I can have any woman I wish. I do not need you." He eyed her. "Besides, you are hardly attractive now. You are as thin as a rail. And with child."

Meg did not remind him that the child was his.

Robin smiled at her. "We will talk later." He signaled Timothy and the younger man followed him out of the room. Meg turned to stare at the wooden door, listening as the bolt was dropped into place. She had one hope. Zach knew that O'Leery was alive and pursuing her. Surely he would realize what had happened to her and he would rescue her once again.

"O'Leery," Zach did not extend his hand. "My name is Hollander. Zachary Hollander."

O'Leery made no move to stand. He was sitting at a table in the barroom of his Broad Street saloon. It was not yet noon, but the mahogany bar was already doing a brisk business. O'Leery was seated by himself, but the moment Zach had appeared on the threshold of the saloon, two oversized Irishmen had come to stand protectively behind him. He settled back more comfortably in his chair. "I know who you are," he said, not amiably.

"May I?" Zach asked, but he did not wait for a reply before pulling out a chair. He sat down facing O'Leery. "It is time for you to drop the charges against Meg O'Neil."

O'Leery smiled. "This is why you have sought me out?"

"Yes. Your pursuit of her is nonsensical. There is nothing to be gained by it."

O'Leery fingered his scar. "There is justice to be gained. She tried to murder me."

Zach leaned forward; his tone dropped. "If you wish to discuss justice, then you tread dangerous ground, my friend. Justice would be your paying a high price for what you have done to Miss O'Neil."

O'Leery stared.

"Do you deny being the father of her child?" Zach said coldly.

"I have no idea who the father is. I was hardly her first, nor shall I be her last."

Although his words hurt Zach, he remained impassive. It was hard to control his temper, though. He fought to do so. "Do you deny forcing your attentions on her?"

O'Leery laughed. "I do. She forced herself on me. For the sake of gaining a job," he added.

Zach saw red. He was on his feet. The two thugs stepped closer to O'Leery, but Zach did not care. He lifted the table, which contained a glass of whiskey and a whiskey bottle, upending it onto O'Leery's lap. O'Leery's chair flipped over to the floor, the big man still seated in it.

The thugs grabbed Zach by the arms. He did not try to shake them off. "I have grown very fond of Miss O'Neil,

252

O'Leery. Fond enough to make her my wife — if she will have me."

O'Leery was pushing himself to his feet, his face flushed with anger. But he could not hide his surprise. He blinked before recovering. "Do not expect congratulations from me," he said harshly. But he signaled the two thugs and they released Zach, taking a step away from him.

"I am not only protecting a servant now," Zach said. "If my future wife and child are harmed, then you shall pay with every single hair on your head. Have I made myself clear?" Zach asked.

O'Leery smiled. "You could not have been clearer, Hollander."

Zach turned abruptly and walked out.

The lantern had burned out. Meg sat on the floor beside a stack of kegs, having no desire to go anywhere near the table and chair O'Leery had used. She did not know how long she had been incarcerated in the storeroom. But she was thirsty, hungry, and she had to urinate. Worse, she was still afraid.

What if Zach did not rescue her? What if he could not figure out what had happened to her? She would not put it past O'Leery to leave her in the storeroom until she died of starvation. He was capable of such cruelty.

Meg wiped her eyes with the hem of her sleeve. She must not give up hope. It seemed impossible that she and Zach had come this far, to the brink of sharing a precious love, only for her to lose her life at the hands of a man who had already abused her so badly. Yet life was not fair. For if it were fair, her mother, brother, and two sisters would not be dead. And she would not be carrying the child of a man she despised.

Meg tried not to cry. How she wished she could pray to God, but while she believed in Him, she had not been able to pray to Him since leaving Ireland. Meg closed her eyes. "Mama," she whispered, "I know you are near. I need you now. Please help. Oh, please, Mama — send Zach to me."

It was the housekeeper who told Zach that Meg could not be found.

He had requested Meg be brought to the library. He was confident that O'Leery understood, and if not, he himself would press charges against the other man, for assault at the very least. He was certain that a settlement would be reached in no time at all. He imagined Meg's reaction, her relief, at being told that her nemesis was taken care of.

Of course, he was still afraid. But not of Robin O'Leery. He was afraid of daring to love again, yet his desire for Meg was so strong that he realized he had no choice but to take the risk — or wonder forever what might have been. Life was so unpredictable, a fact he had learned firsthand ten years ago when he'd returned from Canton to find Angeline and Michelle dead. There were no guarantees. But if Meg allowed him to court her, if their love continued to unfold and grow, if she accepted his eventual proposal of marriage, he would guard her and her unborn child with his very life. He was stepping out on a limb, but this time, he had no intention of crashing to the ground.

Zach was aware of how excited he was to see Meg — as if they had not spoken but a few hours ago. Yet now Mrs. Green was telling him that she was not to be found.

Zach stared. His pleasure, his smile, faded. "I do not understand. What do you mean?"

"I have not seen her since last night, actually, sir. And she is nowhere to be found. It is as if she has disappeared," Mrs. Green said worriedly.

Zach stood, placing his hands on his desk. "Summon all

the staff." He reined in his alarm with great difficulty. "Find out who saw her last, and what she was doing. Or if she told someone that she was going out." But he distinctly recalled that he had told her to stay put. She could not have mistaken his meaning.

"I have already asked the staff, sir, and no one has seen her since last evening," Mrs. Green said. "She must have walked out."

Zach's heart turned over hard. Would she have directly disobeyed him? Surely not after he'd revealed his feelings for her.

"I will ask everyone again to search the house," Mrs. Green said into the sudden, strained silence. "Do not worry, sir, I am sure she is all right."

Before Zach could reply, Rebecca spoke up from the open doorway. "That will not be necessary," Rebecca said smoothly, entering the library. "Would you leave me and my brother, please?"

When Mrs. Green had left, Rebecca touched Zach's sleeve. "You are green. And all because that Irish girl cannot be found?"

"I told her to stay out of sight. Her life is in danger," Zach said tersely. "She would not disobey me, not in this. She was frightened herself."

Rebecca studied his face.

Zach met her gaze. "And I happen to be in love with that Irish girl, so in the future, I would appreciate it if you addressed her by her name. It is Meg."

Rebecca gasped. "Zach! You cannot be serious!"

"I am deadly serious," he said. "I have dismissed her from our employ so I might begin a serious courtship."

"A courtship?" Rebecca turned white. "A courtship?!" She was incredulous.

"I am going to the police," he said decisively.

"Are you thinking about marrying her?" Rebecca cried, following him to the doorway.

He paused, facing her. "Yes, I am."

Rebecca's eyes widened. "Zach, she is uneducated, Irish, Catholic, and dear God, she carries another man's child."

"She is exceedingly smart, and if she wishes it, she can have the finest tutors in Boston. She has the right to choose her own religion, for this is America. But I do wish you would stop harping on the fact that she is Irish. The country of her birth means little to me. And as for the child, he is an innocent victim of terrible circumstance. I will gladly embrace him or her as my own. How could I not?"

Rebecca seized his wrist before he could go. "She is not coming back."

He jerked. "What?"

She did not flinch. Her amber gaze was direct. "She is not coming back. I am sorry to have to tell you this, and please, do not hate me for doing what I thought was right, in order to protect you. I offered her five thousand dollars to leave this house, to leave Boston and never return. She took the money, Zach. She is gone."

Chapter Ten

The limb had broken. The fall was nearly fatal.

Zach stood in the doorway of the small chamber Meg had used during her short stay at Hollander House. He felt far more than abused, he felt empty now, completely drained. All he could think now was *how?* How had he so misjudged her? How had he been such a fool?

How could she have done this to him?

He stepped into her room. He hadn't even been furious with Rebecca, he had been too shocked, too grief-stricken. Had an ass kicked him in the teeth, he could not feel worse.

He did not know why he was there now, in her cubbyhole room.

He walked over to the narrow bed and sank down on it. To his dismay, he thought he caught her slightly floral, musky scent. His heart turned over. It felt like it was bleeding. Zach cradled his head in his hands.

A part of him refused to believe what he knew to be the truth. A part of him clung foolishly to the thread of a notion that there just had to be an explanation.

But he knew that was absurd.

Zach sighed, the sound choked. He dropped his hands. There was no point in lingering in her room. And then he saw her clothes.

Zach froze. And slowly he stood. Her worn gray dress hung on one of the clothes hooks on the wall. His mind began to function.

She had arrived with only the clothing on her back. Why

had she left his home to start a new life in a black uniform that clearly identified her as a domestic servant? Why hadn't she taken a moment to change her uniform for her dress? Why had she also left the shawl behind? Although frayed at the ends, Zach knew good cashmere wool when he saw it. It did not make sense.

He was filled with sudden doubts. Something was not right. Granted, with $5,000 she could walk into a store filled with ready-made dresses and buy something new. But why, why walk out of his house dressed as a housemaid?

It crossed his mind that she had not walked out of the house. O'Leery's image swiftly came to him.

Zach left the bedchamber. He would pay O'Leery another visit.

But five minutes later he realized that wasn't necessary. Because the ransom note had arrived.

"What if she's dead?" Betsy whispered, as pale as any ghost.

Mrs. Green sat hunched over the table in the kitchens, which were deathly silent. The entire staff, some twenty servants, were gathered there. "Don't go talking that way," she said sharply. "Dear Lord, return that sweet girl to us safely," she prayed.

Betsy began to cry.

"She was such a nice girl," Cook said from where she stood beside the stove. "So helpful, so kind."

"She *is* such a nice girl," Mrs. Green retorted.

"Beautiful, too," Peter said in a whisper. He was in shock.

James laid his hand on Betsy's shoulder. "Don't cry, Betsy." He spoke in a whisper, as if afraid to break the unnatural, tomblike silence that had fallen over the entire house. "Did you see the captain's face? He is enraged. I have never seen him this way. He will get her back. I have not a doubt."

"But will she be alive?" Betsy gasped, trembling. "I've heard so many stories about kidnappin's! An' the poor soul's never alive in the end."

"That's enough," Mrs. Green said, ashen. She stood. "We all have duties to do. *Now,*" she said sternly.

The staff dispersed.

"Here it is, sir," the gentleman said, laying a leather valise on Zach's desk.

"Thank you," Zach said to the manager of his bank.

"It is not a problem. I only hope you know what you are about, Mr. Hollander." The man smiled, but with an anxious light in his eyes.

"I do." Zach glimpsed a pale, tight-lipped Rebecca hovering by the doorway. He ignored her, opening the valise. Gold bullion filled the case. "Is it all here?"

"Every cent. Ten thousand dollars' worth."

The two men shook hands and the bank manager left. Zach closed the case. He looked up as Rebecca came forward. "I know you are angry with me," she said.

"That is an understatement."

"I had to do it. I was only trying to protect you," she began, her eyes glistening.

"I do not need protecting," Zach said harshly.

Rebecca nodded. "She refused the money. Zach, I did it because society will not accept a marriage between the two of you!"

"Of course it will. In a few years, no one will even remember that Meg came to this town destitute, fleeing the famine in Ireland."

Rebecca tilted her chin, tears rolling down her face. "Maybe you are right. But what about the child? Society might forget about Meg. But they will not forget about the child."

"I will make that child a prince or a princess, Rebecca. I am not worried about it."

Rebecca held his gaze until she had to look away.

Zach moved to her. "Can you not find some charity and goodwill in your heart for a brave and admirable woman, one who has fallen into terrible straits? For my sake?"

"You must truly love her," Rebecca said.

"Yes, I do."

Rebecca was crying now. "Then I wish you both the best. I am so sorry, Zach." She reached up and threw her arms around him. "Don't hate me," she whispered. "Don't hate me, please."

He held her for a moment. "I could never hate you. I love you, you are my sister." Zach released her. The warmth left his eyes. "Now I have business to take care of."

Rebecca shuddered. "Please. Do not take any chances. Do not get yourself killed!"

Zach only smiled grimly as he lifted the valise and headed for the door.

It was late. A crescent moon had risen in the starlit sky. The alley in Fort Hill was oddly silent, oddly vacant, and dark except for the moonlight. Usually every part of the neighborhood was filled with drunken revelers from sunset until dawn.

Zach saw no one. He had dismounted Saint, and stood beside his horse waiting impatiently for O'Leery. A shadow stepped off one of the dark stoops farther down the alley. Zach's jaw tightened.

O'Leery walked forward surrounded by a half dozen men, one of whom was his son, Timothy. He smiled at Zach. "Good evening, Hollander. Where is it?" His gaze darted from Zach to the horse.

Zach smiled coldly, withdrew one gold bar from his saddlebag, and tossed it so that it landed at O'Leery's feet. "You will get the rest after I see Meg. I wish to know that she is safe, unharmed, alive."

O'Leery shook his head. "My note was specific. The gold first, and then she shall be released."

"I do not care what your note said," Zach said. "If I am not reassured that Meg is alive, you shall not see another ingot of gold."

O'Leery stared at him. Finally he nodded, raising one hand. Zach stared past him, into the dark recesses of the alley. Eventually he could see shadowy shapes emerging from the darkness, moving forward. He stiffened, forgetting to breathe. Two men were holding Meg, walking briskly toward them. She stumbled several times.

And then she saw him — just as he saw her starkly white face and fine features. She cried out and his heart started beating again. She did not look harmed other than a slight bruise on her face. "Are you all right?" he called out sharply.

Relief filled her eyes. "Yes," she said hoarsely. "Yes, Zach."

Zach lifted his hand, never taking his gaze off of Meg or her captors. A horse's hooves could be heard approaching, becoming louder. A rider came into view. He paused a few paces behind Zach.

"Give her over," Zach said tersely.

"The gold first," O'Leery replied, his tone as clipped.

Both men stared.

The silence was deafening.

O'Leery jerked his hand and the two men holding Meg brought her forward so that she stood beside O'Leery. They continued to hold her. She was perhaps ten feet distant from Zach. But all the men surrounding her were armed with pistols and knives.

Zach was also armed.

261

Zach spoke over his shoulder without turning his head. "Bring the case."

The rider moved forward until he was next to Zach. Zach took the case, walked forward. One step, two, three, and dropped the case at O'Leery's feet. Zach's fingers inched toward the pistol hidden in the waistband of his breeches. He glanced at Meg, who was breathless and pale. O'Leery bent over the valise, opening it wide. He took in a sharp, satisfied gasp.

"The girl," Zach said, whiplike.

Meg was shoved forward as O'Leery closed the case. Zach met her halfway, throwing his arm around her. Their gazes met as O'Leery and his men turned to leave with the gold. Zach rushed with Meg to his horse, tossing her astride instantly. As he leapt up behind her, a whistle sounded. Sharp and high-pitched.

"Police! O'Leery, halt!"

Zach whirled Saint, protecting Meg with his bigger body as they thundered out of the alley, gunfire suddenly filling up the night.

At the bottom of Fort Hill, Zach pulled up his blowing, eager stallion. He slid to his feet and pulled Meg down and into his arms. She collapsed against his chest.

He stroked her hair, which was unbound, as he cradled her in his arms. "Dear God, are you all right, truly, Meg?"

She cried a little before she could speak, then looked up at him out of shining eyes. "Yes. I prayed you would come. I never really lost hope, or faith. Thank you, Zach. Again, thank you for saving my life."

He cupped her shoulders. "Of course I came. It took me a while to figure out what had happened. O'Leery sent me a ransom note."

Her eyes widened. He saw her blush. "That was not very smart of him."

He understood her meaning instantly. "To the contrary, it was quite astute. He knew how I feel about you. Do you think I care about the money? Of course I was prepared to pay the ransom. How could a price be put upon your life — any price — when you mean so much to me?"

She was motionless. Then she softly touched his cheek. "You mean so much to me, too. I . . . I am overwhelmed."

He tilted up her chin. "Don't be overwhelmed, my dear. I only want you to be happy." His gaze held hers a moment longer before he brushed his mouth over her lips.

The kiss held, deepened. Meg's arms went around his back. Zach crushed her to him. Finally they both came up for air, gasping like two fish out of water, and then they laughed — simultaneously.

Zach stroked her cheek. "I was so afraid I would lose you when I had only just found you," he said quietly.

"I felt the exact same way," she confessed.

"And I was worried about the child."

Her eyes glistened silver in the dark. "You worried about the child? My child?"

"Of course I did," he said tenderly, stroking her hair. "How do you feel?"

"Fine," she said. "I think I am incredibly lucky."

"No. I am the one who is fortunate. If you agree, that is, to return with me to Hollander House — as my wife."

She started.

He smiled, but his heart was speeding wildly. "I had intended a serious courtship, but that no longer seems necessary. Not in light of all that's happened in these past few days."

She was finding it terribly difficult to speak. Tears tumbled down her cheeks. "What if . . ." She had to stop and fight for words. "What if I want a courtship?"

"Then you shall have it," he said expansively. His smile faded, his gaze was brilliant. "And anything else you wish."

"Of course I will marry you," Meg said, reaching for his hands.

Palms clasped, he said gravely, "Can I court you after we are wed?"

Meg nodded, choking on a touch of laughter mixed with tears. "I love you so much," she whispered.

"And I love you," he said. "You do know what the Chinese say?"

"I have no idea," she said, smiling tremulously.

"They say that when a person saves another's life, their souls are bound together for all eternity."

She gazed up at him. "I like that. I shall gladly be bound to you for all of eternity."

He kissed her again and whispered, "And I to you. Don't cry, Meg."

"But they are tears of joy," Meg said. "And it has been so very long. I relish them."

He understood. How he understood. And he thought of Angeline and Michelle with only a small bittersweet pang. Their images were so very faded, and he knew, without regret, that time had done its work well. Zach folded her against his chest, realizing that he was crying, too. "Yes," he said. "The joy has been a long time coming for us both."

But now, he knew, they would treasure it forever and then some.

HUNTER'S MOON

Fern Michaels

Chapter One

Even in his dream he knew he was dreaming because there was no way in hell Kathryn Bannon would kiss him, not the Kathryn he'd left to swing in the wind after promising to marry her. He groaned in his sleep as her eager lips mashed against his. She was whispering things in his ear he'd yearned to hear for years, sweet words only lovers knew. He responded in kind, his mutterings grinding into the softness of the pillow beneath his face.

He rolled over, his legs thrashing at the covers. "I'm sorry. I need you to believe me, Katie. What can I do? How can I make it up to you? Tell me and I'll do it. It was so good between us and I ruined it. Please say you believe me. If you give me another chance, I swear I'll spend the rest of my life making you happy."

The alarm on the bedside table buzzed. In a half sleep, Hunter Kingsley's arm snaked out to press the shut-off button.

He lay panting, his eyes squeezed shut. One of these days when he had this dream, Kathryn was going to respond. "Yeah, yeah, yeah," he muttered as he swung his legs over the side of the bed.

Hunt eyed the telephone next to the clock. He could call her in a heartbeat if he really wanted to. Someone, somewhere undoubtedly knew where she was. He could say all the things he said in his dreams. In the real world, using a real telephone, he would finally get to hear Kathryn's voice. A voice he'd hungered to hear for years.

He was on his way to the bathroom when the phone rang.

Should he answer it or shouldn't he? He picked it up, said hello, and then frowned. "I'll call you back, Mallory, I'm shaving and I'm in a hurry." Hunt slammed the phone back into the cradle. "I don't even *like* you, Mallory Evans," he said speaking to his reflection in the mirror. Hunt leaned closer to the mirror. "That, my friend, makes you a thirty-five-year-old jerk."

Forty-five minutes later Hunt pushed his suitcase through the open door. He locked his apartment door, his mind racing. He'd turned off the stove and coffeepot, locked the patio doors, hung up his wet towel, dumped out Biz's litter box, and carried out the trash. He wondered how Biz was doing in the boarding kennel as he walked to the elevator.

Hunter Kingsley was going home.

Hunter Kingsley stood for a moment on the sidewalk before he fit his key into the lock on the ornate iron gates. Outside it looked like just another day, just another place. Beyond the brick walls and intricate ironwork, it was another day, but a different kind of place where time literally stood still. At least for him.

The gate closed soundlessly behind him. He walked on the old Charleston brick, careful not to step on the mossy fringes. His old nanny Pearl would have his hide if he disturbed the moss. She'd fry his hide if he so much as picked a petal from any of the blooms that ran rampant in this private place he'd always thought of as a sanctuary. He looked around now at his mother's private garden. It was lush and dim with just enough sunlight filtering through the leaves of the ancient Angel Oak to highlight the narrow brick paths that led nowhere, the tubs and barrels of bougainvillea, gardenias, hibiscus, and oleander that teased his nostrils and flirted with his eyes behind the aviator glasses he wore. From far back in the garden next to a dark green, original Charleston bench, a fountain, one of many, trickled. He'd dozed off on that bench to the peaceful sounds of the water splashing in the fountain hundreds of times, maybe thousands. Overhead there were mourning doves that nested in the tree, chirping and chittering to one another. His deck back in Atlanta held a sorry-looking geranium with yellow leaves, a lawn chair with two missing slats, a rusty iron table, and a pile of unread magazines. He shuddered. More than anything, this garden was what he missed the most. Living in bachelor quarters and working eighteen hours a day in Atlanta didn't allow for much leisure time.

Hunt sat on one of the pristine white iron chairs. He noticed for the first time that the table was set with a linen cloth and his mother's fine china. Well, he had been invited for breakfast. Pearl would serve him a hearty breakfast of ham, eggs, grits, thick sliced toast, her homemade blackberry jam, and fresh squeezed orange juice. He could smell the housekeeper's Jamaican coffee perking. Hunt thought about the breakfasts he caught on the run at Burger King at six in the morning back in Atlanta.

Hunt leaned back to stare at the Angel Oak. Three hundred years old if it was a day. Once he and Lee had fashioned a canvas tree house in the old tree. Pearl had rigged up a pulley and served them fat sugar cookies and ice cold lemonade every afternoon once Kathryn made her appearance. Pearl called it their hidey-hole. His mother had called it an eyesore. Whatever it was, he, Kathryn, and Lee had spent hundreds of blissful hours nestled in the tree.

"Mr. Hunt, is that you?" Pearl said from the kitchen doorway.

"It's me, Pearl. You're lookin' as beautiful as ever." It was the truth. Pearl was a tall, stately woman with a coronet of braids. Her face was unlined and unblemished. Tiny bells tinkled in her ears and silver bracelets jangled on her wrists. She wore a wheat-colored muslin dress that dropped to her ankles and a snow white apron. He'd always marveled that there was never a stain or a crease anywhere to be seen on the apron. To his knowledge the only time Pearl wore shoes was to church. Lee always said Pearl looked like an aristocrat's wife without her shoes.

"Your mama is almost ready. Why don't you jest sit there in the garden and Pearl will fetch you some coffee." Pearl always, for as long as he could remember, referred to herself in the third person. "The garden looks real pretty today. We had a shower last evening. Mr. Hunt, did you step on my moss?"

"No, ma'am, I did not."

"That's a good boy. How long will you be staying? Pearl freshened your room this morning when your mama said you wuz coming for a spell."

Hunt thought about his reply before he sat down on the iron chair. "As long as it takes." He noticed the crystal bowl of yellow roses in the middle of the table. "Are these your famous Pearl Moon roses?"

"They purely are. It's your mother's favorite. She does like a pretty table setting."

"Pearl, is . . . the room still closed and locked?"

"Yes'm, Mr. Hunt. We don't talk about it anymore. Miz Lily says it fair breaks her heart to talk about her young son. He ain't never comin' back. She has it in her head that she wants to move from this place. You best talk some sense into your mama, Mr. Hunt. Pearl ain't movin'."

"She says that at least once a year, Pearl. She wouldn't be happy anywhere else. I will talk to her though."

"Are you on vacation from all your lawyerin'? Your mama

says you is goin' to be a judge someday like your daddy."

Hunt threw back his head and laughed. "I don't think so, Pearl. I'm thinking of packing it all in and going to some mountaintop to live off the land."

Pearl clucked her tongue as she retreated to the kitchen. A moment later she was back with a copy of *The Post and Courier* and a cup of coffee.

Hunt unfolded the paper. He stared at the picture in the middle of the front page. Now he knew why his mother summoned him from Atlanta. The picture was at least forty years old. Constance Bannon, his mother's childhood friend. The caption beneath the picture said Mrs. Bannon was an heiress to a candy fortune. He skimmed the article. There was no mention of Mrs. Bannon's eight or nine marriages or of her daughter Kathryn. There was, however, mention of a five million-dollar donation to MUSC, the Medical University of South Carolina. After Mrs. Bannon's long absence the donation would place her front and center, which was probably her intention from the git-go. He folded the paper just as his mother Lily Kingsley entered the courtyard.

"Hunter, you look wonderful."

"Mom, you smell better than the gardenias." Hunt hugged her, loving the feel of her in his arms. "Did I ever thank you for being my mother?"

"Hundreds of times but do it again. You should be ashamed of yourself, Hunter, you're only five hours away by car and fifty minutes by air. I haven't seen you in almost a year."

"I call every week."

"It isn't the same and you know it."

Hunt propped his elbows on the table and stared at his mother. At sixty-eight she was still beautiful and regal like Pearl. Dressed in a floral summer dress with pearls in her ears

271

and around her throat she was the perfect complement to the garden. "I saw the paper, Mom."

"Constance came back last week. On Friday she showed up at the garden gate and rang the bell. Thirty-four years after the fact. Pearl let her in. At first I was going to ask her to leave. I still don't know why I didn't. We sat here in the garden for a long time. She ended up staying for supper. Pearl insisted. It doesn't pay to argue with Pearl. We talked and more or less came to an understanding."

Hunt watched as his mother fussed with the strand of pearls around her neck. He had the feeling something was wrong, something his mother wasn't telling him. "Keep fiddling with those pearls, Mom, and they're going to break. Those are great-grandma's pearls, right?"

Lily dropped her hands to her lap. "I think we had a pleasant time. At least *I* did. The whole thing was such a surprise. Constance . . . it's hard to tell about her."

"What did she want, Mom?"

"My son the cynic," Lily said. "She wants Kathryn."

Hunt's eyebrows shot upward. "That's when you should have told her to leave."

"I wanted to, but I couldn't. She looked so devastated. She wants to make amends."

The veiled look on his mother's face bothered Hunt and he didn't know why. "Does she now? How do you make amends for turning your only daughter over to strangers and boarding schools? How do you make amends for not seeing that daughter for more than thirty years? You told me it was thirty years, Mom. Kathryn is three years younger than me so that means she's thirty-two. You can't make amends for something like that."

"Doesn't she deserve the right to at least try? I think she does. She's lived in Europe and Argentina all these years."

"There are telephones and airplanes. You got yourself involved, didn't you, Mom? Kathryn isn't going to like that. She'll consider it betrayal on your part."

"You don't know the first thing about Kathryn, Hunt. I haven't seen her myself in more than three years. She does call Pearl though."

"I know what you told me. I also have a very good memory. Kathryn might have been Lee's closest friend but she was mine, too. She always pretended to be so tough and uncaring. Pearl and Lee saw right through that. You were her pretend mother. It might be a good idea to tell me what it is you promised Kathryn's mother. Just out of curiosity do you happen to know what her name is this year?"

"She told me but I forget. I promised her you'd find Kathryn and talk her into visiting."

"You *what!*" Hunt's heart leaped in his chest. "Oh, no. I'm not getting involved in something like that. You find her. Hire a private dick. How hard can that be? You said Kathryn's in law enforcement. The police will help."

"I want you to find her, Hunt. She likes you. She'll listen to you. A meeting. That's all Constance wants. Kathryn can walk away after the meeting."

"I'm not invading her life. No, Mom. Let Mrs. whatever her name is, hire her own detectives. Someone's going to get hurt here. I don't want it to be Kathryn."

"That just goes to show you how little you know about Kathryn. Everyone calls her Kate. She got married for all of ten minutes so she could change her name from Bannon to . . . Jazanowski. She got divorced. Her coworkers call her Jaz. Did you know, Hunt, she came by every day after . . . Lee was . . . After the funeral? She always brought a flower, a book, candy, a picture. She sent cards. Kathryn called faithfully and then in the end, she caved in, she couldn't seem to get a handle on Lee's death. That's why she went into police work. She said . . . It isn't important what she said."

"Is she here in the state?"

"I don't know. For some reason I almost think she is. This is her home."

"That has to be the laugh of the year." Hunt's face was so bitter his mother winced.

Lily's voice was a flat monotone when she said, "Constance provided everything that was needed. Kathryn had the best of everything. The best clothes, the best car, the best schools, a fortune in pocket money. She couldn't give the child something that wasn't in her to give."

"Then she should have damn well pretended."

"Hunter, I didn't know you had such strong feelings where Kathryn is concerned. Is it possible you cared for her and thought . . . Lee? Oh, no, Hunter, Kathryn and Lee were friends, nothing more. Lee used to confide in her about his dates and she'd tell him what he was doing was either right or wrong. Lee did the same for her. She loved him like a brother. When he was taken from her life, she thought she had nothing left. One night Pearl found her by the gate. All crumpled up. She was crying and muttering about life not being worth living. Pearl took her to her room and . . . I don't know what she did or said but whatever it was, it worked. Kathryn is whole and well. That's why I think she can handle this meeting. I *know* she's been in touch with Pearl. Maybe you should talk to her."

"No, Mom."

"Hunter, when, if ever, did I ever ask anything of you?"

"Mom . . ."

"When, Hunter?"

"Okay, you never asked. This is different, Mom."

"Think how wonderful it will be if mother and daughter

are reunited after all these years. If I can put aside my differences where Constance is concerned there is hope for Kathryn."

"You said you would never forgive Mrs. Bannon for having an affair with Dad."

"Your father is gone. I spent too many years being miserable. Hate is a debilitating emotion. My hatred was all directed at Constance. Your father was to blame, too. I actually came out and asked Constance when she had the time to have an affair with him and she said . . . what she said was, between husband three and four. She provided details I didn't want to hear. I know you and Lee thought I forgave your father, but I didn't. At the end all he could ask me was to forgive him. I didn't do that, even when he was dying. I was selfish. I thought only of myself and how humiliated I'd been. I was devastated that my best friend and my husband carried on an affair in my own house while I was playing bridge. If I had it to do over again, I would do things differently. I can't. It's too late for me. I don't want it to be too late for Kathryn."

Hunt looked up into the Angel Oak. For some reason his mother's words weren't ringing with truth. He wondered why that was. Maybe he was imagining things. "Mom . . ."

"If you do this for me, Hunter, I promise I will clean the room. I think I can do it now. It would be so wonderful if we brought everything full circle again. I know Lee would want you to do this."

Hunt's voice was husky, full of emotion when he said, "I think about him all the time, Mom. I guess that's why I don't come back more often. It's like he's still here. He is, he's everywhere. If I close my eyes I can see him in the tree, hear him barreling up the steps, see him sliding down the banister. Hit and run. It was so senseless."

"We've moved on, Hunter. We can't undo it. Each of us now has a mission. You must find Kathryn and I must help Constance."

"All right, Mom. Pearl said my room was ready so I guess I'll carry in my bags."

"Your room has been ready since the day you left. Pearl freshens it up every single morning. It's part of her life."

"Do you want me to . . . ?"

"No. This is something I need to do alone. I'm so glad you came, Hunter. Tell me, am I asking too much of you?"

"Of me, no. Where Kathryn is concerned, only time will tell."

"Talk to Pearl, Hunter. Having breakfast with you was lovely."

"Almost like old times." Hunt avoided looking at the chair in which Lee always sat. He felt his eyes start to burn. He knew his mother was experiencing the same feelings as she rushed from the table.

"I'd give everything I own in the world, everything I ever hope to own, if I could turn time backward and we were all sitting here eating Pearl's pecan pie. Everything. I swear to God, I'd give everything I hold dear," Hunt said to the empty chair.

Pearl stood in the doorway, her eyes wet. She thought she loved Hunter as much as his mother did. "What did you want to talk to Pearl about?"

"Kathryn."

"I love that chile, Mr. Hunter. Did you know she totes a gun? Sometimes she carries it in her purse. Sometimes she wears it in a shoulder holster. If you make her mad, she might shoot off your foot. She don't take kindly to people stickin' their nose into her business."

"I can't say that I blame her. I'll be careful."

"This is her address. You best tell her I give it to you or else she'll run you off."

"Summerville? That's only twenty miles away. I bet she's even listed in the phone book, right?"

"That's wrong thinkin' on your part. You best be takin' one of my pies and maybe some flowers. It might take the sting out of what you're goin' to be asking her to do."

"Pie and flowers aren't going to do it, Pearl. Thanks for breakfast, it was wonderful, just the way I remember. It sure beats a biscuit and gravy at one of those fast-food places."

"Poison, pure poison. Ain't you learned nothin' in all them fancy schools your mama sent you to? Them places have bugs and hairs in the food. Go on now. I fetched your things in and unpacked it all. You git on your way. You git yerself into trouble, you call Pearl. You mind me now, Mr. Hunter. I still have my old fly swatter."

Hunt laughed, remembering how often he'd felt the sting of the old black fly swatter on his rump. "I'll do that, Pearl."

Chapter Two

Kathryn Bannon Jazanowski, Kate slash Jaz to her male colleagues on the police force, leaned back into the softness of the outdoor chaise. Her movements were deliberate when she reached for her glass of iced tea. The cold glass felt good in her hand. It felt even better when she wiped it across her perspiring forehead. There was absolutely no reason she should be perspiring. The temperature was at 72 degrees without an ounce of humidity. She was sitting in the shade and she had on a baseball cap. Her therapy was over and her body had cooled down allowing for a restful catnap afterward. She could feel her left eyelid start to twitch behind her mirrored sunglasses as she took another sip of the frosty tea.

The newspaper on the terra-cotta patio glared up at her. Every word in it was already old news. If there was one thing in this world that she hated with a passion it was old news, especially when that old news concerned her mother. She wished now that she hadn't read the article, wished she hadn't stared at the picture on the front page, wished she didn't look like her mother. Kathryn wished for yesterday.

Constance Bannon, according to the article, returned to Charleston to her magnificent house along the Battery. She was going to garden, sit on the board of the Historical Preservation Society, and overall take her place in Charleston social circles. To prove that she was home to stay after a thirty-year absence, she planned to make generous gifts to charity and to all worthy causes she could identify with.

Kate snorted, a sound between a laugh and a sob. Right

before Mother's Day. How appropriate.

Maybe it was time to move on. She liked the North. Lee had gone to school at Villanova and she'd visited several times. She'd loved autumn with the change of foliage and the snow at Christmas. Hunt had gone to Georgetown. Lee said he loved it. Yes, she'd give serious thought to putting her house on the market and moving on. Charleston, Summerville, and the subdivision of Tea Farms where she now lived would just be a memory.

"Damn." The single word exploded from her mouth like a bullet. Why should I have to leave just because *she* moved back? You don't, an inner voice whispered. However, you just might run into her or she might come for a visit. Better to leave and let sleeping dogs lie. That means I have to give up my job, apply for another one, she argued with the unseen voice. You have savings, money in a brokerage account. Let's not forget that awesome trust account you refuse to acknowledge. You can move it if you really want to. The doctor said you're well enough to report for desk duty next week. Another month and you'll be back on active duty. That means you can leave tomorrow if you want to. This is all assuming your mother is even the least little bit interested in seeing or speaking with you. She hasn't sought you out in almost thirty years so you might be panicking without just cause.

A creature of impulse, Kate reached for the voluminous tote she was never without. She rummaged until she found the cell phone. She called information for Coldwell Bankers and Delta Airlines. Within ten minutes she had an appointment with a real estate broker for the following morning and a reservation for Philadelphia, Pennsylvania, for Thursday evening. It would give her time to pack, say good-bye to good friends, close her bank accounts, garage her car, and do all the necessary things one needed to do when one planned to fly the coop.

The cell phone in Kate's hand started to vibrate. A second later it buzzed to life. Her hello had a cautious ring to it.

"Kate, it's Ellie. I saw the morning paper. Are you okay?"

"Of course I'm okay. I'm putting my house on the market tomorrow morning. On Thursday I'm out of here. I'd leave tomorrow but there are things I have to do."

"Oh, Kate, why? I'm going with you."

"No, you are not going with me. You have a wonderful job and a guy who's begging you to marry him. You belong here. You'd hate Pennsylvania with all the cold weather and snow. She won't stay. She never does. When she leaves for richer fields, I'll think about coming back. It's best for me. Ellie, we've been friends since kindergarten at Miss Prindle's. We'll always be friends. That's never going to change. Look at it this way. You'll be gaining an extra place to visit on your vacation horizon."

"Are you going to tell Lily and Pearl?"

"I'll call Pearl when I'm settled."

"Want to go to Oscars for dinner? I know for a fact the only things in your refrigerator are a dried-up carton of leftover Chinese food, a wrinkled orange, and two slices of cheese that are so hard they're brittle. You also had two bottles of Bud unless you drank them. I'll be the designated driver so you can get soused if you want."

"Sure. What time?"

"Sevenish. By the way, guess who I saw downtown this morning."

"My boss with his new girlfriend?"

"Not even close. Try again."

"Constance Bannon."

"Wrong again. Hunt Kingsley. Kate, that guy is so good looking he makes my knees weak. It's a mystery to me why he's never married. He is thirty-five! I think he regrets your

280

broken affair and he's still grieving over his loss the way you are."

"You have to stop reading those romance novels. This isn't make-believe. This is real life." Kate didn't want to think about the way her heart was racing at the mention of Hunt Kingsley's name. "Guess what, Ellie, in three years I'll be thirty-five. I'll be on my way to being a career police officer and I won't be married, either. Will that be a mystery to you then?"

"Hell no! It will just mean you're stupid. You've been engaged four times, married once for, was it ten minutes or five minutes, and I know you've had at least a dozen proposals? You're saving yourself for . . . tell me again because I forget."

"It was ten minutes. I'm not marriage material. I'm not saving myself for anyone. Let's talk about something else. I really should hang up because I have to pick up my dog at the groomers."

"Go. I'll see you tonight."

Cane in hand, Kate made her way to the Bronco. She returned an hour later with Sophie, her Yorkshire Terrier, a gift from her coworkers when she'd been wounded in the line of duty. The six-pound Yorkie had been a lifeline to hold onto, a warm, snugly body who didn't object to being cuddled and squeezed. Sophie proved to be a wonderful friend during her recovery. To Kate's delight the little dog had turned out to be a magnificent watchdog, barking when anyone strange appeared on the cul-de-sac or approached the house. Within three days she had the raccoons and squirrels on the run, made friends with a nest of baby rabbits, and allowed the mourning doves to nest in the crepe myrtle in the middle of the yard.

Sophie, all six pounds of her, loved unconditionally. Just the way Biz did.

Kate leaned heavily on the pronged cane as she exited the

Bronco, Sophie trotting along next to her. "A beer for me and grape juice for you, okay?" Sophie yapped her approval.

Exhausted with all the effort she'd expended, Kate lowered herself to the chaise. She was asleep in minutes. Sophie settled herself on a towel under the chaise, her small head resting on her paws. She would sleep later when her mistress woke. For now she remained alert.

Kate squirmed, her good leg thrashing sideways the way it had when she'd been wounded. She knew she was dreaming because Lee and Hunt were fighting over who was going to take her to her prom. "I'm not going with either one of you. You're brothers and I won't come between you. I'm going with Ross McIntyre."

"That klutz? He doesn't know how to dance," Lee said.

"He's shorter than you are," Hunt said.

"So what?"

"Oh, Kathryn, how beautiful you look," Lily Kingsley said as Pearl pinned up the hem of the prom gown.

"They're looking at me," Kate whispered.

"Who's looking at you?"

"Your sons. Both of them asked me to the prom. Lee asked me because he thought no one else would ask me. Now he doesn't have a date. Hunt asked me because. . . . I don't know why he asked me. I guess he feels sorry for me. I really wanted to go with him, Lily."

"Lee would have understood, honey."

"He's a college man. He was just taking pity on me. It made me feel good that he asked me."

"I'm late for my luncheon, Kathryn. We'll talk some more when I get back."

"You need to stand still, Miz Kathryn, or I'll jab your ankle. I think you're sweet on Mr. Hunt. I see the way he looks at you. Those rosy cheeks of yours tell Pearl all she needs to know. When he's a full-growed man he's goin' to come lookin' for you. You mind Pearl now."

"Do you think so, Pearl? Truly?"

"Yes'm I purely do."

"Last night when we were in the garden, we tried to count the stars. Hunt pointed to the moon and he said it was his. Oh, Pearl, it was so beautiful, all silvery and bright. It just shimmered in the dark sky. He said he was laying claim to the moon and called it Hunt's Moon. It was a full moon. He said if he ever proposed to a girl it was going to be under his own moon. Lee laughed himself silly. I cried, Pearl, when I went to bed. Why do you think I cried?"

"Because you is sweet on Mr. Hunt. Everybody knows that, even Mr. Lee and his mama knows. Only ones who don't know is Mr. Hunt and you Miss Kathryn."

"That's rubbish, Pearl."

"Iffen it's rubbish then why are your cheeks so flushed?"

"Because . . . because . . . it's hot in here."

Pearl pointed to the paddle fan overhead. "Ain't hot at all, Miz Kathryn. You kin step out of that dress now so's I can hem it. You kin pick it up tomorrow afternoon. Miz Lily says she wants to take a picture of you and your . . . date. Mr. Hunt tole his mama he would be glad to take the picture."

"Oh, no. Oh, no. He'll heckle me and make me embarrassed. Break his camera, Pearl."

"Scat."

Kate rolled over. She smiled in her half sleep when she felt a tiny pink tongue lick her cheek. "Time to get up, huh? I had that stupid dream again. If I had a dollar for every time I went to that damn prom I'd be rich. You know what I *really* think, Sophie? I think Hunter Kingsley is a first-class jerk. I hate dreaming about him. I never know how I'm supposed to feel when I wake up. By the way, we're moving."

Sophie tilted her head to the side. She stared at her mistress with adoring eyes.

"Just you and me, kiddo. For a long time it was just me. Now at least I have you. We'll be just fine."

Chapter Three

Hunt drove steadily on I–26, his thoughts on everything but where he was going and the reasons for the trip. He thought about his caseload he'd turned over to one of the junior partners in the firm, of his new suit he was supposed to pick up at four o'clock, of his messy two-bedroom apartment in Buckhead. He thought about Mallory Evans and her demand to set a wedding date. He had to make a decision where Mallory was concerned. He had an out if he wanted to use it. Mallory hated his cat Bizmark and had told him it was either her or the cat. Some choice. Actually there wasn't a choice at all. Biz was staying with him and that's all there was to it. Biz had been Lee's cat, rescued from a thornbush in a neighbor's garden and presented to him by Kathryn. He hoped the big furry creature was doing okay in the kennel. He made a mental note to call the first chance he got. He wondered what Kathryn thought when his mother informed her he'd taken Biz. Pearl said Kathryn had doted on the fifteen-pound feline.

Hunt slowed as he approached the Summerville turnoff for 17–A. He headed up the highway, his eyes searching for the landmarks Pearl had mentioned. He'd passed town hall, the azalea park, the grammar school. He sailed through the green light at Five Points, rounded the killer curve on Pine Grove and South Main as he made his way to Tea Farm Road. He made a left and then another left, his eyes searching for house numbers on the mailboxes. He made another left on Pekoe, slowed almost to a crawl until he saw the 99 on the mailbox. A blue Ford Bronco was parked in the driveway.

He heard a dog barking in the backyard. He wondered if Kathryn had a dog or if it was a neighbor's dog doing the barking.

Instead of ringing the front doorbell, Hunt followed the flagstone walkway around the back. The moment he set foot on the terra-cotta patio he knew he was in trouble as a whirlwind of motion attacked him, clawing and nipping at his ankles. He let out a yelp when the dog's teeth made contact with his bare skin.

He saw everything about her then, the baseball cap, the mirrored sunglasses, the pronged cane, the oversized, ratty sweatshirt that said Villanova on the front. Lee's shirt. He wondered what she'd done with the one he'd given her that said Georgetown on the back. He almost asked and then changed his mind.

"Kathryn, would you mind calling off your dog? It bit me twice."

Kate snapped her fingers. Sophie ran to her and leaped onto the chaise. The Yorkie's eyes bored into this first-time visitor, her lips pulling back from her sharp, pointed teeth.

"Well, if it isn't the Great White from Atlanta. Isn't that what they call you in legal circles?" Kate shifted her position on the chaise. Even to her own ears her voice sounded cold and bitter. She was aware of how she looked; downright sloppy. Hunt looked . . . neat, polished, confident. She wanted to rise up and slap him. "To what do I owe the pleasure of this visit? Let me guess. You're bringing ten years' worth of Christmas and birthday cards. The ones you promised faithfully to send. Or are you bringing your phone records to show me that your phone doesn't work from Atlanta? Or is it possible you're bringing a marriage license, the one you said you were applying for? Whatever it is you want, the answer is no. Did Pearl give you my address? She did, didn't she? Get the hell off my property."

"Which question do you want me to answer first?"

"Why are you here? What do you want? Answer those two questions, then take your sorry ass out of here or I'll really turn this dog on you."

"Kathryn, this is me, Hunt. Do you want me to leave and come back so we can start over?"

"I want to know why you're here. Nothing else is open for debate."

"I heard about your accident. I came to see how you were."

"When a low life piece of scum shoots out your knee cap, they do not call it an accident. You could have called instead of coming all the way here."

"I could have, but I wanted to see for myself. I thought we were friends, Kathryn."

"Yeah. I thought that myself. We all make mistakes."

"You got any more of that beer?"

"Why do you want to know?"

"I want one. You aren't much of a hostess."

"In the fridge. Get it yourself. You won't be here long enough for me to put myself out where you're concerned."

Hunt marched into the house, his back stiff. He would have had to be blind not to notice the lack of furniture. A frown settled between his brows.

"You don't have any furniture," Hunt said when he returned to the patio.

"I move around a lot and I travel light. Were you snooping? Don't concern yourself with my furnishings."

Hunt sat down and placed his beer at his feet. "Let's start over. Hello, Kathryn, it's good to see you. Now you say, hello, Hunt, how nice of you to visit."

"Put a sock in it, Hunt. What do you want and you're going to have to do better than that first excuse?"

"It's the truth. Do you want me to make up a lie?"

"Go away."

"Let's have dinner?"

"I have plans." The smugness in Kate's voice did not go unnoticed by Hunt.

"Okay, breakfast. I can sleep over. This is a big house so you must have a spare room."

"No furniture. Sorry."

"Pearl sent you a pie and some of her yellow roses."

"I don't eat sweets anymore and roses make me sneeze." Kate propped herself up on her elbow. "I think I might have more respect for you if you really did come on your own, but both of us know Lily and Pearl sent you. You being a lawyer and all, I would think you could lie a little more convincingly."

"Jesus, Kathryn, what's gotten into you? Do you treat everyone like this or is it just me?"

"What do you think? Are you taking care of Bizmark? If you aren't, give him to me. I wanted that cat and you took him. You just snatched him right from under my nose. You didn't even ask."

Hunt's voice was defensive, boyish when he said, "I didn't know you wanted him. Mom's cleaning out Lee's room today."

"Stop acting like I'm part of your family. I don't want to hear what any of you are doing. I'm not interested. Just the way you weren't interested in me after you got what you wanted. Now, go away!"

"We need to talk about *that*."

"Maybe you do, but I don't. In our case, your silence was more eloquent than any other words you can come up with now."

"It was a shabby thing to do. I admit it. Hell, I was afraid. I was looking at my senior year, at three years of law, finding

288

a job. I wasn't ready to make a commitment for the rest of my life."

"Then why didn't you tell me that? A phone call would have sufficed."

"I did write you a letter. I read it to Lee and gave it to him to give to you. He said he would when the time was right. He thought it would be better if I just kind of faded out of your life. Lee always, in my opinion, had a handle on your emotions. I trusted him to give you the letter. I poured out my heart, told you exactly how I felt, told you I would always love you. I didn't have the guts to tell you in person. I had no guts, period and didn't want to hurt you. I wasn't mature enough. What do you want me to say?"

"That's a crock and you know it. Lee never gave me your letter if there ever was a letter. Do you think in your infinite wisdom that your silence didn't hurt me more? Why are we having this conversation?"

"I never knew Lee didn't give you the letter. He and I never spoke of it again. We're having this conversation to relieve the tension? It was a long time ago, Kathryn. I know this won't mean anything to you but I think about you always. I dream about you and Lee and me at least once a week. I can't understand why he never gave you the letter."

"The alleged letter. Isn't that how you lawyers refer to things in doubt? You're right, though. It doesn't mean anything. If it were supposed to mean something, you would have called or written and mailed the letter yourself. You aren't even a fair-weather friend. When Lee died, I needed someone. I was young, naive, and stupid. Having an affair with you was your answer and when you had enough you went back to school and let me hang out to dry. I needed someone then so desperately. The story of my life."

"Kathryn, I'm sorry, I want you to believe that."

"Those are just words, Hunt Kingsley. I wouldn't believe anything you said to me if you were standing on a stack of Bibles. It's time for you to leave now."

"I guess it is."

"Another thing. I'll send your office a memo in regard to my trust fund. I don't want you handling my affairs any longer."

"That's a pretty low blow and unworthy of you, Kathryn. My legal capabilities have nothing to do with my personal life. I work overtime to make sure that fund grows at a healthy rate of interest. You can do whatever you want with it. I'll cooperate with whoever you chose to monitor it. What do you want me to do with the pie and the flowers?"

"Do whatever you want with them."

"What should I tell Pearl?"

"You're probably the best liar I know. You'll think of something appropriate."

"I'm sorry you have such a low opinion of me, Kathryn."

"You know what, Hunt, I'm sorry, too. You need to ask yourself why Lee never gave me your letter. If there ever was a letter, which I don't think there was."

Hunt turned on his heel, his dark eyes miserable. "I guess we'll never know since Lee is dead. I would never lie about something like that, Kathryn. Especially where Lee was concerned. Is the word forgive in your vocabulary?"

"How do you spell it?"

Sophie leaped from Kate's lap to chase Hunt to the driveway. Once he turned to try and talk to the Yorkie but the dog was merciless as she tried to climb his leg, biting him twice on the shin. He managed to shake her loose before he slid into his car.

Hunt looked into the rearview mirror. His heart thumped in his chest when he saw Kathryn leaning on her cane staring

290

at his car. The mirrored sunglasses were perched on the visor of the baseball cap. He almost skidded into a ditch when he saw her knuckle her eyes. Kathryn Bannon Jazanowski crying?

Unbelievable.

"What did you say to that sweet chile so she wouldn't take Pearl's pie and flowers?"

"She said she didn't want anything from this family."

"Didn't you tell her I ain't yer family? I jest work for this family."

"She didn't want to hear anything I had to say. She doesn't have any furniture, Pearl. She didn't have any food in the refrigerator, either. She told me to get my sorry ass off her property."

"Miss Kathryn said that! Are you funnin' with me, Mr. Hunt?"

"No, ma'am."

"She seen the paper then."

"It was on the floor. We didn't mention it. My visit was short to say the least."

"You need to be takin' yerself back there and make things right. That chile don't deserve so much unhappiness. You hear me good, Mr. Hunt."

"Oh, no. Once was enough." Hunt yanked at his pant leg. "Look at this. Her damn dog bit me three times. She didn't even care. What do you think of that, Pearl?"

"I jest tole you what I thought. You best be goin' back there to make things right, young man. Your mama is waitin' for you in the garden with Miss Kathryn's mama. Both them ladies is 'spectin' you to be bringin' good news."

"It isn't going to happen, Pearl."

"Don't you be thinkin' you kin git out of this. They is

'spectin' you so go out there and tell your mama the coffee is almost ready."

Hunt felt like an errant boy when he made his way to the garden. As always, when he walked down the two brick steps into the flower-scented gardens, he felt like he was in another world. He stared at the two women at the table, one fair and blond, the other dark and exotic. Constance Bannon was the exact replica of Kathryn or was that the other way around? He felt flustered.

"Constance, I'd like you to meet my son Hunter. Hunter, this is Constance Bannon, Kathryn's mother. We've been sitting here anxiously waiting for your return. How did your visit go?"

"It didn't, Mom. I'm sorry."

"She must have said something, Hunter."

"She said a lot of things. She said she wasn't part of this family and wouldn't accept Pearl's pie and flowers. She uses a cane. The last thing she said to me after she told me to get my sorry ass off her property was that she was getting another attorney to oversee her trust fund. A trust fund, I might add, that has never been touched."

"Never?" The dark-eyed, dark-haired woman gasped.

"She doesn't have any furniture and there's no food in her refrigerator." For some reason he couldn't define, he felt smug at the women's startled expressions. He threw in what he thought was the clunker. "I think she's getting ready to bolt."

His mother stared at him with wide eyes. "Do you mean leave?"

"It's just my opinion."

"Did you tell her about Constance?"

"No. I was trying to get a feel for her reaction first. The morning paper was on the floor so she saw the article if that's your next question."

"How . . . how is she?" Constance asked.

She sounds like she cares, Hunt thought. "She's hostile, angry, bitter." He looked pointedly at his mother. "She's not the Kathryn you or I used to know. The fact that she wouldn't accept Pearl's pie and yellow roses should tell you something."

Constance Bannon spoke. Her voice was soft, cultured, almost melodious. "Is there any possibility Kathryn was upset with *you*? When women react the way you say Kathryn reacted, usually there's an underlying cause. You didn't tell her the real reason you were visiting. That leads me to believe her reaction was of a personal nature. Wouldn't you agree, Lily?"

Lily's eyes were thoughtful. "Yes, Constance, I do agree."

Hunt felt his neck grow warm as he stared at the two women sitting across from him. They looked like best friends. He wondered how it was possible to set aside their hurts and disillusionment where his father was concerned. He closed his eyes for a second to try and imagine his father in bed with Constance Bannon. In his own way he'd done exactly the same thing to Kathryn as his father had done to his mother. The only difference was he wasn't married to Kathryn. No matter how you looked at it, he was as much a louse as his father. They were waiting for his response. His mind grappled for a suitable answer. True lawyer that he was, he said, "anything's possible."

"Mr. Hunt, Miz Mallory Evans is on the phone," Pearl said from the kitchen doorway.

From the fry pan into the fire. Hunt excused himself. He felt two pairs of eyes boring into his back as he made his way into the kitchen.

Chapter Four

"Mallory, hello. Is something wrong?" Hunt watched Pearl out of the corner of his eye as she tried to make herself look busy.

"Of course something's wrong. You promised to call me back and you didn't. Your office told me where I could reach you. I miss you. I've been thinking, Hunt. I have all these frequent flyer miles so why don't I just fly to Charleston for the weekend. I think it's time for me to meet your mother."

"That isn't such a good idea, Mallory. I'm up to my eyeballs handling some rather delicate family matters. I explained that to you the other day . . . I really don't expect to have any free time. My mother has her own engagements and I'm not sure she could change them at this late date."

"Oh, poo, Hunt, I'm coming. Don't worry about entertaining me. I can take care of myself. Good heavens, I can even make my own breakfast. Even if we just get to spend a few hours together, it will be worth the trip. I miss you, darling."

"Mallory, this weekend is bad. Save your miles for an important trip."

"If the weekend is bad, I'll take a flight tomorrow and spend the night."

"Mallory . . ."

"I don't want to hear another word, Hunt. I'll take the first flight out in the morning. Meet me at the gate. I'll be the one who's smiling. Bye, darling."

"Goddamit!"

Pearl turned around. "Is company comin', Mr. Hunt? You best tell your mama. She don't take kindly to unannounced visitors 'ceptin' for Miss Kathryn. It purely breaks this ol' heart of mine that she din want my pie and flowers."

Hunt wrapped his arms around the old housekeeper. "It didn't have anything to do with you, Pearl. It was me. She was making a statement. When she thinks about it, she'll call you and apologize. Kathryn loves you more than anything in this world."

" 'Ceptin for old Biz. I miss that ol' cat being under my feet all the time. Your mama promised that ol' cat to Miss Kathryn and then you up and snatched it away from her. Everybody been doin' that all that poor chile's life. You need to be ashamed of that, Mr. Hunt."

"I didn't know. Nobody told me the cat was promised to Kathryn."

"You shoulda asked."

"I should have done a lot of things, Pearl. I screwed up and now I don't know how to make it right."

"Starin' at me ain't goin' make it right. You broke that chile's heart."

"Did Kathryn tell you that?"

"She din have to tell me. I seen it in her eyes. She sez you don't even send her a Christmas card. That's a shame on your mama. She brung you up bettern' that. Now, who is comin' here tomorrow? I need to know so I kin fix the bedroom."

"Mallory Evans. She's a friend, Pearl."

"The kind of friend who sleeps in her own bed?" Pearl asked bluntly.

"Yes. Absolutely."

"Is she bringing Biz?"

"She hates Biz. I put him in the kennel."

"You locked that old tomcat in a cage! God is purely goin' to strike your *daid* for that. Biz will die. He ain't never been locked up. You best have your friend fetch him tomorrow."

"It's the best kennel in Atlanta. Everyone I know boards their animals there. Okay, okay," Hunt said when he saw the grim set of Pearl's jaw and her angry eyes. "I'll call the kennel now. Is Mrs. Bannon staying for dinner?"

"Yes'm."

"I just remembered I have an appointment. Tell Mom I won't be late. Tell her about Mallory too, okay, Pearl?"

"Tell me, true, Mr. Hunt, where are you goin'?"

"Back to Summerville. That's what you would do if you were me, right? Tell Mom I'm taking her car, mine's almost out of gas."

Pearl smiled. And smiled.

Kathryn studied herself in the mirror hanging on the back of her bedroom door. She looked nothing like the sloppy-dressed waif who had words with Hunt Kingsley earlier in the day. She looked good. Too bad Hunt couldn't see her now. Not that she gave a damn about Hunt Kingsley. Tomorrow when she went to MUSC for her last checkup she would stop and apologize to Pearl and say good-bye. Maybe she would call ahead and have Pearl meet her at the straw market so she didn't run into Hunt. Then again maybe she wouldn't do anything but show up for her checkup.

When Ellen's horn sounded, Kathryn made her way downstairs, taking the steps one at a time. Sophie scooted ahead. She handed the little dog a chewie that was almost as big as she was before she turned on the light under the overhang and locked the door.

"You look rather fetching but your outfit doesn't go with

the angry look in your eyes. Do you want to talk about it now or over drinks?"

"Hunt showed up in my backyard this afternoon. If you can figure that one out, let me know. He acted pretty much like the gentleman he is and I acted like a shrew. I didn't give an inch. I got right in his face. I did that to . . . to cover how light-headed I felt. I was dizzy and giddy at the same time. I thought my heart was going to pound out of my chest. Sophie bit him a couple of times. I didn't acknowledge the bites. He could sue me, I suppose. As if I care. I fired him so now I have to get another attorney to oversee my trust fund."

"Is that the same trust fund you don't care about, the same one you never touched?"

"Yeah, that's the one. He has little bits of gray in his hair. He's aging nicely."

"How'd you look?"

"In a word, shitty."

"How'd you feel when you first saw him? You know that quick, instant feeling."

"Like I was kicked in the gut. He can still do that to me. I'd fallen asleep earlier and had that same cockamamie dream about the prom. I should have left here a long time ago. I wish I was anyplace but here. I have this strange feeling that someone's watching me. Cop's instinct."

"Nah. You're on overload. Don't start spooking yourself. Do you want me to let you off at the door or do you want to walk?"

"Walking is good for me. I'm up for a whole lobster tonight. Bacon-wrapped shrimp for an appetizer and a pecan tullie for dessert. Two bottles of Oscars' finest wine. One for you and one for me. You can only have one glass. I'll drink the rest of yours along with my own. I intend to get blitzed."

Hunt angled his car sideways so he couldn't be seen by

297

the two women. He slouched down in his seat as Kathryn and Ellen walked past his car talking animatedly. He felt a sense of loss and didn't know why.

He watched them as they stepped aside to allow an older couple to go ahead of them. She was dressed in a swirl of yellow. He wondered if there was a crown jewel the same color. Kathryn half turned, her eyes searching the parking lot. Hunt slouched lower in his seat. He inched up slowly. Even from this distance he could see that she had on makeup and jewelry. She was as beautiful as her mother must have been at her age.

He was spying. He was a goddamn Peeping Tom. He waited ten minutes before he got out of the car. He walked inside and headed for the bar, careful to look through the door first to make sure Kathryn had entered the dining room and not the bar. Relieved that she wasn't seated on one of the bar stools, he sat down and ordered a beer.

Three hours later with six full beers lined up next to him, Hunt noticed the bartender eyeing him suspiciously. "I'm waiting for someone." The excuse sounded lame to his ears. Evidently the bartender was of the same mind-set.

"I'd call it a night if I were you, Mister. I don't think she's going to show."

"I think you're right." Hunt paid his bar tab, left a generous tip. It was a nice night; he could sit in his car and wait.

It was a beautiful evening, dark and velvety with millions of stars overhead. He reeled backward when he noticed the nimbus around the full moon. Hunter's Moon. It was a silly thought. Why was he even wasting time thinking about it? Because, an inner voice whispered, you made promises to Kathryn about Hunter's Moon. They were just silly things young people say. Uh-huh. Right. Sure. Hunt groaned as he slid into the driver's seat. He turned on the engine just long enough to lower the power-driven windows and then turned it off.

What in the hell could two women find to talk about for three and some half hours? He felt flattered when he considered the possibility they were discussing him. Kathryn was really good at talking something to death. At least the old Kathryn was.

In the moonlight he saw the swirl of yellow as the two women exited the restaurant and made their way to the car. With the window down Hunt could hear their conversation. "Look at the moon, Ellen. Somebody told me once it was a Hunter's Moon. Actually it was Hunt Kingsley who told me that. Am I drunk, Ellen?"

"You're close. Drink some coffee when you get home."

"I don't have any. You know my cupboard's bare. That's good, though. When I leave on Thursday, I won't have any food to throw out. Remember now, don't tell anyone where I'm going."

Hunt bolted upright. He strained to hear the rest of the conversation.

"The day is going to come whether you like it or not, Kate, when you have to face your demons. After you do that you can walk away. You're doing this ass backward."

"I don't care. Listen," Kate said waving her cane in the air, "seeing that . . . that lawyer today made me realize so many things. I hate lawyers. They're the scum of the earth. Did I ever tell you my mother was married nine times? In the paper they called her Bannon. I never even got to know my father. He died five days after I was born. Bannon was my father's name. She doesn't have any right to that name. She shouldn't even be using it."

Ellen reached for her friend's arm. "Sort of like you using the name Jazanowski, right?"

"It's not the same and you know it."

"Get in the car, Kate. It is the same thing."

"I hate his guts! Do you know what he did? He stole Biz. Biz was supposed to be mine. I loved that big old cat. Biz loved me, too. I just bet you anything if Hunt Kingsley and me were standing side by side and Biz was there and we both called him he would come to me. That's because Biz loved me as much as he loved Lee. So there. He probably gives him dry cat food."

Hunt almost leaped out of the car to defend his care of Biz. He had the door open and one leg on the pavement when Ellen's car backed up, swerved, and cut into traffic from the access road leading to the restaurant.

The Honda Prelude was three cars ahead of him but that was okay. Kathryn's house was in a straight line and he knew the way. He stopped to pick up two coffees from Grandy's restaurant.

Hunt asked himself over and over why he was doing what he was doing. "I care about her. I always cared about her," he muttered.

Hunt pulled onto the cul-de-sac and was relieved to see that only Kathryn's Bronco was in the driveway. He took a deep breath and got out of the car, the coffee in hand. He marched to the door and rang the bell. He heard the sound of the cane on the tile in the foyer. He sucked in his breath when they stood face to face. "Can I come in, Katie? I brought some coffee."

At the sound of her childhood nickname, Kate's eyes filled. She stepped aside to let him enter. "I have a screened porch. Do you want to sit out there?"

"Sure. Is your dog going to bite me again?"

"Probably. You deserve it."

"Yeah, I guess I do. I sat in Oscars' all night waiting for you."

"I know. I saw you when I went to the ladies' room. Do you mind telling me why? Understand, I don't care. I'm just being courteous."

"We need to talk."

"You need to talk, Hunt. I'm okay with things. I'm not drunk if that's your next question. It's a good thing I had the wine, though, it's taking the edge off this little visit. I could shoot you right here and now and say you . . . the bartender will remember you sitting there all night."

"You'd probably go to jail. My law firm would go after you. In some circles I'm considered a valued member of society."

"And I'm just a stupid, dumb cop, is that it?"

"I didn't say that, Katie. There's nothing dumb or stupid about being a cop."

"Stop calling me Katie. You gave up that right a long time ago. This is an inane conversation. Cut to the chase so I can go to bed. What do you want from me? Why are you here today of all days? I am of course referring to today's paper with the article in it on Constance Bannon. I was disappointed in the article. I thought they should have given out her other nine names. I didn't feel the least bit entertained when I finished reading the article."

"Katie, I didn't want to come. My mother pressured me into doing it. She called me in Atlanta and asked me to come home. I thought something was seriously wrong, so I came. It seems Mrs. Bannon went to see my mother and they had a talk. They made peace after all this time. I find it a little hard to believe she forgave your mother for having an affair with my father. She did, though. The two of them decided I was the logical person to talk to you, to ask you to meet with your mother. I said no. I kept saying no. Mom doesn't know about . . ."

"Our affair?"

301

Hunt nodded. "I didn't have the guts to face you. I'm having a little difficulty even now. I don't have a defense, Kathryn. I'm not going to try to come up with one, either. It was what it was. For whatever it's worth, I do have regrets."

"I guess it doesn't matter anymore. Hatred takes up so much energy. All I want to do is move on with my life and forget about Mrs. Bannon, Lee, and the rest of your family. I want a family of my own. Is this where we shake hands and you ride off into the moonlight? The moon tonight is yours, Hunt. I will never forget about Biz, though. Don't think you can sit there and tell me stories about him, either. I don't want to hear them."

"I heard you tell your friend in the parking lot that you were leaving. Are you going somewhere for a visit or are you leaving as in leaving?"

"For someone who's as smart as you are, that's a pretty dumb question. I'm leaving. This house goes on the market tomorrow. I'm leaving on Thursday. I will never come back here as long as Mrs. Bannon is alive. Mother's Day is just a few days away. Remember how we all used to line up with those ratty presents for your mother and what a fuss she used to make over them? I thought it was wonderful. I always gave Pearl the best one, though. Isn't that ironic?"

"Yes. Why didn't you ever touch the trust fund, Kathryn?"

"Because it came from her. She set it up. That's your second stupid question of the night."

"It was your father's money, not your mother's. She followed the instructions in your father's will. It's a princely amount, Kathryn. Things can't be that easy for you. You don't even have furniture."

"I own this house. Of course there's a mortgage on it. I have a savings account and a small brokerage account. I'm not poor. Whatever I have I earned on my own."

"It shouldn't be this way."

"No, Hunt, it shouldn't. It is what it is. Shall we shake hands now? I'm tired and my leg is throbbing. I'd like to go to bed. It's late and you have to drive back to town."

At the door Hunt jammed his hands into his pockets. He felt like crying when Kathryn said, "You broke my heart, Hunt. I used to think that was just some kind of pat phrase writers penned in romance novels. Think about it, how can an organ break? Guess this is good-bye. Say hello to Pearl for me. I feel like your mother has betrayed me by aligning herself with Mrs. Bannon."

"That's how I feel, too. I guess when you get older it's easier to set aside old differences. They were very close once. Mom has a lot of friends, but your mother was her only close friend."

Kate leaned forward to open the front door just as Sophie ran between her legs to sink her teeth into Hunt's ankle. She lost her balance, teetered forward into Hunt's arms.

Kissing him seemed like the most natural thing in the world. She didn't resist, didn't fight him in any way as she let her mouth melt into his. It was a long, satisfying kiss that left her breathless and wanting more.

"Oh, Hunt, your eyes are watering."

"Your damn dog just bit me. Oh, Jesus, now she's biting my other ankle. C'mere, Katie. That was my hello kiss. Get ready and hold onto your socks; this is my farewell kiss."

Kathryn's world exploded as she met Hunt's ardor with her own unbridled passion. An eternity later she managed to whisper, "Where are your socks, Hunt?"

His voice was little more than a hoarse croak. "I'd like to do that again."

"Sorry. Two's my limit. Other things tend to happen when you . . ."

"Katie, you talk too damn much. Which way is the bed-room?"

"To the left."

Both muttered about belts and buttons and covers as they shed their clothes, Sophie prancing and yelping her displeasure as Hunt and Kate fell back onto the bed.

Kate stared at him through sleepy eyes. He was gold from the sun, lean and hard muscled. His chest was broad. His arms long and powerful, his hips slender and sleek. The golden hair on his chest threaded its way to his belly to grow darker in the grove between his legs. He looked the way he'd looked so many years ago. Just like in her dreams, just the way she remembered.

Her arms opened to him. He slid his nakedness against hers. His lips met hers, his tongue spearing into the warm recesses of her mouth. A low, agonizing moan escaped her lips. His hands seared her flesh as he searched for each wom-anly curve and found the round firmness of her breasts and she shivered as he sought them with his mouth, teasing and kissing.

She reached for him, taking him in her hand, stroked him, her fingers searching for the secrets beneath the dark gold furring.

Hunt allowed himself to lie back, yielding to her hands as he drew her to him. Her mouth found his and was rewarded with his indrawn breath and the arching of his hips.

An eternity passed before he rose over her, bringing her into his arms as he smothered her mouth with his own, his silken tongue coming in to touch and devour hers. She opened herself to him, demanding he fill the pulsing emptiness he had created within her.

He buried himself within her, becoming one with her, feel-ing her meet each thrust with a lift of her hips. She held fast to him with her arms and with her legs, taking him deep inside her.

When the world as she knew it exploded within her, Kate leaned back, Hunt next to her. His breathing was as harsh and ragged as her own.

"Katie —"

"Shhh. Don't say anything. We . . . were . . ."

"Making love. Katie, we need to talk."

"No. I was feeling vulnerable. I had too much wine. I started to remember . . ."

"Katie, I never forgot. I'm sorry if I broke your heart." Hunt propped himself up on his elbow. "Is there any possibility I can mend it? I want to more than anything in the world. I never stopped loving you. I did love you. It just wasn't the right time for us. At least that's how I perceived it then."

"I'm going away, Hunt."

"It's a choice, Katie. You don't have to go away. You can't run forever. Look it in the eye, deal with it, then you move on. Marry me and move to Atlanta with me."

Kate sat up, the sheet clutched to her breast. "Are you asking me to marry you?"

"Yep." The one word response was a lazy drawl.

"Well . . . I . . ."

"Have to think about it? I could give you a day or so."

"No, no, this isn't . . . I need to thin . . . I need more time. This isn't right. My plans don't include . . . You should leave, Hunt. Oh, my God, what's that on your ankles?"

"Dog bites. Your dog bit me at least a dozen times. Did I complain? No, I did not. I figured it was one of those love-me-love-my-dog things. We can share Biz."

Kate's voice softened. "How is he?"

"He hates me. I feed him salmon. I do everything Lee did. I took his scratching post, all his toys. I give him treats. I get his teeth cleaned. He gets checkups. I try to play with him but he bites and scratches me."

"That's because you keep him cooped up in an apartment. He loved your mother's garden. He had his own door to go in and out. He never went out of the garden. He misses that. He likes you to hand-feed him flaked tuna. He'll purr for hours if you do that. He likes a clean litter box, too. You should put something on your ankles."

"I will. Don't you know any first aid, being a cop and all?"

"You need peroxide, iodine, and Band-Aids. Pearl will fix you up. I don't keep stuff like that in the house. I told you. I travel light and fast."

"Katie, I was serious when I asked you to marry me. I wish now in hindsight that I had the guts to ask you years ago. I'll always regret that."

"It's not that easy. I have things I have to work through."

"Let me help you. If Lee were here, you'd run to him and ask his advice. I know what he'd say and you know it, too. Jesus, you have no idea how much I miss him. I hate going home, seeing his room with the door closed like that. He's everywhere, especially in the garden. Pearl knows it, too. She said his spirit is there in that old tree. I think my mother believes it, too, because she spends so much time out there. Even in the winter months Pearl says she sits out there with a lap robe."

"I don't want to talk about Lee. It still hurts too much. Best friends aren't supposed to die just the way parents aren't supposed to bury their children. I go to the cemetery every Sunday when I'm in town. Sometimes I take Pearl. We always take flowers. Do you go?"

"No. I think I'd fall apart if I went. It's been so long and yet it seems like yesterday. I have to let it go. So do you. Maybe together we can work on it."

306

Kate leaned back on the pillow. "I have a plane reservation for Thursday. I gave my notice today."

"Where are you going, Katie?"

"Villanova. It seemed like the right place at the time."

"No. It's the wrong place. You're holding on too tight. Let Lee go. Wherever he is, I know he's anguishing over our turmoil. He'd want us both to live freely and remember him once in a while. I've totally withdrawn from him and you're front and center. Both of us are wrong. He was my *brother*, Katie. Are you having second thoughts about leaving now?"

"I can't waste the plane ticket. Look, you know my feelings where Constance Bannon is concerned. They haven't changed nor will they change in the future. There are no other options. I want to go to sleep, Hunt. This is nice," she said, snuggling in his arms.

Kate lay quietly, her eyes closed tightly, her mind racing. As her thoughts ran amok, her body welcomed Hunt's warmth, his lean, hard body. She could feel tears form behind her lids. This was probably the single most horrendous thing she'd ever done in her life. The wine and her feelings of vulnerability were poor excuses for sliding into bed with an old lover, a lover who had walked out on her years ago.

Marriage? She felt a sob build in her throat. She shifted her position slightly, not wanting to wake Hunt. She turned to stare at the man she'd known since she was three years old. Once, like Lee, he'd been her friend. That friendship had changed in Hunt's junior year in college. It hadn't been planned; it just happened. A soft summer night, silver moonlight, the heavens blanketed in stars had made it inevitable. Hunt had promised marriage after graduation because in her desperate need to belong to someone she had pressured and begged him until he had agreed. The affair lasted until graduation. The day after Hunt had taken off with his college buddies for a backpacking trip that lasted all summer. Lee was the one who told her he went straight to Washington from Oregon. He didn't call and he didn't write. Licking her wounds, she had returned to Clemson, got her degree, and then her master's. She'd done it on her own too, by working part-time, receiving one small scholarship, student loans, and several grants.

She'd never found her niche, though. She taught for a while, worked in an insurance company for a year, thought about joining the Peace Corps, but joined the police force instead. All she'd ever really wanted was to be Mrs. Hunter Kingsley because marriage would validate who she was. Now, what she'd wanted for so long was within her grasp. All she had to do was say yes. If she did that, it would be for all the wrong reasons.

Did she love Hunt Kingsley? Yes, yes, yes. She had never stopped loving him.

The beginnings of a headache started to hammer behind her eyes. Tomorrow would be time enough to make decisions. She stirred slightly. Hunt's arm tightened on her naked body. She found herself smiling in the darkness. This night was hers. She would deal with tomorrow when tomorrow came.

Chapter Five

Hunt opened his eyes and knew exactly where he was and what had transpired hours earlier. He looked at his watch. Eight-twenty. He should get up and go home because . . . because he had something to do. What the hell was it? He mouthed the word, shit, three times before he swung his legs over the side of the bed. Mallory Evans expected to be met at the airport at eight-thirty.

He turned slightly on the bed to stare at the woman he'd made love with all night long. How beautiful she looked in sleep, how defenseless. The urge to gather her in his arms was so strong he clenched his fists. He wished there was a way to wipe the shadows from her eyes. He'd asked her to marry him, but she hadn't said yes or no. He moved gingerly till he was off the bed. The Yorkie stared at him as he slipped his feet into his Docksides. The shoes felt strange on his feet. He looked down, his jaw dropping. The left side of his right shoe was chewed away, as was the heel of his left shoe. "Bad dog," he hissed. Sophie glowered and growled deep in her throat. Kate slept on. "One hour with Biz and he'd whip you into shape," Hunt hissed again.

Hunt dropped to his haunches. "I understand. It's that female thing. She's a girl and you're a girl. I'm a guy and I don't belong here. I feel compelled to tell you I'm one of the good guys. I'm not even going to charge her for these shoes. I can't believe I'm talking to a dog," Hunt muttered as he made his way to the front door.

Hunt knew he was a sorry-looking specimen as he made

his way to the car. His hair needed to be combed, he definitely needed a shave. He knew the Yorkie had slept on his clothes. He looked down at his shoes again, what was left of them. His partners back in Atlanta should see him now. He burst out laughing as he backed out of the driveway.

At the airport, Hunt parked his car in the hourly lot. He loped up the stone steps that led to the main building, losing his left shoe twice. Each time he fit his foot into the Docksides he laughed, a booming sound of delight. He headed straight for the baggage area. He heard Biz before he saw him. The big cat was unhappy, snarling and spitting as he pawed at the grill on the kennel. He offered up identification to the baggage handler. The moment the man nodded, Hunt had the kennel in hand. As an afterthought he looked around for Mallory Evans. When she didn't appear in his line of vision, he left the building.

Hunt unlatched the grill on the kennel as soon as he closed the door of the car. Biz leaped out and snarled at him, his paws lashing out. "Knock it off, Biz. I'm taking you home." Biz's tail swished furiously as he leaped from the front seat to the back seat and then back to the front. He spit and snarled all the way back to the house on the Battery.

Biz under one arm, the kennel under the other, Hunt managed to open the iron gate leading to the garden. Directly in his line of vision was his mother and Mallory Evans. "Good morning," Hunt said. "Pearl, guess who's here! Some coffee, please," he bellowed.

Pearl stepped down into the garden, her arms outstretched. Biz leaped into her waiting arms. Hunt could hear him start to purr. Pearl crooned to the big cat who just purred louder.

"Hunt, where have you been? You look so . . . disheveled."

"I do, don't I?" Hunt said. "Hello, Mallory. You could

310

have brought Biz with you. By the way, how did you get here?"

"I took a taxi. I do not travel with a cat. I don't like that cat, Hunt."

"Yes, you did say that. I love this cat. I see you two have met."

Lily Kingsley stared at her son and then at the strange young woman seated at her breakfast table. Biz leaped onto her lap. "I've missed you, you big baby," Lily said. To her son she said, "where have you been and why do you look like you do? What in heaven's name happened to your shoes? Are those bites on your ankles?"

"Here, there, and everywhere. Yep, they're bites. I had a hell of a time. How long are you staying, Mallory?"

"Three days. I expected you to pick me up at the airport, Hunt."

Hunt stared at the lacquered, coiffed, manicured woman sitting across from him. He wondered what he'd ever seen in her. He rather thought his mother was wondering the same thing. There wasn't one thing spontaneous or exciting about this young woman. He marveled again that he'd spent so many months with her. Gutless. He propped his chin on his elbow to stare at Mallory. It occurred to him that he'd never seen her without makeup. She wasn't interested in uninhibited sex because she didn't want to muss her makeup or hairdo. Had he been blind? Obviously, he'd been deaf, dumb, *and* blind.

"I was there. You were gone. I told you I had a full schedule. You're going to have to amuse yourself. There's not much to do here, Mallory. Give some thought to returning to Georgia. I'll call you when I get back. I made a decision where Biz is concerned. I'm not getting rid of him."

Mallory's perfectly made-up eyes narrowed. Her bright red lips became a thin tight slash in her face. She shrugged. "I find it almost impossible to believe your devotion to a cat." She made the word *cat* sound obscene.

Hunt shrugged the way Mallory had just done. His face registered awe when Pearl set Mallory's breakfast in front of her. The brown-crusted scrambled eggs rested on a robin's-egg blue plastic plate. The paper napkin was wrinkled. The orange juice was in an old jelly glass. Just yesterday he'd seen a plant growing out of it on the window sill. The toast was very dark and it looked cold. The less-than-crisp bacon dripped grease.

"This . . . this looks . . . wonderful," Lily said.

"I'm ready for seconds already," Hunt guffawed. He swigged from his jelly glass.

"What kind of coffee is this?" Mallory asked. She wrinkled her fine patrician nose to indicate she didn't much care for it no matter what kind of coffee it was.

"The kind that comes in them little bags. The same kind like tea," Pearl elaborated. "You jest dip it in the water." Hunt almost choked on his greasy bacon. His mother looked pained.

"You told me Pearl was the best cook in Charleston," Mallory said, dabbing at her bright red lips. The inference was that Hunt had lied.

Hunt smiled. Mallory looked like she'd just bitten into a lemon. "You should taste her pancakes."

"Her waffles are very good," Lily said.

"Hunt, Mallory tells me you're getting engaged. Should I plan a party of some sort? We could have it right here in the garden. Pearl can do all the cooking," Lily said.

"Mom, Mallory and I are friends. There's a host of things to be worked out before I would ever take that kind of step. For one thing, she doesn't like Biz. Mallory wants to move to Savannah and I want to stay in Atlanta. There is no engagement on the horizon." It was all said so bluntly Lily halted her fork in midair to stare at her son.

Mallory's penciled eyebrows raised a notch. "That isn't what you said a week ago, Hunt."

"You know what, Mallory, you listen but you don't hear me when I speak to you. I did say exactly the same thing to you last week. You choose to put your own spin on everything. We shouldn't be having this conversation at all. Now, if you'll excuse me, I have to shower and change." To Pearl he said, "As usual, Pearl, you outdid yourself." Inside the kitchen he whispered, "What the hell kind of breakfast was that, Pearl? I need a dose of Pepto."

"I was makin' a statement, Mr. Hunt."

"Oh."

"Where you been? I ain't never seen you look so raggedy lookin'. Not since you wuz a small boy playing in rain puddles."

"Kathryn's dog chewed my shoes. I have nine bites on my ankles. I stayed all night, Pearl."

"That chile let you stay all night! Mercy."

"I'm going back as soon as I get cleaned up."

"What about . . ."

"She invited herself, Pearl. You have my permission to make as many statements as you want." He hugged the old housekeeper and whispered, "This is a secret, Pearl, between you and me. I asked Kathryn to marry me. She didn't say yes and she didn't say no. Keep your fingers crossed."

"Yes'm, Mr. Hunt," Pearl twinkled. She did love a secret.

Thirty minutes later, clean shaven, dressed in creased khakis and an open-necked white shirt and new Docksides, Hunt was on his way to Summerville.

At the same moment, Kate backed her Bronco out of the driveway on her way to the Coldwell Banker office. She signed the contract at the exact moment Hunt swung his mother's

BMW onto the Interstate. Thirty minutes later the Bronco was heading east to Charleston.

Hunt noticed the absence of the Bronco the moment he turned the corner onto Pekoe Court. His high spirits sagged immediately. They rose again when he decided Kathryn might have gone out to breakfast. He'd wait. At this point he had nothing but time.

Kate rang the Kingsley's garden bell. She knew she could open the iron gate if she wanted to. She didn't. Things were different now. She no longer considered herself a member of the Kingsley family. She waited.

Pearl, regal as ever, walked toward the gate. "Miss Kathryn, you look mighty pretty today. Come in, come in. Mr. Hunt ain't here. He said he was goin' to Summerville to see you. Miss Lily went to a luncheon but there is somebody here who is goin' to be mighty happy to see you. He's waitin' over there on the green chair."

"Biz! Oh, Biz!" Kate scooped up the big cat in her arms, tears trickling down her cheeks. She hugged the cat so hard he screeched and then started to purr, his pink tongue licking her cheek. "He didn't forget me, Pearl. I want to steal him away."

"That fool cat is so happy to be home he ain't moved since Mr. Hunt brought him this mornin'. Ain't no place like home."

"I wouldn't know about that, Pearl. This place, this house, it was the closest thing to a home for me. I live in a house with no furniture. I came by today, Pearl, to apologize for not taking your pie and flowers. I was having a bad day and acting stupid on top of everything else. Hunt was the last person I expected to see yesterday. I'm sorry if I hurt your feelings. I want you to know I would never knowingly do anything to offend you, Pearl."

"Pearl knows that, chile."

"I want to say good-bye, Pearl. I'm leaving and I won't have a chance to get into Charleston again before I leave. I didn't want to say good-bye on the phone. I just love you to death, Pearl. I don't think I'd be who I am today if it wasn't for you. I'll write, okay?"

"Yes'm. What about Mr. Hunt?"

"Oh, is Hunt back?" a trilling voice called from the kitchen.

Biz snarled and wiggled in Kate's arms at the sound of the high-pitched voice.

Kate blinked when Pearl introduced the young woman.

"So, where's Hunt?" Mallory asked craning her neck to stare into the garden.

Pearl shrugged.

Kate stared at the perfectly made up face, at the intricate hairdo, the designer clothes, and the acrylic nails. "He doesn't seem to be here," she said.

"Now I know who you are. Hunt speaks of you from time to time. You're the rich homeless waif. Let me see if I can remember your name. It starts with a K . . . Kathryn, right?"

A homeless waif. Was that how Hunt thought of her and then gave voice to that same thought? "And you are?" Kate said smoothly. She would not allow this plastic excuse for a woman to know how badly her words stung.

"Hunt's soon-to-be fiancée."

"It ain't true," Pearl hissed in Kate's ear.

Tears blurring her vision, Kate turned to hug the house-keeper. "It doesn't matter, Pearl," Kate said, her voice tortured. "I knew it was too good to be true. I should have listened to my instincts. Tell Hunt I said good-bye. On second thought, tell him to drop dead."

"But . . . he said . . . what about them dog bites and them

shoes?" Pearl's eyes were dark pools of soft licorice. She kneaded her pristine apron until it was a mass of wrinkles.

"It was a game with Hunt. Just like the last time. And I fell for it like the last time, too. He called me Katie in that soft, husky voice of his. I'm ashamed to say I ate it up. You better hold Biz when I leave. You don't want him to go out on the street." It was all said in a low-voiced whisper so that Mallory Evans couldn't hear. "It was nice meeting you, Miss Evans," Kate said over her shoulder as she trotted to the gate.

Pearl called her back. "You git yerself into my kitchen, young lady, and take that pie off the counter. The roses are in the milk jug. I'll settle Biz fer you. You mind Pearl, now."

It was easier to obey Pearl than it was to kick up a fuss. Kate headed for the kitchen while Pearl opened the gate.

With seconds to spare Pearl placed the big cat on the floor in the cargo area of the Bronco. "You stay now. You hear me, Biz? Kate's goin' take you home with her. Mind your manners."

"Do you have Biz, Pearl?"

"He's safe, Miss Kathryn. You listen to me, that *hussy* showed up here with no invite. I heard Mr. Hunt hisself tell her he wasn't gettin' engaged. Miss Lily didn't like her for nothin'. Don't you be makin' up a story in your mind about somethin' that don't mean nothin'. She purely hates Biz."

Kate's voice was brittle, her eyes moist when she said, "ask me if I care. Take care of yourself, Pearl. I promise to eat all of this pie and I'll dry the flowers. When I get settled, I'll call and write."

Pearl hugged Kate one last time. She stood at the gate watching as Kate maneuvered the Bronco into traffic.

"Hunt's friend is certainly rude. There's absolutely no excuse for bad manners."

"Miz Kathryn is Mr. Hunt's very special friend," Pearl said through tight lips.

"How special?" Mallory asked, her eyes glinting.

"Very special." Pearl's full lips tightened to a firmer, tighter line.

"She's a cop. Cops carry guns. That isn't a fit profession for a woman."

"Who sez that?" Pearl demanded.

"Why . . . I . . . ladies have genteel professions. Police deal with low-life people. Sooner or later it's bound to rub off. I happen to know the divorce rate in police work is scandalous," Mallory said, her voice huffy, her eyes spewing sparks.

"Iszat so?" Pearl walked back into the kitchen. "Bring your plate, ma'am."

"Bring my plate?" She might as well of said, you want me to go the moon on a ladder!

"Everyone in this house carries their dishes into the kitchen," Pearl snapped.

There was nothing for Mallory to do but obey Pearl. She sniffed her displeasure as she slammed her plate and coffee cup onto the kitchen counter.

"Are there any recent magazines or new books in the library?"

"I don't know, ma'am. I can't read," Pearl lied.

"You can't cook, either," Mallory muttered under her breath. "I had no idea this was such a hostile family."

Kate was on the Interstate, three miles from home when Biz leaped onto the headrest on the passenger side of the front seat. Startled, Kate yelped her surprise. Biz snaked his way over the console to sit in her lap. "I don't even want to know how you got into this car."

Tears puddled in Kate's eyes and then rolled down her

317

cheeks when Biz started to purr as he snuggled in her lap. She stroked him with her left hand as she tooled down the Interstate. "Possession is nine points of the law. That means you're mine. I gave you to Lee so I should have inherited you by law. I'm keeping you. You're in my truck so that means you want to be with me. As soon as we get back to the house, I'm throwing my stuff in suitcases and we're outta here. We'll drive to Pennsylvania and save the plane ticket for another time. You're gonna love Sophie, Biz."

Her eyes tear filled, Kate didn't see the BMW on the west-bound lane of the highway.

Angry with himself, angry that Mallory was still at the house, angry with his mother, Hunt stormed into the garden bellowing Pearl's name. His angry eyes searched the garden furniture for Biz. He called out to the cat.

"You need to stop that bellerin', Mr. Hunt," Pearl said, her bare feet slapping hard on the stone path that led to the center of the garden.

"Where is everyone?"

"Who you lookin' for, Mr. Hunt?"

"My mother, Biz. Is Mallory still here?"

"Your lady friend went shoppin' 'cause there weren't nothin' here to read. Leastaways that's what she said. Your mama is upstairs changing from her fancy clothes. Don't rightly know where Biz is." Pearl's voice was sly when she said, "Miss Kathryn came by to say good-bye. She took the pie and flowers. Your lady friend said mean things to Miz Kathryn. She tole her you wuz gettin' engaged. Miz Kathryn had tears in her eyes. She is a hussy, that one. Miz Kathryn ain't never gonna forgive you for that woman."

Hunt felt his shoulders sag. "She wasn't home, Pearl. I waited. Do you think she took Biz?"

318

"How would Pearl be knowin' that, Mr. Hunt?"

"You know *everything* that goes on here. What should I do, Pearl? I screwed up the first time. I thought I had a chance this time around, but I screwed up again. Lee wouldn't have . . . Jesus, I miss him. If there was ever a time to talk to a brother, this is it."

"Mr. Lee is *daid*. All you got is Pearl and your mama. I know you is a growed man, Mr. Hunt. Iffen I tell you to do somethin', will you do it and not ask me any questions?"

Hunt stared at the old housekeeper. He didn't think he'd ever seen Pearl so agitated. Her apron was wrinkled, too. He nodded.

"Pearl wants you to shinny up into that old tree and be quiet. Company is comin' for tea."

"Are you asking me to spy on my mother and her company, Pearl?"

"Yes'm, that's what Pearl is askin' you to do."

"What the hell . . . Okay, Pearl. What time is the company coming?"

"Real soon."

"Do I have time to call Kathryn?"

"Iffen you do it real quick."

Hunt dialed Kate's number knowing there wouldn't be an answer. He left a long, detailed message, ending with, "I have to do something for Pearl and then I'm heading back to Summerville. I meant everything I said last night. Don't give up on me, Katie."

Pearl waited until Hunt hung up the phone. "You best be hurryin' now, Mr. Hunt. You ain't no small boy no more. It's goin' to take you longer to shinny up that ol' tree. You be careful and don't fall out."

"How long do I have to stay in the tree?"

"Till you hear everythin' you need to be hearin'."

"I don't believe I'm doing this," Hunt muttered as he sought for handholds and footholds. He was breathless when he settled himself in one of the many deep V's of the old Angel Oak. The lush foliage and hanging moss gave him excellent cover from prying eyes. I could stay up here until Mallory leaves, he thought.

Hunt peered through the branches. He had a perfect view of the Bannons' backyard. He looked for the gate, the gate that was locked from both sides for many years. Even with the bright sun he couldn't see any trace of a lock. Maybe it was finally gone. How well he remembered the day his mother had ordered Pearl to nail the gate shut and then two days later a man had appeared to install a lock. To his knowledge no one but his mother ever had a key. It was strange that as a child neither he nor Lee had questioned the lock and the lack of a key. Kathryn had questioned it though. No satisfactory explanations had been forthcoming. From that day on, Kathryn had climbed on two milk boxes and he and Lee had boosted her over the fence. They'd done the same thing on their side of the fence when it was time for her to go home.

The French doors opened onto the Bannon patio. Kathryn's mother walked across the yard to the old fence, lifted the iron handle that would give her entrance into the Kingsley garden. So, Constance Bannon was his mother's company. Since he was in a spy mode he wondered if he'd be able to hear their conversation. Obviously, Pearl thought so.

He waited. Pearl set his mother's best crystal pitcher filled with iced tea in the center of the table. Sprigs of mint clung to the sides of the fragile glasses. A plate of paper-thin sugar cookies was brought out next. He heard his mother say, "Close the kitchen door, Pearl." Hunt's eyebrows shot up so high they almost met his hairline. Pearl had always been privy to all the Kingsleys' secrets. Why was today different?

He listened.

"In many ways it feels like old times, doesn't it, Lily?"

"It was a long time ago, Constance."

"You need to make it right, Lily."

"You can't ask me to do that, Constance. It isn't fair. What good can possibly come of this?"

"How can you ask me such a question, Lily? I want my daughter. I want to put my arms around her. I want her to know me. It's my right. You've denied me that long enough. Neither one of us is getting any younger. I think you've punished me long enough. Do you have any idea, any idea at all, of what it's been like for me all these years?"

"I haven't exactly had a picnic, Constance. It was your doing, not mine. We made a pact. We agreed this was best."

"That was then, this is now. I want my daughter."

"She doesn't want you, Constance. She has her own life and it doesn't include you."

"Because of you, Lily. I was young and vulnerable back then. I have regretted every single day of my life that I allowed you to talk me into this cockamamie scheme."

"You did agree. It was all legal."

"How can you say stealing my daughter was legal? You said you would never say unkind things to her about me. You promised to love her and you damn well promised to take my place in name only. Don't force me to get an attorney, Lily. At this stage of my life I don't care if this dirty little secret comes out or not. Between the two of us we can make this right. If you don't agree then I will explore other options."

"Hunt —"

"Your son is a man. My daughter is a woman. Neither one are children to be protected. I want my daughter, Lily. I mean to make it right if it's possible. If it isn't, I want to know I did everything I could. I want this Mother's Day. I deserve this Mother's Day. I've never had even one. You, Lily, had one every year of your married life. It's my turn now."

"I'm not denying that. There has to be a better way."

"Name it and I'll give it consideration."

"I won't be able to hold my head up. I'll have to go into seclusion."

"Try the word exile. That's what you did to me. You forced me into exile for thirty years. It's my turn now. You didn't even have the guts to tell me about Lee's death. I had to read about it in the paper my attorney sent me. That, Lily Kingsley, has to be the most unforgivable thing you've ever done in your life."

"I was so overcome with grief. I . . . I'm sorry about that, Constance, truly I am."

"Did you clear out his room?"

"Yes. Everything is packed and in the garage."

"When are you going to bring it to my house?"

"As soon as . . . as soon as I can get someone to carry it over."

"I want *my son's* belongings by six o'clock this evening even if it means you have to carry those belongings over yourself. Now that I think about it, you should be the one to bring them. Not Pearl, not Hunt. Six o'clock, Lily, not one minute later. Now, I'm ready to talk about the promises you made in regard to my daughter and didn't honor. You promised to raise Lee and Kathryn as brother and sister. In your home. That's what I agreed to. I did not agree to Kathryn being raised by housekeepers and nannies in my house. You said she would live with you, have her own room. You promised she would have a happy family life. You defaulted on every promise you made to me. I believed you, Lily. All you were interested in was your own selfish reputation. You and that lecher you called a husband, convinced me your way was best for the children. My God, I was such a fool. My son is dead, a son I never got to know and my daughter thinks I'm . . . I don't know what she thinks at this point. You never told Kathryn Lee was her brother. How could you do that, Lily? How? You are the sorriest excuse for a human being I've ever run across. Six o'clock. By the way, I hired private detectives to document everything. I'll locate Kathryn on my own. You betrayed me, Lily."

"And what did you do to me? You went to bed with my husband and created a child. Don't talk to me about betrayal."

"Your husband raped me. He sneaked into my house and raped me right in my dining room. I hardly call that betrayal. You knew what he was like. You used to cry on my shoulder about his womanizing. You've lied to yourself all these years. It's time to clear your conscience and give me the happiness you've denied me all these years. I have a record, Lily, of all the monies that were sent to you by my attorneys all these years. It is a princely sum, none of which was used on my daughter. Think about how you're going to explain that to the courts. Your husband was destitute. You lived off my money. You sent Lee and Hunt to college on my money. You pay Pearl out of my money and you pay the taxes on this house with my money. The money stopped the day I moved back here."

"That can't be true," Lily gasped.

"Your husband arranged it all. I had money, he didn't. The attorneys handled it all. You could lose this wonderful house, Lily. I'm going home and the thing that will make me happiest is if I never see you again as long as I live."

"Constance, wait. I thought . . . you said we were going to be friends, that it would be like it was before . . . before the tragedy."

"I didn't know all these things then. Make it right, Lily."

Lily sobbed into her napkin.

The leaves of the Angel Oak rustled as Hunt made his way down the monstrous trunk. He literally dropped to his knees at his mother's feet. He risked a glance at the kitchen door. He saw Pearl standing sentinel.

"Mom —"

"Oh, Hunt. What am I going to do?"

Hunt took his mother's hands in his own. "Was she telling the truth?"

"Yes. I didn't know about the money. I thought when the check came every month it was from your father's estate. I swear I didn't know about that."

"Lee is Kathryn's brother."

"Yes." The response was a tortured whisper.

"Mom, how could you let Kathryn think all those terrible things about her mother all these years?"

"At first I didn't think I could love Lee because of the circumstances. I was proved wrong. He loved Kathryn more than he loved me or you. Even though neither one of them knew they were blood relations, their bond was strong. I resented it. I was good to Kathryn."

"Mom, Mrs. Bannon said you promised to have Kathryn live with us."

"I know. She's right. She was such a beautiful little girl and she reminded me of Constance so much. It just ate at me. Lee looked like your father. I don't have any defense, Hunt. I have to make it right. Constance was right about everything. Even Lee's death."

Hunt took his mother in his arms. He swore she aged at that minute, right before his eyes. "We'll go together. We both have a lot of making up to do."

"I have to take all of Lee's things over to Constance's

house. No, Hunt, not you, me. It's the least I can do. You sit here and drink some iced tea. It's going to take me a little while."

"Get Lee's old wagon out of the garage, Mom."

"That's too easy."

Three hours later Pearl had to forcefully restrain Hunt from helping his mother. "Miz Constance is mad as a wet bumble-bee. You leave things be between your mama and that lady. Your mama has a bushel of makin' up to do."

"You've always known about this, haven't you, Pearl? Is that why you've been so good to Kathryn all these years?"

"Yes'm. I love that chile. What your mama did was wrong. How do you feel about this, Mr. Hunt?"

"Right now I'm numb. At least now I understand the bond between Lee and Kathryn. I was never able to figure that out. It's going to break Kathryn's heart."

"That chile's heart been broke so many times there ain't much left to break. Miz Kathryn will understand. I don't know if she'll forgive your mama, though."

Hunt sucked in his breath as his mother made yet another trek through the gate, her arms full of Lee's things. "One more trip and I'll be done," she called over her shoulder. Hunt took the time to dial Kate's number. The phone rang and rang. The answering machine didn't click on.

"She's gone, ain't she?" Hunt thought the old housekeeper's words were ominous sounding.

"I don't know. Probably. I guess she didn't believe me. I can't say I blame her. You gave Biz to her, didn't you? It's okay, Pearl. Kathryn always loved Biz and he loves her. Now, more than ever, it's right for her to have him."

"Yes'm."

"I'll wash my hands and we can be on our way, Hunt. First, though, I want to give you something I found among

Lee's things. I'm sorry to say I read it. I thought . . . hoped it might be a letter to me. It was a silly thought on my part. Lee didn't know he was going to die so why would he write a farewell letter. It was sealed. It's the letter you wrote to Kathryn a long time ago. No wonder that child . . . Never mind."

Hunt thought his hand was going to burn right off his wrist the moment he touched the letter. His proof that he wasn't the jerk Kathryn thought he was. He hated the feel of the dry, crackly letter. He jammed it into his back pocket. He couldn't help but wonder why Lee had kept the letter all these years. He'd said he would give it to Kathryn when he thought the time was right. He didn't want to think about that now. He had to think about his mother and the dark secrets she'd kept from him.

Would those secrets change the way he felt about his own mother? Everyone made mistakes, some more serious than others. He was, after all, living proof that everyone made mistakes. He couldn't take back the love he felt for his mother. Nor did he want to. Love, according to Pearl, was unconditional. They'd work it through and hopefully, be stronger for the effort.

"I think she's gone, Mom," Hunt said when Lily returned to the garden. Was that cool, reserved voice his?

Lily's shoulders started to shake. "Then we have to find her. I'll just be a minute."

"You plannin' on going out in public dressed like that?" Pearl asked.

"Yes. The old days are gone, as Constance pointed out. I think I'll get a job, Pearl."

Hunt laughed. He sobered immediately. "Mom, I can support you. People your age find it difficult to get jobs. It's the way it is."

326

"Then we'll have to change that, won't we? You'll have to take a cut in pay, Pearl."

"Yes'm."

"I'm ready, Hunter. The first thing I'm going to do is sell this BMW. I don't need a car. Pearl will let me cruise around in her clunker if I need the use of a vehicle. I don't know what to say, son. I'm ashamed, I'm sorry, and I'm embarrassed. The guilt I've carried all these years has been horrendous. I'm glad it's all coming out. I have to find a way to make it right with Constance. Getting her and Kathryn together isn't enough."

"No, Mom, it's not enough. How did all those stories get around town about Mrs. Bannon if she was in exile?"

"Me."

"Mom!"

"I used to send Constance updates and she always responded with a proper thank you and a short note about what was going on in her life. I didn't . . . what I mean is . . . I just mentioned certain things to certain friends. I didn't make up anything. I was so wounded, Hunt, with your father's infidelities. Constance was my best friend and I thought, believed, she betrayed me. Your father's story was so different from Constance's. I *needed* to believe your father.

"Oh, oh, here comes your friend, Hunter."

"Get in the car, Mom. I'll take care of this."

"Mallory, I only have a minute. Listen, I really don't think this is going to come as any big surprise to you, but I don't want to get married. I'm in love with someone else. I think I've been in love with her all my life and didn't know it. That makes me a pretty stupid guy, wouldn't you agree?"

"I see."

"I want to wish you well. I'm sorry it didn't work out, Mallory."

"Does that mean you want me to leave?"

"Stay as long as you like. Pearl loves to cook for guests. I don't know when my mother and I will be back." Hunt leaned forward to kiss Mallory's cheek. She reared backward.

"Don't. You'll smear my rouge. I think I'll call a cab to take me to the airport and go back to Georgia. Let's stay in touch. Is it that police person?"

"Yes." Mallory's trilling laughter followed him all the way to the car. Hunt grinned from ear to ear.

"I love Kathryn, Mom."

"I know."

"Did Pearl tell you?"

"No, Lee told me a long time ago. He said you two were meant for each other but that you were too dumb to know it. He said Kathryn loved you from the time she was seven years old. He said you'd come to your senses someday and realize she was the one for you."

"I always thought she would end up with Lee. It was that special thing the two of them had. I didn't know then that . . ."

"I'm sorry, Hunter."

"I know, Mom, I know."

Chapter Six

Kate crossed the border into Virginia just as dusk began to settle on the horizon. She drove for another two hours before she veered off the first ramp she saw that announced gas, food, and lodging. Forty minutes later she'd registered in a small motel, gassed the Bronco, and bought two bags of take-out food, one for her and one for the animals. She showered, washed her hair, and then settled herself in the comfortable double bed, the television turned to CNN while she ate her food. Biz settled himself at her feet, his eyes on Sophie who was trying to decide where her place was. When Biz started to purr, Sophie belly-whopped her way to the cat and snuggled close. Biz's front paw pulled her closer. Kate closed her eyes, a smile on her face.

Hunt turned on his signal light before he slowed the BMW to the shoulder of the road. "This is wrong, Mom. We need to go back home. I know Kathryn and I don't believe she's going to go to Villanova. My instincts tell me she's tired of running and hiding. She's going to turn around and go home. She may already have done that. I know her. I saw things in her eyes she didn't mean me to see. Your call, Mom."

"No, Hunt. I have never made good decisions. This is too important for me to . . . to . . . to do something wrong now. If you feel your instincts are sound then that's good enough for me."

"Any cops around?"

"I can't see any," Lily said craning her neck in every direction.

"Good, I'm going to break the law and cross the median."

"What if you're wrong, Hunt?"

"Then we'll both have to live with it. This highway isn't going to go away. If I'm wrong, which I don't think I am, we can make the trip tomorrow."

"Tomorrow is Mother's Day."

"So it is," Hunt smiled.

"Is that why you think she'll go back?"

"That plus Biz. My money's on that old cat."

"Remarkable," was all Lily could think of to say.

Kate woke slowly, her shoulders stiff and tense from the long ride. She'd slept but it had been a restless sleep. She rubbed sleep from her eyes as she thought about the long drive ahead of her. She stirred, her shoulders mashing into the soft mattress. Her feet started to tingle. She almost laughed aloud when she saw Sophie, all six pounds of her, lying on her back, her feet straight in the air, Biz's big head on her belly. His long tail swished once to let her know he knew she was awake.

Kate stared at the animals for a long time. They were strangers to each other. A dog/cat mix that wasn't supposed to work. Yet, here they were, sleeping together, Biz the gentle protector, Sophie the fragile female. Obviously nothing was all black or white. She felt her mind racing, her thoughts chaotic.

Kate watched the sleeping animals for a long time, a smile on her face. A person could learn a lot from animals if they took the time to observe them.

"Rise and shine, guys, we're going *home*. First, though, we're going outside."

An hour later, Kate was tooling down the Interstate, English muffin in hand while Biz nibbled on fish sticks and Sophie gobbled a sausage biscuit.

It was one o'clock in the afternoon when Kate pulled into the parking lot of Stuckey's furniture store in Summerville. She whizzed through the showrooms, picking and choosing from the floor models. Delivery was promised for four o'clock since she lived only four blocks away. Her second stop was the realtor's office where she canceled the sale of her home. She made a third stop at Rainbow Crafts and emerged a short while later with three huge cartons loaded onto a dolly. Her fourth stop was the Piggly-Wiggly supermarket where she spent $180 on groceries.

The animals secure in the house, Kate removed the FOR SALE sign from her front lawn, carried in her purchases, and got down to business. Thank God the realtor had talked her into leaving the power and water on in the house. She'd balked at leaving the phone on and had it disconnected. She did have her cell phone so the outside world was within reach should an emergency arise.

Kate slid a tray of stuffed peppers, her favorite all-time food, into the oven just as her front doorbell rang. She used up another hour telling the delivery men where to place her new furniture. When she closed the door behind them, she looked around. It all looked very new. She needed plants, knick knacks. Junk. Stuff. Monday would be soon enough. She had food in her refrigerator, furniture, animals, a litter box, and a pile of Sophie's poop by the kitchen door that Biz was eyeing with disdain.

Home.

Kate worked steadily at her new dining-room table. She stopped once at nine o'clock to eat the stuffed peppers. She cleaned up, took Sophie for a short walk, returned, called

Ellen to tell her to scratch Pennsylvania from her vacation list before settling back down to work.

Twice during the long night Sophie ran from room to room, Biz behind her. An intruder? Hunt? No way. A raccoon? Absolutely. Each time she went back to work, her granny glasses perched on the end of her nose, certain it was only an animal scent outside that was making Sophie skitsy.

At four-thirty, she turned off the lights and headed upstairs to sleep in her new bed with her new sheets and blankets. She eyed the deflated air mattress she'd slept on for almost a year. Monday morning it would go out in the trash.

Kate slept deeply and dreamlessly for three hours, waking at seven-thirty. She showered and then dressed in her best outfit.

She was going visiting. Decked out in her best bib and tucker as Pearl would say.

Kate loaded the Bronco, Sophie and Biz watching her from the back seat. She made one stop at the Krispy Kreme donut shop for six jelly donuts loaded with powdered sugar and two giant containers of scalding hot coffee. Fifteen minutes later she was on I–26 heading east to Charleston.

At ten minutes to nine, her stomach churning, her hands shaking, Kate rang the doorbell of the stately old mansion on the Battery. She took two steps backward, Sophie and Biz at her feet. Her throat was so dry she wondered if she'd be able to speak.

"I'm Kathryn," Kate said in a choked voice to the beautiful woman standing in the open doorway. "I came to wish you thirty-two Happy Mother's Days." She stepped forward, tears blurring her vision.

"I would have known you anywhere, Kathryn. Please, come in. How wonderful of you to come today. I guess God does answer foolish old women's prayers."

"And stupid young women's prayers. I brought breakfast," Kate said holding up the two Krispy Kreme bags in her trembling hand. "They're loaded with sugar. I like sweets. Actually, I love sweets."

"Amazing. I love sweets, too. Do you need some help with those boxes?"

"No. They're just bulky. Is it okay for Sophie and Biz to come in? I'd like it if you'd open the gate so Biz . . . so Biz can . . . go home."

"Of course it's okay. The gate is open. I noticed it this morning when I looked out the window. I don't think Lily closed it yesterday. I hate things that are locked. It means keep out or don't touch."

Kate nodded. "If you let Biz out, I'll carry the boxes in. Where should I put them?"

"Wherever you like, Kathryn. I want to put my arms around you. I want to say so many things to you. We have so much to talk about. We'll take it slowly, one day a time."

"I don't want us to be strangers. It will take time. Time is all I have these days. I'm partial to kitchens," Kathryn said.

"Then the kitchen it is. I can't wait to eat the donuts. How many did you get?"

"Six."

"Is that all? I can eat six by myself."

"I didn't know that, so we'll have to share. I'll bring a dozen next time." They were having a normal, sharing conversation. Just her and her mother. It felt good. It felt better than good. It felt damn good.

Biz streaked through the open kitchen door, Sophie on his heels. "He's in the garden, Kathryn."

Kate nodded. "I knew he wanted to go home. I learned a lot from him in a day's time. I guess what I'm trying to say is, I wanted to come home myself."

"Did . . . Lily ask you to come here?"

"No. Why do you ask?"

"Was it Hunt?"

"No. I came here on my own. They don't know I'm here. Are you saying I should have told them?"

"Not at all. It doesn't matter. I'm just glad you came."

Mother and daughter stared at each other across the kitchen table, the cartons Kate carried in next to her plate. "These are for you. Happy Mother's Day, thirty-two times," Kate said inching the boxes closer to her mother.

"I don't know what to say."

"I kind of feel the same way. They aren't anything spectacular. It's the kind of thing kids make in school. I used to give my presents to Pearl. She said she loved them. I know she still has them all in her old trunk. It took me all night to make these."

"I don't know what to say."

"You already said that. Go ahead, open them." Kate propped her elbows on the table, her eyes never leaving her mother's face. She felt giddy at her mother's genuine delight over the cigar box with the gold macaroni glued to the top, at the orange full of cloves, the small pine stem in a milk carton, the colored clothespins with a magnet glued to the back, the picture of her in her prom gown, the frame decorated with pinecones.

"Oh, Kathryn, this is so wonderful. I don't know what to say. I'm so overwhelmed. I never thought this day would come."

Kate smiled her pleasure.

Next door, Pearl ran upstairs as fast as her old legs would carry her, her bare feet slapping at the stair treads as she beat the bottom of a metal bowl with her wooden spoon. "Miz

334

Kathryn's next door and she's all gussied up. The gate is open and Biz is back. Wake up, Miz Lily, you too, Mr. Hunt. Didja all hear Pearl?"

Hunt bolted from his bed, his eyes wide with shock. "Did I hear you right, Pearl?"

"Yes'm. You best git down there. That poor chile don't know the truth."

"You were right, Hunt. Give me a minute, Pearl."

"You done used up all your minutes, Miz Lily. You need to be tellin' that chile the truth right now. Her mother ain't goin' tell her nothin'.'"

"At least let me get my robe."

"Me too," Hunt said. "Happy Mother's Day, Mom."

"Uh-huh," Lily said, tying the belt to her robe. "We're moving as fast as we can, Pearl."

In the Bannon kitchen, both women looked up when Lily and Hunt knocked on the French doors off the breakfast room.

"Good morning, everyone," Hunt said cheerfully. "Donuts!"

"Lily, this isn't a good time. Let things be. We can talk about it later."

"No. I need to do it now. Kathryn, I have something to tell you. I want you to listen to me very carefully. When I'm finished, I'm going to leave and you'll never have to see me again. I hope you'll find it in your heart not to let what I'm about to tell you interfere with whatever is between you and Hunt."

Lily looked old beyond her years when she rose from the table a long time later. "I am so very sorry, Kathryn."

"I knew. So did Lee," Kate said softly. "Lee said Pearl talked in her sleep. At first we thought it was a joke. Of course we were very young then. Later on we thought Pearl was just having a bad dream. Not knowing if it was real or not, we pretended. It was our secret. That's why we were so close. It doesn't matter anymore, Lily. The past is gone. I brought Biz back. I don't know what to do about Sophie. For some strange reason those two bonded. Maybe we could share custody or . . . something. I'm going home now so I'll say good-bye. I just want to give Pearl a present."

"I'll call you, Kathryn," Constance said.

"I'd like that, Mom. Bye, everyone."

"That's it, good-bye!" Hunt bellowed.

"How many ways are there to say good-bye?" Kathryn demanded.

"I can name quite a few. Are you going to marry me or not?"

"I don't know. I have things to do, places to go. My mother and I have some plans."

"Oh, yeah. Well I have a few plans of my own."

"Plans are good. Do they have telephones in Atlanta that can reach here?"

"Hell yes."

"Do they have planes that fly to Charleston?"

"Damn straight they do."

"Can your car make it here if you put gas in it?"

"Absolutely. They even have a mail system." Hunt reached into his back pocket. "This is the letter I wrote you a long time ago. Mom found it in Lee's things and gave it to me yesterday. You need to read it, Kathryn."

"No, I don't want or need to read it. It's baggage. I rest my case."

"What about Biz and Sophie?"

"You need to work on that," Kate said as she winked at her mother.

"I want to get married at Christmastime."

"Christmas is good. I think I can free up some time then," Kate called over her shoulder.

"She said okay. Did you hear that? She said okay."

"We heard," Lily said. "Don't screw it up, Hunt."

"I'm going to be watching you like a hawk, Hunter Kingsley," Constance Bannon said, a huge smile on her face.

"Pearl's goin' be watching all of you. You best take yerself into my kitchen and pro-pose like a real gentleman, Mr. Hunt. You mind Pearl now."

"Yes, ma'am."

"Christmas is a wonderful time for a wedding, Hunt. What will we do if there isn't a Hunter's Moon?" Kathryn asked, her voice suddenly shy.

"We'll make one out of yellow paper and hang it from the Angel Oak."

"I do love a man who has innovative ideas."

"You should see what else I can do," Hunt leered.

"Talk's cheap. Show me. I love the word performance."

"Never heard of it. Don't go thinking I'm easy. Katie, what made you come back? I need to know."

"You. My mother. Biz. Me. It was time I guess. When you love someone, taking that last big step is the most important. Loving someone means you put that person first. Isn't that a true measure of happiness? So, it's definitely Christmas for us?"

"Most definitely."

"Shouldn't you kiss me or something? Everyone's watching, so make it real good."

He did.

"Can we make peace now, Constance?"

"I think so."

"You can have this house, Constance. Pearl and I are going to move into an apartment in town. We talked last night and we agreed to open a small flower shop on King Street. There's a perfect little building with room for a small tearoom. I think the two of us can handle it."

"Lily, I don't want your house. I never did. That was my anger and hurt talking yesterday. You and Pearl could never be happy anywhere else. I refuse your offer. By any chance, do you need a partner for the flower shop?"

"I think a partner would be wonderful. We can do the flowers for Kathryn and Hunt's wedding. At cost."

On the other side of the garden, Hunt whispered, "I know the three of them are cooking up something."

"Whatever it is we'll be the beneficiaries. Kiss me again."

"I'm gonna wear my lips out."

"Aaahhhh."